Grace Monro[...] [...]
Linda Watson-B[...] [...]
1960, and graduated with a law degree in her early 20s.
Soon after she began her traineeship, Maria met her
husband-to-be, Gordon, already a partner in a rival firm.
The couple now have four children and live in Kingussie,
in the Scottish Highlands. Maria stopped practising law
some years ago and since then has worked as a hypnother-
apist, stage hypnotist, badminton coach, and fertility coun-
sellor amongst many things. A completely new start in
the Scottish Highlands has afforded Maria the chance to
start the next chapter in her life – as a writer.

After ten years as a Politics lecturer in Scottish universi-
ties, Linda Watson-Brown began a journalistic career as a
columnist at *The Scotsman*. She went on to write on a regular
basis for the *Daily Mail*, *Big Issue*, *Daily Record*, *Sunday Herald*
and *Independent* amongst others and also developed a career
as a ghostwriter. Her first ghost-written book, *The Step Child*,
was published in 2006 and quickly became a *Sunday Times*
bestseller. She is now working on a screenplay of the book,
as well as continuing with ghost-writing and fiction. She,
her long-term partner Paul, and their three children are
planning to move to the North-East coast of Scotland later
this year.

In 2003, Maria and Linda met and became firm friends.
They soon realised that they should put their talents and
experiences together and write as a team. *Dark Angels* is
the first novel in a planned series featuring Brodie
MacLennan. For more information on the pair, visit their
website at gracemonroe.net

Visit www.AuthorTracker.co.uk for exclusive updates on
Grace Monroe.

GRACE MONROE

Dark Angels

AVON

AVON

A division of HarperCollins*Publishers*
77–85 Fulham Palace Road,
London W6 8JB

www.harpercollins.co.uk

A Paperback Original 2007

First published in Great Britain by
HarperCollins*Publishers* 2007

Extract from *Blood Lines* © Grace Monroe 2007.
This is taken from uncorrected material and does not
necessarily reflect the finished book.

A catalogue record for this book is
available from the British Library

ISBN: 978-1-84756-034-6

Set in Minion by Palimpsest Book Production Ltd,
Grangemouth, Stirlingshire

Printed and bound in Great Britain by
Clays Ltd, St Ives plc

f156,762
€10.00

Mixed Sources
Product group from well-managed
forests and other controlled sources
www.fsc.org   Cert no. SW-COC-1806
© 1996 Forest Stewardship Council
FSC

FSC is a non-profit international organisation established to promote the
responsible management of the world's forests. Products carrying the FSC
label are independently certified to assure consumers that they come
from forests that are managed to meet the social, economic and
ecological needs of present and future generations.

Find out more about HarperCollins and the environment at
www.harpercollins.co.uk/green

From Linda:
Lots of love to Jenny Brown (aka The Loveliest Agent in the World) at Jenny Brown Associates for her help, support and huge amounts of coffee. Similar amounts of thankful and cuddly stuff to the team at Avon, especially Maxine Hitchcock and Keshini Naidoo. Their adoration of Glasgow Joe and Jack Deans is much appreciated, as are the very important discussions about weird crushes and diets.

From Maria:
Thanks to Maxine Hitchcock and Keshini Naidoo at Avon, as well as my agent, Jenny Brown. Thanks also go to the Law Society of Scotland, without which this book wouldn't have been possible.

For my family
Maria xx

For Paul – I do appreciate you really.
Linda xx

PROLOGUE

Edinburgh

The cotton sheets feel smooth and crisp between her fingers as she grips the covers. The knuckles on her hands are white and bloodless, the contrast stark. As she weakly reaches for the mask, sweat slowly trickles down from the inside of her armpit. She gets what she wants but the heady smell of rubber almost overwhelms her before the gas and air mercifully take effect.

'The quicker the hell, the quicker the peace.'

The voice of the woman rasps the tired adage.

The girl will have to look elsewhere for comfort. Here, she will find only contempt. She looks around, as she has done many times in the many hours since she was brought to this place. The panelled walls are adorned with ancient smoke-damaged oil paintings, of thin lipped ancestors: no succour will be found there either.

The girl throws her head back against the plump, pillows, her black curls sticking to her damp forehead. Another wave of pain overwhelms her, pushing her further down into the abyss. She almost welcomes the pain: she has ignored the ache within her heart for so long that concrete physical agony serves to remind her that, despite everything, she is still alive.

The handcuff around her left wrist cuts deeply into her flesh. The skin is red and swollen from earlier attempts to escape. She no longer has the enthusiasm to plan her getaway. Reluctantly, she accepts she is securely chained to the antique brass bed frame. Her desire, her need to be free, has waned. She is sapped of strength, resigned to her fate.

Giving birth has that effect.

She gasps one word: 'Water,' adding 'Please,' as an afterthought.

'Do you really believe that being polite is going to change my plans?' The nurse expects an answer. None is forthcoming. There is a battle for life going on in the bed in front of her, and strength cannot be wasted on unnecessary words. 'You must be even more stupid than I gave you credit for.'

The girl tries to wet her lips. Her pulse visibly pounds in her neck. Her mouth tastes like rusty iron filings. Her mind races from one thought to another – the taste of terror reminds her of the dilapidated railings near the school gate.

Frantically, her eyes search for water to cleanse her mouth. In every situation the girl looks for something to be grateful for, at this precise moment she is thankful that she cannot imagine what might happen next, appreciative that her mind has narrowed to the extent that all she can think of is water.

There is only so much she can do. This baby has plans of its own. It will be born with or without her cooperation. Without concern for its own fate once it enters this world.

The nurse will not give her the courtesy of silence. 'Don't lie there feeling sorry for yourself. Start pushing, and get this little bastard out.'

A soft, scraping sound fills the room as the nurse bustles importantly, her tights rubbing on her thighs and drowning out the sound of the clock. The girl still knows without the help of any clock – her time is running out.

She may not have water – but she needs fresh air. 'Open the window.'

She despises the way her voice sounds. Reedy and helpless. This time the nurse obliges. The girl/child painfully screws her eyes shut, as the heavy red velvet curtains are drawn back, flooding the room with brilliant sunshine. Through the Georgian sash and case windows, she can see the garden trees in full leaf. From below, the sounds of elegant street life waft in the open window, and birdsong fills the air. Neighbours genteelly pass the time of day, agreeing that it is, indeed, another lovely morning.

The waves of pain are coming faster now, and it is harder for her to recover between contractions. A screech of wretchedness escapes her lips, and resounds around the room. Her cries for help and understanding remain unanswered.

'You made your bed. Lie in it.' The bed is wet, dishevelled and bloodstained. Nurse McIntyre knows that her instructions are that the flat is not to be soiled, and yet the mess is everywhere. Someone else can take care of it – she's a midwife, not a cleaner. She justifies her neglect and cruelty by reassuring herself that it won't matter in the end. She is taking care of the baby, and that is all she has been paid for.

The smell of fear is pungent. It seems as if the odour is emanating from the very walls of the elegant room. The girl screams again. Nurse McIntyre watches dispassionately, as the girl throws her sick bowl across the room. Only when it ricochets off the Waterford crystal chandelier knocking a marble bust of Sir Walter Scott to the floor and smashing the nose off the statue in the process, does she feel a flicker of concern – for the broken things, not the broken girl.

Their eyes meet and the nurse recoils from the hatred she finds in the panicked velvet brown depths of her patient/prisoner. She recoils still further from the sight of the girl holding the nurse's own scissors in her hand, scissors left carelessly on the nightstand beside a manacled child thought too pain-wracked to move.

Anger and venom flow through the girl's veins giving her strength. She holds the gaze of her tormentor, silently daring her to come closer. As her head tries to grab onto some plan, some thought for escape, her body lets her down yet again.

She feels herself rip in two as the baby's head appears.

The girl lies back on the pillows breathing softly, until she feels the urge to push again. Pushing, she feels her baby turn. Pushing, she feels her baby enter the world.

Nurse McIntyre has not yet found the strength to approach the new mother but the scissors fall from her hand as she reaches down between her legs. She lifts her child to her face. They stare silently into one another's eyes, recognising each other.

Locked in love, the girl does not hear the nurse approach.

She is unaware before the silent needle pierces her skin.

Her heart stops as she feels the jab, and she knows they are undone, she and her baby.

At 9.24a.m., the good citizens of Edinburgh see no more than a bustling, uniformed nurse leave an impeccable flat with a swaddled baby in her arms. Without a backward glance, Nurse McIntyre stuffs the keys to the handcuffs into her pocket.

In the room of hell that she has just departed, a small droplet of blood forms around the entry point of the syringe as the massive dose of heroin takes hold: it is the only sign of life on the unconscious thirteen-year-old girl who has just given birth.

The nurse's stout, flat feet beat along the pavement of the New Town.

'There's no time to dwell on the dead,' she mutters as the baby begins to whimper.

'Not while the living are so impatient . . .'

ONE

Edinburgh, Monday 16 August 2004

The fact that it was raining outside came as no surprise for two reasons. Firstly, this was Edinburgh. Secondly, it was the arse end of 'Fringe Sunday', one of the highlights of the summer festival in which all weather forecasts could be shortened to one phrase: pissing down.

I had fallen asleep to the persistent downpour, to the sound of water drumming on the Georgian window-panes of my flat. I like the rain; it comforts me – which is handy given that I've chosen to live in Edinburgh. That comfort was short lived.

As night disappeared into the misty first hours of Monday morning, the dream came again. I saw an unformed face in the dying embers of my bedroom fire, a face I knew, but did not know.

I came back from sleep quickly and stared blindly into my darkened room. The dream was quickly slipping and I didn't really know what had pulled me from it until the telephone rang again. I groped until I found the receiver. I knew the form – no one ever called you in the middle of the night with good news. Callers only think your sleep can be disturbed by death, police at the door, or work. In my case, it was often all three. People often like to think that lawyers can't sleep because they are so bothered by the ethical dilemmas of their work – the boring reality tends to be that the bloody phone won't stop ringing no matter the time of day or night.

'Brodie McLennan?'

'Yes?' I reached for the bedside lamp and switched it on as I answered the call. It was 1.00a.m. My heart was puncturing my ribs, a combination of late-night coffee, unbroken sleep for as long as I could remember, and the anticipation that comes from a straightforward phone call that rarely gives any indication of what the next case will involve.

'Sergeant Munro here, St Leonard's Police Station.'

Just when I thought my night couldn't get any worse. Munro was a copper with an unnatural love of paper-work and a continuing, oft expressed, feeling that 'wee girls' shouldn't be doing big men's jobs. I was most definitely a wee girl in his eyes, and probably taking bread out of some poor bloke's mouth by playing at lawyers while I waited for my natural calling of having babies and getting myself suitably chained to a nice shiny kitchen sink.

'What can I do for you, Sergeant Munro?'

'We have a woman in custody, Miss McLennan,' he informed me as if I would be astounded. He also seemed to emphasise the 'Miss' part of his sentence a bit too heavily. I was knackered and I was pissed off already – how should I react? 'Gosh, really Sergeant Munro? Someone in custody, you say? At the police station? That sounds awfully exciting. Sorry though, I'm too upset about not being married to be able to do anything about it.' Thankfully, Munro was in official mode, so there was no time for anything but the sound of his voice.

'We're about to charge her with murder, but she asked us to inform you. She was quite specific about that. Asked for you by name, Miss McLennan. You'd better come now because we want her processed quickly.'

Munro always wanted anything that involved processing done quickly. It was a moveable feast though, and it generally got ignored.

'Did you hear me, Miss McLennan? It's vital that your client get processed as quickly as possible.' There was the slightest hint of hesitation in his voice. 'We want her to appear later today. How soon can you get here?'

She was probably a screamer. They wanted her out quickly because the noise was interrupting their telly-watching down the station. Or she was that drunk that the stench of vomit was getting too much.

'Yes, I heard you, Sergeant Munro. Quick, quick, chop, chop. You haven't told me my client's name yet though.'

I sat on the edge of my bed, pencil poised over a yellow legal pad. Did he hesitate, or did I imagine it?

'Female, mixed race, forty-one years old.'

I scribbled the details as he went on.

'A taxi driver had found the alleged suspect with the body of the deceased. The nameless male victim was pronounced dead on arrival at Edinburgh Royal Infirmary. Are you taking all of this down, Miss McLennan?'

I wanted to butt in with: 'No, I'm thinking about recipes and marrying policemen, Sergeant Munro,' but managed to keep quiet.

'Miss McLennan, will you be here shortly? Miss McLennan?'

'I'll be in to the station, Sergeant Munro, as soon as you give me my client's name.'

There was definitely hesitation this time.

In retrospect, I wish it could have gone on for longer.

'You may be familiar with the name, Miss McLennan,' he said.

'Coutts. Your client is Kailash Coutts.'

TWO

Kailash Coutts. Edinburgh's most notorious domina-trix. The word that said it all. Kailash was named after one of the most sacred mountains in the Himalayas. Pilgrims trek around it three times for purification and blessings, for it is thought to be the gateway to heaven. Never has anyone been more inaptly named. That woman was a signpost on the road to hell. As I hung up, my feet were already on the old wooden floor-boards and the adrenalin hit my nerves like a bucket of cold water.

The house was quiet – as normal houses should be at that time of night – but I had begun to dread the hours between midnight and 3.00a.m. While the rest of Edinburgh sleeps, the violent and deranged call on my services. Ordinarily in practices they have a rota of on-call solicitors, but we weren't an ordinary partner-ship. I was the only solicitor advocate in Lothian & St Clair Writer to the Signet who touched criminal work.

The partnership where I worked was founded when Robert Louis Stevenson was a boy. Our client list read like a Scottish Who's Who. Lothian & St Clair was officially a corporate firm dealing with acquisitions and mergers, business deals and documents, and such like. However, clients would keep being naughty. I made it clear: crime (and the profits which come from representing it in court) should be kept in house.

It was not, by any stretch of the imagination, a popular idea. I'd have been as well to suggest that we ban double-barrelled names and holidays in Aspen. The price I had to pay for pointing out the obvious was that I got lumped with the whole bloody lot.

The tide turned somewhat two years ago. Rather than scumbag clients (whether well-to-do scumbags or not), it was one of our own who needed help. Senior partner Roddie Buchanan's picture was splashed all over the tabloids. There was some justice in this. The man's mantra had always been, 'There's no such thing as bad publicity.' Somehow he seemed to question the validity of that stance when pictured on the front page of *The Sun* naked in the dungeon of an S&M whorehouse.

I kept Roddie Buchanan's file at home – away from the prying eyes and empty wallets of summer work experience students who might think to supplement their grants by rehashing old news, or selling pics to their pals. When I opened the folder, loose clippings fell to the floor, scattering around my feet.

A hidden camera had snapped a masked Roderick Buchanan Esquire, trussed up like a Christmas turkey. And here was where my past met my present – Kailash Coutts, clad in black leather basque and fishnet stockings stood over him, a large syringe in her hand.

11

Apparently, Roddie had paid her to inject his testicles with water until they were the size of footballs. And they say men don't have any imagination.

On the day *The Sun* led with the story, Roddie didn't deign to come into the office. It didn't matter. He was irrelevant. I was asked – no, told – by my colleagues to represent him. It was up to me to determine what line such a representation would take. I didn't need anything real. I just needed to throw Roddie and his wife a bone, so to speak.

I sued *The Sun* for three million pounds thanks to a technical error in the wording of the story. In Scotland, if you want to avoid being sued for defamation, then every word printed has to be correct. The article stated (actually, the one-handed hack job leered under the headline: NO BRIEFS, MISS WHIPLASH!!!) that Roddie Buchanan ('posh Edinburgh legal bigwig') paid Kailash Coutts ('infamous pervy S&M Queen') to inject *both* of his testicles. I got Kailash to sign an affidavit, in front of an independent Notary Public, to the effect that he only wanted one bollock dealt with.

The paper settled, for a derisory sum, but they gave us the all-important apology (notwithstanding that it was printed on page nine). Roddie could now say to everyone that he'd been defamed and his wife could broadcast her husband's absolute innocence in every drawing room in the city. After all, if the nasty tabloid could lie about the number of testicles involved, it stands to reason that the whole thing could be made up – doesn't it?

In the immediate aftermath of the case, appearing

in court was awkward. I was initially greeted with messages for Roddie. The whole business kept every would-be stand-up comedian in a wig and gown going for months, generally along the lines that Roddie had wasted his money given that half of the Edinburgh legal establishment would have been willing to kick his bollocks for free anyway.

Turns out that Buchanan was right in one way – there was no such thing as bad publicity. My career – and my fees – rocketed. A grudging respect from him would have been nice though, given that I was the one who had cleared up his scandal – somehow, he just didn't seem to be able to show that little bit of gratitude. I didn't take it personally; it wasn't just me he didn't like: he may have paid other women a fortune to whack him off with a whip or inflate his bollocks to within an inch of their life, but he wasn't that fond of the fairer sex. I wasn't too surprised – I had met Eilidh Buchanan on a number of occasions.

Now I was going to have to ask Roddie's permission to take on this case. Kailash Coutts must have been behind *The Sun* getting the pictures of Roddie's hobby in the first place. She certainly knew that we had asked her to be complicit in getting an apology from the paper on a technicality that didn't matter one bit – in fact, we were all sure she must have had a dozen photograph albums made up of much tastier pics than the paper ever published. There was a clear conflict of interest, and I thought that I should withdraw from acting. My opinion was irrelevant until it had been past Roddie Buchanan.

It was a lovely prospect. I had to face calling him at home to inform him that his favourite prostitute was in police custody and that she wanted me to represent her. That was bound to go down well with his wife.

My mouth was dry and I felt embarrassingly nervous as I rang his home number. I could have kicked myself the moment the receiver was picked up and I recognised Eilidh Buchanan's voice. I remembered Roddie was in Switzerland, putting a deal to bed.

Details were unnecessary. No matter what, I had to tell her that Kailash Coutts was in custody and I did not want to represent her.

She listened as I spluttered out the sparse information.

'You will contain this,' she said condescendingly. 'I will not tolerate the firm splashed all over the gutter press again.'

Edinburgh lawyers' wives – they're the ones you don't mess with. They're the ones so warm and cuddly that their men pay good money to get whores to dress them up in rubber fetish gear and inject their genitals for fun.

'I can't stop it. The trial will be a matter of public record. Open to the tabloids. I don't doubt that they'll ... erm, re-open old wounds, but there's nothing I can do about it.'

'Well, now . . .' replied Eilidh Buchanan. 'You've just laid something on the table, Brodie. I think we need to examine your attitude closely. If you can't stop what needs to be stopped, we'll need to find someone who will.'

'Is that a threat?' I asked.

'I'm just stating a fact. For the record.'

My pet hate is pointless conversation, and nothing could be gained by continuing this tête-à-tête, so I said goodbye and within seconds had grabbed my scuffed black biker's helmet, worn from years of use, and left for St Leonard's Police Station.

The night air was damp and earthy; a soft haze covered the slate rooftops. There were no lights in the windows of my neighbours' houses. I threw myself onto the kick-start, praying the pistons were on their firing stroke, otherwise I would be thrown off the bike. Not that it was just 'a' bike; it was my pride and joy – a 1970 Ironhead Fat Boy Harley, and it thankfully roared into life, the huge 1200v twin engine with straight through pipes woke half the neighbourhood in the process.

I looked up. I wasn't too bothered about waking neighbours, but there was one person I cared about and I cared about the fact that he never got enough sleep (not that I would necessarily ever tell him). I didn't want to be the one responsible for waking him if he had finally dropped off. The bedside light was still on in the first floor bedroom in our house. Fishy must still have been awake anyway. This must be another night when he would be plagued by his worries, where sleep would evade him, and he would ponder over his work until morning. This would be one more day, when I wasn't there to listen to him. Fishy and I went back a long way – we had met on our first day in the Law Faculty at university and he was the only student to win more prizes than I did.

When I first bought my flat, I adored the isolation. I revelled in the space and light, and particularly in the fact that I could have anyone to stay over without withering looks or comments from others. Of course, by 'anyone', I mean men – my track record meant that few of them ever stayed more than one night. My romantic dreams of finding someone a bit more permanent were as much coloured by my habit of pushing away most men who tried to get close as by the fact that they were generally losers anyway. It wasn't that I didn't get on with men – far from it; some of my closest friends were afflicted with excess testosterone, and I wasn't averse to non-committal relationships based purely on a nice backside and a lie-in – but as soon as any man started to get, as my mum would have put it, 'serious', the shutters came down and the metaphorical locks got changed.

By the time I realised this, I also realised that I was spending a hell of a lot of time alone anyway. I decided that a flatmate was in order and texted lots of old pals from university and around – Richard Sturgeon and I had got on well when we were students together, and I was delighted when he got back to me and said he was working in Edinburgh and needed somewhere to stay.

I had hardly seen him recently. We both shared a house, and, when we had time, shared laughs too, but those times were rare just now. Not only were we both working ridiculous hours, but the bone of contention which was always between us seemed to be even more problematical than usual. I wasn't fighting Fishy – I

16

was fighting DC Richard Sturgeon. I had always thought Fishy had thrown his talent away by joining the police force. I knew how good a lawyer I was, and the thought that the one person who I thought was better than me had actually chosen a different path was unfathomable. His job appeared to be just as stressful as mine, judging by his insomnia and weight-loss, but I didn't have much sympathy. I just couldn't understand why he was taking this career path – I wasn't just being stubborn; I genuinely thought he would be better out of the police force, especially given that he seemed to be miserable all the time anyway. Still, as every women's magazine on earth would tell me, I needed to be there for him as a friend rather than a constant critic.

In truth, Fishy was just another one to add to my list. Another one hacked off at me, another one to push out of my mind as I headed off to the station. Sergeant Munro would be there having a fit at my lack of promptness, and Eilidh Buchanan was already gunning for me.

Roll on Kailash Coutts – could it get any worse than a tart who already disliked and had tried to bankrupt me, now demanding that I represent her in a murder case?

THREE

There was no traffic – quite right too, normal people should be in bed at this time of night/morning. The cobbles were greasy and wet though, and I had to keep my speed down to stop the bike from skidding on the road.

Driving conditions were treacherous. I had no time to enjoy the beautiful buildings as me and Awesome climbed Dundas Street in the heart of the New Town.

Stuck at the traffic lights at the bottom of Hanover Street, the Sphinx sitting atop of the National Gallery stared down ominously at me. If she was foretelling something, I couldn't read her warnings, but I knew that the day would bring a stark new world for someone. Out there, somewhere, a wife was waking up to the news that her husband was dead. Does he have children, I wondered? If so, how will they feel? They will be expected to walk upright, go to work or school, and keep a roof over their heads. Crime rips people apart and I see it every day, it's what pays my mortgage and it's what keeps me awake at night. It surprises me that more people don't seek revenge.

The lights changed, and my musings continued. I always think on my bike, solve problems, but Kailash Coutts eluded me. What could this man have done that was so heinous it warranted his murder? Kailash was the self-appointed dissolute ruler of the city. Her wealth, which was considerable, was built on men's depravity, but to acquire her fortune, she must have seen everything (and been well paid for it). What could have been so new to her, or so terrible, that she felt she had to deal with it – permanently?

I wanted to know who this man was who had been dismissed by her. He was probably white, with the usual number of fingers and toes; he was doubtless older than my twenty-eight years. He would be ordinary by most standards, and I'd imagine his wife and work colleagues would have no idea of his secret life. Or would they? One thing my work has taught me: you can never tell someone else's vice, unless you have that particular sin in you. It was a truth I often saw in my work. Edinburgh is the city of split personalities, its establishment was the inspiration for the original schizo-boys, Dr Jekyll and Mr Hyde, and there were plenty of men out there who still led pretty effective double-lives of suburban normality married to episodes in the likes of Kailash Coutts' dungeon. There wasn't much I could say in favour of Kailash herself, but at least what you saw with her was what you got, or in any event, it was after the Roddie Buchanan scandal.

Edinburgh Castle sat, impenetrable on its rock,

shrouded in mist, as I turned down the Royal Mile, past Deacon Brodie's pub. The sign on the tavern wall told the true tale of his downfall and continued the myth of two-faced Edinburgh denizens: 'worthy by day, a gentleman burglar by night, hung on the very gallows he invented'. As a child, I had stood with my mother in front of the painting of the hanging Deacon, relentlessly questioning her: was he my namesake? Was I named after Deacon Brodie? To my disappointment, she always blasted my romanticism out of the water, repeatedly telling me that I was named after the old tea factory that our thirteenth-storey flat overlooked. I still clung to the hope that I had more in common with a licentious, gambling, thieving criminal hanged for his sins than a packet of tea.

On the opposite corner to the pub that still drew me in, outside the High Court, sat a statue of Hume, the father of Scottish law. Draped in a sheet, I felt the artist could have used some aesthetic licence – the sagging pectorals of the carved man made me swerve every time I drove past, although it appeared that only the pigeons and I took any notice of him.

I increased my speed and Parliament House sped by. The route to St Leonard's was a trail of the crime history of Edinburgh, and the narrow closes where body snatchers and serial killers Burke and Hare plied their trade to keep university anatomists busy flew past. Now a city of repute, the Capital could not easily erase its disreputable past. The new Scottish Parliament building at the foot of the Mile did nothing to expunge its notoriety – a series of architectural and financial disasters had led us to a point where the whole business had made Edinburgh a laughing-stock and bought only a few dodgy constructs with what looked like bingo-winner stone cladding.   F156,762

On every corner in Edinburgh, I see an imprint of crime overlaid onto the landscape. I looked up at Arthur's Seat, the Salisbury Crags looming ominously in the early morning skyline, and remembered the German bride thrown over its cruel edges to her death. Not too heartbreaking for her new husband as he collected the insurance money. Everywhere was the same, every place had a story of cruelty or jealousy or lust or evil. St Leonard's Police Station nestles at the foot of Arthur's Seat, in the heart of Edinburgh's Old Town, and is not averse to putting a few new nasty stories into the history of the city. Ordinarily, the streets around the station are, by and large, deserted. But as I approached it in the early hours, it looked like a three-ringed circus. This spelled trouble.

Reporters with notepads and tape recorders, like flies on a corpse. They were everywhere. A television crew was on the street, a man in a sodden trench coat talking into a microphone, his face serious as a grinding camera recorded him for the morning news.

They were all waiting impatiently, for my arrival. I could have kicked myself for not stopping to put some make-up on, but I genuinely hadn't realised there would be this much interest in Kailash so early on in the case. Someone at St Leonard's must have made a tidy backhander alerting the hacks to this one. Reluctantly, I parked and made my way towards them – I didn't want to look dazed and tired in a million homes tomorrow, but without the benefit of a full-blown Jo Malone overnight kit and emergency make-up box in my back-pack, I'd have to accept it.

Jack Deans was the first one to notice me as I pulled off my helmet. I always feel obliged to say, 'Jack Deans, prize-winning investigative journalist' when I introduce him to anyone. I preferred not to recognise that I still got a very worrying flutter every time the fucked-up waster looked at me. Christ knows why. He was a decade past his best – and that would have been if he had spent his best years sober. A former international rugby player, he towered above me. His eyes slowly lowered to meet mine. They were deep, deep blue and he managed to draw me into his stare – or maybe he was sleep-deprived too and couldn't focus very well.

Deans was definitely handsome, in a worn out sort of way. In his younger years, he covered war zones and corrupt dictators; in his latter years he had lost himself in a morass of laughable conspiracy theories and discovered that he couldn't quite find enough clarity at the bottom of a bottle of Laphroaig. He claimed he wasn't drinking these days, but I'd seen him slip enough times to know that he didn't have a permanent pass for the wagon. I had to shake myself out of my very private but still highly mortifying crush on Deans – he'd never let me live it down if he ever found out. His grey black hair flopped over his right eye as he approached me and I drew myself to my full height (five foot four plus the three inches I got from the rather snazzy Cuban heels on my hand-made biker boots).

'Brodie!' shouted Deans, his voice shaped by a past affair with whisky and cigarettes. ('No! No! No!' I told myself. 'It's shaped by booze and fags and cancer and hardened arteries and all sorts of manky stuff. He is *not not not* sexy.')

'I take it you're here for Kailash?'

The woman had turned into Madonna – she needed no surname. I was tired and I did actually resent his familiarity, even if I did, on a dull night, often want to get into his no-doubt-vile-but-very-well-filled pants.

'No comment,' I said tersely.

'I've been standing here, in this pissing rain, for almost two hours – give me something. Please? Please, Brodie? Pretty please?'

The rain had plastered his hair to the side of his grizzled cheek. Although it was raining, the night air was still – after about thirty seconds with the man, as usual, my bizarre crush had worn off and I just wanted to slap him for assuming he had any right to information from me. I was also not so smitten that I didn't wonder how he could have been there for nearly two hours unless someone had called him pretty bloody sharpish.

I ignored Jack Deans and made my way to the front door of the station and he followed me. His past glories were still sufficiently bright in the eyes of the other journalists present for them to hang back deferentially.

The man was tracking me. I felt his eyes bore into me but continued to ignore him, until he grabbed my arm. Instinctively, I smashed my helmet into his knee: to his acolytes (and the CCTV outside the station door), it looked like a clumsy accident, but we knew differently. He crashed to the ground, like a newly cut Christmas tree.

Magic moment officially broken.

He grabbed my ankle on his way down. Almost toppling, I angrily held my balance. I stared at him, now just wanting this fine gentleman of the press to bugger off out of my way so that I could get on with my job. Rather than look annoyed, or even pained, the face of Deans was the picture of smugness.

'You don't know, do you?' he whispered.

I wouldn't give him the upper hand, wouldn't start our usual tit-for-tat.

'You don't know, do you?' he asked again, slightly louder this time.

I waited all of five seconds before breaking.

'No, Jack, I don't know. I don't know which schemy wee copper has phoned you out of your stench-filled pit at this time of the morning. I don't know how many Big Macs or cans of cash-and-carry lager you've paid him for his trouble. I don't know why so many half-bit hacks are gathered outside when all they're going to do is run more pictures of tarts in mini-skirts with a cut-and-paste job pretending to be a story. But I bet, I just bloody bet, you're going to tell me.'

I stood with my hands on my hips, feeling quite pleased with myself. Losing your cool and shouting outside a cop shop while on professional duty was always a good way to start a case.

Jack Deans stood back from me and mirrored my pose, a smile creeping onto his lips. He let his eyes

24

wander all over my face, and, for a moment, I thought I almost saw a flicker of sympathy.

'Brodie?' he asked, as if I'd know the answer. 'Brodie? They haven't told you, have they?'

I kept my silence this time. If he had news of Kailash, he'd be bursting to tell me anyway.

The next words out of his mouth were a statement, not a question.

'You don't know who she's murdered.'

A smile of satisfaction crossed his face. I had to hand it to the grandstanding bastard – this round was going to him.

'Why didn't they tell you, Brodie?'

The same question was beginning to float through my mind.

'If I was you, Brodie, I'd figure out who wanted to throw me to the wolves.'

Jack Deans knew that his special status was coming to an end, the press pack descending, and me running out of patience.

He propelled me through the doors into the police station in one fluid movement.

'Alistair MacGregor,' he whispered in my ear.

I had no time to answer him.

I had no time to think.

I could only assume that I hadn't heard him correctly.

FOUR

What was wrong with Kailash Coutts? Could she just not keep her hands off the Scottish judiciary? Like most of the men she came into contact with, Alistair MacGregor had another identity – but this one didn't involve bondage and baby nappy fantasies. No, this one was a shitload more complicated. The dead man wasn't known as Alistair MacGregor. He was known by his full title, Lord Arbuthnot of Broxden, Lord President of the Court of Session, or, to make things simpler: the highest Law Lord in Scotland. No wonder Sergeant Munro was so keen to get this one processed quickly, and no wonder the entire Scottish media was camped outside St Leonard's in the wee small hours.

I didn't have any time to wallow in the misery that was hurtling towards me – times were bad when Jack Deans seemed to be the only one giving me a hand – as the full wonder that was front-house in an Edinburgh cop shop opened out in front of me. The smirks on the faces of the police officers at the desk could have made me regret some of my past harsh cross-examinations, but I was more concerned with trying to block out the truly awful rendition of 'Rawhide' that was going on as I made my way to the desk. No introductions were necessary. I'd spent far too much of my time here in the past. Desk Sergeant Anderson waddled towards me, red faced and huffing from the exertion of moving two feet without a pie in his hand. His cheap white shirt was see-through, and puckered over his vast gut, the only accessory being some worn-in underarm sweat stains. A veteran, coming up to retirement age, he made it known he'd seen – in his words – young 'punks' like me come and go. Given that I was also pretty sure he dreamed of himself with a shiny 'Sheriff' badge pinned to his chest, I wasn't exactly bothered. What did worry me was the fact that he was breathing so heavily he was either going to have an orgasm in front of me, or he was working up to some godawful joke that he'd laboured over since the last time we met. At least the first option might be funny.

'I'd *like* to take you to the cells, Miss McLennan . . .' he wheezed, pausing for dramatic effect as the lackeys around him waited for the punch line. 'But you might call me a liar.'

Had the Marx Brothers suddenly been arrested, dragging in Laurel and Hardy with them? Had Tommy Cooper come out of cryogenic hibernation to announce a new career in law enforcement with Ricky Gervais and John Cleese as his loyal sidekicks? Or had some fat sweaty bastard of a useless copper just tried – in vain – to score a lame point against someone who wouldn't shite on him if he paid Kailash rates? Whatever the reason, St Leonard's erupted with joy at the witticism launched into posterity – Anderson wouldn't be able to move for bacon butties and Irn Bru for the rest of his shift given the joy he had bestowed on his colleagues with his pathetic introduction. I vaguely recalled our last meeting – a police assault case involving some wealthy young pro-hunt protesters. I won, although the verdict owed more to the judicial loyalties of the bench, than any great legal point on my behalf. Every dog has its day, and this was Sergeant Anderson's. His young posse were enjoying his bravado, especially the ones who had also received a tongue lashing from me when they had appeared in the witness box.

Just as I was trying to boost myself with the facts of my incredibly superior existence and immaculate professionalism, I caught sight of my reflection in the plate glass windows of the station. Normally, my best feature is my hair; at the moment it looked like the stuffing that escapes from horsehair settees. Dark auburn curls had turned to frizz with the help of the damp night air and my motorbike helmet. The rain and spray from the roads had soaked through my leather jacket, leaving me no alternative but to remove it. I should have known better. I was wearing my favourite t-shirt, soft, grey, and very worn. The kind of garment you wear to bed when your mum says you look a bit peaky. Unfortunately, in this scenario, I don't have the sort of cleavage which makes a police station full of men look away. They didn't like me personally and they hated what I stood for – but all that could be forgotten amidst the amazing revelation that I possessed breasts. Sergeant Anderson's moment of glory was stolen as an entire cop shop launched into a communal wet-t-shirt fantasy. It could be worse, I told myself, before remembering that the belt buckle holding up my leather trousers bore the Harley legend: 'Born to Ride'.

As I followed Sergeant Anderson to the staircase door leading to the cells, I tried to block out the hilarious comments being lobbed my way. There was no denying that I enjoyed the attention that came from being a court lawyer when it suited me, and on my terms, but tonight, going into whatever lay in front of me, I could do without anyone's eyes and remarks. In fact, I'd have paid good money for an uptight Marks and Spencer suit and button-down shirt. I didn't exactly look the picture of legal respectability, or the embodiment of my infamous claim to fame as youngest solicitor advocate in Scottish legal history. Still, no matter that I could hide behind all sorts of professional titles such as Writer to the Signet (alongside Sir Walter Scott, no less) – in this place, I was the lowest of the low: a lawyer and a woman. Even my client could probably expect better treatment than me. God knows what she would make of my appearance – actually, she'd probably think that she was being visited by one of her peers, and not a very good-looking one at that. Alongside wondering how Kailash Coutts would interpret me, I also briefly thought of what my mother would say – discomfort made me shut that voice off pretty sharpish.

Sergeant Anderson and I formed the start of a

cavalcade as we moved down into the bowels of the station. We weren't alone for long – passing by offices, we were joined by their occupants on spurious errands. They all wanted to see it. To witness the showdown between myself and Kailash Coutts.

How would I react to meeting with the woman who was accused of killing another member of my profession?

How would I react to meeting the woman who had asked for me by name to represent her even though we had nothing but a history of mistrust and deceit?

How would I react to meeting the woman I had always suspected had called the papers to set up Roddie Buchanan and almost ruin me in the process? Although I was Roddie's junior partner, under Scottish law, I was jointly and severally liable for the debts of our entire firm. This meant that the creditors could come to me for the money had the scandal ruined Lothian & St Clair. I, in turn, would have had to sue Roddie to see a penny of that money ever again. It was a close thing. The scandal and gossip arising out of the Kailash Coutts debacle threatened the very existence of the firm. Clients were bleeding away. Our overheads, mostly high spec offices in Castle Terrace, were prohibitive, and the bank had called in our overdraft. Unpredictably, the last moment change of heart from Kailash Coutts saved us. By signing the spurious affidavit about Roddie's single rather than dual bollocking, she gave me the ammunition to raise the defamation action.

As our motley crew continued downwards to the cells, the smell assaulted me. I felt myself gagging. The noises from behind the locked steel doors made me think of Bedlam. Ruby the turnkey shuffled towards me. I always thought of Ruby as symbolic of this place – nothing was quite right, but there was enough of a superficial attempt to make outsiders think everything could hold together just a bit longer. Thirty denier black tights attempted to cover her gnarled, varicose veined legs. They failed. Her peroxide blonde hair had the vague look of something that had seen a hairdresser once, but the visit had resulted in locks the texture and consistency of a scouring pad. It was in a very fashionable style – for the 1950s, which was approximately the last time any man had considered her attractive.

Her real name was Jean, but she always seemed like a Ruby to me in honour of the bright red lipstick she slashed over her gash of a mouth. To be honest, I had been torn between naming her 'Ruby' or 'Blue' – the latter would have been equally appropriate in recognition of the two slabbed cakes of eye shadow adorning her drooping lids. Ruby was oblivious to her failings, but she eyed me up as if I was something she had trodden upon in the street. Obviously, I did not fit her notion of glamour. Fag ash hung from her mouth and keys at her side. Deftly she fingered the collection, recognising every one by touch alone. She unlocked the door – I had never noticed any of them creak before, but when a small crowd is silent, holding its breath, every little noise is exaggerated.

The door swung outwards from the twelve-foot cell, briefly obscuring my vision. Epinephrine was surging through my body, heightening my senses, so that I became aware of a scent, delicate and sweet, dancing towards me.

I had been taken aback when I saw Kailash Coutts in the flesh for the first time.

There are women whose eyes meet for a moment, and, although they are not friends, they know each other. Instantaneously, they sum one another up, their eyes flicking from hair to shoes, and for a second their souls unite. When I met her, I thought: I could be friends with you. We are women at the height of our respective professions, daily we fight men to get on top. In my case it was, thankfully, only figuratively.

I recalled the bald details given to me about my client: Female, forty-one years of age, mixed race. Those empty words didn't come close to describing her, the photographs I had seen didn't do her justice.

Kailash Coutts was a woman gifted by nature – and what nature didn't give her, she went out and bought. And she certainly knew where to shop. Her long, black hair fell glossily to her shoulders, as she turned to look at me it rippled like a waterfall. A few seconds in her presence and I wasn't sure whether the voice inside my head sounded like Mills & Boon or Loaded.

'You've got five minutes.' Sergeant Anderson's voice was hoarse with excitement. 'I've got paperwork to do if Ms Coutts is to appear in court today.'

I was astounded at the respect he was giving my client. And perhaps a tad resentful that I was never accorded the same. What was it about her, and why didn't I have some of it? Kailash was the product of an affair between a married Donegal nurse, and a young surgeon from the Punjab. Her father disappeared home to an arranged marriage, her abandoned mother threw herself on the charity of her cuckolded Irish husband. In his generosity, he agreed to keep the child, and raise it as his own provided the baby was white. When she was born, it was immediately obvious that Kailash's olive skin did not pass the paper bag test. If her skin were lighter than a brown paper bag, she would have been kept and passed off as a genetic throwback to the Spanish Armada that wrecked itself on the rocks off the west coast of Ireland. Unfortunately for the young Kailash, mixed-race babies are often very dark skinned in the early days of their lives. Her fate was sealed. Home for her was a series of fostering residences. Nobody wanted to claim the dark eyed child as their own.

Times change. My father abandoned my own mother, yet it was acceptable in society for her to raise her fatherless child alone. My mother adored me – in her own way – and was always determined to give me every opportunity possible, with or without a man by her side. If I had been consigned to the life that Kailash had led, would I have walked in her footsteps?

I'm a sucker for any fatherless child. As I looked into the black eyes of Kailash Coutts, I swore that I would do everything I could to get her off. I knew that I was in danger of committing professional suicide. The woman who had almost ruined my firm, almost ruined me personally, was now about to be charged with the murder of one of the highest Law Lords in the country. And, on the basis of us both being deserted wee girls, I had decided she was my new best pal.

I grabbed her arm as she walked out to Sergeant Anderson. 'You have the right to remain silent,' I reminded her. 'Use that right. This morning there will be a court hearing. We will make no plea or declaration in response to the charge of murder. Later, there will be a judicial examination. It will be tape recorded, and at that stage we must state your defence, otherwise the Crown can found upon our silence.'

'Our.'

I was already linking myself emotionally to her. I would have to pull back, but as Kailash smiled at me, I realised grimly that it wasn't going to be any time soon. I hoped she understood what I was saying, hoped she recognised the coded message in my words. I did not want to hear that she was guilty, as that would place me in an awkward position as an officer of the court. I was giving her time to think up a defence.

I stood for a moment, watching her walk away to be charged with murder, and I silently cursed my own absent father. I was in her web now, and I was sure Kailash Coutts was not going to let me go.

FIVE

'You look rough.'

'I feel worse than I look.'

'Well they do say beauty comes from within, so try to cheer up.' Lavender smiled at me as she handed me a steaming cup of coffee. In that instant I could have forgiven her anything. Even the fact that she was sitting in my chair didn't bother me – neither of us harboured any illusions over who really ran the show in my office. Lawyers may be the public face, but the real power lies with their secretaries.

I sipped gingerly on the burning liquid, staring out of my office window at Edinburgh Castle, as Lavender began to read out today's cases from the diary.

The court diary is the most important record in a legal firm – a missed court date or a misplaced trial is a sack-able offence. The consequences of such a mistake can't be overstated – it is imprisonment for the client, and even worse for the solicitor. If a punter does not turn up at his trial date, a warrant will be taken for their arrest – if the lawyer doesn't attend they face contempt of court charges.

Going over the court diary was a ritual that Lavender and I did every morning at 7.30a.m. if we could, we gave it the respect it was due even when a huge case like that of Kailash Coutts was going to blow everything out of the water. So much of my time was going to be spent on her, that I needed to ensure that nothing else was going to suffer.

'How many trials?' I asked Lavender.

'One jury, and a continued High Court job. Robert Dunlop already has his papers, he'll do it for you, and I'm sending the first year trainee in to sit with him. On top of that,' added Lavender, 'we've got five summary trials and two of them are in Kirkcaldy.' Her voice got lower, and although she didn't exactly mumble, she certainly hurried through the next part of her list of points.

'I instructed Eddie last night and I dropped the files off at his house.'

She fumbled with the pages of the diary as colour flooded her face. I didn't have the energy to tease Lavender about her unrequited love for Eddie Gibb. Eddie was a brilliant court lawyer whose genius at the bar was exceeded only by his excess in the bar. I was never quite sure whether it was me or Lavender who kept forgiving Eddie his misdemeanours. I do know that Lavender had to pull him out of the pub on so many occasions we had a code name for it – Eddie was in court nine.

Most of the Sheriffs knew about Eddie's difficulty and forgave him for it. I reckon that we all knew we had a bit of Eddie in us.

'You know I like Eddie as much as the next person, Lav, but we're shooting ourselves in the foot to put him in Kirkcaldy on his own.'

'So Sheriff Robertson hates him? He's not too fond of you either, Brodie.'

'I'm not talking personalities here, Lav – if Eddie has hit the bevvy at lunch time who's going to pull his arse out the fire? You can't be in Edinburgh running the show, and Kirkcaldy watching over lover boy.'

'Beggars can't be choosers, Brodie – I had to keep other agency lawyers on standby to deal with Edinburgh, leaving you free to cover the custodies – you didn't call me last night to let me know if you were overstretched and I didn't want another lecture on "Delectus Personae". I did my best, and I think Eddie can do this.'

Lavender's blonde curls bobbed merrily – in contradiction to her mood. Her forty-three-year-old face was untroubled by wrinkles, fat was the filler she preferred to keep her face smooth, and it suited her. She was gorgeous and I loved her like a sister. Never a size 8, her figure was a walking Rubensesque fantasy. She generally drew men to her like moths to a flame, but Eddie's love of the booze meant that he always seemed one step away from her, even though he relied on her so much.

Lavender knew as much as any solicitor on the team at Lothian & St Clair. She understood what it meant to build a successful criminal practice, and Delectus Personae meant that there were some clients who would only stay with the firm if I represented them.

Her intuitive instincts were buzzing last night – she knew we had a client; a Mr Big who would demand my undivided attention.

She just didn't know who it was yet – I hadn't summoned the courage to tell her.

Lavender was indispensable to me. After the Kailash affair, the firm's serious financial trouble meant that my life hung in the balance – the bank balance of Lothian & St Clair. The only way for me to find freedom was to make the firm financially successful again. To do this I took on every case I could – but there was one difficulty. Although I was prepared to work every hour outside the office, I couldn't be in two places at once. I didn't have the resources to take on extra bodies, so I had a team of agency solicitors. Agency lawyers are like Japanese Ronin – Samurai without masters. They are lone warriors who owe allegiance to no one. The Japanese didn't trust them – but I didn't have a choice. Anyway, it was generally left to Lavender to keep them in check.

She interrupted my thoughts. 'I'll find out you know.'

'What?'

'The secret you're trying to keep from me – I'll find out. I always do.'

It was true, no one could have any privacy whilst Lav was about. You simply had to accept it because, as well as running my life for me, her gift of hacking into computers was so useful at other times.

It all started with eBay. Lavender began buying and then selling. Buying from the fifteen-year-old shoplifters and then passing it off on the net. Quite the entrepreneur. No one was any the wiser and her computer skills developed until her natural inquisitiveness got the better of her.

There was a man – with Lavender every story could begin that way – and she wanted to know more about him. When does infatuation become stalking, as she is so fond of saying? Anyway, this man was interested in computers so Lavender took a course on computer security – how to keep company firewalls safe from hackers. To build firewalls you have to know how to take them down, and the secrets hidden behind those walls were irresistible to her.

The mystery man worked in a city bank, and the Metropolitan police completely misunderstood Lavender's interest in the bank's security systems. The outcome was leaving her former life in London behind and a change of name – Lavender Ironside, stolen from a gravestone in a Highland graveyard. We were made for each other. Lavender needed me as much as I needed her.

I looked over to see what was keeping her so busy.

'You could at least wait until I left the room,' I said.

'You're showing no signs of going,' she retorted, unashamedly rifling through my briefcase. 'You're so untidy – don't you realise I have to try and make some sense of all this scribble?' She pulled my notes closer to her face.

'Kailash Coutts?' Her eyes narrowed in contempt.

'I knew we were desperate to get clients, Brodie, but I didn't for one moment think things were this bad.'

'How do you think I feel? I've been up half the night because of that woman.'

'Why didn't you say "no", then? You're the one who's prostituting yourself if you can't say "no".'

'I tried – but Roddie wouldn't let me. Well, his wife had some say in it too.'

'I hope that sounds as pathetic to you as it does to me,' she retorted.

'Look at me, Lav – look at my life.'

'You haven't got one – you work all the time trying to dig yourself out of a hole caused by Kailash Coutts. A hole that's getting bigger. We've got one jury and three summary trials plus the custodies to be covered in Edinburgh today, and it could all blow up in our face because of that woman. Again.'

'Well, here come the cavalry.'

I could see movement through the glass panel in my office door.

In they trooped.

Robert Girvan – smart and sharp as any bankrupt could be. He had a restricted practising certificate because his senior partner had messed up the firm's accounts and, like me, Robert was jointly and severally liable for the debts. He was my warning. If at any time I felt like bunking off, I thought of Robert and a shiver ran down my spine. We both knew that was why I gave him work.

Danny Bishop – nice guy shame about the face. He was scarred from his cheek to his chin. Legend had it that he went out with his client's girlfriend and was offered the choice – his balls or his face. Most people knew that although he had chosen the latter, the experience had taken his balls anyway.

The trainee was following him, smart-suited and

40

relatively eager, she wasn't to know that they all looked the same to me; even the ones who were pretty much my own age.

Trailing up the rear, both physically and metaphorically, was David Bannatyne. He had his own firm until he left his wife and developed a habit of picking up young men and taking them home only to find that they had loaded his gear into his car and driven off into the sunset without him.

These were my Ronin, the ones who were going to save the day. In spite of their personal problems, if you could actually get them into court, they had a flair not often found in the more clerical amongst us.

They perched their backsides on any available ledge and looked at me expectantly. As was usual, Lavender handed out the coffee before I dispatched the files and instructions for the day's work. I started with the trainee.

'HMA v Marjorie Pirie; it's a High Court trial. Donnie Dunlop has already been instructed and he appeared on the last date in court – it was continued from the fifth of June because a crucial prosecution witness went into premature labour. It's straightforward. Just do exactly as counsel tells you and don't bad mouth the judges to the client.'

'Why would I do that?' the youngster protested.

'A friend of mine agreed with a divorce client that the Sheriff was a bastard for giving his wife an interim aliment settlement of £250 per week.'

'So?'

David Bannatyne shook his head and got up to refill his coffee.

'Have you never heard of murmuring a judge?' he asked.

The bemused trainee shook her head.

'Well, it's a criminal offence – a judge can say anything they want to you, but if you make any smart remarks back, inside court you'll get done for contempt, outside court, it's called murmuring.'

'Thanks, David – I've put you down for the jury trial. It's on the list for today but it's unlikely to start. I think, as usual, they will have a number that will plead. This won't – inside the file I've put a list of recent cases. Andy Gilmore was stopped by police – they searched his car because it was messy with CDs – and they thought the CDs were stolen. In the course of the search they discovered cocaine – it was an illegal search because it's arguable that they didn't have justifiable cause to stop and search in the first instance.'

'Cheers, Brodie – take it you thought I was the man for this case because I could argue that my car is messy?' He pulled the file from my outstretched hands – a smile curled round his lips.

'What am I doing today?'

Danny Bishop looked tired, he was in his early fifties and, although the scar had faded, time was pulling the left side of his face down faster than the right giving him an odd lopsided grin.

'A two cop breach – in the district court.'

'Cheers.'

I turned to face Robert Girvan who was looking at me expectantly.

'You're going to be watching my back in Edinburgh Sheriff court – I'm covering the custodies.'

He looked at me as if to question whether that was everything – I knew that I should warn him that all hell could break loose around me, but somehow I couldn't find the words.

'The two summary trials are pretty straightforward. Smile at the fiscal and see if you can get them both put in the same court. One is a breach of the peace. My client assures me the witnesses won't turn up.'

Robert winked at me. 'That's the kind of trial I like.'

He liked it because I still paid him for a full day in court.

'And the other?' He waited with interest.

'The other one is solicitation – Maggie Jones giving a client a blow job in his car.'

'For Christ's sake, Brodie, why are we taking this to trial?'

A grimace flickered across his face. I hadn't fancied doing this trial either but Maggie was a 'good client', namely she was a heroin addict who did anything and everything to fund her habit. Repeat business was always handy.

'Okay, Brodie, tell me the defence to this one – please don't say it was because she didn't swallow.'

Our humour at anytime of the day is black or lavatorial – preferably both.

'No, it's not – better than that, Rob. The arresting officer didn't see any money change hands – so our argument is that she wasn't soliciting, she was doing it for fun.'

'Terrific – at this point I'd like to state it's me who has to make that argument in court, not you.'

'Trust me,' interrupted Lavender. 'Brodie would rather be making any spurious point than what she's got to do today.'

My eyes locked with hers, daring her to say anything more. As usual she ignored me.

'Well – you're not saying anything and they'll find out soon enough. Brodie, in her wisdom, is representing Roddie's whore.'

'Which one?' asked Robert. 'Not Kailash?'

Lavender nodded.

Robert stood up. He tilted his head and spoke softly. 'Why?' is the last thing he said as he left for court.

I had stopped asking myself the same question – I was already in too deep.

SIX

At around 9.45a.m., Edinburgh Sheriff Court resembles 'Paddy's Market'. Squalor and clamour abound, as young men with cheap suits and even cheaper tattoos scramble for justice. At the same time, lawyers with overdrafts and considerably more expensive suits clamber for clients – it's hard to work out who is more desperate.

Preoccupied, I pushed my way through the throng. Journalists jostled with juvenile delinquents, and all of them seemed to want a piece of me.

'Hey, Brodie!' A young man, proudly sporting a tattooed blue line across his neck with the immortal words 'CUT ME', called out to me. 'I'm thinking of changing my lawyer.'

Tattoo Boy knew that the press were here to see me and he wanted to be part of the action. Young men like him are known as 'dripping roasts', highly prized at the Edinburgh bar for being cash cows. Their criminal activities, and subsequent trials, bought most of the Mercedes cars parked outside court. I didn't like to turn down such a plea as his, but I had other things on my mind. For one, Jack Deans was bearing down upon me.

'I hope you're not feeling as bad as I am, Brodie.' His voice sounded rough, like heavy-duty sand paper. I was feeling dreadful and he was always guaranteed to bother me one way or another. I'd ignore him. That was always classy.

'So, Lord Arbuthnot is no more,' Deans mockingly intoned. 'How does it feel to be representing his killer? Real step up the old career ladder there, eh?' I kept ignoring him, this time because I had no answer, not for Jack Deans or myself.

BBC Scotland moved in to the gap that had opened up as I moved away from Deans. I had no comment for them either. Disconcertingly, I heard a reporter describe me on camera as the rising star of the Scottish bar. For how much longer, after I'd dealt with this corpse of a case, they didn't deign to tell me.

The public space in front of the courthouse was even more crammed than usual. Everywhere, people mixed cheek to jowl, everywhere, that is, except for one tiny corner. This wasn't just a piece of ground – this was territory. It belonged to the Dark Angels. Instantly recognisable, their garb was almost a marketing strategy. Long black leather coats. Peroxide white hair worn long and poker straight for the girls, spiked crew cuts for the boys. Black hats, and short black painted nails were obligatory for both sexes, as were the silver-topped black walking sticks they all carried. Their skin was alabaster white, as if they would shrivel in the sun.

They were into everything, but, strangely they were never caught, or, at least, never brought to trial. Urban myths existed about their cases being returned to the police marked 'No Pro', no matter what they were accused of. The 'Dark Angels' were, for some reason, not to be prosecuted. It was a source of speculation in the bar common room as to how they escaped detection. It certainly was not the case that they blended into the background.

In the centre of the pack, their leader, Moses Tierney, stared at me sullenly. Moses was his real name, not a carefully chosen brand addition like everything else to do with his gang, and he was born during a brief period in his mother's life when she was junk free. I had heard that she called him Moses because he was to be her deliverer. Predictably, this wasn't to be, and after his mother's death, Moses was taken into care. Her only legacy to him was an overactive imagination and a flair for the dramatic. I had never observed Moses Tierney at court, nor had I glimpsed the 'Dark Angels' in daylight before, but I knew who he was, who they were. My gaze locked with that of Moses; he had the stare of a wolf, with pale grey, dark ringed eyes. In all this commotion, he held my attention. I suddenly felt as if he were presenting the Dark Angels to me – he wanted me to see them. To his gang, he was their Messiah, and I had to concede he had kept them out of trouble – so far.

'Charismatic, isn't he?' Jack Deans had sneaked up on me again. 'Are you wondering why they're here?'

This time, I nodded in answer. 'I think we all are.

What's brought them out of their hidey holes at this time of the day?'

I was fixated on the Dark Angels. As I stood watching them, as one, they all stared at me, lifted their walking canes and raised them towards me. Almost in salute. There was no danger in their action. They then turned and slowly filed away.

'That answers it,' resumed Jack Deans. 'They came for you.'

I pulled my eyes away from the bizarre homage in front of me and shot round to face Deans. 'Are you enjoying baiting me? Winding me up about Kailash and now about Moses Tierney?'

'I feel that's a trick question, Brodie,' he answered. 'A part of me knows you want me to say "No" and be gallant and mindful of your feelings and all sort of pish like that. But another part – roughly ninety-nine per cent – wants to ask you if you're officially off your fucking head? Of course I'm enjoying it. You're squirming, you have no idea what to do – I'd have to be, at the very least, a practising lawyer not to get any pleasure out of that. And you get a lovely wee blush to your cheeks when you're mad at me.'

'Anything else you want to add before I leave with a highly satisfying picture of me kicking your bollocks from here to Princes Street?' I asked.

'Oooh, you been getting ideas from your client?' Deans mocked. 'No, I'm pretty much done – I'm happy with my lot.'

I moved towards the sanctuary of the revolving court doors – not quickly enough, as I could still hear Deans shouting something about how he preferred what I'd been wearing last night to my court attire.

Kailash Coutts was waiting for me in the cells. She looked like an exotic caged beast, completely out of place. Pacing backwards and forwards, she was 'motoring'. Distressed prisoners do this, but my senses didn't indicate that she was troubled. Her brow seemed to be furrowed, quite an achievement given the amount of Botox in there, as she muttered under her breath.

Something was wrong though. Kailash was immaculately dressed. Someone had brought her in a fresh set of couture clothes. The way the accused presents themselves is crucial to the outcome of a case. Generally, the better looking you are, the more chance you have of being found innocent or receiving a lighter sentence. But Kailash was an unusual case; she was turning the theory on its head.

'I never thought I'd have to say this,' I started, 'but you look too . . .' I was fighting for a tactful way to say it.

'Expensive.'

Obligingly, Kailash finished my sentence.

'Absolutely!' I nodded, foolishly believing she might go along with my ideas. It was pretty unusual for a lawyer to have to tell a prostitute client they looked too tasteful – in this case, Kailash just seemed too good for her surroundings and I was worried the judge might be completely thrown. Murdering whores don't often look like Halle Berry taking the day off to meander down a catwalk.

In return, and with brutal honesty, Kailash looked

me over. I had brought my bike to court so that I could park. I'd worn my leathers and changed into a suit in the agents' room. A well used high street label, my court wear looks even worse crumpled, but it usually suffices. Looking down, I could see some of my buttons were in the wrong holes, giving me an odd rumpled effect. As usual, my striped blouse was unironed. With regard to my shoes, it is sufficient to say that I could not see my face in them. In my favour, my legs were smooth and tanned although bare legs in court is deemed inappropriate in some quarters.

'Take a look at yourself,' she sneered as I tried to pretend there wasn't a problem.

'You are a professional,' she informed me. 'A woman of some importance, and you are dressed like . . . Well, you are dressed like . . .' she couldn't quite bring herself to spit the word out, and I wondered what descriptive term could possibly make a tart sound as though it was the filthiest word in the dictionary.

Kailash's French manicured fingers stroked her flawless complexion, as she searched for the proper insult.

I tried to help.

'A student. I look like a student. I'm always being told that.'

'No,' she said, wagging her index finger back and forth, as if no student ever looked that bad. She gave up on the put-down, there was clearly nothing awful enough to describe me – and continued the lecture.

'Brodie, you are unique. How many people have escaped from their upbringing? Truly escaped? You are educated, which is rare where you come from. You are respected – to an extent, but it is still an achievement. And Brodie,' I could have sworn her voice softened, but I could have been misled by the fact that I was starting to wonder just how she had managed to Google me while in St Leonard's, 'you are beautiful, no matter how much you try to deny it.' I've read that if you can speak at the rate of a human heart, you can sell anything. Kailash had that gift and I needed to fight her mesmerism.

Her voice returned to normal. 'We must work on your image.'

I struggled past the image of me striding into court à la Julia Roberts, styled by Stella McCartney, with a Nobel Prize in one hand and an Oscar in the other. It was hard to decide which fantasy was best, so I went for reality instead.

'No, Kailash. Right now, we work on your defence.'

Worryingly, I was beginning to notice that Kailash was doing everything she could to avoid talking about what had actually happened. We hadn't yet had the conversation I have with most clients, where I spend my time trying to get them to shut up. She already knew I didn't want to hear that she had murdered Lord Arbuthnot, but this was deeper than that. No one pleads guilty to a charge of murder. It is simply not worth it, because there is only one sentence: life. If she told me she was guilty, it would make my job impossible, but she was being even quieter about it all than it usually required.

'The three defences to murder that apply to you are ...'

Kailash stood impassively in the corner smoking an

imported cigarette. I prayed she was listening to me. This was all a damn sight more important than taking me for a makeover.

'Alibi. That means it wasn't you. You were somewhere else when the murder happened. It helps if you have a credible witness to back you up.'

Fleetingly, I wondered if she knew any credible witnesses. To be openly associated with Kailash Coutts was social, and professional, suicide. A cold, slow, shiver ran down my back, like an ice cube meandering down my spine. I was in that category now.

'Then, there's self defence,' I continued. 'But, you are only allowed to use reasonable force, and in your case it might be tricky, given that it is the Lord President who's dead.'

Kailash raised an eyebrow quizzically, as if I did not know my own profession. Regrettably, she might be right.

'Lastly, and it's difficult, is the defence of accident. That means you were there. You were the cause of death. But it was a mishap.'

Kailash said nothing. The clock on the cell walls showed 10.30a.m., as a disembodied voice called me over the tannoy.

'Brodie McLennan to court six.'

A young police officer rattled the bars of the cell.

'You're here,' he said, stating the obvious. 'Sheriff Strathclyde is on the bench. He's waiting for you.'

Standing straight to catch his breath, he blocked my exit. I pushed past him, running at full pelt out of the cells, my black gown flying as he called after me.

'By the way . . . he's been on the bench since ten.'

With barely a nod to Kailash, I ran and ran. I didn't stop until I reached the entrance of the court. My adversary for this morning, Baggy Sutherland, lurched against the doorframe. He had a droopy hangdog look that comes from a lifetime of disappointments. Gifted in court, when he was sober, he could bring a tear to any juror's eye. His black court gown was in fact green with age. On occasions when I had forgotten mine, his was the only one left hanging in the agents' room. Wearing Baggy's gown was like putting on the mantle of Elijah.

'You're in trouble.' Baggy stopped me, and started pulling at my gown. I had no time for pleasantries, I pushed forwards, but he wouldn't let me go.

'It's on inside out,' he offered by way of an explanation for the mauling which was taking place. Rather deftly, for a man with tremors in his hands, he removed my gown, and turned it right side out.

'The mood that old bastard's in, he'd do you with contempt for wearing it that way.'

Baggy was serious. Sheriff Strathclyde had a severe problem with me – even before I acted for his wife in their divorce action. He could find me in contempt of court for anything, even my clothes. I would win it on appeal, but he still had the power. I was anxious to do nothing to offend him.

I could almost hear his breath as I walked in. Sheriff Strathclyde is small, very angry, and with a body shape that favours a toad. I intended to walk straight in and proceed with business. He, of course had other plans.

He wanted me to suffer. His ball-like face, which looked as if it had been chewed by a large dog trying to remodel its own arse, signalled red for danger.

All heads, but one, had swivelled to watch my entrance. Kailash looked intently at the bench. She had taken the direct route from the cells, and had arrived much faster than I could.

'How kind of you to find the time to join us today, Ms McLennan.' Sheriff Strathclyde's voice was chilly, deep, and rich, the product of a very expensive education.

'Give me one good reason why I shouldn't find you in contempt of court,' he spat at me. 'Right now.'

'Well, how about the fact that you have absolutely no right to?' I countered. 'I was consulting with a client on a very serious charge.'

It took about a second for me to realise this wasn't quite the approach I should have gone for.

'No right, no right!' Purple in the face, Strathclyde looked as if he were about to explode.

'No right!' he continued. 'It's my court! I can do as I please! Anything! I can do anything!'

Raising himself up to his full height, he leaned over the bench. For a moment, I thought that he would topple onto me. I was squaring up to him. This day was getting worse with every passing minute and he was a bully. Anyway, surely he wouldn't respect obsequiousness?

'Find me in contempt,' I challenged him, 'and I will appeal you straightaway.'

No judge likes to have his or her decisions appealed. I had my pen poised noting down every word he said.

Strathclyde was well acquainted with the appeal procedure. He knew that judicial words spoken in anger did not go down well over the road in Parliament House.

Disdainfully, he flicked his manicured hand in my direction. Feeling more relief than I would ever admit, I took my seat in the well of the court, opposite the Procurator Fiscal.

This case, in technical lawyer speak, had all the makings of being a Right Royal Bastard.

SEVEN

The Fiscal and I had been at university together. Frank Pearson was a mature student when we were both studying together, but the age gap made no difference to our friendship. I always had time for him and I liked the way he never made assumptions about me or my competitive streak.

The sheriff clerk looked disparagingly at me as she called the case. I was grateful that indictments are called in chambers, which meant that no member of the press or public was allowed. As things stood, the people who were allowed to be there were causing me enough trouble without any help from outsiders.

'Are you Kailash Bernadette Coutts?' The clerk's voice rang out around the courtroom.

The surprise caught in my throat. Bernadette? But then I recalled her Irish mother and realised it could have been worse; she might have had my first name.

The clerk's voice went on as I waited impatiently for my turn.

'How do you plead?'

That was it. My cue. My curtain call. I leaped to my feet.

'Brodie McLennan. I appear on behalf of Ms Coutts, who makes no plea or declaration at this stage.'

On indictment charges, you do not plead guilty or not guilty, you do not declare your position, you do not give anything away. I expected to be out of that oaf's court as quickly as possible, because I couldn't ask for bail on a murder charge, and I was determined to leave no clue behind me. Kailash would be remanded in prison until the trial, and I would have a chance to reconsider my position at that point. I could already see myself this evening, languishing in a bubble bath, working out whether I should go on with this case, working out how to get out of it. My reverie was soon broken.

'Ms McLennan, approach the bench.'

Frank Pearson was already there, and deep in discussion with Sheriff Strathclyde.

'The Fiscal has moved that we carry out the judicial examination now in view of the media interest in this case.'

Frank raised his eyebrows in apology to me. This clearly wasn't his decision – the word had come from much higher up. I felt as if I had been ambushed and took little comfort from the fact that Frank probably felt the same way.

I didn't have many cards to play.

'I haven't had time to discuss this with my client.'

Kailash's performance at the judicial examination was crucial to the outcome of the case, and I didn't want her to be thrown in there before I had a chance to discuss matters with her.

Sheriff Strathclyde was quick to put the boot in.

'I hope you're not suggesting, Ms McLennan, that you would be coaching your client?'

As it is illegal in Scotland to prepare witnesses, I hastily denied it. Under the circumstances, I had no objection that would be upheld. Swiftly, I moved towards the dock. Unlike me, Kailash seemed unperturbed. She was eyeballing Sheriff Strathclyde and he shifted uncomfortably under her gaze.

'Kailash? I can't stop this judicial examination.'

Her face did not even register my presence. Trance-like she continued to stare at Strathclyde. I assumed that her stares were to unsettle him, and I assumed that she was trying to unsettle him because he was – or had been – a client of hers. That was all I needed. Maybe she thought she could bribe him or embarrass him into calling off the case. If so, she must have conveniently forgotten just who she was accused of killing. I was losing patience.

'Kailash!' I called as loudly as I dared. 'Listen to me. The Fiscal is about to ask you questions. However, you are entitled to refuse to answer them.'

My heart was beating, a mixture of adrenalin and anger. She wasn't listening to me and was bound to throw away any slight chance she may have. I had to press on – professional ethics meant that even clients who wouldn't deign to give me a moment of their attention still had to be advised.

'You don't have to answer any questions, and my

normal advice would be to say nothing as that is the safest option, but – and it is a big "but" – if you have a good defence, and don't state it, the Crown can comment on your failure to the jury. Kailash, I don't know whether you have a good defence or not. This is your call. It really depends on how brave you are.' I finished my whispered comments to Kailash feeling more of a need to shout explicit advice rather than leave so much to her judgment. She was much calmer than me.

Again, no reaction. Her lack of emotion was worrying me. How was she going to act and react when she got up there? Was she going to take the psychopath route? The wounded tart with a heart? Or continue her mad staring at Strathclyde? It mattered to me. It mattered a lot. When a trial lawyer gets started, the victim and the accused are lost. It is merely a fight, a game with the prosecution. And it's a game I like to win.

'Kailash, this matters. This will all be tape recorded and go before a jury.'

She surprised me by clutching my arm and nipping it.

'Did you say this will be tape recorded?'

I nodded my head, resentfully rubbing at the place on my arm where her nails had dug in.

'Is there any way the tape can be interfered with?'

'No, of course not. It's kept and authorised by the Fiscal.'

'And do you trust him? Do you trust that process?'

'Kailash, what's going on? Of course I do. I know Frank Pearson. He's a good man. But I also know the process. They're the ones who want this to happen. They're not going to scupper their own procedures. It's nothing to be scared of.'

'Scared?' she almost spluttered. 'Why do you think I would be scared?'

'Well, if you're thinking from the other side and actually believe you, or someone you know, could get in and wreck the tape if you don't come out of it too well, you can forget that right now. No chance,' I warned her.

She chewed her lips as she was thinking. I have the same bad habit – it saves my nails, but the inside of my mouth resembles a slasher movie.

'Don't stand in front of me when I am being asked questions. I want to see him,' she informed me in an emotionless voice.

'Kailash, it won't work. I don't know how you know him – although it doesn't take much imagination to guess – but that won't cut any ice here. It doesn't matter if he likes to dress up as a schoolgirl or get his arse smeared with peanut butter while a whippet licks it off, you've been accused of murder. That's all that counts.'

'You've got quite a vivid imagination there, Brodie,' she responded. 'I could use you.'

'Don't bother flattering me. It's standard practice for lawyers to act as a buffer between clients and the bench.'

That was true, but I was also put out at being side-lined. I wasn't a bit player in this. I was a star attraction and I liked it that way. Nonetheless, I continued.

'I can't stop you if you are specifically instructing me that way, Kailash, but remember that you still retain the right to consult with me before you answer any questions. I can't interrupt in the proceedings so it has to come from you.'

Kailash had already moved on. She hadn't even heard the last comments. She was, however, the only one ignoring me. Sheriff Strathclyde had his beady little eyes focused right in my direction.

'If you are quite finished, Ms McLennan, perhaps we may have a moment of your time to begin.'

He was looking anxiously at his watch. It wasn't any concern for procedures or the fact that he was a dedicated workaholic – rather he was keen not to have a late lunch. Rumour had it that it was generally liquid anyway, and I had certainly seen him carried from the bench on more than one occasion.

Sheriff Strathclyde was sweating profusely. Was it Kailash's gaze, or the effects of last night's whisky? The sheriff clerk, switched the tape on, and it began. I didn't listen to her give her basic details, I was just praying my client would speak up.

Ordinarily, the less an accused says the better, but this case was unique. We had to come up with a good story – and stand firm.

'At 11.30p.m. I was walking home.'

Kailash's clear voice cut through the silence of the court; the only other sound was the whirr of the tape recorder.

'Alone,' she added on reflection.

We held our breaths as we waited to hear how Lord Arbuthnot of Broxden had died.

'At present, I do not think it is necessary to state

whose company I had enjoyed earlier in the evening. Latterly, I was at the Balmoral Hotel.'

Sheriff Strathclyde continued to shift uncomfortably under her stare. I was annoyed. It sounded as if she was hiding something. Also, there was absolutely no emotion or contrition in her voice. It would not go down well with a jury. Public speaking is the number one fear amongst people – dying is second. That means most would rather be the corpse than give a eulogy at a funeral. But Kailash sounded calm, as if she were reading a bedtime story to a child.

'I had a couple of glasses of champagne. I decided to go home before I had finished. I brought the champagne flute out with me.'

Her voice was controlled, as if this was perfectly normal behaviour.

'I crossed the road and was sipping champagne as I examined the large statue of the bronze horseman. This sculpture fascinates me. It is anatomically correct in every detail, except one -its tongue is missing. The artist committed suicide, when he realised this . . .'

She was rambling. Kailash Coutts still stared at Sheriff Strathclyde, as if they were having a private conversation at a dinner party.

'Strange,' she continued, 'I always thought it was our tongues that got us into trouble.'

Lifting her head even higher, she gestured towards him.

'Don't you agree, M'Lord?'

Without waiting for the reply, that would never come, she continued.

'In the wall of Register House is a seismograph. It is behind glass, and it measures earthquakes.'

Pausing as if speaking to imbeciles, she added: 'On the Richter scale.

'It is extraordinary how earthquakes can hit Edinburgh, M'Lord.'

To his credit, Sheriff Strathclyde only flinched a little bit before Kailash continued with her story. I was pretty sure she was enjoying herself as much as anyone could in this situation, but everyone's patience would run out soon if she didn't start coming up with the goods.

'I first saw them in the glass of the shops,' she went on. 'Teenagers of both sexes – a gang of about ten.'

For the first time, her voice cracked with emotion. I had an unsettling feeling that she was putting it on, a consummate actress. Why should that surprise me, given her profession?

'Next, I heard a strange drumming sound.' Her voice was becoming higher, her own fingers and nails drumming on the edge of the stand. I had to hand it to her – the audience was sitting on the edge of its seat.

'They were banging. Old fashioned walking canes, I think. Banging them off the pavement, off the pavement, time and time again.' She sounded breathless now.

'They gathered round me . . . black leather coats . . . their hair was white . . . and they were frightening. Any exit route was blocked off. I was trapped. Trapped between the wall of Register House and the horseman.'

Kailash asked for water. There was an almost palpable sigh of relief. We all needed a breather

'The boy . . . their leader . . .' her voice was faltering now, 'he began the taunts. Asking me for a price list.'

Impressively, Kailash dropped her head, but kept her eyes up, never breaking the stare with Sheriff Strathclyde. She continued in a staged whisper.

' . . . for my services.'

I knew she was being polite, but I had hoped, against hope, that we could have kept her profession out of the trial. Although practically everyone in Edinburgh knew exactly what Kailash Coutts did for a living, I had hoped to raise objections if any assumptions about the reason for her movements were made. Surely even notorious prostitutes had perfectly innocent nights out from time to time? As soon as I had the thought, I realised I wasn't even managing to kid myself. I knew I was clutching at straws – but straws were my only hope at this stage. In my dealings with Kailash, I had kept strictly to the golden rule of cross-examination: never ask a question to which you do not know the answer. I had broken it on only one occasion when I had asked her if Lord Arbuthnot was a client. She had replied that he was not, so I would argue that her sexual reputation was irrelevant if the dead man did not use her 'services'.

'Menacingly,' Kailash went on, 'he danced around me, weaving in and out, tapping me on the body with his cane. I was in no doubt that my life was in danger.'

Gasping for breath, she pulled a handkerchief out

and began wiping her eyes. I breathed a quiet sigh of relief that she was conforming to such a clichéd, but useful, weeping stereotype.

'I reached into my bag.' Her voice wavered; she rested her hand against her breast shakily, as if reliving the moment. 'And I pulled the empty champagne flute out. I was terrified. I smashed it against the wall to protect myself. All I could see was that evil boy, and his strange, strange eyes. But then . . . nothing that happened next makes any sense.'

She collapsed weeping, and everyone else seemed taken in, but I have studied body language and while Kailash Coutts was a bloody good actress, she was actually a crap liar. When we speak, our body communicates the truth. In court, my senses are heightened by adrenalin. I had watched the micro movements of her eyes when she spoke. She looked down to the left, an indication that she was, at best, hiding something. If she had been telling the truth, Kailash would have looked up to her right, to recall facts. Our bodies do seventy per cent of our communication unconsciously, but Kailash must have missed the lesson on that when she went to stage school.

After sipping on some water, Kailash began again.

'I smashed the glass against the wall, not to use it, but to threaten them, to keep them away. I was screaming for help, but I thought that no one could hear me.'

The Dark Angels had chosen a busy spot in the East End of Princes Street to attack her. I guess some might interpret it as a sign that Moses Tierney and his crew

65

thought they were above the law, although they would have been hidden behind the horseman and the wall in a very short, narrow alleyway.

'His arms encircled me. I screamed, lashing out with the broken glass. I was so sure it was him, that boy with the strange eyes, and I was scared, so scared. Only when I felt its sharp edges pierce the skin did I notice whoever was holding me did not have a leather coat on – he was wearing a rough green Harris Tweed jacket. Someone had heard me – someone had come to help, and I had rewarded this, this *saviour* with a broken glass.

'He started shouting: "Am I cut badly? Am I cut badly?" Kailash gulped for air like a stranded fish as she recalled the night's events. 'But the blood just kept gushing out of him.'

So Lord Arbuthnot had died a hero attempting to save a woman in distress. I wondered if he would have rushed to the rescue if he had known who she was?

'The bunch of criminals fled, but not before they lifted my handbag . . . and I was left alone with Alistair MacGregor,' she concluded.

I sat up sharply in my seat. She had called him by his own name. She would not have known that, unless she knew him well. Lord Arbuthnot was his judicial title, assumed when he took his seat as a senator in the college of justice. Judges don't always take judicial titles but his father, Lord MacGregor, was, at the time, still sitting as the Lord Justice Clerk, the second most powerful judge in Scotland.

The MacGregors could trace their judicial lineage

back for four centuries. But that bloodline ended last night, on a Princes Street pavement. Alistair MacGregor died without issue.

Sheriff Strathclyde sat watching Kailash, visibly moved by her story, and somewhat impressed that his deceased colleague had performed such a chivalrous, if fatal task. If a lauded man had to die, how much better that he should die in the pursuit of a noble deed, even if the heroine was a whore. Kailash wiped some tears away and decided she had a few more words to add.

'I held him in my arms, but the blood just kept flowing.'

She paused and looked at the tape recorder before continuing.

'I don't know where he came from . . .'

She paused again, as though considering the dead man's options. She lifted her eyes from the whirring tape inside the machine and reverted back to staring at Sheriff Strathclyde.

'Oh . . .' she whispered, before her voice became steadily stronger.

'He must have come from the toilets.'

Sheriff Strathclyde leaped to his feet as a slow smile spread across Kailash's face.

'Stop that tape now! Stop it! I demand that you stop it!' he shrieked at the stunned clerk.

'Yes,' went on Kailash Coutts. 'I think he did. In fact, I'm positive. Lord Arbuthnot came from the public toilets. He came from the toilets.'

Sheriff Strathclyde was now on his feet, blustering, moving back and forth.

'I order you to stop! Just stop speaking now, woman!'

Kailash looked at him one more time, looked at the still-whirring tape machine and pronounced:

'Certainly. I've said all I needed to say. Thank you, M'Lord. Thank you.'

EIGHT

After the court was cleared and Kailash escorted back to the cells, I left as quickly as possible. I didn't want, or need, to speak to my client just now, but I did have to go over what had just happened. Alone.

Ordinarily, I would have tried to nip back to the flat. Some mornings, some afternoons, some trials just left me needing time spent with nothing more strenuous than a cookbook in front of me. Running often worked, drinking too, but there was nothing more satisfying than taking your frustrations out on a block of meat or chocolate. Today wasn't shaping up to be the sort where I could slip in a bit of kitchen action – Kailash's outburst had seen to that.

Strathclyde's behaviour was unheard of – judicial interference with a witness's evidence may happen, but never so publicly, and never on tape. I couldn't blame Strathclyde for his outburst. The toilets at the East End of Princes Street are a notorious gay haunt, particularly favoured by those keen on a nice wee bit of cottaging to go with their double lives.

Could it really be that, seconds before he died, the Lord President was ensconced in a grubby toilet cubicle, with a stranger? He was married, without children, but Alistair MacGregor and his wife Bunny had a public life that did not allow for any whispers or revelations. They were patrons of a children's cancer charity, regular visitors to opening nights at the Festival and King's theatres, and expected attendees at anything involving a *ceilidh* and small-talk that happened in the city.

Actually, I had some sympathy with Sheriff Strathclyde's reaction. Lord Arbuthnot had died a hero – what had his sexual preferences to do with his death, or the memory of him?

As I left the court, the first editions of the *Evening News* had already hit the streets. As there had been no media present when Kailash had dropped her bombshell, I didn't expect anything to be splashed across the front page – but it was only a matter of time. I grabbed a copy, just to be certain, and was reassured by the usual headline informing residents that traffic was worse, parking was impossible, and the Enforcers (the Dr Who-type name for the Capital's traffic wardens), were evil personified. No change there.

However, it wouldn't be long – helped by the selfsame papers – before Edinburgh would be reeling with shock. Particularly the Establishment. Ordinarily, the city was a peaceful place for them. Fist fights, brawls, even murders were common enough, but they were usually the work of what they still considered to be the lower classes who hung around pubs and such dreadful places. Every Friday and Saturday night, a thug would take a fist to his neighbour or his wife, and each weekend there was at least one stabbing in the pubs in Leith. These episodes were just part of life. For those who could buy themselves out of such a world, things were very different. They may worry about credit card fraud, or getting their purse pinched as they leave Harvey Nicks, but what had happened to Lord Arbuthnot would shatter their cosy little world.

Public opinion would soon decree that this was no ordinary murder. It had money, titles, gangs and sex – it was a story waiting to happen, and I gave it twenty-four hours tops before the shit wouldn't just hit the fan: it would splatter us all.

With a television crew camped outside my office, I parked in the only spot in Edinburgh where I knew that I would not be harangued by the press. Outside the home of the deceased. Even in death, the elite are accorded privileges. If this had been a 'normal' killing, the media would have set up shop – in fact, there would be someone in there right now, persuading the bereaved that telling all to a tabloid followed by a stint on a talk-show would cure everything. Money doesn't just talk – it buys peace and quiet too, and that was exactly what was happening on Heriot Row.

As I surveyed the scene from outside the private gardens opposite Lord Arbuthnot's home, a small card-board cup filled with steaming espresso was pushed under my nose.

'Stop dreaming, Brodie,' a familiar voice intoned. 'Keep your eyes open if you're set on making enemies.'

71

Jack Deans had emerged from the exclusive private gardens behind me, holding two cups of coffee and a bag of muffins. If past experience was anything to go by, he would have made his purchases in Rose Street at the police box coffee bar. To get to where he was now harassing me, he would have walked down to Heriot Row using the private Queen Street Gardens as a shortcut. Deans couldn't have known I was parked in Heriot Row – he wouldn't have seen me, over the high hedges that guarded the occupants' privacy until the last moment. How had he known I was there? I knew it was pointless to ask him, as futile as asking how he, a mere commoner, had obtained the elusive keys to Queen Street Gardens. Deans would merely state he had his sources. He was a man who got himself into places no one else could. And, I guess my vanity would have to accept that, perhaps, he wasn't looking for me; perhaps he had decided this was where he needed to be irrespective of who else was hanging around.

'Beautiful, aren't they?' Jack Deans was staring, openly envious, at Lord Arbuthnot's Georgian townhouse.

'Rarely come up for sale these houses.' Scanning, his eyes appeared to be noting every architectural detail.

'One of the best addresses in the world,' he went on, as much to himself as to me.

'Robert Louis Stevenson lived at number seventeen. They're passed down through families or sold privately to a suitable purchaser.' Jack Deans' mouth crumpled at the sides, giving him an air of disappointment, although I doubted if he had ever been in a position to buy one.

I didn't join him in his reverie. I savoured the hot, strong espresso as I observed the house. Sure, it was elegant, but this street has always spooked me. These houses are not homes. They gleamed like the prized possessions they were, but I doubted there was often the sound of children's laughter or happiness coming from them. Their owners did not even contribute to their appearance – well, only financially. They were largely owned by rich men with wives who lunched. The late Lord Arbuthnot and his wife, Bunny MacGregor, were no different. They'd have a legion of help to keep their little jewel shining, but the place would have no heart like all the others on the street.

The house had no front garden; you simply climbed three stone steps from the pavement to get to the door. This did not make it accessible. To the right of the doorway, a plain brass name plaque was fixed, declaring that Alistair MacGregor, Advocate, lived there. Judges remain advocates even when they are senators of the college of justice. Frankly, it would have been dangerous for the plaque to proclaim that this was Lord Arbuthnot's residence. He was a hard man, a tough sentencer, who publicly and frequently stated that justice must not only be done, it must be seen to be done. The voice in which such statements would be delivered was – had been – rich and sonorous, honed by Eton and polished by Christ's College, Cambridge.

'He's been in the Enlightenment since he was nineteen.'

Jack Deans came back to life and I immediately knew

73

the reason for his interest in this case. My hands gripped the tiny cup that was still warm from the coffee. Turning to face him, I stared with what I hoped was a withering look.

'So?'

'You as well, Brodie? Another unbeliever.'

He was well used to this reaction.

'I'm meant to get all excited about a debating group for public school boys? For people who should know better?' I asked him.

'Brodie! It's a secret organisation that rules Scotland! Over eighty per cent of the judiciary are members.'

'Jack, I've heard it all before. From you. Time and time again. I don't care what little groups little boys join, not even when they keep their membership going when they're grown men. If they want to shave their left leg and dribble toffee on their right nipple while pledging allegiance to some Faerie Queen of the thirteenth century, good luck to them. If they're busy with that, maybe they won't interfere in my cases and *real* lawyers can get on with *real* legal work.'

Jack Deans paused, before continuing as if I had never uttered a word.

'And, as I was saying, all of them became members before they had finished their law degree. Like Lord Arbuthnot.'

He actually did have a point, but I'd be buggered if I'd tell him. Either the Enlightenment Society was the most incredible talent spotting organisation ever or there was something more to it.

'Listen to this, then, if you think it's all so innocent.'

Deans was winding himself up to begin a full-blown rant. Behind him I could see that we were being observed by someone hiding amongst the curtains in the late Lord Arbuthnot's house.

'In its official biography, it states that if ever judicial interests conflicted, with the interest of the Enlightenment Society, then the society's interest must be primary.'

This guy was sad and clearly obsessed with conspiracy theories. So what if Arbuthnot and the old guys had got their jobs through nepotism, surely things had changed now?

Jack Deans was launching into a history lesson, but I was edging myself back into the shadows of the hedge so that I could see the goings on without being seen. My uninvited companion was making this very awkward.

'The Enlightenment Society was founded in 1774, by two Masons from the Central lodge. Robert Louis Stevenson and Sir Walter Scott were both said to be members, and given their membership of other societies, I wouldn't be surprised. The Enlightenment Society still meets every week at the University of Edinburgh. Its members pepper the highest offices in the land. At least eighteen Scottish Law Lords are members. This matters, Brodie, it matters.'

'Jack, I. Don't. Care. It's irrelevant. The MacGregors are an ancient family, man and boy they have pledged their allegiance to the widow's son.' I started to use Masonic terminology, just to wind him up and to show that I was not completely ignorant.

'Very good, Brodie. You've read a wee article some-where, but obviously not the right one as you're still so bloody sceptical. Did you know that the Masons began in Scotland?'

I didn't. We are a small and largely barren land. I could see no good reason why an organisation that has been credited with some of the major changes in world history, such as the French and American revolutions, would begin in the homeland that I love dearly but still think of as a tad parochial. Besides, I was too inter-ested in what was going on within the house.

Shaking his head from side to side, Deans lit a cigar-ette. A sign of the times, he did not offer me one. I was grateful – in a moment of weakness, I would have accepted. He generally claimed it was his last one, and he was in the process of quitting, but he'd wound himself up so much this time, that he didn't even bother with the pretence.

'You've got so much to learn. And you've got to start learning sharpish – for your own safety. I'll start at the beginning.'

I groaned theatrically, but he still cleared his throat.

'The Knights Templar fled to Scotland after Philip IV of France and Pope Clement V had their leader, Jacques de Molay, burned at the stake. You'll know his face, it's on the shroud of Turin.'

He just tossed that one in, as if everyone thought as he did.

'Oh, that's right, Jack. I remember reading that was a pretty recognised thing these days. In fact, I think the Pope has just issued a press release.'

Jack didn't seem that interested in the black saloon that drew up outside the house. A subservient man in a sombre suit deferentially approached the front door. The undertaker, come to discuss funeral arrangements. I knew that he didn't yet have the body, because I was due to attend the post mortem later that day. I didn't get bothered by post mortems – or so I told myself and everybody else – but suddenly, I became acutely aware of the muffin sitting heavily in my stomach. Another reason to resent Jack Deans.

'In March 1314 they roasted Jacques de Molay over a slow fire on the Ile de la Cite in the Seine. He cursed Philip IV of France and Pope Clement V, ordering them to join him before God's seat within the year. They were dead under suspicious circumstances within months . . . and so started the powerful Templar legends.'

'Thanks for the history lesson. Got any more on how to shut the fuck up?' I snapped.

The undertaker was now safely ensconced inside. I did not see who had opened the door as it had been such a seamless movement.

Annoyingly, and predictably, Deans continued with his discourse.

'Christendom was a dangerous place for the surviving Templars. Where could they run?'

'Shame your brain wasn't around in those days, Jack – I hear that's a pretty vacant space.'

I had to hand it to him – he was a born storyteller. He couldn't keep the dramatic inflections from his voice, and he loved an audience, even a reluctant one.

'Only a country, where the Papal Bull did not extend would accept them. Robert the Bruce had been excommunicated, and so these learned wealthy knights were welcomed into Scotland.'

Pausing to light another cigarette and draw breath, he continued.

'There are more Templar graves in Scotland than anywhere else in the world . . . outside Jerusalem.'

The undertaker left the house. He had been inside for less than ten minutes, insufficient time for a cup of tea never mind to organise a funeral for a Knight of the Thistle.

Jack Deans was looking at me expectantly, probing me with his eyes.

'What?' I hissed and threw my hands in the air. What did he expect me to say?

'Is that all you have to add? Scotland's premier judge has been murdered, and, even off the record, you have no comment. Ach, Brodie – you're not the girl I thought you were.'

'My comment is . . . it was an accident,' I said, trying to ignore the flutter I got from him almost complimenting me and almost admitting he thought about me. I almost managed.

Incredulous, he continued. 'It's the first time a judge has been murdered in Edinburgh. Now you know his background, and you know he was bumped off by a prostitute. Do you *still* say it was an accident?'

'Yeah.' I answered like a snotty teenager.

He looked let down.

'Not everything is part of some hidden agenda, Jack. Sometimes, most times in fact, things are exactly as they seem.'

The house seemed to be stirring, an old cleaner, dressed in a floral crossover pinny, busily polished the brass nameplate, as if someone of importance was awaited. Not the master of the house obviously.

Surprisingly, Jack Deans had no interest in the comings and goings of the house. I was the sole focus of his attention. Scrutinising my face, he sought unknown confirmation of something. Satisfied, he nodded to himself.

'You've a lot to learn.'

'So you've said.'

Placing his tongue between his surprisingly white teeth, he paused for a moment. Thinking better of what he was about to say, he changed his mind.

'If you see things as they are, and believe that's all there is, you've led a sheltered life.'

I couldn't deny it. He was right. I had led a charmed life to date. Although my father had forsaken me before my birth, my mother Mary McLennan moved mountains to give me the future she thought I deserved.

Mary was born in a fishing village in the north east of Scotland. It bears no importance to my life, except for one stroke of good fortune: its proximity to Gordonstoun, the school for the Royals.

Gordonstoun provides nine free places to children from the surrounding fishing villages. Mary McLennan lied and cheated my way into one after primary school was over. It wasn't easy. I was an outcast, but, over the years as I saw my peer group take up soul-destroying jobs or sign on the dole, I was grateful for every time she shouted at me and made me study.

I never quite understood her passion, to push me up the social ladder, because she was perfectly content with her own life. It just wasn't good enough for me. Mary worked two jobs to give me the finest. I promised I would repay her selflessness one day.

We were both cheated. If there is a God, He saw fit to deny her greatest wish – to see me graduate Suma Cum Laude from the Law Faculty at the University of Edinburgh.

Dying from the cancer running rampant throughout her body, doctors were unable to control her pain. Delirious with morphine, she repeatedly begged my forgiveness, crying over and over again that I was meant for better. Without seeing me graduate, she would never know that she had achieved what she dreamed of. I had reached my potential. I had succeeded. Mary was a humbling mother in many ways, and the root of my addiction to work, I freely confess in moments of introspection, came from being a slave to her ambition for me.

My reverie was shattered as Jack Deans grabbed me by the shoulders. He swung me round, directing my eye line to the car that had just pulled up outside Lord Arbuthnot's home. An ancient two-seater Morgan roadster. Racy, with maroon and silver paintwork. The driver parked on the kerbside, directly in front of the house. Flouting the yellow lines he ignored the parking bays where we were. Obviously not an *Evening News* reader. Jauntily, a tanned old man jumped out with a spring in his step, which belied his years.

'I thought I told you, Brodie,' said Jack. 'You've got to keep your eyes open.'

He paused before whispering:

'I was wondering if he'd show up.'

NINE

Jack Deans was going to be tight-lipped about this one until he alone decided it was time to speak. This man was obviously important, not merely because of Deans' reaction, but because of the aura he had about him and which even I could sense from my vantage point amongst the bushes.

My heart played knock and rattle with my chest. I knew this man from somewhere but I couldn't say where. He stopped at the foot of the steps, his back unbowed with age, and his hair silvery white. We were feet from him, as I tried to blend in with the shadows of the hedge.

Turning in our direction, as if aware that he was being watched, he looked hard. Intense blue eyes pierced out of his tanned, weather-beaten face. If eyes are the windows of the soul, his was icy cold. At best he could be described as purposeful.

No resident of Scotland had skin like that. This man had clearly lived abroad for years – so how did I know him? Pedigree hung about him, like mist at dawn. Surely only mourners would darken the doorstep of the deceased today – but on this man, no trace of grief showed. Breeding had strengthened his upper lip.

Jack Deans was still silent as the man turned on his hand-made leather brogues and walked up the stairs. The door was open before he arrived. His appearance was evidently expected. The door had swung open, as if by some ghostly hand; the person opening it remained unseen. Deftly, the old man disappeared inside.

I felt a gnawing at my insides. I ached to know who he was. Shamefully, I was willing to trade anything. My voice was high and excited as I spoke.

'Right, Deans, spill. If you want any inside information, scoops, whatever, now's your chance. Tell me who he is.'

'Calm it, Brodie. Don't be so impatient. Or so desperate. It's not your most attractive feature.'

Since childhood, I have found it impossible to believe that patience is a virtue. My right boot tapped a salsa rhythm on the cobbles beside my bike. When anxious, I fidget. Jack Deans was enjoying my discomfort, although he seemed at a loss to understand my urgency.

'Impressive old bloke, isn't he?' he teased me as I nodded assent.

'I'm surprised you don't know who he is. He was a fighter pilot during the war . . .'

'Well, I wasn't around then, and an obsessive interest in military history seems to have passed me by,' I answered. 'So, if you could get your self-importance out of a place where the sun doesn't shine, maybe it wouldn't kill you to actually tell me who the old codger is?'

Jack Deans stared at me.

'You don't even recognise him?'

It was a question to which he expected an answer. I was not prepared to give him any insight into what the sight of this old man made me think – I didn't quite know myself, other than the vague sense of recognition.

'Of course I do, Deans. It's just that I so enjoy our never-ending verbal sparring that I thought I'd keep begging you to tell me just for fun.'

'It's Lord MacGregor,' he revealed.

'The old Lord Justice Clerk?'

'If you want to put it that way, yes. Personally, I think his role as father of the murder victim is more important.'

I wouldn't have recognised him from court because he retired from the bench long before I was called. The only thing I knew about his career was that some still said he had retired too young and that the Law of Scotland had suffered as a result of his lack of influence.

The need to know how I knew him still gnawed at me. A traffic warden passed his car, stopped to look at it, then, magically moved on. I was still puzzling over this. Edinburgh wardens are mean and vindictive, and generally deserve their press coverage. I personally had never witnessed one walk away from such easy pickings.

Speaking of easy pickings, I turned my attention back to Jack Deans.

'Why were you surprised that he turned up? Surely, a father-in-law would be the first one to comfort the widow.'

'I wasn't surprised,' he sounded huffy, 'I just said I

wondered if he would. There's a difference. I like to keep an open mind on all things.'

I snorted before snapping, 'Oh, for God's sake, just tell me what the score is here.'

Resigned, he spoke. Slowly at first, as if trying to formulate it all in his head.

'They fell out years ago. I don't think they were ever close. No one knows what the cause of the argument was but Lord MacGregor refused to sit on the bench with his own son.'

Jack Deans chewed on the end of his pen, trying to formulate his own answer.

'The members of the Enlightenment wouldn't get involved, wouldn't even try to sort out the mess and old MacGregor resigned.'

I ignored the way Deans had managed to bring his conspiracy theories in again and asked: 'Was Lord MacGregor involved in the law at all after that?'

'No,' answered Deans. 'He severed his ties and left the country, although he did keep his flash pad in town. He was a widower, so he took to wandering the globe. Finally, he settled in Thailand, and I understand he married again and has a young family.'

The lives some people lead. At his age, I would have thought he was more in need of a pipe and slippers than a mail-order bride. It was all interesting enough, but still didn't explain where I knew him from. I waited anxiously for Lord MacGregor's exit from the house.

'There was only one connection that Lord MacGregor kept up,' added Deans.

I turned to face him, but he toyed with me like a game

show host pausing to increase the suspense. I moved away, keen not to let him see my interest in this matter.

Eventually he gave in.

'The only link that Lord MacGregor maintained was his post as governor at Gordonstoun School.'

Looking at me in anticipation, he continued:

'Coincidentally, he severed that tie the year you left.'

Again with his conspiracy theories.

This time trying to drag me in.

'Oh, for Christ's sake, Jack, it's not unusual for old boys to remain in touch with their schools. Some judges even take their judicial names from their school house.'

Jack Deans cut me short.

'He went to Eton.'

I couldn't think about this latest piece of information. The black-painted front door was opening, the brass lion knocker looked positively menacing. It seemed as if nothing was happening, and an inordinate amount of time passed between the opening of the door and the eventual emergence of Lord MacGregor. He walked out of the house alone.

'Interesting. I would have thought if that pair had buried the hatchet, then Lady Arbuthnot would have seen him to the door,' commented Deans.

'Perhaps she's too upset by her recent bereavement to move.'

'You obviously don't know Bunny MacGregor. Appearances count for everything. Even in death.'

He looked at me conceitedly, and I, for one, was getting heartily sick of this game playing.

'Jack, I didn't know we were in a competition. I'm

a lawyer remember, not some half-bit hack trying to steal your crown.'

I have learned that where men are concerned flattery gets you everywhere, and Jack Deans was no exception. He softened as he looked at me (and I softened as he softened – to my shame).

'You're quite right, darlin' – and there's no telling what trouble a rookie like you could get into if I wasn't there to help.'

I ignored him – again – and continued to watch Lord MacGregor. Pushing myself further back into the large privet hedge, I felt confident enough to ogle him. He seemed in no hurry to leave as he squinted his eyes, blocking out the August sunshine. Perched on the top step, he kept watch, and instinct told me he was waiting for someone. The heavy red velvet curtains in the house twitched several times. The unseen observer was also clearly wondering what Lord MacGregor was up to.

Jack Deans inclined his head towards Lord MacGregor.

'His relationship with his son was always troubled. Did you know he was expelled from Eton?'

'Who? Lord MacGregor?' I asked.

'No, Lord Arbuthnot. He was officially given the chance to leave, so that he could get into another school, but rumour has it that it was serious.'

'Serious? In what way?'

I had any number of friends who should have been expelled from school, but it's very hard to turn away twenty thousand pounds a year.

Lord MacGregor was pacing back and forth now.

He was obviously not a man used to being kept waiting. A cloud of darkness shifted across his face and, momentarily, I felt sorry for his son. I would not like to cross Lord Gregor MacGregor of MacGregor.

Centuries seemed to fade, and I could see him in the role of war chief. Perhaps I should find out about his record in World War II. After all, he was not a man who had mellowed with age. Now glancing at his watch, the famous Highland temper glowed red, under his already sun darkened skin.

'Are you listening to me, Brodie?'

I bit down hard on my lip.

'Lord Arbuthnot was expelled when he was fifteen. For being a peeping tom.'

'What? I thought it was something awful or murky or at least illegal. He was just a bit of a teenage perv? If snooping on women getting dressed or on couples having it off makes young men criminals, I can retire now. On top of that, what relevance can you – even with your bloody conspiracy theories – think that pretty straightforward adolescent behaviour has on his murder decades later?'

'Well, the Jesuits would have disagreed. They believed you could tell the character of a man at seven.'

I repeated the old adage back at him.

'Give me the boy until he is seven, and I will show you the man. But the Jesuits weren't in charge in this instance, Jack. And from what I know, it would take more than a bit of schoolboy high jinks to get them to chuck out a blank cheque. For the sake of political correctness, let's assume the theory applies to the female members of the human race too. Do you want to know what I was like at seven?'

I didn't wait for him to answer.

'Fixated on my mother, terrified she would leave me, and clandestinely longing to lead a cloak-and-dagger life like Deacon Brodie. I was a psychiatric case in waiting. Hormones levelled out and now I am the delightful, normal vision of womanly perfection you see before you.'

Silence fell between us, until Jack spoke again.

'Christ, look who's coming.'

Moses Tierney was sauntering up the street. A child of the shadows, he spotted me immediately. Raising his cane once more in acknowledgment, I marvelled at his grooming. Black nail varnish must show every chip, but his was immaculate. White blond hair, dyed, spiked and gelled to perfection.

Moses walked up the steps of the Heriot Row house. He and the father of the deceased greeted one another like old friends: two dapper gentlemen together.

Lord MacGregor placed his arm around Moses' shoulder in a gesture of support. Together they stood in front of the Georgian panes, staring at the twitching curtains. Whoever was behind them did not come out to acknowledge this silent vigil. Lingering for what seemed to be ages beneath the windows, I was perplexed.

Lord MacGregor was, in effect, harassing his daughter-in-law. And he was doing it alongside the individual who had been pointed at by Kailash Coutts that morning as the real cause of Lord Arbuthnot's death.

Jack Deans nudged me overzealously in the ribs.

'What do you make of that, Brodie?'

'I don't know – unless there's a problem with the will or inheritance. No matter what the sum involved, death brings out the worst in the relatives. Old families have their inheritance rules laid out from way back. Probably the MacGregors are governed by the law of primogeniture. Primogeniture is a feudal law, it means only the eldest son can inherit. And the dead man has died childless. It's a fight in the waiting.'

My lecture was shattered by the sound of their leather soled heels, crunching, as the two men turned to face me. Dread cracked through me like a whip and weakened my legs. I moved onto Awesome, the leather bike seat feeling comforting beneath me. I moved faster than I thought possible, thrusting my empty cup at Jack Deans. I jumped up, whamming my foot onto the kick-start, and Awesome roared into life. The noise of the engine momentarily stopped Moses Tierney and Lord MacGregor in their tracks.

I drove from Heriot Row, faster than the law allowed. I moved from the land of the living, to a place of death – and I welcomed the change.

TEN

I rarely see dead people. I try everything I can to avoid it, but when faced with the inescapable I do as I'm told. And this was something I had been told to do.

'Stand aside, Ms McLennan. Unless you are intent on performing this autopsy for me.'

On the word of the pathologist, I threw myself back against the wall. Squat and easygoing, he required space in which to manoeuvre his considerable girth. Gowned in green surgical robes, he edged past me, buttocks rubbing against the side of the wall. He held his gloved hands aloft: the tips of his fingers were already bloody, as if he hadn't been able to wait and had already been poking about in the body before we arrived.

Professor Patterson, police pathologist and holder of the Chair of Forensic Medicine at Edinburgh University, was now in his sixties. Born with a port wine stain that smudged over half his face, including his right eye, most of his life he had endured the nickname 'Patch'.

Patch was always picked last in games as a child, but

he didn't mind, rationalising that he wasn't exactly a born athlete. Yet, even in the classroom where he had shone, he wasn't favoured. Frustrated by this treatment, he turned to his studies and graduated as a doctor. Highly sensitive and intuitive, Patch Patterson recognised as a junior registrar that his patients were frightened by his appearance. A resilient boy from the Western Isles, he embraced the only branch of medicine where his patients could not judge him – the study of the dead. Patch had been my Professor of Forensic Medicine at university, and had also taught Frank Pearson too. He kept people at a distance, but when he liked you, he made it obvious in his own way – he had always been kind to me as a student, and, despite the fact that he sometimes still treated me like one, he had continued his kindness towards me in my professional life.

The body, still covered by a sheet, lay on the table, not two feet away from me. Ironically, I had never been this close to the man underneath while he was alive. In life, red silk gowns trimmed with white ermine proclaimed his status. Now, I was doing my best not to stare at the toe tags dangling from the veined blue feet with the usual collection of bunions and corns.

Unsurprisingly, the morgue had a distinctive odour, the stale stench of death no amount of air freshener could mask. Had I been led here blindfolded, I would still have known exactly where I was. The clock on the wall showed that it was 2p.m. At this hour of the day it smelled even more unpleasant.

'Death is the great leveller,' began Professor Patterson, jovial as ever and keen to chat.

'Always nice to host a reunion.' Patch gave the welcoming smile of a genial host. 'I met him several times at functions,' continued the Prof as he threw the corpse a sideways glance. I was pretty sure I heard him say, under his breath, to the cadaver:

'And a right arrogant bastard you were too.'

I looked up sharply at Patch. He smiled and nodded in my direction. My eyes met Frank's over the gurney. Simultaneously, we rolled them upwards. Although it had been several years since we had been in his class, Patch's irreverent attitude to death could never be forgotten. Nothing, except children, was so horrific or sacrosanct that he wouldn't make a joke about it.

'Lord, Lord, let's start the cutting.'

The lilt of his voice was high and poetic; it reverberated round the austere, windowless room. Patch had left Stornoway on the Isle of Lewis over fifty years ago, but living amongst the Sassenachs had not dulled his accent. Adhering still to the traditions of his childhood and a staunch member of the Free Church of Scotland, he compounded his position as an outsider. Social pariahs acknowledge one another, and like all fatherless children I collected father figures. I was as close as Patch would come to a friend, and it cut both ways.

With the flourish of a magician, he yanked the sheet away. Lord Arbuthnot lay pale, naked and bloodless. The silence of the dead hung heavy in the room, as we came to terms with our own thoughts. I thought of the droves of reporters outside – how much would a photograph like this command? Perhaps Patch was thinking along similar lines as he shouted: 'I don't want anyone within fifty feet of this room, is that clear?'

The young morgue assistant responded to his high sharp command, and shuffling off, replied: 'I'll see to it, sir.' A dynamic nod followed, as he affirmed, 'I'll keep an eye out ... I sure will.' Hobbling out on his loose-laced skateboarding shoes, the young man did not return to the autopsy room.

The four of us were left alone. Lord Arbuthnot hardly counted, although he was the reason we were there. My eyes explored inches of his exposed flesh at a time. Age had undermined his muscle tone and he lay flaccidly before us. Nonetheless, I could see that in his youth, he had been an athlete, and as my mother would have said prior to his demise, he was still 'a fine figure of a man.'

Ordinarily, death masks are peaceful. Lord Arbuthnot's face seemed irate. Most of the blood had been washed from his body, but it was still accumulated between his fingers and under his nails. In life, I was sure his hands would have been immaculate – in death, they were downright grubby.

'He literally bled to death.'

Patch had read my mind – he had an uncanny knack of doing that.

'Hardly a drop of the red stuff left in him.'

His gloved finger pointed to a jagged scratch on Lord Arbuthnot's neck.

'Insignificant, isn't it?'

Patch was now poking into the small puncture hole.

'I've had worse nicks than that shaving.'

Frank Pearson's mouth was slightly agape, staring incredulously at Patch's actions.

'Could that really be the cause of death?' he asked.

'It was the means by which he appears to have died. However, if Ms Coutts had merely placed her forefinger like so . . .' Patch pressed down hard with his finger, 'he would be alive . . . and looking down on us all.'

Accidental death? My mind was racing ahead to petitioning the High Court for Kailash's release from prison. I wasn't really present in the room, my mind was so busy on the next job. I almost didn't hear Patch speak again.

'So simple to have saved him, to have saved the life of Scotland's highest Law Lord.'

Patch's voice always got higher, when he was onto something. To my ears, he was almost squeaking. My heart was sinking as I knew that this case was just about to get difficult again.

'Rudimentary first aid was all that was needed. A Girl Guide could have saved this man.'

Patch was almost singing now.

'I seriously doubt that Kailash Coutts was ever in the Girl Guides,' I interrupted. 'Although she's probably got the uniform these days.'

It was an off-the-cuff remark I was shortly about to regret.

'Presumption rarely leads to the truth, Ms McLennan, and when you assume facts, you are invariably led on a wild goose chase.'

Patch smiled at me condescendingly.

'What evidence do you have that Ms Coutts was not a perfectly ordinary child?'

'It was you who taught me, Professor, that aberrant behaviour in adults has its roots in childhood.'

'How very Freudian of you, Brodie, but the aberrant behaviour you have accused your client of – is it murder or prostitution?'

Frank Pearson stared at me like the adversary he was. I had forgotten he was there. At university he was so insignificant. Obviously the Fiscal's office had honed his wits. I stared at him with a new respect.

'Who's the deviant?' I asked, trying to regain lost ground. 'The man who pays ten grand to get his arse whipped, or the woman who does it to him?'

'I guess we'll have to ask Roddie Buchanan that one,' sniggered Frank. He caught himself quickly, clearly recognising it was inappropriate to be laughing as he stood over Lord Arbuthnot's naked corpse.

'If I may continue . . .'

Patch spoke sternly as if addressing two school children. He switched on his tape recorder and spoke clearly.

'Although, the entry wound is small . . . observe the jagged edges of the lesion . . . it would appear to be consistent with a blow from a broken glass . . . the downward serration . . . would indicate the glass was propelled from above the carotid artery . . . severing it immediately . . . the assailant was left handed . . . and strong.'

Patch switched off the tape recorder. He never did that. It was against the standard operating procedure.

'In view of the deceased's position and status, details of this autopsy must be held under the strictest security.'

He looked shiftily around. Clearing his throat he continued.

'It has been proposed that the Lord Advocate may place a one hundred year banning order on some of the papers in this case.'

'They can't do that. It's a murder trial.' Frank Pearson sounded outraged.

'They did it with the Dunblane Report initially,' I reminded him. 'They had no good reason to do that, and it would have remained sealed unless some people had fought to get it changed.'

'Brodie, they didn't have a trial there. Thomas Hamilton was shot dead after he massacred those children.' Frank Pearson had forgotten himself, and was leaning across Lord Arbuthnot's body. I was wincing at the sight of it, but we court lawyers love a good argument. The rights and wrongs get lost in the fight.

'Thomas Hamilton was a paedophile. As far back as 1968 if talk is to be believed. Police officers had been questioning his right to run boys' clubs for years. In particular, in 1991 a police report said he should be prosecuted for the way he ran his boys' clubs, and his gun licence was revoked. But the report was returned marked "no-pro." No prosecution by the Fiscal's service, Frank, because, according to some – nonsense conspiracy theorists in your eyes, I'm sure – in the reports three other people were mentioned: two Scottish politicians and a lawyer.'

Frank Pearson glared at me as I continued to shout at him across the cadaver.

'The Fiscal's office didn't prosecute, Frank. And on 13 March 1996, Thomas Hamilton walked into Dunblane Primary School and shot sixteen children and a teacher . . . with a licensed gun.'

I was so incensed, I was almost frothing at the mouth. The brutality of those murders had shocked the world but especially Scotland. Nothing like it had ever happened before or since, but I couldn't understand the link here. Why was I being told the same thing might happen with my case as had happened with Dunblane? Lord Arbuthnot's death didn't justify a cover up just because he was a pillar of the establishment.

'Why does this need to be confidential?'

Patch turned to look at me. He seemed relieved that I had finally asked the question which needed to be spoken.

'I understand that someone – I don't know who – will have a "watching brief".'

I could tell that Patch would have felt more comfortable discussing such matters privately. Guilt stabbed at me. Like Fishy, he had been neglected by me. I figured he felt he had to speak to me now, or he might not get the chance again until the trial. It wasn't a wise decision. A watching brief meant overseeing how events unfolded, and if anything untoward were to come out then the individual given it would have to act. What form that action would take, I had no idea. A watching brief certainly explained Sheriff Strathclyde's extraordinary behaviour at the judicial examination.

Kailash Coutts was a powder keg, and everyone knew that she would not go down alone – as long as she didn't take me with her, I felt I could cope.

The whirr of the blade and the crunch of bone brought me back to reality. Patch had switched the tape-recorder back on and was cutting through Lord Arbuthnot's ribcage. Snap, snap, and he was in. Stealthily, like a burglar, he reached inside, droning on into his microphone. I preferred not to listen, concentrating instead on blowing air onto my heated face.

Scales were on the bench beside him. He plucked the still heart out of the body and placed it to be weighed. The ancient Egyptians believed that after death, your heart was weighed against a feather; if your heart was heavier you were not admitted to heaven. They understood that you had to receive joy and give joy, and they believed you should be rewarded or punished accordingly. To my fanciful eye, Lord Arbuthnot's heart looked heavy on those scales. He didn't give or receive joy from his father. Had he shared such an emotion with anyone else in his life?

'I hardly knew the man in life – I didn't like him then and I certainly don't like him after dissecting him.'

Patch sounded disapproving and it snapped me back to attention. It wasn't hard to breach his moral code because of the strict tenets of his religion. In fact, it was a surprise to me that he tolerated my behaviour, although he did often say it was because I knew no better. I was sure that wasn't a compliment.

'As I said before, to have saved this man's life would have been so straightforward. It turns out it was only a question of time anyway.' None of the condemnation had left Patch's voice.

I followed him to the metal side table where he had placed the heart. Scalpel in hand, he progressed with the dissection, shaving slivers from the heart. He stained the shavings and invited us to look down the lens.

Chivalry has no place in law. Frank Pearson moved forward to examine the slide first. Nervously, he cleared his throat, and again he coughed. Either he didn't know what he was looking at or he was reluctant to say.

'So, Frank, what do you see?'

It was like an oral exam at university. I shifted uncomfortably. So many years had passed – he wouldn't be able to remember. I didn't want to risk putting myself in the same position.

'Some fibres are missing their nuclei, indicating necrosis or death of the tissue.'

'Very good, Frank.'

Patch turned to face me.

'Now, Brodie, what else can you see?'

Reluctantly, I looked down the powerful microscope.

'There's inflammation, old scarring, and narrowing of the coronary arteries.'

Lord Arbuthnot was sixty-four when he died – nothing unusual so far. I was missing something. There had to be evidence in the heart tissue of wrongdoing, that was the only phenomenon that could have incited Patch's moral indignation.

'Trust your intuition.' He used to drum that into me. 'It comes from your subconscious mind that knows far more than your little brain.'

I relaxed, and spoke more freely. It was obvious once I stopped looking at a Law Lord and just saw a corpse.

'His heart tells us more than that. It tells us in death what he would never have wanted us to know in life,' I coldly stated.

'Lord Arbuthnot was a chronic drug abuser.'

ELEVEN

I could hear Frank Pearson's sharp intake of breath. I had committed myself so I might as well carry on.

'Chronic ischemia, fibrosis of varying age, plus an absence of coronary artery disease or cardiomegaly, and patchy necrosis . . . basically a coke heart.'

'Well done, Brodie,' said Professor Patterson. I glowed under his approval. I had won the prize for forensic medicine at the Old College, and Patch had hoped at the time that I would take it further. Maybe I would have had it not been for two things – the desire of my mother to see me as a lawyer, and my own preference for the vibrancy of the living – with all their flaws – rather than the stench of the dead.

I looked across at Frank. He had wilted under my display, and his newfound confidence had left him. The words of Jack Deans came back into my head – I didn't want to make any more enemies than were strictly necessary.

I caught Patch's eye, silently pleading with him to bring me down a peg or two.

'Of course, it's not strictly correct, Brodie . . .'

Frank heaved a sigh of relief.

'Drugs such as narcotics, synthetic narcotics, whatever the addict can get their hands on, will destroy the heart just as effectively as cocaine. Elvis Presley is a sad example . . .'

Patch's voice trailed off on the slight technicality as a smile lit my face. Elvis was his one failing. In terms of the 'Wee Free Kirk', any singing or joviality is frowned upon. Patch had to keep his infatuation with the King well hidden from the brethren.

Slowly, it sunk in. The Lord President of the Court of Session was a cokehead. I found it hard to believe, but the toe tags confirmed that it was indeed Alistair MacGregor, aka Lord Arbuthnot, lying there on the slab. And I had seen inside his body with my own eyes. At least it explained why he had fallen out with his father. Why his father thought he was unsuitable material to be a judge. Old man MacGregor went up in my estimation; it was a hard step to take to report your own child, but that must have been the real reason behind their argument.

'Why was this information not known?'

Frank Pearson looked as I felt – shell-shocked.

Patch was staring despairingly at us.

'Again you are assuming facts. How do you know that it was not known? Simply because this is news to the people in this room does not mean it was unknown to others.'

Patch is always pedantic; right but hair-splitting. Unless, Lord Arbuthnot was manufacturing the narcotics himself, someone had to know.

'If the authorities knew about it, then they should have made him resign.'

Frank's voice was indignant, but quiet; as if he was mindful that no one outside the room should hear of this.

'What about blackmail? He left himself wide open to it.' I stated what we were all thinking.

'There's no evidence that he was being blackmailed.' Frank Pearson looked annoyed with me for even having mentioned it.

'Funny though . . . when you consider . . .' Patch was wandering, but a point would arrive soon. 'The MacGregors were the original blackmailers.'

He ignored my warning glances.

'It's true. The MacGregors stole cattle and "sold" it back to their owners. Rob Roy MacGregor was a black-mailer. Poetic justice if it happened.'

It wasn't enough that Patch had revealed to us the flaws of character in the present MacGregor, he sought to destroy a legend as well. I could see that he was enjoying himself, so I did not react. One thing did concern me – Patch had switched his tape-recorder off again, and none of this information regarding the heart was being recorded. Patch was meticulous, he would not have done this by accident. Either he had made a decision, or someone had made it for him. This information was going no further.

The chest cavity on the cadaver was still open. Patch, bloody after his earlier excavations, was looking over both his shoulders. He moved cautiously forward, towards Lord Arbuthnot's feet. Then he placed his hands on the deceased's hips, and rolled him in my direction.

Horrified, I stepped back, Patch's irreverence knew no bounds. The body groaned as gases escaped, pressure widened the hole in the chest wall and I could see right inside. I knew that I would be having nightmares about this for weeks to come.

'Stop lolly gagging over there and come and see this.'

Patch was staring at Lord Arbuthnot's backside. I could see no way that this could get any worse. Frank Pearson was already green to the gills, and if there had been others present I would have been running a book on how much time he had left before he was sick. I shouldn't have been so smug.

At first I couldn't make out what I was looking at. It was faded with age. Patch swung his large magnifying glass in front, and we stared mystified.

'What is it?' I asked.

'What does it look like?' Patch sounded irritated by my puerile question.

'It looks like a tattoo,' Frank replied, unabashed.

'Well, it's not. It's a burn.'

'Like a cattle brand?' I had found my voice again.

'Precisely!'

The autopsy room fell silent. Far away in distant corridors, I could hear the rattle of trolleys. Porters shouted greetings to one another, normal life continued. In this room, it had stopped; nothing was as it should be. We stared in quiet communion at the mark, burned long ago into the rear end of Lord Arbuthnot.

'Have you ever seen anything like it?' The words tripped softly out over my lips.

'I have obviously seen burn marks on children made by cigarettes and heated objects,' answered Patch, 'but I have never observed first hand such a brand. Note these indentations – also old burn marks.'

Patch's plum eyelid twitched, as he observed the oddity. His curiosity was aroused, but from past experience, I knew he would add nothing to his disclosures. We were lost to him now as he studied the grooves and indentations on the flaccid, bloodless, buttock.

I felt the vomit rise into the back of my throat, acidic and sour it burned its way up my gullet. Fire flushed through my system. Last time, I barely made it to the ladies room. The race was on, no time for niceties. I grabbed my helmet off the steel table by the mortuary room door. I had no time to say goodbye, or to hear Frank Pearson's muffled guffaw.

The place was a maze. I ran directionless through the corridors, searching for a toilet. No luck, so I pushed down hard on a fire exit handle, praying it wasn't alarmed, and escaped into the fresh air of the car park.

The autopsy room had been windowless; the storm clouds outside took me by surprise. My lungs gasped for cool clear air, but to no avail: the afternoon was warm and muggy. A summer storm was building. My t-shirt clung to my back; small streams of sweat ran down my neck, as I sprinted towards Awesome. The sun was hidden behind heavy clouds, and even Awesome gleamed dull in the flat light. The shine had been taken off everything.

Escape was all that I had in mind. I needed something more than I could get from my Harley. Heading for Arthur's Seat, I was sure to find solace. Unfortunately, I didn't find good sense and the black saloon car behind me with tinted windows was nothing but another bit of traffic to me.

The car was of the same mind, but the driver was obviously too taken with the sight of Holyrood Palace to pay attention to the road. His wheels – I assumed he was male as they cause ninety-five per cent of accidents – just missed my back tyre.

Fat drops of rain fell on my visor as the heavens poured. I opened up my throttle and increased my speed. I had to shift to lose that idiot. The rain came down faster. The rumble of thunder travelled over the River Forth as I climbed Arthur's Seat.

Dark and stormy, I continued to climb higher. Puddles of water lay on the road, the sprayback on the engine made Awesome sluggish.

The black saloon caught up with me as we reached Dunsappie Loch. Every sinew in my arms was tight as I struggled with the conditions. The car moved out to overtake on the single track, one-way road. I tried to facilitate his manoeuvre but I wasn't fast enough. His bumper caught my exhaust and shunted Awesome across the road. The tyre caught the kerb and I spun over the handlebars as the first sheet of lightning cracked the sky.

The thick leather of my jacket protected me as I skidded along the road. I stopped, face down in a puddle of muddy water. The water, mingling with my blood, rose up my nose. Coughing, I tried to lift my head up. At speed, the car reversed back towards me, its tyres spewing muddy water over me in a deluge.

Too late I recognised the vehicle. I had last seen it outside Lord Arbuthnot's house. The storm raged on, even the ducks took refuge in the reeds at the edge of the pond. The grumbling thunder masked the sound of his footsteps.

Mercifully, blackness descended shortly after I received the first blow.

TWELVE

Fortunately, the drugs clouded my consciousness. Foolishly, I welcomed sleep. Unconscious, the nightmare truly began.

Inner turmoil makes for restless slumber. The hand on my shoulder was firm but friendly. Fishy shook me awake.

'You've got a visitor.'

His blue eyes crinkled with laughter. Relief flooded through me. I was going to recover, or else Fishy would look worried rather than bemused.

My eyes strained to adjust to the light. I blinked and blinked, but I appeared to have brought a strange apparition back with me from my dream state. No matter how many times I opened and shut my eyes, the bizarre man at the foot of my bed didn't move.

Red tartan trews emphasised his elegant limbs – dancer's legs once upon a time I'd guess. Black patent shoes, polished to within an inch of their life. No greater contrast could have been found to my scuffed black courts, lying discarded in the corner. Placing his hat on the chair, the man removed his black velvet jacket. I pushed myself hard against the pillows as he began to amble towards me.

Suspicion must have shown in my eyes, as he began to speak softly like someone singing a lullaby.

'Hush now, child. Kailash has sent me to care for you.'

That was a frightening prospect on its own. She was paid to hurt people – it was her job. And right now I didn't know who had sent my attacker. For all I knew it could have been Kailash herself. One of the few things I had been able to stammer at Fishy when he found me, was that he was to tell no one, until I had figured out who had sent my baseball bat message.

I was angry at him for betraying my confidence, for not protecting me better. Maybe the responsibility of caring for me was too much. Perhaps I should have gone to hospital, but official police involvement was not the wisest course of action. I had made too many enemies, and I was starting to get as bad as Jack Deans with conspiracy theories. I didn't know who to trust.

Fishy stood staring at the doorway eyes protesting his blamelessness. I broke contact with him; he would be dealt with later.

'You're in terrible shape, Brodie,' Fishy began huffily. 'You need a doctor or you need a miracle – he's the best you've got.'

I raised my fuck you finger at him but he didn't move. The man we were referring to did – gently pushing my hand into a ball to remove the offending gesture.

'I'm Malcolm.' He had been filling his eyes on me

110

since I had noticed him – and for God knows how long before that. As he introduced himself, his liver-spotted, manicured hands gave me a tiny white pill and a glass of tepid water. Suspicion must have shown in my eyes.

'Do I scare you?' Malcolm asked. Never one to admit weakness I shook my head.

'Well, then open your mouth . . . it's only lady's slipper.'

As I still looked confused, Malcolm continued with his explanation.

'A Native American remedy.'

'For?'

'Calming your nerves, stopping you greetin'. It's an extract boiled from the roots. It's good stuff.' He failed to tell me it was also superior to opium in inducing sleep.

I hadn't had the energy to cry. Yet. His little tablet must be to stop the tears that would surely come once I thought about what had just happened to me.

Deftly he placed the pill under my tongue.

'Keep it there, and let it melt.'

Malcolm bent down and picked up a battered brown leather physician's case.

'You're the strangest looking doctor I've ever seen.' I blurted it out.

Malcolm hesitated for a moment, then sat down beside me. He looked at my face, at the bruises and the swelling and the blood, and I saw a change come over his face.

'You may be right, Brodie McLennan. But by name and by bloodline, I am related to a healing tradition that stretches back a thousand years.'

I looked at him expectantly.

'My family name is Beaton and our history was as bone-setters and healers. Not many options for me – there weren't many chances for . . . Well, in Inverness in the sixties I was what they called a pansy. It wasn't the most swinging of places then. Or now.'

Clearing his throat he added: 'I was maybe a wee bitty obvious.'

From his get-up, this didn't come as a huge shock, but I kept my tongue silent as distant pain flickered over Malcolm's face.

'I tuned in, dropped out and headed for San Francisco. Learned about Native American remedies. I found people who appreciated my skills – and who did not denounce my . . . personal habits.'

'How did you meet Kailash?' I asked.

'Ordinarily, I never talk about her. People . . .' Malcolm appeared to be searching for the correct word, 'misunderstand.'

Organising himself in silence, he placed ointments and unguents on the bedside table. Outlandish aromas from his pots and potions quickly filled the room.

'Please? I'd like to understand her . . .'

Sensing he would do anything for Kailash, I deliberately hit his hot buttons.

'If you want to protect Kailash, Malcolm, if you want to keep her out of jail, then give me your help. The more I know Kailash, the better able I am to defend her.'

It was enough. I had played my part well. Without stopping to catch his breath, he launched into their history.

'When I met her, in the eighties, in Amsterdam, she was just a wee slip of a thing. Doing the only thing she could to make ends meet.'

Education had obviously never been part of her curriculum, but I refused to accept that the only escape route for a young girl was prostitution. I thought it wisest not to voice my opinion.

'Initially, she was the injured party in rich men's sadistic sex games. That's how we met. I used to patch the girls up and send them out again. Kailash is a smart one. As soon as she realised a certain type of man paid more to be hurt, then she found she had a talent for it.

'Freud said that the sexual history of an individual begins at birth, and sexual pleasure in the beginning has no aim or object. The only way it can get an object of desire is through experience. This is complex and it can go wrong.

'With all the clients in Kailash's place in Amsterdam, that process had most definitely gone wrong. Successful businessmen who crave humiliation and pain.'

He paused – presumably running a few scenarios through his memory bank.

'There are older ladies I've worked with who earn a small fortune dressing men as babies and changing their nappies.'

'I can't understand why the women do it,' I interrupted.

'For the money, lassie. So what if they have to change shitty nappies? They'd be doing the same thing working as a carer in an old folk's home – only there they'd get minimum wage. Not every woman has the opportunities you have.'

Malcolm turned from me to prepare ointments, leaving me to think about my senior partner. Roddie Buchanan's predilection was harder for me to figure out. Where did he come up with the notion of having his testicles injected so that they swelled to the size of small melons? How did he explain that to his wife? I assumed that part of his thrill was the excitement of getting caught.

The drug was taking effect; my mind was fuzzy. It was getting harder to distinguish between reality and the dream state. I tried to fight Malcolm as he removed my nightdress, but the drug had lowered my inhibitions. A strong woody scent filled my nostrils as he applied warm oil. Vaguely aware that Fishy was in the room, I felt protected rather than horrified by the presence of my friend.

'Black birch oil . . . its astringent properties will help her wounds heal.'

Malcolm's voice was soft and low as he spoke to Fishy. His experienced hands kneaded the oil deep into my flesh and I felt myself drifting in and out of consciousness.

'What do you want the vodka for?'

Fishy was keeping a watchful eye on Malcolm.

'Have you warmed it?' queried the older man. His voice had changed to brusque and efficient. 'Vodka is a spirit I use, because it is readily available, to help me make a poultice. Do you see these lesions on her back?'

I could not hear Fishy's reply. I felt as if I was floating away from them both.

'These wounds were not caused by a baseball bat. When you picked her up, did you see a thin metal bar or a baton lying around?'

I still could not hear Fishy.

'Yes, I suppose so,' agreed Malcolm in response to a comment I had not heard. 'These red marks across her back could have been caused by a walking cane.'

Drifting into my nightmare world, I fought hard to stay awake but the drug overwhelmed me. Moses Tierney interlinked with my absent father, tormentors together, scornful of my efforts. There was something I wasn't seeing. I have always abhorred stupidity – particularly my own – but, without realising it, Malcolm's intention to make me sleep while my body healed plunged me into my own personal hell.

I was past caring when he applied the leeches to my swellings. Somehow he managed to convince Fishy that standard medical practitioners were once again using them. They didn't hurt as he positioned them on my body to release their natural anaesthetic. Leeches, Malcolm assured Fishy, would also release a powerful antibiotic into my bloodstream. When they were satiated with my blood, they dropped off naturally and the inflammation was reduced.

Uncomfortably, I drifted in and out of consciousness, unsure of my surroundings and the faces that came to see me. By the time Jack Deans turned up, white plate in hand, stacked with pancakes, I wouldn't have been surprised to see Mother Teresa doing the dusting.

THIRTEEN

'How's Sleeping Beauty?' he asked, as if we'd been having a perfectly ordinary chat seconds earlier. The plate that he put down clanged off the bedside cabinet as I stared at him in disbelief.

'Ambulance chasing now, Jack? You're sinking lower than even I predicted.'

'You've been out for three days, Brodie. Fishy had to go to work . . . so I offered to babysit. Looks like it's going to be a thankless task.' Jack Deans busied himself, straightening my bedclothes as if the situation was a perfectly normal one.

'Where's Malcolm?' I asked.

'He's just left. I had to throw him out the door – poor old sod's been with you the whole time. Now it's my turn – I'll attend to your every need. Cups of tea, bowls of soup, commode, bed bath, inside stories on your colleagues – you name it. Particularly the bed bath.'

'How did you know I'd been attacked, Jack?' I wasn't in the mood for our usual verbal sparring. I knew he had his sources and I was panicking that word on the assault on me was out. Lavender would cover me as best she could at work – and that was nothing to be sniffed at – but if Roddie and Co. actually knew that I had been attacked, that would put a completely different complexion on things. As I waited on his answer, I became aware that I was absolutely starving. Reaching over, I pulled the plate of pancakes towards me, and pain shot down my right arm. I had an instant memory flash – after I had gone over Awesome's handlebars I had landed awkwardly on my right shoulder.

'You in pain?' asked Jack.

'Nothing like asking the obvious to show your shit-hot journalistic credentials, is there?' I looked at him grumpily, now too sore to eat.

He answered by shoving a pancake into my mouth. It tasted better than I would ever let him know.

'The old guy left pills for you, but I think they're a bit dodgy, no packet or anything. At the risk of repeating myself – which I'm sure you'd never let me away with – you need to watch yourself, Brodie. I had a bad back and the doctor gave me extra strength pain killers. I brought some in case you needed them.'

I refused his medicine, leaving the pills on my bedside cabinet. Jack Deans had no healing skills that I could see and he seemed oblivious to the irony of me taking his pills over those from Malcolm. The man was hardly a walking 'good health' advert.

'Do you know what happened?' he asked.

'Sniffing out another scoop, Jack?'

'Aw shut it, Brodie. I'm actually genuinely concerned – and genuinely bothered given that I'm forsaking my valuable time to be passing you bloody Lucozade and grapes. Show a bit of gratitude, will you?'

I'd do the shutting up bit, but that was all he was getting. I was still getting over the irony that he was in my apartment, and I was in bed, but we were both fully dressed and eating pancakes rather than doing what was a damn sight more appealing.

'It's just that I spoke at length with Fishy, and he filled me in on the details. I thought perhaps, well, after the accident your recollection might be hazy . . .'

My mother had always insisted that I did not speak with my mouth full; now managing to stuff the warm pancakes into my mouth, old habits died hard and I nodded at Jack, urging him on.

'Fishy received an anonymous call at the police station. It came through on his mobile.'

Jack knew the import of what he was saying. Anxiety gnawed at my stomach, making the pancakes suddenly hard to digest. Fishy's number wasn't easily obtainable; someone had gone to considerable lengths to find it. Either that or they knew it already.

'They said that you'd met with an accident near Dunsappie Loch.'

Jack Deans sat down on the bed, his bulk pulling the covers tightly over my legs, so that I was suddenly aware of pain in places that had hitherto seemed fine. Ignoring my wincing, he grabbed my hand.

'Brodie – they said it was a warning. You don't mess with these bastards.'

'That's the problem, Jack. I don't know who they are so I don't know who to stop messing with. Did they say what they wanted me to do?'

'I suspect they think we know more than we do.'

'Is Roddie Buchanan a factor in all of this?' I asked, feeling an urge to pace while still unable to move. 'Maybe they think I found out something when I was acting in his defamation action.'

'What, more than what was splashed over the papers?'

'Seriously . . . can you imagine how edgy some people are feeling just now? Kailash is a loose cannon. If she's going down – and it looks as if she is – then I bet she intends to take every member of the establishment that has ever come within five feet of her right down there too.'

Sheriff Strathclyde's behaviour at the judicial examination had certainly convinced me things could blow.

Something else was bothering me.

'How did Kailash know to send Malcolm? She's in prison.'

Jack Deans got up and circled the bed. For the first time I noticed the creases in his shirt, and the heavy circles under his eyes. Had he been keeping watch with Malcolm, or had he thought it necessary to stand guard?

'Something else I don't know. The guy's like fucking Mary Poppins, but more effeminate than Julie Andrews ever managed. He just turned up at the door.'

'Is that when Fishy phoned you?'

'Yep, he wanted to check him out, to see if I knew anything about him. But he's a shadowy figure in

119

Kailash's life. Don't know what the old guy's hiding, but he's covered his tracks pretty well.

'Obviously, Fishy was worried about you. You were bleeding so much and he wanted to take you to hospital. Stroppy cow that you are, you refused. I can't even imagine how hysterical you must have been to get him to agree.'

Too many questions were in my head. I knew that Fishy had recently had his doubts about his superiors in the force. His sleepless nights weren't for nothing. Like me, there were cases that niggled, details that made sleep impossible, but, for Fishy, it had been going on for too long as far as I could see. It had been a while since we had stayed up till the wee hours chatting over a bottle of wine, but even I could see the dark circles under his eyes, notice the weight falling off him, and recognise the jumpiness from sleep deprivation. I had the impression that someone he worked with was making things hard for him – phone calls abruptly finished when I walked in, he took days off when I knew he wasn't ill. I'd had enough run-ins with cops to know how difficult they could make things – was Fishy being picked on by one of his own? Had someone given his mobile number out? If they had, how did they know who had attacked me? Who was involved with what here?

The front door bell rang. Jack's face tightened with anger, he seemed genuinely concerned about me and I was close to being touched by it.

'Jack – where does Kailash Coutts fit into all this?'

'You'll get a chance to ask her yourself. Madam Kailash wants to see you.'

As he stomped off to answer the door, he added: 'And the all-involved Malcolm says you're fit enough. That's him now.'

I could barely see Malcolm's face as he staggered in under a mountain of clothes and designer bags. Nice to know he was still able to manage a bit of retail therapy in the midst of his concern for me.

'Been enjoying yourself, Malcolm?' I asked.

He looked at the pile he was creating in the middle of my floor as if surprised that they had got there in the first place.

'You're meeting Kailash – did no one tell you?'

'I've been informed that an audience is scheduled, but I still don't see what that's got to do with you maxing out your credit card.'

'Well . . . last time you met, Kailash was a tad *concerned* about your appearance.' He nodded, as if he had explained everything perfectly.

'Kailash insists *all* her girls look the part.'

Malcolm began derisively throwing all my clothes into the middle of the floor, as Jack Deans smirked, hanging around the edges of the wardrobe, hoping to catch a glimpse of a PVC corset.

'I am not Kailash's girl,' I spluttered. Adrenalin propelled my legs onto the wooden floorboards, and the endorphins over rode my pain. I bent down to pick up my own clothes with one hand, throwing Kailash's offerings aside with the other.

Catching sight of myself in the mirror, I was stopped in my tracks. My hair looked redder than its usual auburn and its curls had not been tended to for three, hard days. Raising my hand to touch my bruised, grazed cheek, I thought of Patch, and pity welled up inside me. I didn't recognise the woman before me; I saw instead the scholarship girl, huge dark chocolate eyes staring out of a pinched pale face. Malcolm was right – I was a mess.

As I stood there with Kailash's offerings in one hand and my own sorry articles in the other, the feel of the expensive cloth between my fingers slipped through. It felt good, even in this state -why was I fighting?

Isolation is the cruellest of punishments. Before I went to Gordonstoun, it had never occurred to me that I was something less than human because I couldn't afford to look like others. Survival was my only hope, success my only revenge. I'd thought those days were behind me, but this had brought it all back.

Clinging to my downtrodden costume went deeper than the clothes. Letting them go meant releasing the final vestiges of my mother. Four days ago, on a thundery night at Dunsappie Loch, my assailant hadn't won – whoever he was had beaten courage into me.

I thought I could hear Mary McLennan cheer. This wasn't going to get me – this was something I could do. Something I could win.

Jack picked up the Armani suit, and passed it to me just before he excused himself, leaving me in Malcolm's hands.

FOURTEEN

Jack Deans insisted on driving me to Cornton Vale, explaining I would be too tired to drive back. In any event Awesome was my only source of transport, and she had been towed to the garage.

Heading out of Edinburgh along the M9 to Stirling, it was obvious Jack had fallen on hard times – as if I needed proof. His Jaguar XJ6 was at least twelve years old and smelled like an ashtray. Actually, I liked its faded elegance. The white leather seats were cracked with age, and I could feel a draught on my forehead where there was a hole in the soft top.

The crown on top of Linlithgow Palace was visible for miles. Jack drove in thoughtful silence, intent on getting me to the women's prison as fast as he could.

I, however, was in no rush to meet up with Kailash Coutts. There were too many unanswered questions between us. From my brief encounters with her so far, I held out little hope of getting any straight answers.

On top of that, our history was almost too much. This woman had nearly destroyed me; I could easily have been a casualty in her war with Roddie Buchanan. If her antics had resulted in the financial collapse of the firm, my life would have gone into freefall; starting with bankruptcy. A domino effect would have resulted in me losing my home and my practising certificate. In effect I would have had to put out a begging bowl to any firm that would take me.

Edinburgh lawyers are not known for their charity. I don't exempt myself from this charge, but I'm well used to taking care of myself whenever I can. What had happened between Kailash and Roddie had taken things out of my hands – it was only by getting Kailash to sign that affidavit that I had managed to get some control back. Throughout it all, I had felt uncomfortable that she was pulling the strings more than I was willing to admit – and this was the root of my difficulty now. My intuition kept telling me I was once more a pawn in Kailash's games, and I could not yet see the path to safety.

Such thoughts roiled around my mind as the flames from the petrochemical plant at Grangemouth lit the sky. The M9 is a straight road cutting through the heartland of Scotland, an industrial past sitting easily beside a shortbread tin image. All too soon, the phallic monument dedicated to William Wallace, Scotland's greatest patriot and the tourist icon of *Braveheart*, was visible; it meant my meeting with Kailash would soon be upon me.

My mood plummeted, and Stirling Castle reminded me of its past glories. I didn't want my best days to be behind me. I had just started and, to be honest, work was all I had, something I didn't want to dwell on too much. Kailash would have to be handled if I was to get out of this how I wanted.

Cornton Vale is Scotland's only women's prison, notorious for the high suicide rate of its inmates. Clearly, imprisonment affects the psyche – some of my clients loved it; they enjoyed the routine and the easy access to drugs. But Kailash was a different type, more akin to a crooked accountant than a street junkie, and such people found loss of freedom much more difficult to accept.

If I was hoping to gain a psychological advantage over Kailash, it was dispelled the moment she walked into the small, sterile consulting room. Once more the air was filled with her scent. Prisoners who are on remand are allowed to wear their own clothes. As ever, she surprised me wearing a white and gold salwar kameez with a duppatta around her neck.

Her silk kameez rustled softly as she moved towards me. Smaller than I remembered, her stature did not diminish her presence. Like Marcus Aurelius, she had found that room inside herself. Peace radiated from her. Given her circumstances it was extremely disconcerting.

'Was Malcolm able to help with the pain?' she asked, without the padding of social niceties.

Maybe she was wondering whether the effects of what I had been through were even beyond Malcolm's skills. Her voice had an ambiguous quality. It was difficult for me to identify her roots. I was listening intently to the inflections of her voice so that I did not answer her directly.

'Brodie?'

It was the first time I had heard her raise her voice. Moving my head slightly to minimise the pain, I made eye contact.

'You've got to float above the pain, and keep your wits about you.'

She paused for a moment her eyes lingering on my face.

'You're in danger, girl.'

'And you're not?' I retorted.

'No, I'm in trouble. There's a difference. A big difference.'

Looking at me as if I were a silly child she continued. 'The worst case scenario is that I get life in prison. In Scotland that's nothing. I'd be out in ten.'

'What makes you think I'm in more danger than you?'

My voice sounded unconvinced. Kailash moved in to make her point.

'There has been no threat to my life. Recently.'

She had a point, but if Kailash wasn't behind the attack on me, then it was logical to assume that whoever was, was hurting me to get at her. As I silently considered my options, I was unguarded. At a glance Kailash understood my reasoning.

'Stop chewing your lips and listen to me.'

Her harsh tone grabbed my attention. Suddenly aware that I was biting down hard on my lower lip, I stopped and looked at her.

'I don't mean to be callous, Brodie, but if a hit man wiped you out, I could easily get another defence lawyer.'

As a salve to my ego she then added:

'Not one as good or as trustworthy, of course.'

Kailash sounded as if she meant it, but then she always did. For my part I felt a twinge of guilt cross my conscience at her words. It was true – removing me would not necessarily harm Kailash. But if that were the case they could have disposed of me at Dunsappie Loch. The caller had told Fishy it was a warning. Usually when people receive a cautionary thumping they are told what action they must take to avoid further beatings. That had not happened, which meant anything I did at the moment could incur their wrath.

Kailash reached inside her embroidered salwar, and pulled out a battered recorded delivery envelope. Even before she handed it to me, I could see that it was well thumbed. It looked old but the postmark was dated only the week before Lord Arbuthnot's death.

'I need you to see this, Brodie. I must warn you the contents of the envelope may shock you – to be truthful when I received it, when it was sent to me, I was confounded.'

Why would I be shocked, and Kailash merely perplexed? I was not a novice in the seamier side of life, and her condescension was irksome. Reaching into the envelope, I was aware of Kailash's scrutiny. I deliberately took my time, enjoying her unease. I could feel that it was a photograph. I pulled it out but it had been folded in two.

Pausing before I unfolded it, Kailash reached out and touched my hand – now *I* felt uneasy. Involuntarily, the muscles in my throat tightened making it hard to breathe.

I spread the paper out on the table before me.

Staring back at me, a computer generated picture.

My own face superimposed on the body of a dead, uniformed schoolgirl.

Revulsion travelled through my fingertips to the rest of my body. The girl was ritualistically posed, almost as a crucified corpse. She was young – she would have been young. Her skirt was pushed up and she wore no underwear, her legs were splayed open – and my face was on top of that grotesque image.

'I would never have shown it to you if you hadn't been attacked.'

Kailash did not seek to reassure me. Her world was a place where such threats were taken seriously. She was personally aware of what human beings could do to one another. I sought to comfort myself.

'It could just be a sick joke,' I said, my voice sounding feeble.

'Try telling that to the girl whose body it is, Brodie. This is a corpse, a corpse with your face over it.

'It looks violently ritualistic to me. Unlike the recent attack on you – so that was either a warning as claimed . . . or something to whet their appetite.'

Kailash waited for me to say something. As unsavoury as it sounded, what I had gone through was merely a canapé, a starter. Bile rose in my throat at the thought of some sick bastard getting sexually excited by my pain.

I felt vulnerable again but that would only stimulate his appetite. I had to pull myself together.

'Any theories?' Kailash asked

'I'm guessing it's a man. Nearly all sexual violence seems to emanate from the Y chromosome, doesn't it?'

'Not necessarily, you could have a killing team. Dominant male, submissive female, because that's what it usually takes to get a malleable young female involved in extremely violent behaviour. Ask yourself, Brodie – why would this young girl have allowed herself to be taken to her death? Wouldn't she have needed to trust someone? And aren't we all encouraged to believe that all women have the nurturing instinct? That they are all, by nature, safer than men. Brady needed Hindley; Fred West needed Rose West; Ian Huntley was trusted because of his relationship with Maxine Carr.'

If Kailash had agreed that it was likely to be a man, then it meant that I could at least have felt safe with half the world's population. Now, things were changed psychosocially, everyone was a suspect.

'Hey . . .'

I realised Kailash was talking to me.

Her eyes were curious. 'Brodie, are you all right?'

'I'm sorry I didn't hear what you were saying.'

I just wanted to get out of there. I needed to get back to some sort of normality. I stood up and said goodbye, inadvertently leaving the photograph behind on the table. Kailash stood up and handed it to me.

'This is yours.'

Like a poisoned chalice, I would love to have handed it on. I knew Kailash was better able to deal with such matters, and I did not relish the learning curve I would have to go through to survive all of this.

I briefly shut my eyes and rubbed my forehead.

'We've touched the photograph with our bare hands, meaning our prints will be on it, but maybe the killer's will be too?'

Kailash shook her head.

'I ran it past a friend, nobody else's were.'

I like a world where my survival is limited to books, exams, and bad tempered judges. This didn't feel like my world – and I never wanted it to be.

FIFTEEN

I got Jack Deans to drop me off in George Street when we came back from Cornton Vale. I'd spent most of the journey in silence again, not because Jack had annoyed me, but through sheer physical exhaustion. I may have been out cold for three days, but I didn't feel anywhere near rested. Every part of me ached, and the visit to Kailash had taken more out of me than I was willing to admit. Willing to admit to most people, that is. I needed Lizzie.

I jumped out of the car at Whistles before an Enforcer could slap a ticket on us, and walked a few yards to the coffee kiosk nearby at the edge of the pavement. It was Jack's favourite outlet in the city, but that status wasn't due to the quality of the hot drinks. Lizzie Collins was renowned more for her ability to turn any man to slush than for her barista skills. Gorgeous, petite, blonde and manipulative, it would be easy to hate her – I preferred her as one of my best friends than a mortal enemy. Life wasn't good if Lizzie got you in her sights for some perceived slight or misdemeanour.

As soon as the occupant of the tiny kiosk turned round to face me, my heart sank. She wasn't there.

'Hi, Brodie,' said the dreadlocked and lanky streak of piss behind the counter. 'Looking for Lizzie?'

I nodded – there were lots of people in this city looking for Lizzie, but at least my intentions were honourable. I just wanted a shoulder to cry on and someone to share eating with – most of Lizzie's seekers were after something a bit more carnal, even if they suspected they'd never experience it.

I grabbed the proffered cappuccino from Gregor (and said I'd tell his dad he was OK next time we both met at work; most of Edinburgh's dodgy looking characters were generally likely to come from affluent, middle-class backgrounds, and most of them had at least one member of the legal profession in their genetic make-up), and headed along George Street.

It was always hard to keep track of Lizzie's movements. I knew that she'd been in Milan for a week or so – the result of her latest dalliance. I also knew that she'd come back loaded with handbags and shoes, but her travel-mate would still be carrying the same number of condoms that he'd left with. Lizzie would almost put Kailash to shame with her ability to play men. We'd been friends since university, the only difference being that Lizzie had attended lectures for three weeks before deciding it wasn't for her. The student life, however, was most definitely her thing, and she acted her way through four years of a degree without being found out. After her 'graduation', she had most of the skills in place to have transformed herself from working-class nothing into darling of the world.

Lizzie had always meant a lot to me. We both came from nothing, but while I admitted that my background often pushed me in a very negative way, Lizzie only saw hers as an audition. She wasn't what birth had made her, she was what she had decided to be. No one would have guessed that the beautiful, fragile creature who swam from one admirer to the next had started life in a Wester Hailes drug den and had only started to blossom after being fostered by a succession of well-meaning but, ultimately incapable, families. Lizzie would learn what she needed to from each then move on. She hadn't moved on from me yet, and I hoped she never would. I wanted to go over what had been going on but it would have to wait – I should have guessed she wasn't back as she would have taken over in place of everyone else at my sick bed given half a chance.

Walking more quickly than my aching legs wanted to, I headed towards my next choice. People who drank were going to hell in a hand basket according to my teetotal mother. Right now, I didn't give a damn.

'Double Glenmorangie, please,' I shouted. The young barmaid eyed me suspiciously, hesitating before supplying my order, as if she was thinking of redirecting me to some more appropriate hostelry. She was new there. Although the Rag Doll bar on the corner of Coburg Street was virtually deserted, the regulars interrupted their game of pool and nodded almost imperceptibly, acknowledging my presence.

It was a hard pub, the type of place it wasn't always

entirely safe for a stranger to wander into, but I wasn't a stranger. Each time I came here, I felt as if I had come home. The Proclaimers were singing 'Sunshine on Leith', and I felt safe. I also knew exactly who I was looking for, and as my eyes skimmed around the room, I didn't see him.

'Three pounds, please.'

Snatching the amber liquor, I almost threw the money over the bar.

'Your money's no good here.'

His voice was deep and rough, as if trawled from the North Sea. An arm the size of a leg encircled my waist pulling me to him; I surrendered, and took refuge in his chest.

'Long time no see, honey…'

Pointing to the glass, his voice sounded disapproving – especially for a pub landlord: 'Have you got some kind of problem with whisky now?'

He pushed me away, his eyes taking in every detail of my appearance, fingering my Armani suit with the light touch of a connoisseur.

'The clothes are fine, but give me the name of the bastard that did this to you.'

His voice cracked as his hand gently pushed back my curls and stroked my bruised cheek. Sitting down on a bar stool, he put both arms around me and pulled me towards his chest again. I could hear his heart beat, strong, and steady. We stayed like that for some time, with him patting my back in consolation.

In that moment, I could almost feel sorry for the shit, or shits, who had assaulted me.

When stirred, Glasgow Joe is a hound from hell. But he was my hound from hell. I had come to the only person in the world who I knew could protect me against whoever had ordered the attack. Joe is my friend, but more importantly right now, he is an assassin.

Six feet six in his stinking stockinged feet, he likes to wear a kilt during the Edinburgh Festival. None of the women who flock to him during those three weeks have any idea what they're really getting as they fall for the vision of Viagra on legs walking down George Street.

Joe and I had met on the first day at St Mary's Sweet Star of the Sea Primary School. Newly arrived from Glasgow, his thick accent would ordinarily have made him an automatic punching bag, but even then his size kept the bullies at bay.

Joe said I was "Clyde built". The shipyards on the River Clyde made the finest ships in the world, but the only boat I resembled was a tug. No threat to anyone, I was hounded from the start.

'Are you a green grape or orange juice?' shouted the boys from the Protestant school.

Was I a Catholic or a Protestant? I hesitated, finally recognising that my green blazer was a giveaway.

'What's it to you – you radge?'

Joe walked up to the gang, his red hair glittering in the sun, and whispered it in the leader's face before butting him on the forehead. Scattering, like coins thrown at a wedding, the boys disappeared in the direction of the Water of Leith.

That incident took place twenty years before, not half a mile away from where we stood today. Both outsiders, we clung together from that moment on. I had as much faith in him now as I did then.

'Tell me about it, darlin'.'

He led me away from the bar, across the bare floor-boards to a bench seat covered in ripped, red leatherette. I leaned on the Formica table nursing my drink. The Rag Doll in itself was not a big money spinner, but it was a convenient front for Glasgow Joe.

At the age of nineteen, he had run away from police questioning. Joe always said he had two options: the French foreign legion ('Rubbish for my lovely Celtic complexion, all that sun and sand' – He was the oppo-site of me. I don't have the usual redhead's complexion, my skin loves the sun and tans easily) or America ('I always wanted to be a cowboy, doll'). An easy choice.

Joe never did talk much about his time abroad. At one point, I had visited him in the States, but, even then, he managed to hide most of his life from me. It had brought consequences that neither of us wanted to address even to this day. All I knew was that, while there, he had honed the skills I was about to rely upon. Evidently whatever he had been up to was profitable – he had plenty of money in his pocket, and a declar-ation that he never wanted to see the back of Leith again.

'The face bashin' – who did it?'

Joe's voice was insistent, as he repeated his earlier question.

Telling him about the assault at Dunsappie Loch was difficult. Hurt flickered through his eyes because he hadn't been called to the scene. He'd been there for schoolyard scrapes and broken hearts – where was he when I really needed what he was best at?

'Where's the bike?' His second question seemed more practical, but he knew how much Awesome meant to me. As soon as I answered, he was on his mobile arranging for his mechanic to uplift her from the other garage and tend to her wounds.

Those ministrations out of the way, he cut to the chase.

'Why the fuck didn't you call me sooner?'

'That you all out of sympathy, Joe?' I asked, knowing full well that he would have been at my bedside like a shot had I contacted him. 'I've been out of it for days, not exactly in a state to give you a wee ring and a natter. Or maybe you expected Fishy to call you? Is that it? Have you forgotten that you won't even let him in this bloody place without a search warrant?'

'He got in when it was your birthday party,' he replied huffily.

The whisky burned my gullet as I swallowed it too quickly; smoke irritated my eyes and I could feel them watering. I had put off showing him the photograph that had been burning a hole in my pocket since Kailash gave it to me in Cornton Vale. Strangely, I had to fight the urge to let Jack Deans see it first. To resist temptation on the way back from the prison, I pretended to sleep.

'Ok, honey . . . what are you hiding?'

137

I must have looked surprised at his perceptiveness.

'Look, you know it's my job to notice when people are concealing things. Drugs, guns, secrets – all the same to me.'

'I'm acting for Kailash Coutts,' I admitted.

He raised his eyebrows, and rubbing his chin, let out a sigh.

'Aye, the jungle drums have been beating on that one. My only question is – why?'

'Well, she asked for me. But,' I admitted hesitantly, 'Roddie Buchanan – or his wife really – is insisting I "contain" this.'

'Look, doll, MI5 couldn't contain Kailash Coutts. If he's so keen that your firm represent her, why doesn't he do it himself?'

'You know that he doesn't do any criminal law . . . and they have a bit of history in case you've forgotten . . . and, as I told you, she asked for me.'

'I know this might come out wrong, but why does she want you?'

Annoyance flashed across my face, so he quickly added:

'Given her history with Roddie? With the firm?'

'I don't know, Joe, I don't know much just now. But . . . she gave me this.'

Unfolding the photograph, I laid it out in front of him. Swearing loudly under his breath, he clasped my hand. He was obviously repulsed and unwilling to pick up the eight by ten black and white photograph.

'Kailash said she received it by post . . . the week before Lord Arbuthnot's death.'

'Murder.' He corrected me.

138

'We've got a defence of accident.'

'Look, Brodie, with that woman there is no royal "we". Kailash Coutts looks after number one. You better do the same. Can you be sure she received this when she said she did?'

'Well, she showed me the original recorded delivery slip . . . and it was dated.'

'Jane!' he shouted at the barmaid.

'Get the bottle of Bruacladdich from the back, and bring two clean glasses. Proper clean ones from the back as well.'

After sorting out our beverages, he turned to face me.

'This sick shit always makes me need a drink ... I cannae lie, Brodie, it's serious. That lassie,' he said, forcing himself to look at the picture again, 'that's real, Brodie, that's real.'

Glasgow Joe had garnered the strength to pick up the photograph. Ostensibly it portrayed me in what would pass for a school uniform. Sensible shoes, knee length socks, white short sleeve shirt and a black mini skirt. I was obviously dead, an elastic band of the type used by nurses to plump up veins before drawing blood was tied tightly round my elbow, an empty syringe lay discarded by my body. Some sicko had posed the body in a pseudo-'Playboy' pose, as if I were offering sex on a plate.

'It's not your body.' Glasgow Joe spoke seriously. 'Your thighs haven't been that thin since you were ten.'

I kicked him hard under the table, but he continued to hold my hand. The fear we had both felt moments before had been broken, but I knew it would come back. Placing his thumb and his forefinger under my chin, Joe raised my head to make eye contact with me.

'What's Fishy saying to all this?'

'He doesn't know. Kailash only gave it to me this morning. I haven't seen him since I got back from Cornton Vale.'

Joe kissed me on the forehead.

'I'm going to phone Fishy and fill him in on the details. Don't move from that spot . . . you're safe here.'

I watched Glasgow Joe pull his mobile phone out of his sporran and walk outside. Before he left, he pulled a young man away from his game of pool to guard the door. I shifted uneasily under my babysitter's unrelenting gaze. An unwritten law was if you worked for 'Glasgow Joe' you did exactly as you were told, and you did it well.

The music for the pole dancers had started, and the pub began to fill up for the late afternoon show. I was steadily drinking my way through the bottle of Bruacladdich on my own, tapping my right foot to the music. Jane the barmaid interrupted my drink-fuelled trance by bringing me a cheese and onion toastie. Obviously, wherever Joe was, he was still worrying about me drinking on an empty stomach. He needn't be too concerned. I was living the high life here.

SIXTEEN

The door opened and the regulars fell silent. It was obviously an event of cataclysmic proportions – on cue, Fishy walked towards me, carrying a briefcase and looking neither right nor left. Things must be bad if Glasgow Joe was letting cops in his pub. As Fishy called my name, I numbly stood to attention, allowing him to hug me and kiss me on both cheeks. He didn't let go. I stepped back, and he began to apologise.

'I'm so sorry, Brodie . . . I had to go to work . . . I'd already missed two shifts and Malcolm assured me you were on the mend. Jack Deans offered to help . . . . I should never have gone.'

His face was lined with fatigue as he spoke at the rate of gunfire to me. Closing his red weary eyes he exhaled slowly, and dropped his chin onto his chest.

'Stop wittering on like an old woman, Plod. Still going to be fucking apologising when she's dead, or will you be back doing your knitting by then?'

Joe was always hard on Fishy, and Fishy believed it was because the Glasgow hard man was in love with me. Maybe one day I'd tell Fishy the true story behind that particular angle, but not now. In turn, I believed that Joe himself was jealous of Fishy who was most things he was not – but I was too fond of my kneecaps to ever mention that theory to my supposed admirer.

'Brodie, show him the photograph.'

Joe was in working mode. I did as I was told, going through the same procedure of unfolding the photograph and placing it before Fishy. He bent his head over the image.

'Do you think it's the same?' asked Glasgow Joe, peering over Fishy's shoulder as he examined it. Fishy rolled his head, from shoulder to shoulder, his stiff neck popping gently. He looked from the photograph to my face, backwards and forwards, backwards and forwards.

'Yes, it's the same.' His voice sounded cold and flat. Conversely, Glasgow Joe showed all his emotions.

'Oh sweet Jesus . . .'

He sat down heavily beside Fishy, and they looked at one another, blocking me out.

'Will you two stop it? You're frightening me.'

My voice sounded like a squeal. Fishy got up off his seat, and came round to me, placing his arm on my shoulder. I was kind of praying it was just because he didn't get on with Joe, but my sinking heart knew better.

'Ach, Brodie – I've been too preoccupied for months to spend time with you. Ships in the night and all that. I've been on the graveyard shift most of the time. It's been shit – and now this.'

I understood. I'd been just as bad myself, and felt I

hadn't been supporting Fishy even though I knew he'd been having problems, knew of the sleepless nights.

Over his shoulder, the first dancer sashayed onto the makeshift stage to the strains of Rod Stewart. The girl was too heavy to be wearing a sequinned G-string, and I could see her stretch marks from where I was sitting – nonetheless, her small group of admirers whooped enthusiastically.

'Brodie, are you listening?'

Glasgow Joe's voice was sharp; I sat up.

'Now see, that's what your mother was always complaining about . . . you go off into your dippy, wee daydreams – and quite frankly you look thick.'

Glasgow Joe was right, it did annoy my mother. On one occasion she paid for an artist to come to the house to draw me. I drifted off, a far away look in my eye, my jaw slack, and mouth open. Mary McLennan refused to pay: she wasn't parting with her hard earned cash for any picture that made her daughter look 'feil'. Reminding me of her, however, wasn't going to get my attention back to the matter in hand.

'Brodie, you listen to what Fishy has to say, or I'll clear the pub – and that girl . . .' he pointed to the gyrating woman on the stage, 'won't be able to feed her bairns. A scoosh of Big Macs twice a day every day adds up, you know.'

Then he turned on Fishy.

'And as for you…' he pointed, 'get on with things. Is that all your fancy school taught you? To be a gobshite and mess lassies about? Brodie needs looking after – get to it.'

Duly chastened I sat straight and tried to sober up.

'Six months ago this came through the post to me.'

Laying a green Moroccan leather photograph album on the table, Fishy pushed it towards the picture of me as a corpse. 'It contains four separate sets of photographs.

'The photographs relate to four different girls. They've all been photographed post mortem.'

As Joe would put it, I must have looked pretty thick again.

'Christ, Brodie . . . it's the girls from "the bodies in the bag" murders.'

'Are you telling her or am I?' interrupted Fishy. 'You might care to remember I've been working on this for six months . . . you've known for about ten minutes.'

Things went ominously quiet while the two men considered what had just happened. Answering Joe back was pretty brave – coming from Fishy, it was even braver. Limbs could be lost any second.

'Fair due.'

That was what passed for an apology with Glasgow Joe.

The bodies in the bag murders were infamous in Edinburgh. They spanned almost three decades, all four remained unsolved, and the cases were closed due to lack of evidence. The last body was found in 1990.

Fishy and I studied the facts in our Forensic Medicine class with Patch Patterson. They were his greatest disappointment. All pathologists have cases that, for one reason or other, they cannot solve, and, in spite of

Patch's brilliance, he had a few of those. The bodies in the bag murders were taken by him as a special affront, perhaps because they involved children. The knowledge that he had never found out the identity of any of the girls seeped through as he taught us the few findings of the case.

'Before you open the album, Brodie, I should warn you that the person who generated that picture of you is aware of this album.'

'Oh for Christ's sake, Fishy, you sound like a fucking bank manager. Look, Brodie, whatever sicko bastard sent this photograph . . .' Joe waved it in the air, 'was the hand behind these ones.'

'We assume so at this point. I don't suppose we can really say with one hundred per cent certainty,' cautioned Fishy.

'Look, pal, my bones are telling me that the bodies in the bag killer is behind Brodie's photo. I've had to rely on my instincts to survive for years – and they've never let me down.'

'I just don't think there's any point in panicking her.'

I grabbed the album and inserted my fingers at random, into the thick black sheets of the book. The page fell open and I was staring at an identikit photograph of the one Kailash had given me. The clothes, the paraphernalia, everything was the same, except the face. This girl was young and unblemished. Flicking through the pages, I could see that the other three sets of pictures were the same. The bodies had been posed, slightly differently for each shot, but each set contained three identical positions.

'Maybe it's just some smackhead behind this,' suggested Glasgow Joe hopefully. He knew he could outwit any addict and keep me safe. A sadistic serial killer was quite another matter. Was I on some hit list? Had I been targeted? I'd like to believe Joe's idea, even superficially, but it was so obviously not possible that I didn't have the heart to lie to him or myself.

'No. Opiates are great pacifiers. A sex fiend like this,' I pointed again at the picture, 'wouldn't take anything that would blunt his libido.'

'Fishy, I know that the photographs look the same, but Brodie is too old. Whoever did this – the guy is a paedophile. Brodie doesn't fit his MO.' Glasgow Joe motioned his head in the direction of the album.

'What's the score with these investigations?' Without waiting for a reply he spoke again. 'Why haven't your crowd ever caught the bastard?'

'Because this is what they had to go on.'

Fishy, laid another set of photographs before us, all in the same format. I found myself wanting to gag as I looked at the bloodied dismembered body parts, sticking out at odd angles from the black plastic bin bags.

I had seen these photographs before and, at that time, in my student days, I had been strangely unaffected by them. But that was long before I felt that the 'girls' and I had been brought together in some bizarre sisterhood.

Fishy started speaking, louder this time to be heard above the music.

'There weren't enough body parts recovered to identify them. No heads and even the fingertips had been removed. We had bits of bodies in bags, and we had clear evidence of a series of murders, but we didn't know who the victims were and we soon ran into a brick wall without that to go on.'

The dancers had changed, a skinny little slip of a thing now strutted her stuff, unfazed by the fact most of the men she was thrilling were old enough to be her father. Her grandfather. She continued slithering up and down a pole as Fishy's voice caught my attention.

'On each occasion, each discovery, the police received an anonymous call telling us where the body would be found. Bear in mind these girls had never been reported missing – or, at least, we didn't think they had.'

It didn't make sense. Bodies are usually found by neighbours complaining of strange smells, or by dog walkers. Killers ordinarily take great care to conceal the evidence of their crimes.

'Arrogant bastard isn't he?' Glasgow Joe sounded angry. 'Why couldn't he hide the body, the bodies, like any normal murderer?'

I didn't let myself wonder how many bodies Joe had disposed of in his time.

'I've thought about this for six months,' said Fishy, 'and it actually seems pretty clever to me. He controls the discovery of the body and he knows exactly what evidence we have and what state it's in.'

'Very Masonic of him . . .'

We both turned to look at Glasgow Joe.

'Well, it is,' he brusquely defended his position. 'I might not have a degree like you pair, but I do know crime, and the murderer wants to keep his identity a secret, like murderers tend to do, so he's hiding it in plain sight . . . like the Masons. All their secret symbols are there to be read – if you know what to look for. It's a basic rule – you want to hide anything well, do it in the open.'

Fishy ignored Glasgow Joe. 'When I was sent the album out of nowhere, I asked my superiors to reopen the cases.'

'You didn't tell them about this album did you?'

Glasgow Joe was worried on principle. His basic philosophy was never volunteer information and it had kept him out of Barlinnie on at least one instance that I knew of.

'No . . . thank God. They asked me why I was suddenly interested in these cases. The last one happened while I was still at school. I just said I'd heard a rumour in Leith.'

'You weren't quick enough – or quiet enough,' Glasgow Joe admonished him.

'It pains me to say it, but you're right,' admitted Fishy. 'Within an hour I was transferred out of Leith into the traffic division. I've been working the grave-yard shift since then, chasing fixed penalty dodgers.'

'Anything else?' asked Joe.

'I was meant to get a promotion, and it's been stalled.'

'Still got your bollocks though? You're lucky they're just trying to bring you to heel. If you step out of line and let them know you're still interested in these cases . . . you're up shit creek.'

Fishy sighed, rubbed his eyes, then decided more drink was needed. Watching him rub shoulders with half-naked dancers with highly unlikely breasts, I felt frumpy and knackered.

'That wee bastard's hiding something,' interrupted Joe.

Standing at six foot one inch, no one else called Fishy small, but Joe belittled him at every opportunity. I was sure he was wrong – Fishy wouldn't hold out on me.

'Kailash thinks it might be a killing team,' I told Joe.

'Does she now? That changes things. If that's her opinion I'm with her, no matter what Sherlock Holmes over there says.'

Fishy was weaving his way back to the table; it was taking him a long time, as the Rag Doll regulars were making the most of an opportunity to nudge the local police. Fishy thumped the drinks tray down onto the table.

'Not missing anything am I?' he asked.

'That's exactly what I wanted to ask you,' said Joe.

Rifling in his pocket, Fishy pulled out another photograph and placed it on the table.

'I think I've found out the identity of one of the girls. Her grandmother has been looking for her since 1990. Meet Laura Liddell. This was taken that year at a Church of Scotland outing for under privileged inner city kids to Gullane.'

The faded colour photograph was quite different from the others, it curled up at the edges and I smoothed it out to get a better look. Laura Liddell smiled out at me from a sunny beach; her bikini strap had slipped from her shoulder showing the redness of her chest, which promised her a painful evening.

Squinting her eyes to smile into the camera, her light brown hair hung around her shoulders in ringlets formed by the salt water. Even in this photograph there was an air of doomed predestation about her. I was almost more bothered by this picture than the others.

Childhood memories flooded back, times of running through an abandoned graveyard with Joe, where one old stone always made me want to cry.

> *Here lies the body of a child who died*
> *Nobody mourned – Nobody cared*
> *How she lived – How she fared*
> *Nobody knows – Nobody cared*

It might have been written for Laura – but her body wasn't in a marked grave. Her existence had been erased. No face, no memories, no identity.

At school we were taught the Westminster Confession of Faith: By the decree of God, for the manifestation of his glory some men and angels are predestined into everlasting life, and others foreordained to everlasting death.

Had Laura, and others like her, been predestined for torture? And now, did the killer think I was like her, like them? What was my future – was I predestined for hell too?

SEVENTEEN

Icy water ran in rivulets down my neck and back, waking me up. Standing under the power shower, leaning against the large limestone tiles I watched my hands turn a shade of blue.

I needed this time to think. I had to consider what I knew – or didn't know – so far. I wasn't being allowed to get out of this case; a case in which my client had specifically asked for me as representation despite our past history. I couldn't get the image of Kailash out of my mind as she stood in court, eyeballing Sheriff Strathclyde – but I had even more difficulty with why he had reacted the way he had. For now, I was going to ignore Jack's conspiracy theory and his witterings about the Enlightenment Society, but I couldn't ignore the fact that the black saloon that knocked me off my bike at Dunsappie Loch was the same one that I had seen outside Lord Arbuthnot's house in Heriot Row – minutes before Lord MacGregor arrived at his dead son's house to meet with Moses Tierney. I also had to face up to the fact that whoever had clobbered me

could very well have done so with a walking stick –
and with that I was right back, full circle, to Moses and
the Dark Angels yet again. What the hell was going on?
What was I caught up in, and why had someone decided
that this needed to get personal? I felt that there were
so many clues wafting around, but maybe the knock
I'd taken when I was attacked was just making me a
bit more stupid than usual (although I know there
would always be some who would say it was often my
approach to things involving my own safety). I knew
without a shadow of a doubt that the car was the same.
I knew that I had seen the grieving father talking with
Moses Tierney, and I knew that the Dark Angels were
caught up in this somehow. But what was I missing?
What if the baseball bat marks on my back were from
a different source? What if they *were* cane marks as
Malcolm had suggested? A blatant calling card of the
Angels, but why would they do that to me when I had
never really had that much to do with them? More
confusingly, why would they attack me after making
such a public display of their – perhaps feigned –
worship outside the Court?

Ever since the post-mortem, the facts that Patch had
uncovered had been spinning round my head. Not so
much the information about Lord Arbuthnot's long-
term drug abuse, but the image of the brand on his
arse. The condolence I got from Patch's raising the
possibility of accidental death only offered a glimmer
of light. There was too much darkness coming from
other aspects of this case to make me feel much hope.

What sort of warning was I being sent by my attacker?

And why wouldn't they tell me what I had to do to avoid further attacks? My heart told me this all had something to do with the super-imposed photograph that Kailash had shown me, but to make the leap from that to the notion of a serial killer team who were now out to get me, seemed ludicrous. My stomach didn't seem to recognise the ridiculous nature of the premise though – it had been churning for ages now.

Why was Fishy being dragged into all of this? How had my attacker got his mobile number, and who had sent him the photograph album six months ago? The same person? I didn't know where the four body in the bag murders fitted into all of this, but now that we had a name for one of the victims there was at least one lead to go on. And it was closer to home than I had ever realised.

As the shower trickled to an end, I pulled myself away from considering things I could do nothing about, to get back on track. I am a creature of habit – every morning at school, I was woken at six, forced to have a cold shower and then run ten miles. I find it hard to break this Spartan routine; I've even learned to enjoy it. It seemed I was alone in this.

'For Christ's sake, Brodie – is this necessary?' Glasgow Joe was an unwilling participant in my early morning habits, even though he'd chosen to be there.

'No one asked you to come.' I reply tersely, still fighting a hangover. The first twenty minutes of any run are difficult, your legs are heavy and your body does everything to make you stop. It was the first time

I had been out running since the assault, and I didn't want to have to deal with Joe's whinging too.

'You know that I can't leave you on your own. Your safety equals my bloody torture.'

We left the flat, and his face was already puce and sweaty as we started down Dundas Street. Glasgow Joe wasn't built for speed – not in these circumstances. The roads were almost deserted; a solitary early morning cleaner passed us on her way to work. We had passed the longest day and the morning was as bright as noon as we turned into the cycle path that leads down to the Water of Leith. I felt as if we were the only two alive. The ground was flat, and because of Joe we took an easy pace. In spite of the pain, I increased my speed, leaving Joe struggling in my wake as he ran over the cobbled bridge. Swans swimming in the dirty, litter strewn water, greeted him, as if acknowledging his endeavour. Sensing that his last burst of effort had knocked the resistance out of him, I slowed down and allowed him to catch me.

'I take it you recognised her?'

As soon as he spoke, I felt sadness overwhelm me and it was difficult to keep moving.

'Of course I recognised her – that photograph . . . Laura looks like it was yesterday.'

I was still reeling from the shock of what I had quickly realised. Joe and I had gone to primary school with Laura Liddell, and when I saw the picture of the little girl smiling on the beach, it was disturbing. She looks the dead spit of her mother too – I always found it hard when we were all at primary school together to imagine Shirley as a Mum. She didn't seem like any of the other ones. Didn't seem the type to have a child weighing her down.

'Half the time she didn't know she had one,' muttered Joe.

We were at the door of the Rag Doll. Joe's pub stood on the corner, opposite the old tea factory I had been named after. Looking down the narrow street, the skyline was dominated by the high-rise flats where I had spent the first years of my life. Squinting, I could see the yellow balcony on the thirteenth floor, where I had spied on the other children who were playing street games.

'Maggie still lives there. I'll phone her after breakfast . . . she's getting on a bit now,' said Joe as he opened up the pub. I was immediately assaulted by the smell of stale fag smoke and spilled beer. Standing in the middle of the empty bar it looked even tattier than it had the night before.

'God, Joe, this place is a tip.'

'The regulars like it like this – it discourages the wrong type,' he said.

'What? Folk that have baths?'

'Aye – Edinburgh ponces,' he smiled back at me.

I followed him through to the back of the pub. The window had bars on it; an unnecessary precaution I would have thought. There wasn't a smack-head or nutter around who would mess with Joe. He put the kettle on and I took the opportunity to nose around. Joe lived on the premises in what was basically a bedsit. In sharp contrast to the front of house, his private quarters were austere; they took minimalism to new heights. The kitchen contained a white enamelled cooker that was only on display in one other place – a museum. As Joe supervised the sizzling sausages and bacon, I considered the monastic air of the place, spoiled somewhat by the enormous Victorian wrought iron bed. Joe was a wealthy man and the only place it showed was here. A goose feather quilt with an embroidered white linen cover lay on the bed: it was spotless. Piled high with pillows, it was the sort of bed that Goldilocks would have chosen. At the foot of the bed a white fur cover was neatly folded. The thick original floorboards were polished and covered in part by a sizeable rug from the rare brown Orkney Jacob's sheep. The bed was reflected in an outsized white French antique mirror that leaned against the wall. Joe wasn't vain, so I had to shake my head to dispel thoughts of why it was there.

The smell of bacon lead me back to the kitchen, and I could hear Joe singing 'I'm Gonna Be (500 Miles)' from the shower. Even with the enhanced acoustics of the water he sounded like Shrek on a bad day. I felt better for my run too; stronger, less afraid.

Wandering in with a large white bath towel wrapped round his waist, Joe turned the sausages.

'I've left some gear for you in the bathroom.'

Glasgow Joe had once been a member of an infamous Hell's Angels chapter and yet was anally retentive about cleanliness. I knew he wouldn't let me eat until I had washed again, so I headed off to the shower.

Until Joe bought the place, it was still serviced by

156

an outside loo. Long and narrow, the high cistern toilet was now at one end of the tongue and grooved room; a long cast iron bath filled one wall.

To shower, I had to step into the bath and pull a curtain round. A wicker basket on the floor contained a large selection of exclusive Swiss products that I knew could only be bought in Harvey Nichols – after I had stayed at Joe's one night when locked out of my flat by accident, I had complained about the cheap shower gel and supermarket shampoo on offer. I'd bunked down at his many times since then, and had never had cause to complain again. He took good care of me, did Joe.

After rubbing the skin rejuvenating cream into my legs, I slipped my feet into the clean cashmere socks provided. It was like being in a health spa, not the back room of one of the scummiest pubs in the city. Recalling Malcolm's admonitions. I rubbed the black birch oil which Malcolm had given me into my wounds, conditioner into my hair, and shaved my legs. I may not be Kailash's 'girl', but my appearance and health could do with a bit of a helping hand just now. I wasn't going to willingly put leeches on myself – not all of Malcolm's advice was quite so easy to take. Struggling into the spare jeans and t-shirt that I always left there, I wondered about Joe's private life. Did he ever bring anyone back here? And, if he did, what did they think about the signs of me that littered the place?

Joe came in just as I finished.

'I phoned Maggie – she's expecting us.'

He handed me two filled rolls, and headed for the

door. Evidently, we would eat our breakfast on the hoof. We took our time to walk the short distance from the pub to the flats and by the time we got there, I was on my second roll. I didn't want to risk my mouth being filled with the smell of piss if we used the lift, so we started the climb to the nineteenth floor. I tried to ignore the graffiti, which had always been there, but the place had definitely deteriorated in the last ten years.

Joe rang the doorbell, and I could hear Maggie Liddell shuffling inside. It took some time before the door was opened and a morbidly obese woman peered out. Her life had been hard, and her commitment to food was understandable. She had given birth to six children, and only one of them was not HIV positive. Maggie was a good woman who had done her best as heroin swept through Leith like wildfire.

'My God, son,' she shrieked at Joe, 'you're making an old woman very happy – you look good enough to eat.'

Maggie clasped him to her enormous bosom – it might have been my imagination, but I thought I saw him quake. He was probably regretting wearing his kilt by now. I barely received a nod. It was generally perceived by the red Leithers where I had been raised that I had sold out and forgotten my roots. I'd certainly tried to – yet now that I was in trouble, it was the first place that I had come running.

It was like stepping back in time, from the orange swirly carpet to the copy of Gainsborough's *Blue Boy* that hung above the gas fire. The fire was on full blast, and the room was stiflingly hot. Maggie's chair was placed next to it. I could see that her legs were badly mottled with fireside tartan.

'So, son – you're here about Laura. Do you have news for me? Is she safe?' Maggie Liddell knew the truth, but Joe had told me that for years she had fooled herself that Laura was in London, alive and well.

Glasgow Joe shook his head and Maggie began to cry; long, heart rending sobs as she rocked back and forth letting her grief pour out.

'Aw, son, I can hardly believe it. That wee lassie. That wee bairn. I should have saved her – I knew she was in trouble. I went to the polis, I honestly did, but they didn't believe me – respectability counts for a lot.' She spat out the word 'respectability' as if it had nothing to do with morality or decency.

'You told them she was missing?' asked Joe.

'Oh aye, was at their door every day. Laura was my youngest grandchild – and after the bother I had with my six . . . I was already looking after three grandchildren and with my diabetes and my arthritis – I couldn't take another one. I knew she was in trouble, and I thought that the polis would come through for her.'

I had heard that Maggie had taken some of her children to court to assume parental rights of her grandchildren. An ardent activist, she had mobilised a group of grandparents in the area to assume responsibility for the offspring of their wayward, HIV positive children.

'What do you mean she was in trouble?' I asked.

Maggie did not lift her head to look at me. Her hands covered her face and the folds of flesh on her arms wobbled as she continued to rock back and forth.

'Laura was in care, son,' she answered, as if Joe had asked the question, not the wee upstart she was ignoring. 'That's never a pretty picture, but that wee lassie went through a lot.

'Whilst she was in the custody of the council . . . I think she was interfered with. Some dirty bastard taking advantage of kids with nothing left anyway. I'd rip their bollocks off and hang them up to dry, so I would.'

Maggie stopped to catch her breath and blew her nose with ferocity. Composing herself she began again. I had more questions, and as long as she was answering them, I didn't mind if she channelled it through Joe.

'Interfered with in what way? Was she abused? Raped?'

Maggie stared resolutely at Joe.

'I used to bring her home for weekend visits when I could. She was always such a lovely lassie, but she changed after being in that home for a while. There was nae chance of her getting fostered – snotty weans fae druggies on schemes never seem to attract yer Hollywood stars looking for a cute wee bairn to take into their lives.

'She eventually said when it was just me and her one day – the other ones were away up the Walk to pinch fruit fae the Paki shops . . .' Maggie's words came out naturally. Children shoplifting, local shopkeepers being the butt of racism, it was all as easy to her as going to the bingo and dodging the loan sharks on the estate.

'We were sat here watching the telly when she said

it,' Maggie's eyes watered at the thought of what her granddaughter had revealed.

'When I say, interfered with – I don't mean once or twice –she told me she was hired, loaned, to high heid yins. When I went to the polis – they'd have none of it.'

Glasgow Joe and I listened in silence as she spoke. We had already agreed that we would not show her the photographs; there is only so much the human mind can bear.

'So I decided to deal with it myself. I didn't take her back that Monday morning, no' right away. I took Laura to the doctor and had her examined – she agreed, said that she had been interfered with. I think she went to the polis as well, she must have done, because they came banging to the flat as soon as I got back, accusing my son who'd been staying here at the time. That meant every access visit from Laura had to be supervised by the social – word got out . . .' Maggie turned to Joe and nodded at him for confirmation.

'That my son was a "beast" for assaulting Laura – he was hammered in the lift and just left.'

Joe nodded at her, supporting her; reaching out he held her hand, gratefully she squeezed it.

'Davy, my son, couldn't take it . . . he would never have harmed her. He had full blown AIDS by that time and it wasn't even safe for him to come home. I couldn't even let my laddie die in peace . . .'

Tears ran freely over the red broken veins on Maggie's cheeks; pushing, she lifted her great bulk from the chair, and hobbled to the kitchen. The arches in her feet had fallen as a result of her weight; she moved slowly and with difficulty, dragging her tartan slippers across the threadbare carpet.

I could hear the kettle being switched on, and Glasgow Joe went through to the tiny kitchen to help Maggie. There was no room left in there for me and I wouldn't have been wanted anyway. I stood by the balcony window whilst I waited for my cup of tea. The one redeeming feature of our flat had been the view. On a clear day I could see straight across the docks to Fife. The Firth of Forth was mesmerising in any weather. I loved to watch the ships come in and out. If I had lived on Maggie's side of the building, perhaps I would have turned out like Shirley. It's hard to visualise a better life if all you see is concrete.

'Maggie was telling me the last time she saw Laura alive, was the 23rd September 1990, just before her fifteenth birthday.'

Joe was carrying a huge tray laden down with Tunnocks teacakes and caramel wafers. My heart sank as I knew we would have to eat our way through a considerable number of them to avoid offending Maggie even further.

Joe spoke loudly, so that our hostess could hear.

'Maggie asked around after Laura told her what had happened. She used some of the people she knew through the grandparents' groups, and some of the addicts that her kids were friendly with. Maggie reckons there's a ring of men – and they've been grooming children round here for years. There's also a rumour on the street that one girl escaped – and that she has evidence that could send them all away.'

Maggie stopped her sobbing to interrupt him.

'And I thought that girl was my bonnie wee Laura – I kept expecting her to walk in and we could put those bastards behind bars where they belong.'

Maggie had reached her chair now and she manoeuvred herself into it like an oil tanker docking. Her knobbly hand tapped my knee forcefully, to gain my full attention or to beat me into submission.

'I'm talking to you, lassie. Maybe I'm no' playing with a full deck now – but that girl exists . . .'

Maggie's rheumy eyes stared into mine, they still shone with unshed tears.

'I deliberately fooled myself that it was Laura – but you can't blame a granny for hoping, can you? Especially when there's no' much to hold onto.'

I placed my hand over hers, and promised that we would find the vanished girl, but I didn't tell her what I really thought. The truth was, if the mystery girl was still alive, she wasn't missing – she was in hiding.

EIGHTEEN

My stomach was aching from all the teacakes and caramel wafers I'd polished off, and we again decided to take the steps rather than the lift. Our route was empty and it gave me a chance to think what to do next. I switched on my mobile to check for messages – there were several irate texts from Roddie Buchanan but I didn't want to meet him yet. My cases were being covered, Lavender had seen to that, when Joe had initially phoned her to say what was going on, so I could tell myself that there was no need to call him back.

The sound of our feet echoed through every storey, and my hip was beginning to hurt – maybe I should have waited before I went out running.

'Do you think that girl really exists?' Glasgow Joe asked.

'I want to believe . . . but she could be an urban myth. There are plenty of them round here.'

I understood Maggie's self-deception, and bought into it to some extent. I needed to trust in this girl's existence because my own life might depend upon her.

'Maggie's theory about the paedophile ring didn't sound right though, Brodie – there have only been four deaths over the years.'

'Maybe there's something unusual about those girls – something I have in common with them,' I ventured. 'Why would it go from them, their killings, to me? It can't be random, that's not how killers like this usually work. From what I know of the cases, there are certain things this killer needs to do, there are things that he – or she – do to get their way of working all over the murder, so there needs to be something that makes me next in line. What is it, Joe? What am I missing?'

Joe ignored my last comment; we all see, and hear, what we want to.

'But Maggie said they had already tried to report the men to the authorities – so the children were no threat to the ring, they knew that even if they did disclose, nothing was going to happen, the police weren't going to do anything.'

'Yes, but those girls jeopardised the security of the abusers, even if it came to nothing – perhaps they view me as a threat too?'

'How could you be a threat to them? You know nothing.' Joe was stating the obvious, again. But he was wrong, I did know something – and that was that I did not want to die. I was perplexed. I wanted a quick solution but I just couldn't see things clearly. Pinning my hopes on Fishy, I waited on him to phone, which he did as soon as we were out of the flats.

'Where have you been? I've been worried sick – I've been phoning all morning.' He rattled on, his voice high and laced with anxiety. Highly-strung, I could hear him unwrapping his antacid tablets and felt guilty for upsetting his ulcer.

'I've got to give evidence in Edinburgh Sheriff court this afternoon – meet me in Chambers Street Museum before that,' he demanded.

Joe and I headed away from Leith, back to his lockup. We needed transport, and he had a collection of possibilities that would make an aficionado drool.

Glasgow Joe has probably lost count of the motorbikes he owns. Awesome was his present to me on my twenty-first birthday, and remains the best gift I've ever received. He disapproved of the name I had chosen – but I was still tickled by how many teenage boys got hard-ons just looking at my bike, all of them mouthing 'Awesome' as they considered riding nothing trickier than a mini-scooter themselves.

I thought I should be keeping a low profile, so I was surprised when he took the keys to his customized trike, a bespoke three-wheeled bike, hand built in Texas, with a chopper front and two seats at the back. The petrol tank was crafted into the shape of a coffin, practically impossible to get petrol into, but the practicalities weren't what had attracted Joe to his toy.

The paint job on the trike would outshine a Ferrari, and probably cost as much. Even the seats are specially made black leather, with a hand-stitched embossed skull. Joe had decided we were going cruising. The point about a normal motorbike is that wearing a helmet affords you a certain amount of anonymity – on a trike you don't wear a helmet, but you can give up all hope of not being noticed anyway.

I knew Glasgow Joe had a plan; he just hadn't bothered to tell me. Reluctantly I climbed on board, but not before he had handed me a jacket. I took one look at it, and protested loudly. 'Bad Ass Girl' was written in shocking pink gothic script between the shoulder blades. 'Christ, Joe – did you get me this specially or do you keep it just in case you want to impress *really* classy women?'

The roar of the engine announced our arrival two blocks away. We drove up Ferry Road, the early afternoon shoppers assuming we were a Festival act and waving us along. Joe was heading for Muirhouse and Pilton, some of the most deprived housing estates in Edinburgh, but he didn't finish there.

By the time we made our way up town and finally parked in Chambers Street we had visited the Edinburgh that is strictly off limits to tourists. For a reason. Glasgow Joe was showing anyone who might be interested that I was under his protection now.

Chambers Street Museum is a vast, red sandstone edifice built by the Victorians. To get to its revolving doors, you have to climb a myriad of steps – maybe that's what puts the lawyers off. Within its hallways I have enjoyed many contented hours, at all stages of my life. As a child with my mother, I would spend long periods dangling my hands in the sizeable fishponds, trying to entice the Carp and the Koi fish to nibble at my fingers. When I was older with Glasgow Joe, the fascination with the fishponds remained, but this time we were intent on collecting the coins from the bottom. Later, as a graduated law student it was a stone's throw from Old College, and I sought a respite from professional exams within its peaceful, tranquil walls.

Fishy was waiting for us in the café. After Maggie's enormous spread I couldn't eat a thing; Joe suffered from no such inhibitions. He went off to get haddock and chips, and an espresso for me.

'You look very smart,' I said, commenting on his navy, pinstriped court suit. He was obviously about to give evidence.

'What time is the trial starting at?'

A look of fury covered his face.

'The accused pled guilty just before lunch, so, there's another wasted day.'

There wasn't much I could say to that, I had done the same thing myself too many times before. We sat in uncomfortable silence waiting on Joe: whatever Fishy had to say, he obviously didn't want to have to repeat it.

Joe finally arrived, and we all squeezed round a table that was far too small. His elbows kept nudging Fishy as he worked on his meal, and I watched Fishy's irritation grow. Pushing himself back from the table he began to speak.

'There's no easy way of saying this . . . the files that I saw six months ago have been removed from central filing. The records department maintain they've been lost for years, ever since the move from the annexe to the main building.'

'But that's not true, you handled the files, you saw them,' I interrupted.

'Well, their computer records back up the lie. I didn't want to make too much fuss – the lower the profile we keep on this the better.'

I thought of Glasgow Joe's escapades this morning, and was not surprised when he refused to make eye contact. Joe left the table on the pretext of obtaining salt for his chips.

'I'm sorry, Brodie,' said Fishy. 'All we've got to go on is this.'

He pulled the photograph album out of his brief-case. If I had the choice I would never look at that bloody album again, but choice was exactly one luxury I didn't have. I made a mental note to try to avoid the pictures of Laura Liddell until I felt stronger. This proved to be impossible.

'I think it's in chronological order, starting on the back page.'

I could feel Fishy watching me intently, as I reluctantly followed his instructions.

'Have you no idea who sent you this . . . this fucking atrocity?' I shivered as I used my fingers to open the book; the pages were sharp, cutting into my fingertips.

'I've already told you; it just arrived in the post.'

I turned my attention to the first item. It was a series of newspaper clippings, yellow and brittle with age. I handled them carefully to avoid disintegration. But the newspaper articles did not refer to the murders, instead they gave details of a newborn baby thrown into the sea and washed up on Portobello beach in November 1976.

In the run up to Christmas, the discarded baby

caught the imagination of the townsfolk of Portobello, and they determined that the child would not suffer a pauper's grave. Local businessmen set up a fund, to commemorate the baby's short life.

'Sickening isn't it? Their mawkish sentimentality determines that a dead baby needs a six foot marble angel on its grave, but five miles along the coast they wouldn't have given two bob to keep a vulnerable kid like Laura Liddell safe.'

Joe was back with his salt and we let Fishy rant. I was thinking of Maggie Liddell – no one is more maudlin than her and I'd have placed good money on the fact that she had contributed twenty-eight years ago.

The angel on the grave was a marker, a symbol of hope and decency when life is callous. Fishy still had to learn. You couldn't solve all of the world's problems; you have to start with the ones that you find on your doorstep.

There was another article relating to the baby. The police were looking for its mother in case she needed medical help. Such was the public furore that the wretched woman, who must have been beyond desperate to throw her baby away, would have been charged with infanticide if they had ever caught her.

The local newspaper had devoted two pages to the erection of the angel. There were tales of local primary schools running jumble sales, women's guild selling crocheted pram covers; it appeared that all the neighbouring communities had contributed.

'Look closely at the photographs.'

I stared and stared – what was I looking for?

'Jesus, Brodie, look! Is that who I think it is?' Glasgow

Joe poked the paper excitedly. 'It is! God, she looks good – she looked like that when I first met her.'

I removed Joe's finger to get a closer look. Sure enough, in the background at the raising ceremony stood a woman I couldn't fail to recognise.

My mother.

A shiver ran through me. Mary McLennan, still slightly plump after giving birth to me, stood in the fashion of the time with her hair-piece piled high upon her head. She did look well, but, more than that, she looked sad. I wasn't surprised – after five miscarriages, I was her last hope to become a mother, and cruelty towards children was something that was beyond her ken.

'No!'

The exasperated word hissed through Fishy's pursed lips.

'I wouldn't have recognised your mother. I didn't know her when she was a young woman.' Fishy sounded impatient.

'Look again. Look at who I was showing you in the first place.'

This time he pointed, directing my eye to the appropriate image. Amongst the list of dignitaries, Mrs Bunny MacGregor, wife of the late Alistair MacGregor QC, Lady Arbuthnot.

'Christ – that's some coincidence,' said Joe.

I felt my face tighten with anger and Fishy looked the same.

Coincidence is a word you use when you can't see who's pulling your strings.

NINETEEN

The clock that sits on top of the Balmoral Hotel resembles Big Ben. It has four faces with one clock face always five minutes fast. It showed eleven o'clock now. The hotel once belonged to the railway and the management wanted to ensure that the passengers were punctual. As a student I worked at the Balmoral as a chambermaid. I started work late and left early according to whichever face suited my needs. As I waited on Jack Deans, I had time to reflect upon the fact that now I was the one who needed at least four faces.

'Admit it, Brodie, he's stood you up.'

Glasgow Joe was striding up and down Princes Street, edgily dodging the admiring tourists trying to take his photograph; I was loathe to admit he was right.

Raging, I tried to salvage the situation. Grabbing Joe's arm, I crossed the street to the locus of the murder. Standing beneath the statue of Wellington on a horse, I retraced Kailash's steps. Observing the bronze in all its detail, I conceded that from a purely professional point of view this impressive beast would captivate her – in laywoman's terms, he had a huge whanger.

Unusually for Edinburgh during the Festival, the air was warm. Typically, the ambience was European street life, with performers on every corner – except one. Not a soul was standing outside the gents' toilets Kailash had claimed Lord Arbuthnot had visited in the moments before his death.

I sent Glasgow Joe in to ensure that the coast was clear for me to enter. Despite the fact that I was still standing at the horseman, I could hear Joe kicking toilet doors open and shrieking:

'Get out of there ya dirty old poofter – does your wife know you're in here?'

Joe's sentiments cut through me like a hot knife in butter; at least it proved that, had Lord Arbuthnot been in the toilets, he would have heard the screaming Kailash. Following in the wake of Joe's tirade, like rats leaving a ship (rats with their flies undone mostly), men of assorted ages ran out. I wanted to shout apologies to them but they sought anonymity, quickly slowing to a walk once they were safely away so as not to draw attention to their identities or activities.

Though deserted outside, it appeared to me that the toilets were one of the busiest venues in town – that being the case, someone else would surely have heard Kailash scream?

Glasgow Joe guarded the entrance.

'Sounded to me as if you were unnecessarily harsh there, Joe.'

'Some stupid old bastard thought Christmas had

come early when I walked in – you can guess the rest.'

Joe was righteous with indignation, inflamed by the fact that his suitor was a minister.

Victorians took their sanitation seriously – their moral codes were a bit dodgier and had probably laid the groundwork for the man of the cloth who'd just tried to jump Joe in a public lavvy. They had built the toilets underneath Princes Street, away from the noses, and prying eyes, of the citizens. I walked down the steep spiral staircase; the steps were narrow and Glasgow Joe moved slowly trying to accommodate his galumphing great feet.

The walls were lined with bottle green glazed tiles, cracked with age. At dado height the tiles were narrow, and formed a raised rope pattern. Above that line white oblong tiles increased the sense of height and theatricality; by the time I reached the urinals I was anticipating a spectacle. The dark teak water closets were substantially built, and there was plenty of room to accommodate a party of two. Original Thomas Crapper high cistern toilets were still in situ. It was actually a place with a good deal of atmosphere if you ignored the two matters of what it was for, and what generally happened there.

Privacy was a problem; there was a gap of ten inches between the floor and the wood. If you were so inclined, it enabled you to count the number of feet thereby discerning the amount of occupants, and perhaps having a wee look if viewing was more your thing than participating.

In recent times police have been known to place

surveillance units on such toilets. To get round this, visitors make sure they carry high-priced carrier bags with them to such venues. The ones from posher stores are better able to withstand the wear and tear rather than a cheapie from Asda. As I investigated the scene, I found it difficult to imagine the Lord Arbuthnot I knew standing with a Harvey Nichols shopping bag getting a blow job in a bog.

If this had been one of the last places he had visited before he died, what did it mean? Obviously he laid himself open to blackmail, but if Kailash was blackmailing him she wouldn't want to kill that source of income.

The sound of footsteps came dancing down the stairs. The little man with the weak chin was crestfallen when he spied me before he spotted Glasgow Joe. I acknowledged him with a nod before leaving the almost empty toilets. I carried his sense of disappointment and the smell of the cheap pine cleaning fluid with me as I reached street level with Joe at my side.

Jack Deans was waiting for us when we reached daylight.

'I don't like to be kept waiting,' Glasgow Joe snarled at Jack Deans.

'Well then, you shouldn't get distracted by your hobbies,' Deans nodded in the direction of the toilets. 'Anyway, I thought I was meeting Brodie, not you – if I had known, I'd never have bloody bothered anyway. "Hairy-arsed wideboy shags scum in public khazi" isn't much of a headline.'

'Better than you usually manage,' answered Joe, clenching his fists, itching for a fight.

I was only half-listening to them. They had done this dance before, many times. What really bothered me was how much I was going to tell Jack Deans. I realised just how little I had told the reporter already – our trip to and from Cornton Vale had been pretty much silent, and I hadn't even told him anything by way of thanks for how he had helped look after me when I was recovering from the attack. I had a decision to make – was he trustworthy enough to receive full disclosure? In my heart it was a decision I wasn't ready to make but I was concerned that others had made it for me.

Deans offered no explanation for his tardiness. He had made arrangements to meet up with Fishy at the Pleasance as he had to review some comedy shows for the Sundays, so it looked as though Joe and I would have to tag along. Lost in thought I struggled to keep up with them as we crossed the bridges that link the New Town with the Old.

The Pleasance, which nuzzles in the shadow of Arthur's Seat, was packed with London media types in heavy glasses, and drunken tourists of all ages looking for a good time. It's part of the University of Edinburgh taken over as a huge comedy venue during August; the three of us entered its cobbled courtyard via the old stone archway. Within the courtyard I could just see Fishy struggling through the crowd carrying a tray laden with pints sloshing everywhere as the throng jostled him. He must have been expecting us to come with Deans – how much had they already discussed? How much did Deans know, and how much had Fishy revealed?

Pushing through the crowd towards the long trestle tables, I was taking no prisoners. It was my intention to prepare the strategy, which could, and hopefully would, save my life, and I needed a seat to be able to do it.

Fishy placed a pint in front of me, and Glasgow Joe removed it.

'She'll be needing what little wits she has, so, until this is over, no more alcohol.' At least Joe was joining me in my enforced sobriety; he replaced my pint with a can of Diet Coke.

'I think we can speak freely here.' Jack Deans spoke first. I was sure he was referring to the venue; he appeared to take it for granted that we would trust one another. I wasn't quite so sure, and I wasn't about to let my secret crush on him loosen my tongue.

'I'm glad you're saying that we'll speak freely, Jack, because, as far as I'm concerned, you've been holding things back from me – as usual.'

'It's natural to feel a little paranoid in your situation, Brodie.'

Red rag to a bull time. Telling me – telling any woman – that she was a bit paranoid was as good as asking if she was having her period. I wanted to ask if he would be laughing and joking if he'd been asked to defend someone who had tried to ruin him, been attacked, left for dead, and drawn into a paedophile's murderous wank-fest. I went for the other option – try to make him feel bad on a personal level.

'But you made me feel like that even before I knew about the threat. I'm not paranoid, Jack – I just know too many shitbags.'

Deans' silence condemned him. He was definitely withholding information from me, I could tell from his body language.

The photo album lay on the table between us. I laid my arm across it proprietorially; there was no way Deans was getting to see the contents without telling me what he knew.

He leaned across, and whispered in my ear.

'Did you ever wonder why you had risen so high in such a short time, Brodie?'

It was a rhetorical question, for he barely had time to draw breath before he began again.

'I have. I've often wondered how dirt with a degree – no offence meant – is the rising star of the Scottish Bar. Even getting a traineeship at Lothian & St Clair should have been beyond you. I'll bet Roddie Buchanan secretly despises you. Ok, you're bright . . . but you needed the high profile cases and since I've watched you get above your station, I've wondered just who has been opening doors for you. Have you ever asked the same questions, or are you just so bloody sure of yourself that you assume it's all talent and hard work?'

Jack Deans was too close to the mark; the only thing he got wrong was that Roddie's scorn was open, not secret. Calmly, I removed his hand from my shoulder while he continued to talk.

'Either way, and in case you're interested, I haven't figured out who your invisible benefactor is yet.'

'Break it up, you two,' interrupted Fishy. 'We've got a big enough fight on our hands. First of all, I'd like to bring you up to date on what I did today. The official files are gone – and I don't think they'll turn up anytime soon – so I contacted Frank Pearson and tried to pull a few strings for old times' sake.'

Fishy looked smug, ignorant of the fact he was heading for a fall. I just sat back, and watched who would deliver it. As it turned out, it was Jack Deans who exploded.

'You stupid bastard – do you realise what you've done?'

It was another rhetorical question; Deans obviously thought he had all the answers. He leaned back gathering his energy for the next onslaught. Disconcertingly, I was more aware of how good-looking he was. Even at times like this I could find a moment to curse my father; if a man was mad, bad or sad I was attracted to him. But a man who was emotionally unavailable to me was best of all, and Jack Deans had thrown down his gauntlet.

'I'm dealing with fucking amateurs…' he said disgustedly. I could see Fishy about to answer him, and then wisely, at the last moment, shut up.

'If that book you've told me about is part of what I think it is – and your mate is as thick as you are – then you've just signed his death warrant.'

The colour bled from Fishy's face. Jack Deans was right, and that was more important than Fishy's hurt feelings.

'Christ, we'd better get hold of the poor sod,' said Glasgow Joe, springing into action after watching the show in silence since it began. He took the Procurator Fiscal's mobile and home numbers from Fishy. Before he left the cobbled courtyard to make the phone calls he looked at Jack Deans.

'Don't let her out of your sight until I take over again – it's not too shabby a job, Deans.'

It was an order, and one that was obeyed immediately. As Joe vacated his seat, Jack Deans slipped in beside me. He knew what mattered, and this was more important than their pissing-against-a-wall boy's niggling.

Deflated, Fishy watched Joe with his swinging kilt walk away – so did most of the women and half the men in the crowd. Deans brought him back to the moment.

'There's no room for error here, Sturgeon – let me see what you've been sitting on for the last six months.'

Fishy pushed the album in front of him. Jack Deans let out a moan even before he had opened it.

'I've heard about this,' he said, as I wondered what story lay behind that innocent statement.

Jack Deans normally protected his sources. I watched as he stroked its leather bound cover – if I wanted more information out of him then I would have to make him feel as if we were on the same wave-length. I have always been fascinated by mentalism, old stage acts that pretend they can read the minds of an audience. My interest had led me to America and India in the past to study with old practitioners before their knowledge was lost. Most modern psychological techniques have their roots in magic; it was written in the old grimoires that if you copied a virgin's breathing and then tightened your anus, you captured her soul. I loved that sort of stuff, one day thinking it was nonsense, the next believing it was the truth of the world. There was definitely some useful information in what I had learned. I doubted that Jack Deans was a virgin, I certainly hoped not, but I knew that if I mirrored his body movements, his subconscious mind would believe that we were, in the widest sense, 'soul mates'. I didn't bother to clench my anus as that seemed a tad extreme, but I did wait for my actions to take effect before posing my next question.

'Tell me how you've heard of it?' I asked, expecting an answer and getting one.

'On 7 May 2001, there was a break-in at Fettes.'

His voice was slow, and measured; I sensed trust in his eyes. Fettes is the central police headquarters in Edinburgh. Located in an expensive suburb, it is situated opposite the boarding school of the same name that Tony Blair attended.

Jack was too slow for Fishy, who interrupted.

'That's right, a group of protestors from the Animal Liberation Front broke in and sprayed graffiti on the walls – but nothing was taken.' Fishy smiled at me, seeking acknowledgement that it was good to have someone on the inside. But when all was said and done he was a policeman, and they were sensitive about the embarrassing break-in.

Jack Deans shook his head, and rolled his eyes.

'That's the official line, Thick Boy – or should I say the official lie.' I had learned from my limited dealings with Jack that you had to let him tell his tale in his own style – rambling. Journalists tended to be thwarted storytellers. I was certainly frustrated listening to it unfold, like Fishy I wanted him just to cut to the chase.

'It wasn't protestors from the Animal Liberation Front. The thieves did steal files – all of them have been recovered except one, and I think this,' he tapped the photograph album loudly, 'is part of the missing file.'

He drank long and deep from his pint before continuing.

'That's why I was late, Brodie – I was afraid to come. Afraid of what might happen if I got involved again.'

I found myself warming to him as if we had a deep connection. Abruptly, I pulled myself up. The mirroring of the breath works two ways, and my subconscious mind was starting to believe Deans was Prince Charming.

'Just get it over with and tell me what you know about this album.' I was of the same opinion as Joe; apologies would be no good to me if I were dead. I had noticed that Deans still hadn't opened the album up yet to look inside.

'After the break-in there was a rumour that it had happened. Of course, officially, nothing had gone wrong.'

'You can understand that . . . it doesn't make us look very good if our headquarters is breached.' Fishy was understandably trying to defend his colleagues, yet I found myself bridling.

'Quite.' Jack was terse and off hand. 'I received a call – from a source . . .' Jack was uncomfortable and mindful that Fishy was a cop. He thought long and hard before he spoke again.

'The source informed me that a break-in had occurred – and that it was most definitely not a protest over animal welfare. He told me that files had been taken and directed me to a rubbish bin where he had left some photocopied papers of the files.'

Giving forth that information was noticeably tiring for him, as if he were about to release a burden held onto for too long. Taking a long slow deep breath he began again.

'The papers that I saw talked about this album. I'm not sure whether my life would have been easier if I had it back then – but I'm damn sure I wouldn't be sitting here with you today.'

TWENTY

The PA system crackled and announced the comedy show that Jack was there to review. In spite of the fact that it was one of the most sought after tickets in town, none of us budged. The need to know more rooted me to the spot, and I moved as the pack shifted around us.

We were the only silent grouping in the courtyard – it took several gulps of Guinness before Jack was ready to talk again.

'I had to be very careful regarding the laws of libel . . .' He looked at me accusingly and I knew what he was wanting – contrition. He had been one of the journalists involved in the Roddie Buchanan debacle. I didn't think of that as my attacking Jack because I had sued the newspaper not the individuals involved. It looked as though he had different ideas.

'At least you still have enough blood in you to look shamefaced, Brodie McLennan.'

'Jack – I apologise to no man; or even half-men like you that I feel quite sorry for. I was doing my job and

I'd do it again – anyway the break-in at Fettes was *before* Roddie's case.'

He ignored me and continued.

'The article that I turned in was nothing more than a news report detailing the break-in; it said nothing about the papers or missing files.'

Under his breath, he added, 'Thank God.'

He went on. 'Anyway, before it was even published, I was arrested by the Serious Crime squad. They detained me for six hours and then I was released, pending a formal complaint.'

Rolling his head round I could hear the bones in his neck snap; it wasn't attractive but somehow he still was. A battle scarred war-horse: I was falling for all the stories, and he was laying it on thick.

'That wasn't the worst of it – the article was never published. I was sacked for . . . shall we say, *spurious* reasons.'

'I heard you were fired because you drank too much.' Fishy was on the attack now.

'For Christ's sake man: I always drank too much. I've never met a newspaper man – or woman for that matter – who didn't. Well, none of the ones I'd trust.'

Jack Deans didn't sound angry at Fishy's comments, just resigned. Maybe he'd tried to justify this part of the story too many times before.

'Anyway,' he continued, 'I've never really had serious work since then, which was why I had to resort to working on the "Daily Tat", but your Ladyship put paid to that.' He lifted his pint of Guinness, and raised his glass to me.

'I've always been curious; how did you get that story?' I made eye contact with Jack Deans, and held his stare, every part of me looking for a lie. There was none but that didn't mean that his answer didn't surprise Fishy.

'Kailash.'

The word that said it all.

I composed myself to cross-examine Deans. As the condemned, I felt I had that right.

'Who tipped you off about the photocopies of the files?'

'As I've said, it wasn't the Animal Liberation Front.'

Jack Deans was trying to be difficult, but I could teach classes on obstinacy. I gave him a look that hopefully indicated I would let Glasgow Joe beat it out of him if necessary.

'Jack, I didn't ask you who it wasn't. I want answers – I want them now.'

His eyes looked down to his left; he was recalling and formulating facts. Some minutes elapsed before he spoke, but I can find unknown patience when waiting on a reply.

'It's hard to describe him, Brodie – I keep my sources close to my chest. Never know when someone might start asking hard questions about me, so I like to keep them on side.'

He watched me to see if I was buying this story, but his body language checked out. Unless he was a psychopath, and nothing would surprise me just now, then he was telling the truth.

'How do you know that all the files have been recovered – except this album?'

'I've lived with the consequences of that break-in for longer than I care to admit – my life has been put on hold.' He turned towards Fishy. 'Now, does that sound familiar? I know it's their standard operating procedure – destroying your reputation is always the first hit. In my case they said I was a falling down drunk – who's going to believe a guy like that? You've had some of that treatment too, Plod, haven't you? What was it? Traffic division and promotions stalled? Well – unless you're keeping something from us, you've been bloody lucky. You've still got your reputation.'

'How can you say he's been lucky, Jack?' I exploded. 'How selfish can you be? You were a drunk, you *are* a drunk – they were right with you! But Fishy's the brightest graduate recruit they've ever had. Spit it out, Fishy – you had dreams of becoming the youngest Chief Inspector they'd ever had. This must have ruined that for you?' I looked at Jack Deans as I spoke to my friend: 'Tell that supercilious bastard that he isn't the only one with dibs on hardship round here.'

'Aye, Plod,' interfered Jack Deans, 'what screws are they turning? Traffic division is a nice wee rest not a death sentence. And no promotion? Unless you know the right handshake you were never in line for that in the next decade anyway. What have they *really* done? Banned you from the Jaffa cakes for a month? Said you can't get freebies off the tarts down the docks until after Christmas?'

Fishy looked uncomfortable and I felt it. Just as much, I hated the idea that he would tell me anything new with Jack Deans sitting there. What could be so bad that he hadn't told me before?

'There is something,' he began. 'Brodie, I'm so sorry, I know I should have told you, confided in you, but it's been so hard. You haven't been around, and I just can't get past this. Can't get past it at all.'

'Past what, Fishy?' He ignored me and sat with his head in his hands, staring at the wooden bench in front of us.

'Fishy? Answer me. How bad can it be? I'm a bloody lawyer! We can either deal with it or we can sue – those are great options. Tell me what it is and we'll choose the best one.'

'The word on the street is that I'm a beast, Brodie. You got an option that'll wash that away?'

My eyes flicked towards Jack Deans. This was scurrilous beyond words, and obviously the true explanation behind Fishy's insomnia. 'Beast' is criminal slang for a sex offender. The only honour I have ever found amongst thieves is that they take any opportunity to assault sexual perverts with a predilection for children.

'What grounds do they have for saying that?'

'Grounds, Brodie? Grounds?' asked Fishy. 'They don't need any fucking grounds. Coppers start ratting that one of their own is a paedo and grounds don't mean shit. No smoke without fire and all that.'

Hot fat tears welled up in my eyes and my voice trembled. I wanted to weep at the unfairness of it all.

'But, Fishy,' I said, desperate to fix this, like I thought I could fix everything. 'We can tackle this. They don't have any proof – they can't have any proof because there isn't any. They have to put up or shut up – and the shutting up has to come with a resumption of full responsibilities, consideration for promotion, and an apology with all traces of their allegations removed from your files.'

Jack Deans reached out, and squeezed Fishy's shoulder. I was touched by his gesture and it struck me that Fishy seemed to appreciate what Deans had done more than what I had offered.

'Fishy – forget about no smoke without fire; we can fix this. Now, tell me where to start? Is there anything I need to know that would affect a case?'

Still holding him by the shoulder, Jack softly repeated my question. 'Sturgeon – is there anything else we need to know? Anything Brodie needs to know?'

'They caught my credit cards in a sweep of internet paedophile sites.'

Fishy's voice cracked with emotion, he bit down hard on his lip to maintain composure. I watched as a small droplet of blood formed where his tooth had succeeded.

'That's serious shit, Brodie,' Deans said, turning to me. 'All they need to do is leak that to the tabloids – you'll be crucified,' he added to Fishy. Shaking his head as he envisioned the furore he couldn't resist gilding the lily, 'Plod the Perv; Paedo Cop Named and Shamed; Paedo PC faces Perv Charges. It's piss-easy – and great stuff for any hack. They'd hound you out of Edinburgh.'

Deans wasn't exaggerating. Even the Capital's respectable church going citizens approved of mob rule and public castration where paedophiles were concerned.

'Thanks for the vote of support, Deans,' said Fishy.

'Does it matter at all that it isn't true? Safest way in the world just now to ruin a man's reputation – and how much bloody evidence is needed? Sod all. The fact that the police claim to have evidence that my credit card was used to download images of kiddies being abused for my sexual kicks is going to get a damn sight more coverage than the alleged beast saying "it wisnae me."'

He turned to direct his next words to me. 'It's not true, Brodie. I've never been on any of those sites, not even for work. I've never worked in that unit, never even seen any of that bloody sick shit.'

'Have you been mugged recently, Fishy?' I asked. 'Has anyone attacked you and you've thought nothing was stolen?'

'For fuck's sake, Brodie,' interrupted Deans. 'Get back to your Miss Marple books. If someone wants to nick a credit card they just do. They don't need piss-poor pretend muggings – they could get his details from his rubbish.'

'Maybe some bastard stole it out of my locker?'

'You don't have to explain yourself to us, son. It's that easy to get someone's details nowadays that it's hardly even worth spending the brain time going through the options of where it was – someone wanted it, someone got it. That's enough for just now.'

Jack Deans looked at me to back him up. Too late I reached out to touch my hurting friend, wishing I'd thought of it first. Gratefully, Fishy clasped my hands.

'You'll be next, Brodie – if they think that you are a danger to them, they'll set out to destroy your credibility,' warned Jack.

'That sounds like a threat, Jack. And who is this cloak and dagger "they" anyway?'

'When will you realise I'm not the enemy?'

Straightening his spine he raised himself up to his full seated height. His blue eyes were like forged steel and looking from one to the other of us he appeared to be doing a final sizing up, for a split second I thought he would leave. I realised then that I needed his particular abilities to survive. I vowed to be more courteous to him if he stayed. Making silent promises of improved behaviour is a habit of mine; I've learned to my cost that rarely do I keep them.

'Ok. We're in this together.' His voice was decided. Relief flooded through me.

'And who are "they"? All in good time, Brodie. When I spoke earlier I made them sound invincible, but there is one person who always manages to beat them at their own game.'

His pint was finished, and he reached out to finish Glasgow Joe's Diet Coke.

'Who?' I asked.

'Moses Tierney.'

The Coke spurted from my mouth, hitting Fishy on the face, brown droplets dripped from his nose and chin as I spoke again.

'Moses Tierney? A boy in a long coat with more make-up than is healthy but not the brains to match. *Moses Tierney*? He's an idiot.' I rubbed self-consciously at one of the marks on my back.

'Is he? Think about it, Brodie – we all know he's shady yet neither he nor any of his gang is ever brought to court. I've spoken to Procurator Fiscals who have put case after case up marked for prosecution only to have them returned marked "no pro".

Fishy was wiping my spit, and the Coke from his face but he was nodding vigorously. I could not allow my personal dislike for the boy to interfere with my judgement, and Deans was, unfortunately, right.

'I just find it hard to accept that Moses Tierney is some kind of criminal mastermind. I'll ask Frank Pearson about it when we see him, when Joe gets back.'

I didn't hear Glasgow Joe creep up behind me. He startled me with his reply.

'You'll be a long time waiting, Brodie hen. I've done everything I can to track down Pearson. Unfortunately . . .'

Joe's voice trailed off mid sentence, and I could sense that he felt as I did.

It wasn't unfortunate – it was a bloody tragedy.

TWENTY-ONE

I had woken up morose after a fitful night. I was worried about Frank Pearson, and knew I had been bothered by dreams of him during the few bits of sleep I had snatched. I knew that we would need to do something today, and that I needed to go to Frank's flat with Joe, but I had stress and discomfort surging through my system – and it needed a get-out clause.

Unfortunately, my morning run did nothing to lift my mood. I had stayed too long in the freezing shower, and I still felt chilled from it.

When I'm stressed, I cook. Unlike a lot of people who use the same outlet, I tend to eat it all as well. I was making porridge using my mother's spurtle which had belonged to her mother before her. Generations of McLennan women had been unable to make porridge without it. Joe had just informed me that I could not make porridge with it. His opinion was worthless – he was a Sassenach who thought that sprinkling sugar on his porridge was a good idea, when any fool knew that salt was the one true way.

The mucky looking substance bubbled in the pot, spattering out drops of burning oats – even at the kitchen stove I was in danger of being injured. Luck wasn't with me at the moment.

'The post's arrived.'

Joe dragged me out of my reverie as we ate – I was engrossed in the newspaper, looking for clues without knowing what I was actually searching for. With beginner's luck, I found a self-congratulatory interview from the officer in charge of Operation 'Bluebird'. He confirmed that officers sweeping US child porn sites for credit cards had pulled out the names of over 1000 Scottish residents. Amongst the professions listed were teachers, civil servants, social workers and a serving police officer. 'The net was closing in,' he said, and, listening to the beating of my own heart, it felt like a prophecy.

Walking slowly towards me, his mouth tightly shut, Joe offered me a brown envelope. He looked tired. His hair was coarse and tousled. Roughly he pushed it back from his forehead and in the harsh morning light, I noticed the greyness of his complexion that bore the scars of many battles, most of which I'd romanticised as he never told me any bloody thing. He'd received over a hundred stitches in his face over the years, and although the American surgeons had done a magnificent job of reconstruction, his right eye was pulled down at the side which meant that when he was not smiling, he looked cruel. Like a killer.

'I don't like the look of this – no stamp, hand delivered.'

It was addressed to me and I moved to take it from him. I'd been losing track of the days but it hit me – it was Sunday. There shouldn't be any post.

He jerked back and punched the wall with his fist. 'Brodie – those bastards were here in the night.' He put his hand under his armpit, ignoring the blood seeping out over his white shirt.

I moved again to take my envelope.

'Piss off – you're not getting your mitts on this. I'll get Fishy to check it out. The fewer people that touch it the better.'

He left the kitchen and went into the bathroom, ostensibly to wash his wound, but clearly going to open the letter, assuming that it was a bomb.

In his youth, at the tail end of the conflict in Northern Ireland, Glasgow Joe had been recruited through a Catholic boys' club, and trained as a gun-runner for the IRA. While with them, he had been trained in Gadaffi's PLO camps, a somewhat alternative student exchange, and it seemed obvious that he would have explosives training, even though we hadn't discussed it – like most things.

It was this tuition that led to the charge that forced him to leave Scotland. Joe had never adequately explained how he managed to come home for my mother's funeral. I had my doubts but I was so glad to see him I kept them to myself. During his time in America I suspected that he was still working for the IRA. There were parts of himself that he had to keep a secret from me so that we could still be friends. We were in denial but it had served us well so far.

As I waited with my ear pressed against the door, I could hear him rummaging around. The clock in the hallway ticked one hundred times before he emerged, looking drained and emotionless. When I saw him it startled me for a second time.

'What's the matter?'

He ignored me and my throat tightened into a ball. Tripping on his heels, I followed him into the drawing room.

'Sit down a minute while we look at this.'

Silence followed as Joe struggled to find the words. Fidgeting, I threw myself down beside him on the large cream sofa, the cushions creating a valley in which we collided. The envelope hung limply in Joe's hands that were placed between his open legs, resting on his sporran. I grabbed it from him, and he released it without a fight.

My breath was coming short and quick, but I felt almost sedated as I pulled another photograph out of the envelope – was I the local depository for all the weird pics hanging around Edinburgh these days? I had only taken out a corner before I recognised it – the original hung in my hallway.

It was my graduation photograph. The three of us beamed out at the photographer – me, Fishy, and Frank Pearson. We were all smiling, grinning with achievement – only now Frank had a noose scribbled around his neck in black felt-tip pen, R.I.P. scribbled across his body.

'Well?'

I couldn't answer Joe. What was I going to do? What

could I say? I was drowning in shit, and kept getting kicked back into it. I couldn't scream, because I didn't have anything loud enough within me. What could I possibly say or do?

I heard my mother's voice. 'Stop whining, Brodie, and stop talking to yourself. Get on with it – and fight like hell's furies.'

I reached into Joe's sporran taking out his cigarettes and matches. He watched as I leaned back and lit up. Psychologists say that subconsciously smokers don't believe they have a future. I remembered this and in one swift movement rose and threw the cigarette into the unlit fire.

'Frank – I don't just know where he lives,' I said, 'I know which neighbour keeps his spare keys too – he told me during a drunken heart-to-heart one night that his unrequited love on his downstairs neighbour had only resulted in him asking her to water his one plant when he was away. And that took three years.' Despite everything, we both suspected there was nothing to be done and it wasn't a house call I relished. As I saw it I had no choice. If I believed Fishy, I couldn't leave it to the police. I had to go there myself.

'Why do you think they sent us the photograph?' asked Glasgow Joe. 'Was it a warning or are they gloating?'

'Come on, Joe – you've been in tougher situations than this, but you need to accept that this isn't your fight. Hell, I don't even think it's my fight. But it seems whoever touches these photographs is sucked in and destroyed. Walk away, Joe – I want to take my own chances. And in answer to your question – the bastard's gloating.'

I slammed the door shut leaving him inside. I ran so fast, and hard along the road that my chest ached. I didn't just run to get to Frank quickly, I ran to escape the demons on my back. It wasn't too far to walk to his flat but it was definitely too far to sprint. I leaned over the gutter, and vomited from my exertions. The sourness of my porridge as it revisited my mouth made me wonder if the Sassenach's were right to wallop in sugar.

A hand grabbed my hair and yanked my head up. Yellow stomach acid dribbled off my chin. The sound of my own retching had obscured the noise of Glasgow Joe's trike. A surprisingly clean linen handkerchief wiped my face. He still held my hair even though he knew that it was hurting me. Turning my head so that I was forced to look him in the eye, he spoke slowly:

'It's over when I say it's over, Brodie.' Roughly, he pushed my head away.

We left the trike where it was; it wasn't a day to be announcing our arrival.

'Are you sure this guy's a lawyer?' Joe asked. I had run from my townhouse in Cumberland Street, and turned left in the direction of Leith heading for Broughton Street. Frank Pearson was a public servant, and his annual salary was probably less than I would receive for Kailash's case. The discrepancy in wages was reflected in our homes. Entering the nasty smelling common stairwell, I wondered why people kept cats if they hadn't heard of cat litter. Struck by the gloominess, Joe gesticulated to the smashed stair light. The covering of the light was heavy duty Perspex; it had taken some force to break it.

Frank Pearson lived on the first floor. We tried to climb the stone steps in silence but it was a waste of time given that we'd already announced our arrival by rattling on the door of the keeper of his heart to get the keys. Still Joe and I continued like piss-poor spy recruits – I held my breath as our feet scuffled up the stairs. Trying to lighten my weight, I held onto the mahogany banister and pulled myself up. A cat meowed on the top floor. We stopped until a door opened and the cat went in.

Outside Frank's door there was a simple name-plate. We'd wasted our time with the keys; the door hadn't been forced open. It was 9.30a.m. and whatever had happened looked like it had occurred the day before. It was unlikely that the assailant was lying in wait, unless he had a monumental bladder and great belief in the human spirit.

Nonetheless, Joe insisted on going through the open door first. I followed closely behind, going so far as to hold onto the belt strapped around his waist. Frank Pearson's flat was a typical tenement. The hallway was dark, long, and narrow with a high ceiling. The cornice was ornate and made of moulded plaster. The hall was cluttered with evidence of Frank's sporting life. Unable to see clearly, Joe's kilt was snagged by Frank's mountain bike as we skirted past it. Turning round to pull it free from the bike pedals, he managed to hit his head off the surfboard hidden in the shadows and hanging on the wall. Surfing in Scotland seems a contradiction in terms, yet on the Island of Tiree there are some of the best waves in the world. Surfers on the professional circuit descend in their droves to catch the waves, seemingly oblivious to the cold, and Frank sang its praises every holiday.

I thought I could smell death ahead of me. I doubted Frank would be going to Tiree again unless it was to get his ashes scattered.

Passing the open living room, we popped our head round the door. The brown carpet was a remnant from the sixties, brown onion swirls hid the dirt that lay in its down-trodden pile. The furniture had either been bought at auction as a job lot or an elderly relative had died and Frank had cleared the house. It was obviously a bachelor pad, nothing matched, and in spite of the fact it was tidy, it was apparent he wasn't expecting company. The loneliness of his existence overwhelmed me. We were alike. Who would mourn his passing? Who would really grieve for him? Who would feel that all the clocks should stop because he had gone out of their life?

I didn't want to answer that question in my own life, so I accepted that I would probably be the one doing the ash scattering and moved on.

'Are you sure you want to do this?'

We stood on the threshold of Frank's bedroom, and instead of answering Joe, I pushed him through the doorway. I hadn't known what to expect, but whatever it was, it wasn't what we got.

'Jesus.' Joe let a spent breath escape his lips, and I, for once, was lost for words.

At first I couldn't see a thing as blackout curtains were drawn. I didn't want to open them for fear of being overlooked. I couldn't switch the light on in case a neighbour spotted it. Slowly my eyes became accustomed to the dimness. In the background Frank's radio alarm played softly on waiting for its owner to switch off the button.

I saw Frank's hairy legs encased in American tan tights, the type old ladies wear. Although they were clearly queen size, whoever had placed them on him had done so with great difficulty, rips in the nylons ran freely down Frank's thighs where fingers had been poked through in the effort of pulling them up. In spite of this supreme pulling effort, his assailant was unsuccessful, and the gusset of the tights hung comically half way down his legs. There was no way he could have moved with those on, they would have had the same effect as tying his legs together. Painful childhood memories of wearing woollen tights, with the bum hanging down at the knees ensured that I know what can and cannot be done when clad like that.

In spite of his round face, Frank was neither fat nor big; in fact looking at him I was surprised how slender he was – but, then again, black is generally considered slimming. Frank's genitals were tightly bound in black rubber casing, and a taut PVC girdle constricted his chest. The mask that completely covered his face matched the girdle. It had small holes for the eyes and nostrils; they obviously came as a set, but I wasn't a connoisseur of the outlets where you could get such get-ups. To someone like Kailash, this was as common-place as office stationery.

Frank had been hung like a deer from the ceiling. Whoever had done it was not an expert, and the rope had come loose throwing him on the floor.

'Should we check to see if he's dead?' Joe was reluctant to go near the body; Frank Pearson looked like a ridiculous wrestler, and the manner of his death robbed him of any gravitas. From the moment this became public knowledge he would be an object of ridicule.

'For Christ's sake, Joe, look at his neck. He's obviously dead – you couldn't hold your head like that unless you were.' I was curt, more at the memory of what Jack Deans had said than anything else. They destroyed your reputation to ensure no one took you seriously.

'There's no way the police will buy this as suicide – poor bastard's hands are tied behind his fucking back, Brodie!' Joe had grown more used to the sight of the corpse and was now walking freely around the bedroom. Out of the corner of my eye I was watching him. I didn't want to disturb the crime scene, and let them know that we had been there first. We stood back from the body, side by side for warm human contact. I could hear Joe's breath, and it gave me the courage to examine the body.

'He doesn't look very stiff.'

Joe was right. Rigor mortis didn't appear to have set in. When the muscles relax then become rigid, it is usually within the first twenty-four hours, disappearing within thirty-six hours after death.

'Can you see any purple patches, Joe – because I can't?'

Still standing like two stooges I wanted us to look for livor mortis. When the human heart stops pumping, the blood begins to settle in the parts of the body closest to the ground. The onset of this condition appears almost immediately and disappears within twelve hours. As I looked, I knew that there was no way I could accurately estimate the time of death. He must have been alive thirty-six hours ago, because Fishy had spoken to him – so how could I explain what I was looking at, the contradictions shouted out by his body? When Joe was here yesterday, the door was locked – yet open today. Had Frank been with his attacker when Joe was here? Had he heard Joe and thought that he was about to be saved?

The answer to these conundrums was slowly coming to me. In my rush to get to the body I threw Joe against the wall.

'Call an ambulance, Joe, he's still alive!'

TWENTY-TWO

Prising the noose from Frank's neck I placed him on his side, trying to secure an airway. Even though I had once been forced to do a certificate in first aid training, I was still surprised that it was coming back. His pulse was faint and weak, his hold on life was slight but there. My mother had always believed that if it was your time nothing could prevent it; if it wasn't, regardless of the injuries or disease, you made it. I had always disliked this fatalistic attitude but now I prayed that it was not Frank's time, because fate was about the only chance he had at the moment.

The Medic One team was there in five minutes. Two green suited paramedics didn't shy from the body as we had. One medic calmly took the mask from Frank's face, and began to talk to him, nipping his ear to get his attention. The other turned to us, asking us Frank's details, if he was allergic to anything – they seemed to assume that we knew him more intimately than we did. I tried to explain that it was by chance that we found him.

'He's lucky, then,' answered Green Suit One. 'He's misjudged the timing on this one.'

I looked at Joe who was still staring at the scene before us – 'Timing?'

'Guys who like this sort of thing,' Green Suit Two jerked his head towards their patient, 'they usually have it down to a fine art. It's practically algebra to them.'

'What is?' asked Joe.

'The difference between shitting their load and topping themselves,' answered the paramedic.

'You think Frank did this for fun? Why in Christ's name would anyone want to do this . . . .' Joe nodded his head at the PVC-bound Procurator Fiscal.

'About five deaths a year occur because of asphyxiophilia – no idea how many more die from enjoying it too much.'

We looked aghast at the paramedic as he continued.

'Auto-erotic strangulation? Actually, loads more probably die than the official figures show – when families find the bodies they usually cover it up.'

Joe had cottoned on quickly. 'No wonder. Poor bastards – suicide is hard enough to deal with, but this . . . We needed you here fast so I didn't think to tidy him up.'

'He wasn't trying to commit suicide, mate. It's edgy sex – the ultimate thrill; the problem is there's always a risk of cardiac arrest and usually the first sign of trouble is your heart stops.'

The man looked over at his colleague.

'He's lucky. I think he just passed out because of

lack of oxygen, his heart seems fine – but he knocked himself out on the bedside table when he fell.'

'When I see some things – and I've seen a lot – I can't help wondering: who was the first stupid bastard to try it? What gave someone the fucked-up notion to get this into their heads for a laugh?'

Joe was striking up a conversation to cover his nerves. My response was always to show that I was a walking Wikipedia.

'It's been around for centuries, Joe – the Marquis de Sade wrote about it in *Justine*. When there were public hangings, the corpse often had an erection and then ejaculated on the moment of death – the ultimate orgasm. People wrongly assumed it was brought about by the strangulation – in fact it was caused by the snapping of the spine. And there was also syphilis. Men were often left impotent – often they viewed this . . .' I waved my hand nonchalantly at Frank's feet as the paramedics strapped an oxygen mask on him, 'as a cure.'

I was joining him in his chattering nonsense; the paramedic looked at me, noting the bruises on my face. He wasn't exactly judgemental but he clearly thought that I engaged in such practices myself.

'Is that right, Brodie? Well sorry for me never listening when they mentioned all that to us at primary school – still, not for the first time, you've taught me something.'

The medics had strapped the unconscious Frank to a stretcher and were carting him out of the room. Joe followed them to the ambulance.

I remained behind. I didn't buy for one moment the

notion that Frank had done this to himself – had he also just happened to send me the graduation photo with a noose drawn round his own neck, and assume that Glasgow Joe and I would charge in like the cavalry bang on time?

In contrast to the rest of the flat, heaps of clothes were scattered around and it was apparent that the killer had searched for something: whether or not they had found it I couldn't judge. I searched through the mounds of personal effects. Beneath his bed were a pile of soft porn magazines. The type any normal male would be likely to have, the usual healthy dose of misogyny and dirty-mac-fantasy, but I had no time for sensibilities, so I raked through his clothes rather than wonder about his reading material – inexpensive durable sports clothes, two cheap suits, and a mountain of tatty shirts.

Giving up on the mess, I flicked through his CD collection of classical music. It was apparent as I looked at it that Frank was anally retentive about order – he'd have a fit if he ever got home and saw the trashed havoc that had been left elsewhere by whoever had ransacked it. The CDs were filed according to composer and then alphabetically with reference to the symphony orchestra playing the piece. The only deviation glared out at me – Dolly Parton's Greatest Hits. Dolly smiled cheerily out at me dressed as a glamorous rhinestone cowgirl. I could ordinarily have been tempted to burst into a few bars of 'Jolene', but I just couldn't imagine Frank Pearson singing along. Sticking out of the CD case was a receipt dated the day before. Inside was a plain unmarked disc I slipped inside my pocket.

'Right – let's go,' Joe insisted behind me.

'One last look – in case we've missed anything.'

Wandering into the kitchen we both looked at the cheap Ikea mugs on top of the Formica boards. Two of them. I smacked the back of Joe's hand as he went to lift the mugs, nursing his hand he looked at me resentfully.

'Forgotten your speech to me already?' I asked him.

'There was no sign that the door had been forced so Frank had to have willingly let someone in.' I pointed to the mugs. 'He could have known who did this to him.'

'Come on, Brodie – I'm meant to be the naïve one here given that I've never read any of your historical porn and I seem to be the only bugger who finds this all downright pervy, but has it occurred to you that Frank let this guy in because they'd arranged to do whatever got them going? Then the other bloke took fright when he saw it all going tits-up?'

I lifted a plastic carrier bag and carefully placed the mugs inside. As far as the police were concerned this was an attempted suicide so chances were this evidence would be inadvertently destroyed anyway which, to me, justified withholding it.

I looked at the clock – it was only just after 11a.m., but I felt as if hours had passed within Frank's claustrophobic flat. I kept having flashbacks of him in S&M gear. Who had a motive for, what I was sure was, attempted murder? I couldn't make sense of Jack Deans' theories; who would the Enlightenment Society be trying to protect if they were behind this? I forced myself to walk down the stairs even though it felt safer to stay in Frank's flat on the basis that lightning doesn't strike the same place twice.

As I got outside, I had a feeling that I was speeding fast down a one-way street, that I was almost to the place where I had to get to. So why hop off and try to run ahead? I turned my mobile on. Five missed calls all from the office and an angry text message from Roddie Buchanan warned me that my day was about to get a whole lot worse.

TWENTY-THREE

'If you stand on a crack, you'll break your back. If you stand on a stone you'll break a bone.'

I whispered the childhood rhyme under my breath as I picked my way along the pavement outside the offices of Lothian & St Clair in Castle Terrace. I hadn't been back, or in contact, since my meeting with Lavender. I had, of course, been in touch with the lovely Miss Ironside, but, rather than force flowers and fruit on me, she rightly guessed that what I needed most was for her to hold the fort. To be honest, it was what she did when I was there anyway. I heard a voice calling my name from the other side of the street as I headed towards the building.

'Lizzie!' I shrieked in delight as five feet two of perfumed loveliness hurled itself at me.

'Brodie, darling!' she answered, immediately informing me she was in middle-class luvvie mode. 'God, you look shit.'

'Really? That bad?' I asked, fingering my various facial cuts and bruises.

'Actually,' she replied, 'you look worse. You're way beyond "shit".' Lizzie paused for dramatic effect as she leaned back to survey me. 'Aye – definitely shite on legs.'

She whacked me on the arm as she burst into gales of laughter. Looking around and seeing no immediate sign of Glasgow Joe, she asked, 'Where's that gorgeous man of yours then?'

'He's not mine, but he is around – he's parking. Where have you been, Lizzie?'

'You know where I've been. Bloody Milan. With bloody Luciano. I tell you, he's as Italian as my arse. And that place! You been there?' I shook my head. 'You could *buy* fuckin' Primark with what one handbag costs. But never mind my woes, what've you been up to, silly cow?'

'You wouldn't believe it if I told you, Lizzie. Drink tonight?'

'Abso-bloody-lutely, darling. And make sure that lovely bloke in a kilt is there!'

She flounced off in the direction of the coffee box, Marni coat flapping, as I turned round again to face where I was going.

The slabs on the street had shifted and moved through decades of frosty winters, and left an uneven, dangerous surface. At the height of press attention during the Kailash Coutts affair, Roddie tripped on a protruding stone falling head-first into a parked car, denting the passenger door. He waited until I had extracted an apology from the Glasgow tabloid before suing the council. The dunt on his head had been worth

£10,000 to him; it wasn't one of my finer moments, but it did remind me that Roddie always came up smelling of roses.

In the shadow of Edinburgh Castle, I hesitated outside the firm's offices. It seemed as if years had passed since I last entered its glass and marble hallway. I felt old as I watched a group of young Italian language students dressed in colourful cashmere wander up Castle Terrace, smoking, and talking excitedly, waving their arms in the air. Wearing jumpers round their waists and necks, it was apparent that the summer sun that sometimes frequents Scotland was too weak for their blood. A cavalcade of Fringe performers dressed like medieval mummers wound their way up the side of the castle, rushing to be on time to perform in the Royal Mile. A jester in a pointed purple and gold velvet cap carrying a stick with jingling bells stopped by me to adjust his spandex tights. I could have happily slapped them all. I was in a shit of a mood, and the city at this time of year couldn't possibly help matters.

'Are you going in, or are you just going to stand there – gawpin'?' Joe sounded pissed off; probably because he was. He had dropped me at the corner ten minutes before and had gone to park the bike. I still hadn't made it to the revolving door thanks to Lizzie. After a heated discussion he agreed to wait for me outside the office, but he didn't like it.

'Joe, I don't need grief from you as well – this is hard enough. I'd rather do anything than go upstairs and see that slimy bastard.' I said it quietly for fear of being overheard. Any number of young, and not so young, associates would love to report back and take my place on the headed notepaper. I had worked too hard to throw it away. A montage was running through my mind – as a young trainee, my heart had skipped a beat with pride every time I told someone I worked for Lothian & St Clair. The glory days were more than a bit tarnished now, or, more accurately, had certainly been shining a bit less brightly since Kailash came on the scene.

I nodded to the security guard at the door who was bizarrely dressed as a Rear Admiral, and wondered, yet again, who would be reassured by that type of get-up? It was a formality anyway – I spent more time at this place than I did at home, so identification was not an issue. Waiting on the lift I caught my reflection in the gleaming brass door-frames. I hadn't made the time to go home and get changed. If I was really stretching a legal technicality, I'd describe me as 'highly informally attired'. In all truth, I was a mess in faded ripped jeans held up by my infamous belt. Too late I realised I had one of those bloody t shirts on again, the ones I only seemed to buy when drunk, yet wear when sober – today's informed everyone that 'Good Girls go to heaven but bad girls go everywhere'. Was there somewhere I could buy good sense alongside white shirts and grey suits or perhaps I could just persuade Kailash to keep sending Malcolm round to my flat every morning with a pre-selected outfit?

The office was like the Marie Celeste – only frazzled partners, panicked about their workload, tended to come in on a Sunday. The only person moving in the corridors was Anna, the oversexed immaculately dressed office junior, who had strangely taken to playing the role of office virgin – badly. How on earth could she be so well groomed on her meagre wages? Her blonde streaks alone must cost about a quarter of her wages. Weekend overtime or a sugar daddy? Still, Anna's ambition was to marry a solicitor, and in any business you have to speculate to accumulate – Kailash would have been proud of her.

The corridors of the firm were Anna's own shop window. She'd toss her hair flirtatiously as she lowered files to display her goods. A brilliant white shirt (not a logo-ed t-shirt I noticed) clung to her ergonomically superior breasts; it was like something out of a Russ Meyer movie. When I saw Anna, I saw descriptions hanging above her head (no man in the office would bother looking that high up), and today I would say she was wearing a modest item which hinted at hith-erto unknown delights. A demure black skirt hugged her young hips that swayed in time to the rhythm of her clicking heels. It was powerful stuff, so naturally I despised the frittery cow with vigour.

When Anna recognised the scruff approaching her, those clacking heels went tap-tapping down the corridor, moving faster and faster away from me than such articles probably are designed to, until she reached the ladies' loo.

So that was how the land was lying – even the office juniors were afraid that association would damn them if they spoke to me. I popped my head around my own office door – it was immaculate. Lavender had clearly been there, but there was no sign of her now. She'd either be chasing Eddie around or keeping my nose clean in my absence.

I had to move on, get to the place I really didn't want to be, and then I could get out again.

Roddie Buchanan was alone in his room, standing at the window, looking up at the castle outlined against a clear blue sky. His back was to me, and, as when I had observed him unnoticed previously, it never failed to surprise me what a small man he was, even though he had a huge head. A comedy-sized head really – unless you were the bearer of it (or his mother, I suppose). In fact it was probably the sheer size of his head that made people think he was a big man.

I coughed to announce my presence, and he made me wait by pretending he hadn't heard. Suddenly I felt overwhelmingly tired, and in no mood to play games. The last few days had rearranged my priorities in life, and getting a row from Roddie was way down the list.

I took a seat, and my earlier resolve vanished. I lit up one of Joe's cigarettes; slumping down in the chair I noisily sucked it up for all it was worth, enjoying it even more in the knowledge that Roddie was an anti-smoking fascist. Finally turning round, he looked at me, flicking his eyes from my boots to the top of my head.

'You look dreadful,' he growled.

Something about him reminded me of a cockroach, and I felt my skin crawl. If I cut his head off would he live for a week?

'It isn't catching – you can still live in a sunny little

world if you choose. Whatever I've got – or am getting dished out – isn't contagious.' I hoped he didn't see my fingers crossed behind my back. You could feel the knowledge of Kailash between us. Although the silence was uncomfortable, I decided to sit it out. I was offering no information – not for free anyway.

Roddie Buchanan finally spoke. 'Two pieces of information – one, your office manager is currently not here as she is, once again, on the trail of Eddie Gibb. Two, in case you're thinking of withdrawing from Kailash's case – don't bother. We want you to continue acting.'

'We?'

I couldn't see any of the other partners in the firm taking an interest one way or another – whatever we were at Lothian & St Clair, it was not a united team.

Roddie sat down and motioned for me to do the same, even though I hadn't waited for his permission and was already seated. In his own opinion, he was royalty. He'd remember for life if you had been seated while he was not. The black swivel chair he occupied was at least twice the size of the one that I was perched upon, but that was Roddie – gamesmanship and manipulation at its best.

His dark eyes were cold but he tried his best to convey empathy.

'It's too bad about the judge dying.'

Succinct, I suppose. What else was there to say? In light of my lack of response, he continued.

'I realise it's difficult, Brodie – no one in their right mind would choose to represent the woman who murdered the Lord President.'

I was about to interrupt and protest the innocence of Kailash, but I couldn't be bothered. I was rapidly sensing that I was about to get more honesty from him than I could handle. Over his shoulder I could see Edinburgh Castle sitting on top of its rock. As an early defensive settlement it was second to none, and in times of war the citizens retreated behind the castle walls. The castle itself was virtually impenetrable because any enemy had to scale the rock face to get to the walls. It meant that those waiting there could see their enemies, and pick them off. I obviously had plenty of enemies who were complete strangers to me. I had no idea who they were – but they all knew me. I came back from my reverie to Roddie speaking once more.

'You're doing us a favour.'

His sly voice continued and I bridled. I kept a mixture of Machiavelli and Kailash in my mind – this was one situation where I needed to keep my friends close and my enemies closer. I smiled across at him.

'It's not a problem.'

Astonishingly, the words didn't stick in my throat but slithered from my lips, as if they had been greased with castor oil. Something mucky was certainly in there.

'I must say I'm surprised, Brodie. Some of us thought you might be difficult – principles and such getting in the way of what's best for everyone.'

Tight lipped and smiling, I said nothing. Roddie squirmed a little in his chair before he spoke again.

'In cases of extreme . . .' Roddie searched around for the correct word, '. . . sensitivity, we stick together. Like a brotherhood we look after one another – if one sticks out for the common good then rewards can be expected, Brodie. In this case we require an Amicus Curae.'

I repeated the phrase back to him in English. 'A friend of the court?'

An Amicus Curae is usually openly appointed by the court, and the accused knows all about it. I was labouring under no illusions that this particular manoeuvre was a covert action, and the last person I hoped would find out about it was Kailash Coutts. What was being proposed was beneath me, and it should have been too low a thing for Roddie to contemplate suggesting.

'And just what exactly would this "friend" be required to do?' I continued. He took exception to the tone of my voice, because, whatever he was, Roddie Buchanan was not a fool.

'Brodie – the Amicus Curae will have to do whatever it takes to look after the interests of the court . . . in whatever form that may take.'

'And if . . . "others" are satisfied with my work as an Amicus Curae, Roddie – what will be my remuneration?'

Roddie brightened up. I was talking his language. I was gaining his trust. His eyes flicked over me like a hawk.

'I will have no part of your incompetence should there be any, Brodie. If you don't carry out our instructions, you will be broken . . . and may wish to be permanently so. We would be willing to assist you in that . . . death wish.' I swear I almost saw a smile on his lips.

'And if I do as I am told?'

'You're young and some consider you bright . . . you would have our permission to profit in which ever way you wanted.'

I looked at him blankly, willing him to say the actual words, as he continued to twist the thumbscrews.

'I don't think a judicial appointment is out of the question. It would take some time of course, but, after all, there is pressure to appear politically correct and get more women on the bench.'

Roddie spoke matter of factly, but his insult was not lost on me. I was plainly as repugnant a bedfellow to him as he was to me. This is not unusual in law firms but what was slightly more galling about my situation was that my mother had worked herself into an early grave to give me this opportunity – and I still wasn't good enough.

'Roddie . . . I haven't even taken silk yet.' If I hadn't gone through this procedure of professional rank, I wouldn't be entitled to wear the silky gowns of the Queen's Counsel. I could live with the fashion disappointment, but if I hoped for a judicial appointment, there would be no short cuts allowed.

'That can be arranged. So what if you have to wait? If our plan is agreeable to you . . . then your presence is required at a reception tonight in the WS library.'

It was, in effect, a rhetorical question, indicative of Roddie's usual management style. Reluctantly, I nodded my head. Receptions in the WS library are not known for their drunken jollity.

'Just turn up, Brodie, that's all you need to do.'

As an afterthought he added: 'And try to look presentable. Shut the door on your way out.'

The brass door handle was cool, and smooth on my hand. It should have calmed me. Instead, I paused in the doorway, desperately wanting to tell the slimy little bastard who had just offered me all I'd ever want on a plate to just fuck right off – but a part of me realised there was another option.

I could get through this.

Maybe.

TWENTY-FOUR

Three gin and tonics later, and a swift resume of the past few days behind us, Lizzie and I parted company. I'd much rather spend the evening with her than continue with the plan laid out in front of me, but I knew I had precious little choice in the matter. I'd gone home to get dressed – with help from my new sartorial assistant of course – and then headed towards the High Street.

The crowd cheered and clapped ecstatically, as the young man on the unicycle blew fire into the air. Pushing my way through the tourists, I felt light headed. Trudging on, I tried to make my way to Parliament Hall, and the WS library.

The Royal Mile was teeming with life of all sorts, shapes, and sizes. A lone piper stood on the steps of St Giles' Cathedral. He had eschewed the usual smart but dull uniform, and instead traded on his raw sexuality as much as his talent. Looking like an extra from *Braveheart* he was not afraid to show a muscled thigh. His white linen shirt was open, and dishevelled. I was going to have to admit my penchant for men in kilts sooner rather than later, but my lack of sex life wasn't going to get to the top of the agenda any time soon the way things were going.

Women were queuing up to have their picture taken with the piper – until recently I too had associated photographs with happy memories, but now they were simply sickening reflections of sadistic and taunting minds. That was what I now needed to focus on.

To reach the entrance to the WS library, I had to walk across the cobbled square. Usually, I'd belt along in my biker boots or sensible two-inch heeled matronly shoes, but today I was dressed to impress – myself as much as anyone else. The square had not been made with five-inch Jimmy Choos (a gift from Kailash via Malcolm) in mind. The square is very old and on the left hand side is the main entrance to St Giles' Cathedral. A church has occupied that site since the twelfth century, and during the Festival a medieval market occupies the square, so I was further hampered in my movements not only by my ridiculous (but gorgeous) footwear, but also the higgledy-piggledy stalls.

I spat at the Heart of Midlothian that is set into the stone at the start of the square – not showing off my commoner's roots, but because I dare not risk incurring the wrath of the gods at the moment. I added my wish to the spittle that flew out of my mouth – survival.

Wiping the spit from my chin, I tried again to make my way to the reception. In 1637, an Edinburgh woman called Jenny Geddes started a riot here to protest at the imposition of a new bible – was there any way I could use that as precedent to get out of the function?

I made my way through the crowds, cobbles and stalls by following a German couple intent on entering St Giles'. A shiver passed through me as I went by. The Cathedral has been used for many purposes down the centuries; one of them was that it stored 'The Maiden', Edinburgh's guillotine. I made a final push towards my destination.

The pit of my stomach felt heavy, as I continued to loiter outside the nineteenth century panelled wood and glass doors. I pressed the ancient intercom and spoke my name. A click told me that I been granted silent entry.

The buzz of genteel small talk surrounded me as soon as I passed through the thick stone doorway. A silver buttoned lackey tried to take my pashmina, but I declined to give it to him in case a quick getaway was in order – it was also pretty useful to cover the many cuts and bruises which still adorned my arms and chest. I moved half-heartedly in the direction of the noise, squaring my shoulders and giving myself a pep talk. I was lucky – I had got through everything thrown at me so far and I should be bloody thankful for that. Frank Pearson would love to be walking into a WS reception tonight. To be fair Frank would have loved an invitation to any WS reception at any time, but the likes of him were not invited – with or without S&M gear. I fleetingly thought that maybe there was some-thing in Jack's assessment of my career – I had got very far, very fast, and Roddie had made it quite clear that would continue if I kept to my side of the bargain.

I had a quick recce round the room – tartan trews abounded, but there was no one here tonight who wore them with the panache of Malcolm. I was pleased that I had asked him to help me tonight. I had wanted to make my mark, and his fashion advice had certainly done that (even if my feet would be aching for days, and my breasts would probably be deformed for life given the shape my bra was manipulating them into). I didn't fit in with this group in the slightest – and that was exactly what I wanted. They were dull, badly dressed little sparrows. The male of the Enlightenment Society was no great shakes but still they managed to outshine their female counterparts.

I was both overdressed and inappropriately dressed – and I was delighted by those facts. I had absolutely no competition whatsoever. Some of the outfits on show appeared to have been brought out of mothballs – from the 1930s. The high priestess of appalling fancy dress masquerading as evening wear, Eilidh Buchanan, was bearing down on me like a barracuda. Sadly, her long tartan skirt, although puffball tight at the ankles, didn't hamper her movements. Looking as if she were sucking a lemon, she stood before me, arms folded. On close inspection her blouse looked grubby. It was probably an antique, and worn by her great grandmother at a Royal ball, but with my newfound sense of style, I was unimpressed.

Every woman in the library, including Eilidh Buchanan, was covered from head to toe in tartan in a variety of colours and linen of varying shades of whiteness. The only décolletage on show was mine, but thanks to Malcolm I was more than making up the deficit.

'I told you to contain the situation – not take lessons from that whore,' Eilidh hissed.

'And good evening to you too, Eilidh.' As I had promised myself, the smile remained fixed – until I saw someone who wiped it from my face.

Lord MacGregor stalked purposefully towards me. He must have arrived after I did, for he was a peacock in full highland dress and everyone's eyes were upon him.

'Ms McLennan! It's a delight to meet you at last. I've heard so much about you. Some of it has even been quite good.' A smile split his face at his own final comment. True to form tonight, I laughed ingratiatingly. Eilidh Buchanan was getting ready to wet her knickers – like an excited bitch on heat she leaped around Lord MacGregor. Casually, he clasped my elbow, and with a flick of his hand he dismissed his acolyte as one would an aggravating mosquito. Unable to resist the temptation I looked over my shoulder and gloated, although truthfully I would have preferred to stay even with her, rather than this man – I didn't know much about him, but I didn't like what I had seen so far. His association with Moses Tierney made him even less welcome to me.

Until this hellish day, I could never have imagined such a scenario anyway. Choosing between Eilidh Buchanan and Lord MacGregor? Hardly my usual band of friends. Unable to do anything else, I allowed my new benefactor to parade me round the room like a prize cow. I felt as if I were being taken on a specific route, as Judge after Judge after Judge acknowledged me and my udders.

Lord MacGregor turned to speak at me: 'It's many years since I've been in this place.' The gaggle of women (I use the term loosely) who were coming out in a cold sweat rather than a menopausal flush every time he walked by them were actually right – Lord MacGregor looked pretty good despite his age.

Our parade of two had stopped in front of an over-sized oil painting of an old man in judicial robes.

'He hated that, you know.'

Lord MacGregor inclined his head towards the picture.

'Said it made him look portly and decrepit . . . he refused to allow them to hang it where anyone who mattered would see it. My father was vain like that – and that over there is my grandfather.' He waved his liver spotted hand in a direction over my shoulder.

Was I naïve to think that the red judicial robes of a democratic country should not be passed down the generations like some plumbing business?

As Lord MacGregor held me in his gaze, I sought a diversion. His little procession involving only me and him had induced the intended effect. I was in no doubt who was insisting that I was an Amicus Curae – he was showing me that he could deliver the red judicial robes of my ultimate ambition if I played along.

Over his shoulder I spotted her. She was wearing a black blouse and a frown. As she bore down on us, I felt that I should warn my so-called benefactor but I couldn't quite find the words. As she entered our space I instinctively stepped back.

'Father.'

Bunny MacGregor's word was neither a question nor a greeting. Just a bald statement. I could almost see her father-in-law's heart miss several beats as he stared straight ahead. My own mouth was dry and my heart raced. I knew that I was not just a bystander in this confrontation – Bunny MacGregor was including me in her silent wrath.

'Darling, are you sure you're up to this?'

Lord MacGregor turned, and seamlessly kissed her on both cheeks. I had the suspicion that he was not referring to the reception but to some silent vendetta that raged between them.

'With your continued collaboration,' she answered, the same lack of warmth in her voice, 'I'm sure that I'll pull through.'

Bunny flicked her fingers, and a waiter jumped to attention. I grabbed a red wine from the silver tray, and as I did so, Joe's remonstrations came to me. I ignored them – I always tended to.

I expected the red wine to soothe me a bit, but it was cold and cheap, its bittersweet taste lingered with me, my lips twisted with distaste. Lord MacGregor looked quizzically in my direction, presumably wondering if it was the wine or the company that was making me grimace.

I blurted out an excuse.

'I've got a big case on and a glass of wine helps me relax.' I could have kicked myself.

'My dear, no one here – least of all me – has forgotten about your case.'

Bunny MacGregor's eyes burned into me as she spoke, deliberately enunciating every word. I marvelled at the woman's restraint.

Lord MacGregor produced a racking laugh, shaking like a silver birch in the wind. I put it down to nerves. Some people laugh when they are nervous, don't they? It's nature's way of dispelling the darkness.

As I looked at him, his laughter ceased.

'No parent should have to bury a child, Brodie.'

As he walked away, I thought of Lord Arbuthnot lying on the gurney. Flaccid. Naked. Dead. It was hard to think of him being someone's child, but he was. I suppose they all were, although I had never thought of it that way. Looking around the room I wanted to escape. Einstein may have believed in the power of imagination, but my mother did not; she believed I suffered from an overactive one. Tonight may have been the first time she was correct. As I looked around the hallowed library, I thought I saw the dead girls walk in and out the genteel group. Every step they took they demanded justice; either that or they were reminding me that I was next. In my mind's eye Frank Pearson joined them; thankfully he was not dressed as I had last seen him.

Lord MacGregor returned, dressed for the 'Red Mass'. Despite no longer holding office, like all others high up in the judicial hierarchy, Lord MacGregor was loathe to give up his costume. Indeed he wouldn't be the first to be buried in it. He approached me directly. I observed the red judicial robes; the silk cloak was ankle length, the collar and cuffs trimmed with white ermine. A white silk band ran down the front of the robe, and for the first time, I noted the significance of the six red Templar crosses upon them.

The Equilateral Blood Cross of the Knights Templar.

If the Templars were the forerunners of the Masons and the Enlightenment Society, then why did our Scottish judges proudly wear the mark of the Masons?

What had Joe said?

Hidden in plain sight?

I felt the familiar stirring of nightmarish panic. A hot flush ran through my body and I wanted to vomit. Tiny beads of sweat broke out along my upper lip.

'Are you all right, my dear?' Lord MacGregor was good at sounding concerned, but he held me whilst stepping back, rightly afraid that I would throw up on his hand-made shoes.

The peculiar taste in my mouth persisted, and as I stumbled, he dragged me from the library out into the cooler air of Parliament Hall. Thankfully, the dead remained where I had last seen them. Silence resounded in the great Parliament Hall, and although my mind was fuzzy, I was uncomfortably aware that I had broken my promise to Joe.

'Don't ever leave the group, Brodie. And if anyone tries to get you on your own, that's the bastard you have to watch out for. Well, one of the bastards anyway,' he'd said.

I tried to stand, but Parliament Hall swam round me.

Clutching onto the carved wooden bench, I tried again. Woozily I moved; with great force of effort and will I placed one foot in front of the other. My senses were heightened with fear – and drugs. Someone had spiked my drink.

Every step I took seemed to announce my escape plan to the world.

I just made it across the Victorian tiled floor and was leaning against a wooden bench staring at the south window that dominates the hall. The stained glass is supposed to represent the inauguration of the Court of Session from the Pope. It depicts a man kneeling in supplication. Those in my profession see it for what it is – the first time a lawyer asked for an additional fee.

I rose and was pushing through the antiquated swing door when it was opened from the other side. Falling, I almost knocked Lord MacGregor over. For a slight man, he was remarkably strong. Carrying me easily, he deposited me in the front seat of a car. I seemed to have lost the power of speech and all control of my limbs. A sense of overwhelming doom came upon me.

I was raised Catholic. Since my mother's death, bitterness has forced a wedge between God and myself. I always wondered if I would turn to God as I was dying.

Just before I blacked out, I prayed to all the angels and saints just as Mary McLennan had taught me.

Remember oh most gracious Virgin Mary that never was it known for anyone to flee to thy protection or seek thy intercession to be left unaided.

TWENTY-FIVE

'Whore!'

He shouted at me, beside himself with anger. The purple broken veins in his cheeks, just above his beard, seemed almost luminescent, giving him the look of a mad clown; presumably not the image he was looking for.

'You looked like a cheap dockside whore last night, Ms McLennan.'

'And you, of course, only like the expensive ones, Mr Buchanan,' I replied, trying to ignore the pounding in my head. Roddie Buchanan blanked my comment, but the stiffening of his body showed that the words had registered. Jack Deans was right – Buchanan despised me. He indeed thought I was dirt with a degree – so why had he employed me in the first place?

'I sent you to that reception last night to make a good impression.' Throwing his hands in the air, he paced around the room before stopping directly in front of me. Swinging my chair round, he placed his hands on my armrests.

Hissing into my face, he asked: 'And what did you do?'

He stepped back a little to look at me. Did he expect an answer?

'Apparently, I did nothing more than swan around looking like a cheap tart – rates must have gone up then, Roddie. Have you any idea how much my shoes alone cost? I can't imagine you haven't used the girls' services for a while – so what other reason could there possibly be for you to not know the difference between quality and trash? Do you get freebies? Sympathy shags?'

I thought I was on pretty safe ground if I stuck to insults – the truth was, the events of yesterday evening were shadowy to me. At that moment I would have been grateful for any information, even from Roddie Buchanan.

His left eyebrow was raised and he made a small clicking sound with his tongue. 'You'll go too far one day, Brodie. You're already the talk of the Steamie.'

'Makes a change from you then – or are you ticked off that someone else is stealing your thunder?' I was sick of his holier than thou attitude. 'The Steamie' was originally the public wash house where women met to clean their dirty clothes and gossip. 'The Steamie' to Roddie and me meant any significant gathering of lawyers, principally those who appeared in court. He still hadn't told me what I had done, so I was left imagining what the gossipmongers would be making of something I didn't even know about yet.

'Brodie, you vomited on Lord MacGregor's shoes as

232

he tried to hoist you into the car. My car actually, as his own had returned home not knowing that Lord MacGregor would be pressed into service quite so early in the evening. You were not reticent about leaving . . . *deposits* in my vehicle as well as on his Lordship's shoes.' Roddie's face registered disgust, and I knew a story like that didn't need much embellishment. I made no reply to the charge – he wouldn't believe me that someone had slipped me a Mickey Finn. I knew now that I had been given Rohypnol. The red wine had disguised its blue colour, and it had reacted even more strongly with the painkillers given to me by Jack Deans that I was still taking. He may not have been the one to slip me the date rape drug, but he had provided the jellies sold to him by a source that had made it all even worse. I remembered a client I once represented who had held up an off-licence because he thought the tablets made him invisible, so the fact that I was having hallucinations was now explained. I hoped that I hadn't been ranting as well.

I had swallowed more than the prescribed dose just to ensure I could get through the evening. Ingesting Rohypnol, on top of what I had taken, gave me the adverse reaction. It had probably saved me, foiling the killer's plans. My eyes scanned Roddie – a supercilious smile twisted his face. If that scenario was correct then Roddie had actually helped save my life in a funny way – if his car hadn't been so readily available, what would have happened to me? I preferred to believe an alternative version – that someone had set out to ruin my reputation, and they had done a damn fine job. I may have been between a rock and a hard place but I didn't want to be beholden to my senior partner on top of that.

I left without thanking him. Trying not to skulk I set off to make my way to Parliament House. Maybe there I could find something that would identify whoever had tried to drug me.

The windows in Parliament House continued to rattle, restless like me, reacting to the summer storm that was brewing outside. The place was built in the 1630s, and the Parliament of Scotland met there before the union with England in 1707. It felt old, and weary. I sympathised, before coming up with what I thought was my best idea of the day – I needed to slip Joe's leash to give me time to think.

I sat in the corridor, trying to occupy my mind. The corridor is in fact a law library built by the Faculty of Advocates to connect Parliament House and the National Library of Scotland. It is a long narrow room, with columns of small desks. Old leather bound books line the walls: not just law books but one of the finest antiquarian collections in the world. First editions of Sir Walter Scott and Robert Louis Stevenson were almost common given that they were advocates too.

Although it was August, the Scottish summer demanded that on days like this, great fires were blazing in Parliament Hall, but none of their warmth permeated through to me. I longed for my soul to be warmed.

At one end of the corridor sat Prather's desk. Prather is in charge of everything, and can procure anything you want. Like an East End market trader, Prather has his sources. Amongst his assets are his workforce, a group of octogenarian men who have no name; they are simply known as Prather's men. Silver buttoned lackeys, they fetch and carry for us. If anyone wishes to contact me whilst I am in the corridor, they stop at Prather's desk, and one of Prather's men will come and tell me.

The corridor was quiet today because the court was on summer vacation, and most of my brethren at the bar had other lives. In light of recent events, I found it difficult to concentrate. The atmosphere in the corridor was draining me. I sought a distraction; scanning the corridor I could see nothing, except fellow advocates who like me had nowhere else to go.

Sunlight shone through the glass at the other end of the corridor; the window emblazoned with the crest of Bloody McKenzie. In the dim and distant past, he was the Lord Justice Clerk; the position that Lord MacGregor had occupied prior to his retirement from the bench. Judges in Scotland are split into divisions and houses. The Lord Justice Clerk is the 'high heid yin' of the second division. The judge in charge of the first division is the Lord President. The Lord President is pre-eminent, it must have irked Lord MacGregor that his son had reached a height above his. Way back when hanging was allowed, and Bloody McKenzie was the Lord Justice Clerk, he loved to see them swing. Lord MacGregor's laughter could be seen in a different light if he was anything like his predecessor, for Bloody McKenzie was particularly fond of hanging children. Justice was seen to be done when he himself died slowly and painfully of inoperable kidney stones. They buried him in Greyfriars churchyard, and the children of Edinburgh sang and danced on his grave.

> *Bloody McKenzie, Bloody McKenzie*
> *Used to hang the Weans*
> *Bloody McKenzie, Bloody McKenzie*
> *Died in awfy pains*

Now there was a lawyer. Not a nice one, if there is such a thing, but at least he was a character.

I felt jaded and weary, my injuries were hurting and work couldn't hold my attention. I kept having to remind myself that, despite the agency lawyers, I didn't just have Kailash's case to deal with. For another client, I was writing an opinion on the validity of a family trust. A son wanted me to find a way for him to sell on the family estates. Albeit that he was a member of one of the oldest, wealthiest families in Scotland, I couldn't be bothered to find him a source of cash to fund his cocaine habit. Not that I make moral judgements with clients – I just found it all a bit tedious.

The lone piper outside St Giles' Cathedral was playing the 'Piper's Lament'. The skirl of pipes wafted in, the mournful tune matched my mood, and I wondered if he'd witnessed my performance with Lord MacGregor's shoes. The piper had stamina in abundance; he had played for at least twelve hours yesterday, and there he was back at his pitch.

I could hear the north wind whistling round the windows again, rattling them once more. My nerves were frayed. I tried to switch my attention, and imagine what the wind was doing to the piper's kilt. His hands were occupied holding and playing the pipes. What if the wind blew his kilt up around his ears? The Japanese tourists would get more than they bargained for and maybe he'd get charged with lewd and libidinous conduct. I berated myself for wasting time on more kilted fantasies before remembering that I had read somewhere that when faced with an untimely death, the sex drive increases.

I looked around at some of my fellow advocates and wondered if perhaps the dead didn't walk all year round in Parliament House. Down from me, two desks on the right sat Dr Death – a name the man openly acknowledged – with twisted grey skin. Every inch a Nosferatu, I half expected him to be afraid of the sunlight, not that there was much in Scotland even at this time of year. Previously he had frightened me. How long before I ended up like him? Now I just hoped I would be given that opportunity, not have my life taken away before it had hardly begun.

Prather's man tapped my shoulder. Without speaking, he placed an envelope before me. Disturbance of any sort, and talking in particular, is frowned upon in the corridor. Prather's man tottered off without waiting for a reply to the message.

Meet me in the Octagonal Room now

If a fellow advocate wanted to speak to me about a case, we would walk up and down Parliament Hall, to avoid being overheard. My unsigned note showed that the author was unaware of the customs of this place – maybe they had recently been called to the bar or were a devil? A devil is a trainee advocate who is under the tutelage of a senior member of the bar. They help prepare cases – they do whatever their devil master orders them to do. But there was another, more obvious option – clearly it could be whoever was after me.

I made my way to the Octagonal Room with the voice of Joe in my ears, despite his absence: 'Are you stupid, Brodie? What in hell's name are you doing? No one knows where you're going, no one really knows what's been happening.'

Whoever had written this note needed me – I just didn't know for what purpose. Maybe it was all really straightforward – a devil who had taken a shine to me, or a rookie who needed my help.

'Your recklessness will be the death of me,' my mother had often admonished. I hoped that it would not be the death of *me*.

My deliberation hadn't taken much more than two minutes. I decided I'd better have a cooling off period. Me on one side, my mother and Glasgow Joe on the other. I always think best when I'm walking, so I went to check my box. When called to the bar, all advocates are given a box outside court nine. As advocates retire or become judges, each advocate's box moves through the system, hopefully rising to a better position each time. As I approached my box it was open – if you are working your box is always open – and was gratifyingly bulging. The higher the pile in your box, the greater your standing at the bar. Size equals merit. Size definitely matters.

As I tried to concentrate on the work in my box, my body started to rebel – it wanted to feel the wind on its face, or just to experience something other than my thoughts. My feet sprang over the worn, herring-bone wooden floor. Before I knew it, I had crossed the empty Parliament Hall, and was heading down the Arbitration Steps.

The steps are so aged that, although they are made of stone, they dip in the middle where people have walked for almost 400 years. The carved oak hand-rail is blackened and smooth from centuries of sweaty hands. Normally, the sense of history overwhelms me as I walk down those steps, but on this occasion, I barely noticed.

In the middle of the Arbitration Steps there is a small rectangular landing; hanging high on the wall is the Culloden flag. Worn to the weave in places, it is the flag the Scots carried at that fateful battle. If it was an omen, I again failed to notice, my eyes were looking downwards through the black wrought iron rails. I skipped past it, and headed on down the next flight of steps.

My heart was racing, although I was not running. Exhilarated to be on the move, and out of the corridor, I felt like a child bunking off school. I was aware of the silly grin on my face, which was not appropriate in these hallowed halls.

The corridor at the bottom is a dark one. Deep in the bowels of Parliament House it saw no natural daylight. The ceiling is low, and the walls seemed to come in to meet me. I forced my eyes to the floor, concentrating on the red runner carpet. Dog-eared in places I could see the hessian backing.

Outside the Octagonal Room I hesitated.

The Octagonal Room is clearly so called because it is in the shape of an octagon. Dark panelled wood covers the walls so it feels mysterious and clandestine. Bookshelves line the panels; every copy of Punch ever published is housed there. Large Georgian windows reach from floor to ceiling; tiny lead panes form diamond patterns.

The light had gone but I could see that one of the eight chairs that sat around the octagonal table had been pulled out.

My stomach fell as I looked harder at the occupant of the chair.

He sat on it quietly and rested his hand-made black brogues on the table.

Not a care in the world.

TWENTY-SIX

Somerled Buchanan. Roddie's oldest nephew, and one of the slickest bastards that ever walked the earth. Except that he wasn't a bastard. He was, in fact, son and heir to one of the Highlands' most extensive estates, one of the few estates still in Scottish hands.

'Still recognise me then, Brodie?'

Somerled didn't speak with a Scottish accent, for he had been educated at Ampleforth, the Yorkshire school rich Scottish Catholics sent their sons to once Fort Augustus Abbey had been closed.

Silence reigned as we drank in every detail of one another. Expelled from school for smoking dope, he was a disappointment to his mother who had named him after an ancestor who was one of the greatest Celtic heroes; the original Somerled was given the title of Lord of the Isles for himself and his descendants. The Lord of the Isles considered himself above the Kings of Scotland for his lineage was older – and that was part of Somie's problem. In a prototype brat camp, he had been sent to New Zealand to a sheep farm to reform his character. I doubted it would have worked – and I probably wouldn't have wished it any other way.

Somie's hair was black like coal, with veins of white through it. Deep lines crinkled round his eyes as he smiled at me. The sun's rays weathered his face, and hard work had honed his body in the fourteen years since we had last met. Love can do many things but never underestimate the power of hate – like a strong electric current it ran wildly through my veins. There was no doubt for me that they were two sides of the same coin.

'You look good – I always knew you would grow into your face.'

He gave a small laugh; glancing over me he stood up to offer me his hand. I hesitated. His palm was large and calloused. It hung in midair for a long time – under normal circumstances it would have been embarrassing.

'You still have eyes like a wild cat, Brodie – bronze with little flecks of gold that flash when you're angry . . . like now.'

He was still laughing at me. I could feel his breath warm and pepperminty on my face. Taller and broader than the last time I had seen him, if I held myself back, I'd still have to say he was the most gorgeous creature I'd seen in years.

Taking off his black jacket, he placed it on the back of the chair. My eyes flicked appreciatively over his body, taking in the way his shoulders narrowed into his waist. Looking uncomfortable in his grey striped trousers, he sat down on the chair again and pulled me to him. Feeling the pressure from his fingers on my waist, I was forced to acknowledge that he had beautiful hands, even with calluses. I abhor small, sweaty, soft hands on a man – Roddie's hands are like that; too many men in the law have hands like that, but Somerled was a different type of man altogether.

We continued to stare at one another, while he held me by my waist. Neither of us looked away. It was like a game, the first one to do so would be the loser. Neither of us liked to lose, and I was already one set down. Looking into his eyes had an unfortunate effect. I felt familiar unwanted stirrings. It wasn't him I told myself; it was simply a physiological effect. Looking into another human being's eyes stimulates the feelings of love. When couples first meet they gaze into each other's eyes eighty per cent of the time. Newborn babies fix their eyes on their mothers to establish a bond. I was rambling in my own mind, trying to assert some control over myself. I know these things, because court work is a psychological drama. Knowledge is power.

Pulling me again, this time I was unbalanced, and I landed on his lap. Lifting my legs he placed one either side of him. For Somie the years of childhood friendship, and more, made him feel entitled to act in this familiar fashion. For me, it was more basic. I tried to ignore his growing erection.

'You know, Brodie, it wasn't my fault that I didn't contact you. I couldn't write to anyone for sometime – Roddie screened all of my correspondence.'

I flushed. So Roddie did know more about me than

I wanted him to – had he sent Somie here to get his own back on me for this morning?

'You could have sent a message through Mariella,' I replied.

'Don't fool yourself – my little sister is a bitch. She was always jealous of you.'

'I know about the bitch part, but the jealousy is a new one. At school, she was forever pointing out to me that I was only there on a scholarship funded by your grandfather – I was the outsider: the scrubber she called me because my mother had a cleaning job.' Angry tears filled my eyes – the nastiness that lies between girls can still cut deep years later.

'I was only fourteen, Somie,' I whispered.

'You were nearly fifteen.'

'I was fourteen.'

'Well, I wasn't much older, Brodie.'

He waited a few moments before saying, 'We knew what we were doing. We knew exactly what we were doing. We were starting from the same place and we both wanted the same thing. You weren't a victim, Brodie – you were my equal. You'll never be a victim.'

I bit my tongue to stop myself from telling him everything that had happened recently. I wanted to tell Somie, but I didn't want to tell Roddie Buchanan's nephew. I distracted myself by paying attention to what was happening. Undoing the buttons on my jacket, Somerled slid it from my shoulders, and laid it carefully on the polished walnut table. Betrayed by my body, I wondered if the dead girls had felt the same. Placing the palms of his hands over my already erect nipples, he moved them lightly, slow circular movements on my thin white silk shirt. My head fell back and my eyelids lowered as I gave in to what I wanted. Placing my arms around his neck, he fumbled with the small pearl buttons at the front of my shirt.

'Why so many? I take it you weren't expecting anything like this?' His voice was low with lust.

'Let me.' I took over and undid them all.

'It was all you last time, Somie.'

'Brodie McLennan – that's not how I remember it.'

'It's not how you choose to remember it. How *do* you think it happened?'

'I was in the library at home, bored, looking through my great grandfather's photographs. My sister and her friends were running upstairs. You were tailing after them as usual, being excluded. I felt sorry for you. They always left you out.'

'So you were being kind when you asked me in to the library?' I asked.

'I thought you might want to see my great grand-father's photographs.'

'So . . . it was educational?'

'It depends on your definition of education – my grandfather was a dirty old bastard – those snaps were pornographic; artistic but pornographic none the less.'

I stared coldly at him. Did he know he was bringing things into my mind that I was trying to push away? How much was he aware of? I had loved Somerled but never entirely trusted him. That hadn't changed with the passage of time.

'In my defence,' he began, 'I had just turned fifteen

– and everyone knows that boys mature more slowly than girls.'

'I was a virgin,' I spat out at him.

'So was I,' he answered.

'You didn't tell me that before.'

'All boys like to pretend that they are Jack the Lad.'

'You lied, Somie – you lied about that, and everything else. Those photographs were obscene.'

The castle at Dunmore housed one of the finest collections of Victorian erotica in the world. The family was ashamed of Somerled's great grandfather's predilection for photographs of naked young women. The problems had really started when he pretended he was a camera pioneer and had taken the young girls up to his studio. There was nothing the families on the estate could do. The cottages were tied, and he was the Laird.

'When I entered the library I did it innocently; you asked me to sit on your knee so that we could look at the pictures together – because there was no other chair.' My voice was hot with indignation. I even sounded to myself as if I was protesting too much. Only a fool would fail to see that my body was responding in a completely different way to my words, and Somerled was no fool in these matters.

'Like now, Brodie? Back then you saw there was one over by the window – you just pretended. You were the one who led me on.'

I placed my hand over his mouth, burning at the memory. He kissed my neck, and walked his fingers up my thighs.

'Christ, Brodie, you're wearing stockings. What kind of woman wears stockings in court?'

'The sort that thinks there won't be someone sticking their hand up there uninvited – and that if it is welcome, there might be a bit of reciprocal appreciation.'

'Even the last time we met, you reeked of sex, Brodie.'

'I've told you – I was fourteen.'

'It was two days before your birthday.'

I was surprised he remembered.

'You just keep saying you were fourteen to make me look bad – and you the innocent in all this. I'm telling you, Brodie – I've slept with a lot of women since, but I've never met any who were as ready as you were that day.'

Slipping my fingers onto his lips to silence him again, I started to undo his tie, placing it on the table.

'Let's make a pact, and forget what happened all those years ago,' I said.

'What if I don't want to forget?' Somie replied. 'I thought it was one of the most character forming experiences of my life.'

'It shaped my personality too.' I choked on bitterness and anger. Then I felt him kiss my neck, and the room swam for a bit as I indulged my baser self. I could feel his breath on my ear, and it sent shivers down my spine.

'On top of that, Brodie, you're conveniently forgetting we had sex again that night.'

I reached over to the table lifting his green and blue striped silk tie. Opening his shirt I ran my hands down his chest, the small hairs catching on my fingers. His pectorals were hard and developed. I could see his six-pack had no covering of fat. Holding his tie in my hand, I spoke softly into his ear.

'We disagree over what happened back then, Somie – but let me give you something now you'll remember for the rest of your life.'

Somie's eyes widened, his pupils were dilated, he was having difficulty restraining himself.

'If you don't wait . . . if you move in any way to satisfy yourself . . . then I'll walk out of here.'

'It's a deal.' His voice was husky. Kissing, he held me tightly as I fought to stop losing myself in him. Holding his hand in mine, I pushed it effortlessly behind his back; soon his other one joined it. A knowing smile flicked across his lips. Using a reef knot I tied his hands to the chair (for the first time I was glad about the sailing lessons I was forced to take). Playfully, he pulled his hands but he was stuck fast. Reaching down I tackled his belt, slipping it easily from its notch; Somie closed his eyes to savour the experience as I pulled his trousers to his feet.

We kissed, he held me tight, and I lost myself in him until I strapped the belt round his ankles, fastening him tight. I stood up, and he waited expectantly for my next move.

'Why did Roddie send you?' I adjusted my clothing; my back was to him as I modestly sorted myself.

'He asked me if I could bring you this package,' he nodded over his shoulder to a brown paper package on the table. The chair rocked as Somie moved, a flicker of comprehension lighting his eyes.

'Did you ask Roddie why he didn't give it to me himself?'

'As a matter of fact I did.'

'And?' I said impatiently.

'And he said that he'd had enough of you for one day – and since I was at Parliament House would I give it to you?'

'And you believed him?'

'Right now, Brodie, I find it all too easy to see how you could upset people.'

His face was flushed as he struggled against his bonds; ignoring his plight I ripped the paper from the parcel, and let it stand. A black Gucci handbag, twelve inches long with a pebble leather shoulder strap, and the distinctive GG monogrammed fabric. This bag was so expensive that ordinary mortals had to rent them from the internet or buy cheap copies from Ingliston Market. The owner of this bag was no chav; this was the real deal. There was only one woman I knew who would have the money and inclination for this sort of thing in her wardrobe.

'Why did Roddie give you Kailash's handbag? Kailash's stolen handbag?' I picked it up, without remorse, and hit him across the face with it. Poking it into his chest, I spoke again.

'Admit it – Roddie chose you to do his dirty work because blood is thicker than water.'

I could feel my heart pounding as if it was bouncing between my throat and feet. Somie would do whatever Roddie told him. I pulled out the contents of the bag.

'Do you know what this is?'

He shrugged his shoulders uncomprehendingly.

'This is my practising certificate. What does Roddie plan to do? Phone the police, and tell them I'm withholding evidence?' I poked him again. 'Do you know what would happen to me? I would be charged with perverting the course of justice – do you know what that means?'

I wasn't getting any answers from him at all.

'Two to five in Cornton Vale.' My skin crawled at the thought of the cell where Kailash was currently detained.

The penny had dropped, he nodded his head, and the smile fell from his face. Turning quickly, I held tightly onto the handbag, and ran out of the room, I had to move fast in case I changed my mind. I continued to run up the stairs.

My only stop was when I paused at Prather's desk to report a strange noise coming from the Octagonal Room.

TWENTY-SEVEN

'There's nae flesh so fine but the worms will eat it,' Patch Patterson pronounced the next morning as he walked up and down his tiny overcrowded office inside the morgue.

'. . . Your life's in danger, lassie, why will you not speak to the police? Officially . . .' he added, looking around at the assembled gathering.

Fishy, Glasgow Joe, Jack Deans, the Professor and myself were fighting for air in a windowless office the size of a prison cell. Joe had just come back from the Royal Infirmary after visiting Frank Pearson, and we'd all breathed a sigh of relief at the news that he was going to get through this – whether his reputation would survive intact was another matter. Joe and I may have arrived in time to save his life, but we couldn't stop hospital staff from passing on information about a PF brought in after auto-erotic strangulation gone wrong. Whoever was behind my attack and Frank's hanging had either made two mistakes in leaving us both alive, or had meant to leave us completely baffled as to what the message behind all of this was.

I turned my attention back to my assembled friends, colleagues and other wasters. 'We've already been over it, but I'll repeat it again if it's necessary.' I addressed them as if they were five years old, and a bit slow at that. I moved over to the white board and put up the evidence in the case, perhaps if it was down in black and white the Professor could be persuaded round to my way of thinking.

'The evidence, and events, come from a variety of sources, but I'm going to list them in chronological order, so far as I can. I'll also list who was involved, and where their involvement lay:

23 November 1976 a baby was washed up on the
   foreshore at Portobello
3 March 1977 the ceremony to erect the memorial to the unknown infant
Fact: my mother, Mary McLennan and Bunny
   MacGregor were both present. Coincidence?

As I mentioned my mother and Bunny in the same breath, my heart jumped. But I didn't have the time and this wasn't the place to go over how unsettled I was.

'Patch, this is where you come in.' I noticed that his whole face was now puce from tension as I was about to go over the nadir of his career.

2 July 1980 the first body in the bin bag found
10 October 1985 the second body in the bin
   bag found
15 August 1986 the third body in the bin bag
   found
5 December 1990 the fourth body in the bin
   bag – we now know the identity of the
   fourth girl to be Laura Liddell

I turned to Patch for confirmation. He nodded and added: 'The DNA results came through this morning.'

'And that's the first time you've been able to identify a body?'

He nodded again.

'It's incredible that you were unable to get anywhere with these cases.' Jack Deans meant it as a compliment, acknowledging that Patch was one of the finest forensic scientists in the world, but it did not come out as he had intended, and Patch bristled.

'Every pathologist has cases to which he cannot find the answers – in these cases I simply did not have enough body to work with. The bodies were not dissected with any finesse; so, the killer was probably an amateur or a very clever professional hiding his skills. Every crime scene was contaminated, the bodies were badly decomposed, and there were no reports of missing girls.' He finished defending himself against the accusation that Jack had never levelled, as Glasgow Joe broke the tension.

'I don't know about you lot, but I'm starving.'

I looked at Joe in amazement, how could he be hungry at a time, and more importantly in a place, like this? I was furiously chewing menthol gum to take my mind off the smell of death. Joe was thinking of cheese-burgers. It took me a few moments to realise that he had actually cleverly deflected attention away from Patch and his embarrassment at Jack Deans' innocently intended comment.

Joe took the orders for food and Patch directed him to a nearby café. Sauntering through the morgue oblivious to the metal gurneys and huge refrigerators, Joe calmly held the list in his hand and left the building.

There are no deaths that we know of since 1990

I looked at those still assembled for confirmation.

On 7 May 2001 there was a break-in at Fettes
    Police Headquarters. The perpetrators were
    alleged to have been the Animal Liberation
    Front. Police sources denied anything had
    been taken

'It's from this time on that the rest of us start to get involved.'

At 9.30 a.m. on 10 May 2001 Jack Deans
    received a tip off regarding the stolen files.
    He was directed to a dustbin, where he
    found photocopies of the stolen papers. The
    papers referred to a photograph album
At 10.30p.m. on 10 May 2001 Jack Deans was

arrested under Section Two of the Criminal
Justice Scotland Act 1980 and detained for
six hours, the maximum length of time that
the police could hold him without charging
him. He was released pending a formal
complaint, which never came

'Is there anything else you'd like to add, Jack?'

'I wrote a very straightforward news report on the
break-in. I was sacked. My piece was never published.
After that, rumours were circulating that I was a
neurotic drunk, obsessed with conspiracy theories. I
couldn't get another job.'

In an attempt to hide my discomfort, I turned to
the whiteboard. Jack had neatly summed up my opinion
of him, and he hadn't finished yet.

'I don't care how unpopular my views are – the
murders of these girls would have been solved years
ago if there was no cover-up.'

Avoiding Patch's eye, Jack turned to refill his coffee
mug. Incensed at the slight to Patch's reputation, I
stepped in to defend the Professor.

'Patch is one of the finest forensic pathologists in
the world – there are just some cases you can't solve,
Jack.' My voice was high and wavering as I struggled
to convince myself. But another voice in my head sowed
doubt by reminding me of a much more recent cover-
up that I knew all about – the one Patch had performed
at Lord Arbuthnot's post-mortem. He deliberately
withheld information about the Lord President's drug
abuse from the tape recorder – but surely that was

different? After all, the fact that he was a junkie had nothing to do with his death.

Jack's hands were raised in a conciliatory fashion.

'Look all I am saying is let's keep our minds open to the possibility that important people are involved.'

On 3 February Fishy received the album anonymously

On 10 February Fishy requests "the bodies in the bag" files from central filing

On 17 February Fishy has a meeting with Assistant Chief Constable requesting that the files on the dead girls are reopened. Request denied

On 19 February Fishy has a meeting with his immediate superior and is advised his promotion is stalled

On 22 February he is transferred out of Leith and demoted to traffic control

On 2 March Fishy's credit card details caught in Operation Bluebird. The card had been stolen, and used on a child porn site Motive – to discredit him?

'As you know, I tried to get the files from central filing, a few days ago – and I was told they were missing. The computer record shows that they were lost when we transferred to the new building, ten years ago,' added Fishy.

'But you borrowed them out a few months ago,' I said.

Fishy dropped his head onto his chest, and rolled it round, causing the neck-bones to crack softly. His tension eased he spoke again like rapid gun-fire.

'I've hit a brick wall, Brodie. The sergeant's attitude is that computers never lie. There's gossip all round the station about why I've been transferred, so no one's willing to help me.'

Laughter wafted into the room, as two porters exchanged a joke in the corridor outside. No smiles cracked our faces.

Furiously I resumed writing on the board.

15 August Lord Arbuthnot/Alistair MacGregor murdered before midnight

16 August Kailash Coutts arrested in the early hours

16 August Brodie attacked on Arthur Seat – assailant unknown

19 August Kailash Coutts gave Brodie a photograph that purported to be Brodie in the same death pose as Laura Liddell

Around 20/21 August Frank Pearson drugged, and hung – left for dead. Method Auto Asphyxiophilia. Motive to discredit him and kill him? Evidence recovered: two coffee mugs and a disc

'The coffee mugs did give me two sets of prints – one is definitely Frank Pearson's but the other set is not listed in any database that I have access to,' explained Patch.

'The murderer's evaded capture for over twenty years. You didn't expect that he would be lying in his bed waiting for us – did you?' I held Patch by the shoulders seeking to reassure him.

'You're right. One thing's for sure – the bugger's nae dunce.' His cheeks crinkled as he attempted to smile.

'The disc – what about the disc?' I asked him.

'We'll look at it together – after the briefing.' Nodding at me to continue, Patch resumed his seat.

Impatiently I started to scrawl again.

22 August Brodie given Rohypnol at a Writer to
the Signet function: Motive – to discredit her
or to kill her

'I can't make head nor tail of it . . .' Joe shouted from the door, like a pack-horse laden with coffee and bagels. Jack and Fishy scrambled over the pile of scattered papers to get their order. A double espresso was all I could handle, hot dark-brown and bitter, like jump leads it gave my system a jolt. Leaning against the wall I savoured the burning sensation as it fell down my gullet.

Rubbing his neck as he stood examining the whiteboard, Joe seemed to fill half the tiny room.

'As I said, I'm buggered if I can understand this . . .' His hand slapped the board. 'But there's one person who does.'

'Who's that then, Columbo? The killer by any chance?' Jack cynically drawled at him.

No one spoke as we looked at each other expectantly – Glasgow Joe barely glanced at Jack all through his expletive-filled rant on how it was odd that the word 'journalist' wasn't an anagram of 'wanker' – but I knew the way he thought, so I spoke up.

'The missing girl. But we don't even know where she fits in, where in the time frame, Joe?'

I was now slapping the whiteboard too.

'Is she at the start? In the middle? Or is she the end?'

'Brodie, we don't even know if she exists.'

I threw Jack a look that was supposed to silence him. I needed to believe. Joe reached over, and not too gently pushed me.

'We know some things. You know that your jacket's hanging on a shoogly nail, Brodie, and, you . . .' he looked at Jack Deans, 'should know that self-pity never got anybody anywhere.'

'Much as I'd like to sit here and take life lessons from an acknowledged piss-artist, there are actual facts to consider,' said Jack. 'There was no mention of a missing girl in any of the papers I've seen.'

I turned my attention to the unofficial police presence in the room. 'Fishy, when did you first hear about the "missing girl"?'

'Laura Liddell's granny told me.'

My heart sank. 'I suppose she didn't tell you her other theory?'

He shook his head. 'No, what was that?'

'Only that Laura *was* the missing girl.'

'But she's dead.'

'Correct – but Maggie has been living in hope since she went missing.'

Joe interrupted at the same time as whacking himself on the head with the palm of his hand: 'Christ, Brodie, I can't believe I didn't remember – Maggie also said a posh man had come looking for the girl before Laura was born – so she knew the key to all of this wasn't Laura. I'm so sorry – she must have said it when we were in the kitchen. Does that matter? Does that help to make any sense of it all?'

Fishy waved his hand dramatically at the whiteboard. 'I don't see any of us making sense of this – there isn't any to start with.'

Suddenly deflated I sat down to finish my coffee that was by now cold. I needed a break, my body and mind were knotted like pretzels. The sound of a ringing phone cut through my consciousness. Patch almost elbowed me in the nose as he reached across to answer it.

'Professor Patterson speaking.'

We all held our breath, except Joe who started rummaging amongst the paper bags looking for something else to eat. Patch eyed him icily as he grabbed Fishy's coffee cup and rescued his diary from the desk, flicking through the pages as he spoke.

'I've pencilled it in – but I expect formal citation – in the usual course. Thank you.' He ended the call and turned to us, looking primarily at me.

'That was Crown Office checking my availability for a trial.'

I nodded at him.

'The Kailash Coutts case – it's up this week. They've had a cancellation at the next sitting of the High Court, and they want to put it in.'

Jack Deans whistled. 'That's quick.'

I was reluctant to show any emotion. 'A petition's got to be heard within 110 days – and as long as I have time to prepare my case, I can't object.'

'Are you sure you do have enough time?' Jack asked.

'Absolutely. It's not a problem.'

Actually, I was fucked.

TWENTY-EIGHT

I couldn't tell Jack Deans – or anybody really – that I
hadn't a hope in hell with this one. I didn't have time,
and with everything that was going on I was unlikely
to be able to do my best for Kailash.

But that was the whole point I reminded myself; I
wasn't supposed to get her off. I was supposed to bury
her as quietly as possible, or suffer the consequences.
Roddie's threats had been vague, but Lord MacGregor
had made sure that I knew what I would get if I fell
in step with their plans. From my first day at the Old
College my mother had craved for me the red judicial
robes; only then, she said, would she be satisfied that
she'd done a good job. That twisted the thumbscrews
a shitload more than anything Roddie Buchanan had
ever spat at me.

'You left one thing off your board, Brodie.'

I was pleased to note that Jack didn't look smug as
he pointed out my error. He lifted the black marker
pen, and approached the whiteboard.

On 10 August Kailash Coutts received a photograph of Brodie, purportedly dead
On 16 August Kailash Coutts charged with
murder and appears in Edinburgh Sheriff
Court

The further information, although correct, didn't clarify
anything, it confused matters. It was tempting to view
the Kailash involvement as coincidence, but that was
only because I still didn't know who the puppet master
was.

My phone rang – the ring tone was the music to the
Can Can – and I made a mental note to change it to
something more appropriate. Out of a sense of respect
for the dead I hurriedly answered it, expecting it to be
Crown Office advising me of the court sitting for
Kailash's trial.

'Hi, Brodie.'

I quickly cut him off; this was not a call I was willing
to take in front of people. I excused myself, and walked
outside. The corridors were filled with purposeful
people living mundane lives. Porters ferrying medical
specimens from wards to labs, auxiliaries in colourful
uniforms wheeling tea trolleys round. It seemed as if
ordinary life would be forever out of bounds now, and
I couldn't really explain why it bothered me now,
because for a number of years I have been part of the
underbelly of society anyway.

I found my usual escape route, the unalarmed fire
door by Ward ten, and made my way out into the car
park. The sun had broken through and hospital workers

were sitting on the grass enjoying a quick afternoon break. I steeled my nerves and phoned Somie.

'I knew you'd call back – you're a lot of things but a coward's not one of them.'

'Why would I not call back? Do I have something to be afraid of?' I asked him.

'Not me for sure – but I can't answer for the rest of the world.'

'You're not angry?'

'It was quite funny.'

'Funny – what was funny about Prather's man discovering you naked and tied to a chair?'

'You've got to remember, Brodie, that servants have been getting members of my family out of degrading situations for centuries – it's nothing new. You'll have to try harder next time.'

'Did you just call for a chat and a laugh?' Even if he had, I was grateful for the diversion.

'No, I didn't.' His voice suddenly sounded serious. 'What have you done to piss off Uncle Roddie?'

'Which year do you want me to start with? To cut to the chase – I suppose we could consider me throwing up on Lord MacGregor's shoes in the Signet Library last night, followed by an equally colourful vomiting moment in your uncle's car?'

'Yeah, I heard about that. Still classy I see. No, unfortunately it's not old MacGregor. It's more serious than that.'

Anxiety nipped my stomach.

'Brodie, I also wanted to say . . . I didn't intend to harm you when we were younger and some of the things you said really bothered me – please believe me. Back then, Brodie, I felt . . . I don't know what I felt for you, but I've never felt it since for anyone else. Maybe we should spend a bit more time together in the Octagonal Room and see if we can't work things out?' There was a large spoonful of contrition in Somie's voice, but it didn't last long before he was back to business. 'Have you looked inside that dodgy bag again?' he continued, allowing no room for me to answer him. 'I pulled Roddie up about it this morning – his attitude is, as long as you toe the line, there's no need for you to worry.' He was trying to convince me, and his voice was smooth and soft as I'd always remembered it.

'I'm not prepared to be Roddie's poodle,' I barked back, sounding just like one. 'And whether or not I've been nosing about in some posh tart's handbag is none of your business – you saw the licence; hoping there's more to rub my nose in, are you?'

'There's a lot at stake here, Brodie,' his voice urged in compliance.

'More than you know, Somie.'

'I'm not a daft laddie, Brodie – I'll keep my ears open for you. In the meantime ask your flatmate why he's been suspended without pay from the force.'

'I've got to go.' I ended the conversation and tried to sound emotionless. The walk back to the morgue was too short to solve my dilemma. If what Somerled had said was true, Fishy had lied – he hadn't been demoted to traffic, and if he wasn't going to work, what was he doing with his time? By the time I reached the entrance to Patch's domain I had decided to support Fishy in his lie. He had stood by me for years, we had been through a lot of life's experiences together – if he was lying, it would be for a good reason.

I opened the door and Patch started speaking immediately.

'The photographs.' Patch spoke in the manner of someone who had finally reached an important realisation and wanted the world to know.

'There's something I have to show you first,' I said.

Patch's mouth fell and his upper lip twitched, his moment had been stolen. My briefcase was more like a valise. I placed it on the table not bothering to push aside the academic journals or the scattered papers. Under the harsh artificial light, every crack and scuff on the worn brown leather stood out; but it was deep, and held almost as much as Mary Poppins' bag. I took out the prize item.

'Have you won the lottery?' Joe whistled as I placed the Gucci handbag on the table. He was the only man present who appreciated it for what it was – probably due to having nicked a few in his time.

'It's not mine.'

'Do I need to ask who it belongs to?' Joe queried, his voice worryingly low. I shook my head.

'I hope that's not the bag she was carrying when she murdered that auld bloke.' Joe's eyes were fixed upon me. Imperceptibly to everyone else I hoped, I nodded – he caught the movement.

'You stupid cow – have you not got enough folk to fight with without upsetting Crown Office and the

Serious Crime Squad – that's perverting the course of justice.' He stomped round the table to shake me by the shoulder.

'I know that. I do know the law.'

'You could have bloody well fooled me,' he replied, sounding miffed more than anything else. 'Well – why did you do it then?' I knew he would question me unrelentingly until I gave him the answer that satisfied him. I couldn't do that, not here, maybe not anywhere, so his exasperation with me was likely to last some time.

'Roddie set me up. He got it to me.'

'You could have handed it into the police saying that it had just come into your hands. Or is it important – does it have anything that will help you?'

'It has just come into my hands! I've not been holding onto it for days, Joe!' My voice protested my innocence too loudly. 'I only got it before I came here – I haven't looked inside it yet – I wasn't looking forward to what I might find,' I confessed.

'Fuck your ethics, Brodie – of course Kailash Coutts is guilty, and if the bag contains evidence to prove that, then you'll just have to deal with it.' Beads of sweat had broken out along Joe's forehead, and his left eyebrow twitched as it always did when I put him under pressure.

'There's no motive for murder – and the evidence supports the defence that it was an accident.' I was in defence lawyer mode now.

'Don't be so bloody facetious,' interrupted Jack Deans. 'I know exactly what it is, and so do you – Joe's right, it is bloody dangerous . . . it's the bag that Kailash was carrying with her on the night Lord Arbuthnot died.'

'But I thought it was nicked?' Fishy said.

'It *was* stolen . . . and I think your friend Moses Tierney took it.' I looked at Jack accusingly relieved that Joe's focus had been broken.

'Well, if Moses took it – how did it get into Roddie's possession?' he replied.

'I'd love to know, but in the meantime what's concerning me more is why Roddie sent it to me instead of handing it straight to the police?' My eyes scanned the room looking for answers, other than the obvious one I already had.

Joe was matter of fact. 'Oh, come on, Brodie – there's only one reason, and you know it. Withholding evidence, attempting to pervert the course of justice – you can take your pick. If the police find out that you have that bag they'll throw the book at you.'

'Let's take Roddie at face value,' I answered. 'Maybe there's something in this bag that he doesn't want the police to know about Lord Arbuthnot.' There was something clandestine about rifling through another woman's bag, and I didn't like it. Some psychologists, and psychics, make a study of a woman's personality dependant upon the contents of her bag. Kailash's was obsessively neat and ordered. A woman who needed to be in control, the type who refused to let things go. A politically incorrect pink crocodile skin smaller purse held her make up, a tatty, locked five-year diary, and her mobile.

Grabbing the phone, Jack Deans switched it on and

rifled through the address book. Like a basset hound with a scent, he would keep going until he found whatever he thought he wanted. His heightened focus grabbed my attention. Even Fishy stopped to watch as Jack's intuition told him he was onto something. This shrewdness was the ingredient that had once made him great, I suppose – for my sake, I hoped it would come back and stay pretty bloody sharpish.

'Christ, I've got it!' His hand tightly covered the mobile protecting his source as usual. I placed my hand over his and pulled, hard. My grip was broken by a third hand removing my fingers from Jack's.

'Stop your nonsense – I need you to look at this now.'

Digging his fingers into my arm, Patch pulled me across the morgue to his computer.

The others followed, and we crowded round the computer screen vying for space, jostling to see over Patch's shoulder. As we watched him bring up the images on screen from the disc that I had found in Frank Pearson's flat, we held our collective breath. Fire flushed through my body, as I took in the images before me. My stomach rose to meet my throat, and then I was cold through and through, chilled to the bone.

Laura Liddell lay in the top left hand corner of the photograph.

Armless and legless like a grotesque Venus de Milo. A dissection process was well under way. In the centre of the photograph stood a small boy, aged six or so, taking in every detail. His large eyes were extraordinary, already shaped by the sadistic scenes he was witnessing, and I wondered how such a boy would turn out.

Joe was tapping the screen furiously. 'Maggie Liddell was wrong. It's not a girl who's missing – it's a boy. If he's still around, Brodie – we have to find him.'

And I knew exactly where to look.

TWENTY-NINE

'Are you going to plead?'

The Advocate Depute's voice sounded whiny and insistent, resounding around an almost empty Parliament Hall. It was the last thing I needed to hear at this time of the morning. For the centre of the entire Scottish legal system it was depressingly deserted. Our shoes clattered up and down the diamond patterned black and white tiles. The outsized ebony fireplaces that I love so much when lit had cold empty grates. Between the two hearths stands the entrance to the Advocates Library; one swift glance told me that it too was unoccupied. The painted South Window stood twenty feet above an elaborately carved wooden stall. It was from this place that Court Macers, like middle-eastern mullahs, called the participants to attend court. It too was abandoned. It wasn't the first time that I had been aware of the religious connotations present in this building.

Underneath the South Window you can see through to court nine, and the start of the advocates' boxes. There was no activity there either. The stone floor was laid centuries ago; it's worn and uneven but it looked as if there would be no contributing wear and tear today. I was searching for signs of life, for as befits the Crown's Prosecution, the Depute looked stern and foreboding. I needed to see others around to take away the feeling that it was not Kailash, but me, who was moving towards her doom. In the High Court of Scotland, an Advocate Depute puts on trial those accused of the most serious charges. In order to become a judge, you have to do a spell as an Advocate Depute, even if you have no background in criminal work. This was the case with Hector McVie, a senior silk, with many years' experience behind him at the civil bar, and the man addressing me now.

The civil bar and the criminal bar are two different animals. Like oil and water they do not mix, and generally there is little love lost between them. Civil law books are dry and dusty, they contain no tales of rape, murder or incest, and civil advocates are in general like their books. That was Hector McVie's world.

Characters who inhabit the criminal bar, in common with their clients have many vices: few of them attractive. One trait they have particularly in common is that they are hard; manners and civility have no place in their world.

Hector McVie was a gentleman. I was afraid he was going to add the word 'please' to his next sentence. He brought out the bully in me, and so I barked back at him.

'No . . . she won't plead . . . it's too bad it was the Lord President who died.'

'I heard you were going to cooperate.' Hector sounded hurt, but he reminded me of my obligations.

'Only an idiot would plead their client guilty to murder,' I answered.

'But you have no defence! Surely it would be idiotic to run a trial for which there is no defence?' His ignorance of criminal work astounded me; to actually have a defence for your client's actions is a luxury that is rarely afforded to us. We have to become masters of defending the indefensible. I bit my tongue and gave him the politically correct answer.

'I have a defence.'

'The Cluedo one? It was Miss Coutts in the street with a champagne glass?' he mocked. Perhaps there was a side to Hector McVie which I hadn't seen so far.

'No!' I was in barking mode again. 'Actually, it was an accident.'

Hector stopped pacing up and down Parliament Hall and turned to look at me. Pulling his gold-rimmed, half-moon glasses down his nose, he stopped and peered. Laughter resounded gently round the Hall; he leaned against a marble plinth, his elbows nesting at the feet of Chantry's statue of Lord President Blair. Holding his glasses in his hand, he wiped his eyes and smiled. I couldn't look at him so I turned my attention to the magnificent statue. It was covered in cobwebs. In Parliament Hall there are a number of alcoves where, traditionally, judges sat to hear cases. These alcoves are now filled with sculptures of the great and the good, lawyers from centuries past. They all seemed to be deciding whether to have a wee laugh at my expense too.

'You can't be serious?' Hector smiled indulgently at me. I liked him – as a matter of professional pride adversarial conflicts are rarely personal – but that could change.

'I am serious. Kailash Coutts will not plead guilty to murder, no matter how much you wish this would all just go away.'

Horse-trading is part of the day to day business of court lawyers. It was obvious that Hector thought I was just waiting for a good offer.

'What if I allowed her to plead to the lesser charge of culpable homicide?' he asked.

It didn't look to me like a bargaining point – it looked like desperation. I was beginning to see just how much Hector – and others – wanted this trial to disappear. In negotiations it's never good to let the other side see how desperate you are to settle, but to be fair to Hector he had obviously been told that we were on the same side. He was having his strings pulled, and undoubtedly knew that the same puppet masters had been speaking to me.

The prosecution and the College of Justice were keen to avoid a trial in order that Lord Arbuthnot's reputation would remain unsullied. Perhaps they were even hoping to erect another marble monument to a dead Lord President. The Crown Office should have chosen someone else. If Hector had been a little more experienced and promised me a lenient sentence, then I might have given him what he hoped for: a simple promise to put his offer to my client. Instead I merely said that I would see him in court – not out of any misplaced sense of loyalty to Kailash, but because I wanted her to go down for murder for a very long time. There had been times when I had felt she and I were on the same side, but the Stockholm Syndrome moments had passed, I was pissed off with her for not telling me everything straight away and I wanted her to know that I wasn't her lap dog. As I left the court, I also had to admit to myself that, on top of everything, I hadn't forgiven her for the anxiety she caused me over the Roddie Buchanan scandal.

Face to face time again. The journey to Cornton Vale prison seemed interminable. The M9 was full of small-engined cars pulling lumpy caravans to the Trossachs. I got no joy from riding Awesome, despite it being the first road trip we had attempted since the accident. It felt good to be riding again, but – with the misplaced guilt of the single woman – I was conscious of the fact that I had barely given my beloved bike a second thought since Joe took care of it. I made silent promises to Awesome that I wouldn't be guilty of neglect again. I was too preoccupied with my imaginary plans of shining and polishing Awesome in a dewy-eyed Utopia that I didn't have the time to reflect too much on my imminent showdown with Kailash.

Finally, I arrived and parked the bike. I didn't pay much attention to the barbed wire on the fence before I signed in and asked that Kailash be brought out from her cell.

I chose not to sit down in the small, sparse inter-view room. My battered bike helmet was placed on the narrow Formica table, and I paced with fists clenched so tight that when I finally released them they ached. The muscles in my jaw were unyielding and I could feel the pulse in my neck pounding. The door opened. Kailash was ushered in, wearing a white silk sari – again her guards accorded her the utmost courtesy.

The sari rustled as she moved. Kailash reminded me of Proteus, the sea-god herder of Poseidon's seals. He had the ability to shape shift at will, he knew all things past, present and future but Proteus was unwilling to tell what he knew. Kailash was reinventing herself, and it was difficult to look at the modest, sedate woman before me now, and see her as leather clad dominatrix. She was a great actress, I'd give her that but I wouldn't be taken in by her. I kept telling myself she was nothing but a manipulative hooker who generally got what she wanted. She wasn't the only one – if I colluded with the Enlightenment, or some unknown men in grey, then it was because at this moment I wanted to. I was playing to my own agenda.

As Kailash sat down, she looked at me and uttered one word: 'Why?'

I ignored her and placed her mobile before her. She picked it up in her still somehow beautifully manicured hand, and, as she read the text message, her face momentarily turned grey.

Meet u as arranged. Alistair.

'It was sent the night he died,' I reminded Kailash. 'You lured him to his death.'

I could feel beads of salty sweat forming on my top lip and I became uncomfortably aware of how I must look to her. I was practically foaming at the mouth, whereas she had regained her composure almost instantly.

Placing her mobile on the table, she again asked me the question:

'Why?'

I stared at her blankly, but noticed that she had taken care not to give me the phone back. I wondered: if I made a grab for it, which one of us would get there first. In my heart I knew that she would – she'd need dexterous hands in her profession.

'Brodie, I have asked you a question. Why are you upset by this text?'

'Because you lied to me,' I snapped back. 'I asked you if Lord Arbuthnot was a client and you said he wasn't.'

'I will repeat myself then, Brodie – Alistair MacGregor was never a client of mine.'

I was reminded of President Clinton's reply when asked about Monica Lewinsky. '*I did not have sex with that woman.*' Everybody else in the world considers a blow-job sex, but life and death are in the details. I was after the spirit of the truth from Kailash, and I wasn't getting it.

'That's a lawyer's reply ... you're covering your back. Was he a punter of anyone you employed?'

'Brodie, if it will appease you – I will confirm I have never known Alistair MacGregor to pay for sexual favours.'

'Why should I believe you – you denied any prior knowledge of the man?'

'Brodie, I think if you centre yourself you will recall

that you never asked me if I knew him, you were only interested in whether or not he had ever been a client.'

She was a condescending bitch when she chose to be.

'You assumed that a woman like me could only be acquainted with a man like Lord Arbuthnot if I was his whore – in my line of work I am no one's whore, they are all my bitches.' She smiled for the first time in a long while.

Kailash had missed the point, I was angry with her because she had made a fool of me. I would have presented her defence even if I had been aware of a prior relationship with Lord Arbuthnot, but I was not inclined to forgive her given that others knew of a bond between them. I'd bet good money that Jack Deans knew. Kailash sat serenely at the table writing in a pale pink raw silk notebook (yet another personal possession she had managed to retain) while I stood silently looking at the wall.

Kailash handed me a note. The script was immature indicating a lack of formal education. I needed all my time to find the killer; I did not have the energy to fight this hopeless case. Lack of sleep had dried my eyes. I tried to blink as reading the note was difficult on many levels. Aware that Kailash was watching me, I cleared my throat, and read its contents out loud.

Rulers see through spies, as cows through smell
Kautilya, Indian philosopher, third century BC

'I may not have a law degree,' said Kailash, 'but I am by no means uneducated. My father's people were civilised, and had 360 different ways to cook potatoes when in *your* society there were no potatoes *to* cook.'

I flushed; the heat surged from my toes to the roots of my hair. Like a naughty child I had been found out – Kailash always seemed to be able to put herself above me no matter what the game was. She needed to do that for her ego, and I needed to avoid it for mine. Every time we met, she managed to make me feel worthless, ill-dressed, gauche, uneducated, *less*... What little grace I had left made me shift from foot to foot. My mother's voice admonished me to apologise for jumping to conclusions, but Kailash and I had too much history for that. She stood up and stealthily walked round the table to face me, her feet made no sound on the mottled grey linoleum but her sari rustled.

Another enemy had been made; there was no way that I could see to re-establish the client agent bond. I decided to jump before I was pushed.

'Get yourself another lawyer, Kailash.'

I moved to pick up my helmet and walk out when she issued an order.

'Brodie – I want you in this trial and THEY have ordered you to be an Amicus Curae. As a matter of interest – what did they promise you?'

She passed by me so closely, that I could detect the individual ingredients in her old fashioned scent. Rose oil and lavender. Any herbalist would maintain that it was a soothing combination; I would beg to differ. I felt no comfort.

Placing her forefinger under my chin she lifted it up.

'Ah . . . nothing but the red robes would tempt an ambitious girl like you.'

I wanted to tell her that it was my mother's ambition she was reading not mine – then I remembered my response to Roddie's blackmailing judicial appointment suggestion and I wondered who was really pushing me on – the ghost of my mother or the true me? Perhaps they weren't as different as I'd always tried to convince myself. 'Did they tell you what they would do to you . . . if you didn't go along with their plans?'

'No.'

'They left it to your imagination . . . what a group of very powerful men would do if you betrayed them.'

I nodded, betrayal sounded such an ugly word. I hadn't thought of it in those terms.

'That's good, Brodie, because I too will leave it to your mind's eye to conjure up my punishment for you if you betray me again.'

Squeezing my shoulder very tightly, she led me to the hard-backed chair and had me sit down. Sitting on the corner of the table so that I had to look up to her meant the dice were in her hands.

'Is that a threat, Kailash?'

'No, it's a choice.'

'It doesn't feel like I have many options.'

'There are always alternatives, Brodie – even when faced with inevitable death you can make a decision to be courageous, to die well.'

THIRTY

My heart felt as if it had stopped – was she talking about me, telling me to die well? – but my face was emotionless. What did one more threat matter? Kailash failed to notice my indifference as she continued her monologue.

'Besides, choice is an illusion . . . in most circumstances we opt to narrow it down. Too much freedom would unsettle you.'

My choice was not to die well, but to live well, and to do that I would have to be smarter and a damn sight more wily than I had been to date.

Kailash rose from her seat like a cat and moved from the corner of the table to stand behind my back. I could only feel her presence, which was immense. Her breath was slow and measured in my ear; mirroring her steady heartbeat, there was no outward sign of stress.

'You're tense?' she said, stating the obvious as she pulled my heavy jacket off in two swift movements, giving me no time to protest.

'You'd be better off with someone else . . .' I replied. 'As an officer of the court I can't lead evidence that would suggest that you met him by accident.' It was the first time in my life that I had not fought to keep a client. Even as I spoke, it felt alien to me.

'In life, honesty is a fool's game,' she replied. Letting the mask of graceful concubine slip, she added: 'You're so up your own arse you actually believe people are interested in what you think of them.'

'What do you want me to do, Kailash?'

Her hands bore down heavily on my neck, making me wince.

'Be a source of pleasure.'

A statement like that meant I had to turn to face her. I couldn't ask what the fuck she was on about with my back to her. Was she recruiting me for her brothel or hitting on me? Kailash grabbed me by the arm and I was again astonished at the strength of her grip. Unlike Roddie, I don't enjoy pain.

'Let's begin again,' Kailash decided.

She pushed my head away from her. Facing the table I noticed that the mobile phone had disappeared without me noticing. Manipulating me by the crown of my head she twisted my neck backwards and forwards. A curtain of auburn curls fell over my face as she pushed me downwards.

'An Indian head massage is what you need, it will dissipate the tension in your shoulders, stimulate your lymph glands, and get the drugs out of your system.'

'Drugs? They're painkillers.'

'If you say so.'

Kailash had my left ear pressing down hard on my shoulder, so it was difficult to argue with her. The pressure in her hands had eased as I felt the tension leave my scalp and jaw.

'Effective, isn't it?' she said.

An involuntary sigh escaped my lips.

'It's an ancient traditional Indian remedy, at least 4000 years old. It began in the families; family members would sit behind one another massaging oil into the scalp, promoting and stimulating hair growth.'

Lifting my thick hair back off my face, and smoothing it around my shoulders she added: 'Not that you need help in that department.'

I felt her eyes bore into me: seconds later the phone reappeared, just beyond my finger-tips. One question had lain heavily between us since our first meeting, asking it now could lose nothing.

'Why did you contact the papers about Roddie?'

'Because I could.'

She stared blankly at the wall behind me painted insipid, institutional green.

'No, I'm not letting you away with that. You and Roddie, your actions, nearly ruined me. I'm liable for that firm's financial problems – problems that you helped create.'

'Why are you blaming Roddie? He didn't contact the tabloids.'

'Why shouldn't I blame Roddie?'

'He's done nothing wrong.' Kailash's insistence was like hitting my head on a brick wall. She reached across and touched my hand; hers was elegant, long fingered and creative. Squeezing me forcefully, I looked from our joined hands up to her eyes.

'No. You shouldn't blame Roddie because he's inno-cent . . . he has the papers to prove it.'

'I don't believe you,' I sputtered.

'But you got me to sign an affidavit, so it must all be above board,' she said, playing the part of a wide-eyed ingénue. Slowly her smile widened. Kailash was enjoying playing with me and she made no effort to hide it.

'I thought it was a lie.' I tried to run my hands through my hair but it was knotted and tangled.

'You were meant to think that . . . You know, when I was growing up in Amsterdam, I wanted to be an actress but there wasn't enough money in that to live on.'

'Really?' I answered. 'I had heard that being a porn star was very lucrative.' My words fell off her like snow from a dry stane dyke.

'I was making art house films, with young directors who thought they were bestowing blessings in allowing you to work with them.'

She broke into a dry cough. Opening the door, she asked the warden for some water. I was going to remind her that it was prison, not a hotel, when the warden immediately handed her a fresh glass of cool water. Between sips she continued her story.

'During this period, to supplement my income, I worked as a magician's assistant. He taught me about misdirection: getting an audience to believe a fantasy you have set up.'

'And that's what you did to Roddie? Why?'

'It wasn't to Roddie Buchanan exactly, but to what and whom he represented.'

We were back to Kailash acting like Proteus, with-holding information.

'Give people the fantasy they want, Brodie – everyone wants to see a lawyer caught with his pants down.'

'But what was in it for you?'

'I do not consider myself a prostitute. I am not a prostitute. I am a courtesan. A woman like me earns a great deal of money when she is young, but as she ages . . . well, the outcome is self evident, therefore I had to change the playing field, and Roddie was an announcement to men of a certain persuasion that I was back.'

For once lost for words, I watched Kailash lean against the wall, and slowly light a cigarette. Casually blowing smoke into the air she spoke confidentially.

'I think you'll find that these are yours.' She handed me back the packet of cigarettes that I kept in my pocket to give to clients.

'Don't try to sidetrack me.' I could feel my blood bubbling inside me. 'What you're telling me . . . you mean . . . that was all just an advert.'

Kailash now looked indignant.

'What do you mean "just an advert"? Do you have any idea how much that kind of coverage would cost?'

'So it worked then? Dream scenario – you're never off your back.'

'It's hectic, Brodie – but I never work on my back.'

Kailash had played us all. Lothian & St Clair, one of the oldest law firms in the world, had been brought to its knees by the marketing ploy of a prostitute. I could barely take it in. The woman sitting opposite me looked like a demure Hindu princess – what kind of mind could work in the way she had just described?

Lord Arbuthnot's trial would receive wipeout coverage from press and TV. Kailash was lining up to play the race card. If she went into the witness box dressed as she was, no politically correct jury would find her guilty. And if they did there would be hell to play from the outside world. The prosecution was in trouble, unable to bring up Kailash's past to destroy her reputation because it had nothing to do with the murder.

My choices had become even narrower.

'Did you tell me the truth to make me afraid of you?'

'No . . . because the people you are dealing with are much more dangerous than I am. They've been at it for centuries.'

My mother had worked too hard for me to throw everything away on a whim. I made for the door, turning back to face her, I tried to keep the loathing out of my voice.

'Your trial starts Friday. I'll see you there.'

I snatched her mobile from the table, secure in the knowledge that I had something to hold against my own client.

The roar from Awesome's pipes was drowned out by the sound of Kailash's voice, as I replayed our interview in my mind on the journey back to Edinburgh. I wondered if I could have handled it differently. There was another little niggle that kept pointing out to me that all of my moral musings were totally irrelevant if the killer got me first. The trial was inevitable – my appointment with the killer was not.

I had no advice for myself – but Kailash should have remembered that the bird that walks into the cage on its own sings more sweetly.

THIRTY-ONE

'Don't just stand there with a bottom lip like a wash-hand basin . . . tell me what's wrong.'

Joe turned my bad mood back on me as he stood behind the bar at the Rag Doll. Trade was quiet for a Thursday lunchtime; a few of the regular clientele were playing pool in the dingy back room. The smoke created a fog, which obscured their faces, the only noise was the sound of the balls clacking and the patrons' occasional idle shrieks. To all intents and purposes we were alone. The floor was tacky with spilled alcohol, and my feet stuck to it as I fidgeted. My eyes searched around for somewhere uncontaminated to place my helmet. The air was unpleasantly sweet, stale perfume lingered long after the dancers had left.

'This place smells like the inside of a whore's handbag, Joe.'

My nose wrinkled dramatically. Wiping the stray flies from my face with a handkerchief, I was dismayed to note the dirt that was retained by the cloth. Thankfully, Joe didn't suggest that I get myself a full-face helmet;

he knows that I love the wind on my face, being able to tell the changes in temperature between a forest and an open moor land. He understands that I like to be close to the elements. I could never have stood a nine to five desk job.

He knows all of this but was still growing impatient with my reticence.

'The cleaner's coming in a minute or two . . . just tell me what's happened.'

'Kailash.'

That one word, and the look on my face, made him renege on his earlier prohibition.

'Langavullin or Bruachacladdich?' Seeing that my mood was dark and barren, Joe offered me the peaty malts of the Island of Islay, grasping that only those spirits could alter mine.

'*Uisge beath* the water of life . . . or as your mother used to say . . . more like *uisge bais* tae me. Thon staggerwatter'll be the death of you. You mark my words, the pair of you . . . where you'll end up, you'll have cause tae scream oot for water.'

Mary McLennan was a native Gaelic speaker, a strict teetotaller who abhorred drink, especially on a fourteen-year-old girl. The famous tirade Joe was referring to was when we got drunk at a Christmas dance when I had returned back from school for the festive season, and he had had to carry me home. Grabbing me by the ear, and marching me to the toilet, she shouted at Joe: 'Drink's bad on a man but worse on a woman.' I flushed at what she would think of my drinking now, but it wasn't enough to stop me.

'*Slange.*'

Our glasses met in mid air, and clinked. I took the crumpled piece of paper with the Indian proverb that Kailash had given me out of my pocket, and pushed it across to him.

'Who told her?' he asked me accusingly.

'She didn't say.'

Reaching across I lifted the bottle of whisky, and with my glass in the other hand walked to the leatherette bench seat. After pouring myself a generous glassful, I started to play with the cardboard beer mats, anything rather than look Joe in the eye. The barmaid on duty had returned from the cellar; Joe left the bar and followed me to my table. Striding across the open floor he looked like a Titan; his golden red hair was sleek and orderly for him. For the first time this summer he was wearing jeans and cowboy boots, dressed like that he wasn't in the mood to play.

'What do you mean she didn't say?'

He didn't wait for me to answer.

'Can I get in to see her . . . 'cos by God if I can . . . She'd tell me who her spy is. I'd like to teach her a few tricks on how to hurt people – consultancy like that might boost her business.' Joe emptied his glass in one.

'She does have a spy but I don't want to think who it could be,' I said, refilling his glass.

'Well it's hardly a long list, Brodie – not many people knew that information. There's me, Fishy, the Professor, Jack Deans and you. Take your pick.'

'I think that was her plan . . . to make me suspicious of everyone.'

'Why would she want to do that? She's surely got enough on her plate.' As Joe spoke he handed me a packet of cheese and onion crisps. His eyes said: 'eat or regret it'.

'Kailash thinks that I'm in more trouble than her. She's not too bothered by the murder charge.'

'She's bluffing . . . it's just the way of the street – look after number one.'

I knew Kailash was undisturbed by her present circumstances and something told me she was playing a game. Right from the start I had the feeling that she had caught me in her web, and I would not easily be released. Well, that had been proved correct today, but no one wants a lawyer who doesn't want to act for them; especially a lawyer who thcy believe is already in the pay of the other side. For some reason I was an important player – I just had to find out why.

Glasgow Joe was munching his way through his second packet of crisps as the music started up for the next show. Punters of various ages, shapes and sizes wandered in.

'Joe, I tried to withdraw from acting for Kailash, but she refused to accept it. I'm confused – I can't understand why she is insisting on me, especially now she knows that they want me to act as an Amicus Curae.'

He was now facing the stage, watching the dancer. I, on the other hand, was looking at his broad black t-shirted back. Speaking over his shoulder, one eye still on the stage, he said, 'It's a new girl. I'm interviewing her . . . keep talking, I'm listening.'

'Although they've asked me to be an Amicus Curae,

I haven't agreed and I haven't had to do anything yet that would jeopardise Kailash's case.'

The girl on the stage was obviously new to the game. Stumbling around the pole, she fumbled to take her clothes off. To me, her efforts were laughable compared to the gymnastic excellence I had witnessed the other day. But the men, including Joe were lapping it up, her naïvete made them feel as if they were voyeurs watching a maiden innocently taking her clothes off rather than a bunch of lairy wasters in a skanky pub.

Blushing, with her head downcast, the girl finished her routine to rapturous applause. Inadvertently, whilst bending down to pick up her clothes she gave them a full view of what they were secretly hoping to see. She stayed in that position for some time, her legs straight and open; her young slim hips to the audience. When the money started landing all around her, I twigged her. She had been playing them all along. The men were still fooled – or still wanted to be. Kailash would have been proud.

Giggling, with her clothes in her arms, she struggled to carry all the money that had been thrown. I could learn something from her. She had used her sexuality in a completely different way to the other dancers. There was a charm about her that made the men feel superior, as if they could teach her something, and the way she innocently smiled at them let them think she would let them.

Play the daft lassie, and win.

Let them all think I was doing their bidding but be my own master.

'She was good, wasn't she? For her first time, I mean,' Joe beamed breathlessly, as he pushed himself up from the table to offer the girl a job. I caught the girl's eye as she stood at the bar; our eyes locked, and a conspiratorial smile passed between us.

'Yes, she was good,' I replied.

Music thumped rhythmically, it was loud enough to make my seat vibrate. Around the empty stage, several young men danced enthusiastically like Masai warriors, bottles of expensive premium lagers in their hands. I was bathing in the acrid smell of sweat that accompanied their endeavours, when a bone thin man pushed through their group. I prayed that he was not making his way to me. I should have known my luck was rubbish these days.

'Brodie McLennan . . . you'll maybe no' remember me.'

He was right – I didn't know him, but I did know what ailed him. Prematurely aged, ravaged by illness, black marks upon his face. Scar carcinoma. This man was dying from HIV. Without a cure, the disease demands that the victim takes care of himself. A junkie doesn't love himself enough to do this, otherwise he wouldn't be a junkie. The man proffered his hand; the skin was paper thin like an octogenarian's – tattooed on his knuckles were the letters L.O.V.E.

I stood up to take his hand, his body trembled, but his handshake was dry and firm.

'I'm Maggie Liddell's laddie . . . . Shirley's brother.'

'And Laura's uncle.'

'Aye . . . Duncan Liddell's my name. We've all heard

of you, Brodie. Your ma was a proud woman – you'll miss her.'

Sitting with Duncan Liddell here in the Rag Doll made me feel guilty about denying my heritage, dropping my accent, and never explaining where I came from if I could help it. At times like this I agreed with many of my detractors that I had no place being in Lothian & St Clair.

'I came to say thanks. I got a taxi down from Mile End House – to shake your hand and say thanks,' he repeated, wheezing all the while. Humility is not an emotion that I am familiar with, but Duncan, with his sparse brown hair and cheap clothes humbled me. Edinburgh was once the AIDS capital of Europe, thanks to the shooting galleries of the eighties. That's probably when Duncan became infected, shooting up smack at the garages at the bottom of the flats.

'You confirmed to my mother that Laura was gone and now she can start to grieve. We'll have a memorial service and we can mark Laura's life. I'd like you to speak at it.' His voice was shaky and speaking took a tremendous amount out of him.

'I wouldn't know what to say.' I instantly recoiled at the notion. 'I'm not the right person.'

'You'd find something, Brodie. You're the only one that's got the education to stand up to them, the only one of us.'

'Who do you think I'm standing up to, Duncan?'

He was confused. My words were lost on him. His eyes clouded over, the medication he was on was affecting him and as he began to ramble, I sat back and listened to someone else's troubles.

'Although my ma's had six bairns, she had a lot of miscarriages as well. My father, the drunken auld bastard, wouldnae leave her alone. After I was born she had six miscarriages. In between having us, ma wis depressed and couldn't take care of us. Anyway, just before Shirley was born, my oldest brother and me were taken into care – put in a residential school at South Queensferry.'

Beads of sweat formed on Duncan's brow and his nose began to drip; he didn't seem to notice even if I was fascinated. Retelling this saga was taking its toll on him. He reached across and touched me as I poured him a glass of whisky, and handed him a cigarette.

'I've never told anyone else, Brodie – maybe if I had our wee Laura would be with us the day.'

Glasgow Joe was hovering at Duncan's back; surreptitiously I shooed him away, judging it unlikely that the broken man would speak in his presence. I placed my hand on Duncan's, stroking the smooth bones beneath my fingertips, and feeling his death nearby, urged him on.

'You and your brother were put in the King George V school near South Queensferry . . .' I prompted him out of his drug induced haze.

'Aye that's right . . . stuff was going on there. Men touching the wee lassies . . .' Duncan broke off and started to weep vociferously. 'My ma thought her bairns would be safe in local authority care . . . it was jist temporary, kinda like respite, but those perverted bastards . . . well, they felt up wee boys as well.'

I reached across to wipe away the tears that were

streaming down his blotchy face; he didn't seem to mind that my hanky was grubby.

'Were you one of those boys, Duncan?' I asked, knowing the answer. Nodding he added, 'But we were lucky. We were in and out of that place. Some of those bairns had been there for years.' The whisky was taking effect, loosening his tongue and relaxing his body, but on a damaged featherweight like him, the window of lucidity would be short. I encouraged him once more.

'Duncan, what you're telling me is key to finding Laura's killer.' At that stage I wasn't sure, but evidence was thin on the ground and we had to follow up any lead we had about paedophiles.

'Other bairns weren't so jammy. I was about thirteen and I had a girlfriend that I met in there. Totally innocent 'cos she was totally fucked up by what had been happening to her. Her name was Heather. Heather Beith.' Closing his eyes in remembrance, he reached inside his trouser pocket, and with the hand marked H.A.T.E. he handed me a curled up photograph. Studying it, I remembered, he was good looking once, like a member of a glam rock band, long hair cut over one eye, mascara smudged like eye-liner.

'No' a bad looking boy eh?' He smiled proudly at me. 'The photo was taken at the bus station.' It was a passport sized photograph in black and white, Duncan had his arm around Heather and she had her tongue out.

'We were supposed to go out on my birthday the next Saturday, but she never came.'

'When's your birthday?'

'Seventh of June. When Heather didn't show up I knew that something had happened so I kept reading the newspapers…as soon as I heard about the girl in the bag, I knew it was her.'

'Did you tell anyone?'

Uncomfortably aware that I was cross-examining him, I tried to soften but he was oblivious. The dam had been opened, and he needed to talk, confess before he died, who knew?

'They said they wanted anyone with information to come forward… I phoned the number that they mentioned on telly twice. I gave my name and everything but no one ever came near. I was surprised that no one wanted to know about Heather.'

'Can I keep this?' I held the photograph in the palm of my hand. 'I've seen her face before,' I said, doubting my next course of action. 'I have a book of photographs that show the girls before they were cut up.'

'Shit, Brodie – I guess it doesn't surprise me for she was one sick mother fucker.'

THIRTY-TWO

'She?' I asked.

'A woman? – But everybody thinks it's a man.'

The words exploded from my lips, because everyone had always assumed that the killer was male.

'Yeah, well, she seemed to run the ring, she was the one who got hold of the bairns. The wee ones trusted her, the older ones, well, she made us feel as if we'd asked for it – in some way we'd brought it on ourselves, even that we liked it.'

He took the whisky bottle himself, and poured a generous nip.

'Do you know what that does to a boy?' He paused, and took a swig. 'It makes him a man like me, a pathetic man, with a wasted life. I've heard people say that if there's a killing team then the woman's only involved because of the man's influence. That cow was nobody's patsy. If she hadn't been there, none of us would've been touched.'

I considered that unlikely, but I didn't want to distress Duncan any further.

'Why did nobody phone me back, Brodie? Did Heather's disappearance mean nothing? The polis were shit hot at nabbing me when I robbed a few lousy cars for drugs.'

'Did you tell any of the teachers at school what was going on?'

'Do you think we were dafties? Of course we did – but they just belted us for making up stories about our betters. It's too late for us, Brodie – most of us are wrecked, but maybe there's still some hope for the memories of those other kids. Maybe you can do that for them, and put some ghosts to rest for other families like you have for my mother.'

Depression rolled over me like a heavy North Sea haar. Duncan was clearly worn out from his trip here and from talking.

'Do you want to go back, Duncan?' I asked.

'Aye. Nae choice really. I can hardly get myself the strength to walk for a piss these days never mind anything else. This is like a fuckin' Christmas outing for me,' he laughed bitterly.

The taxi jolted over the cobbles as we left the Rag Doll. Joe insisted on accompanying me, and Duncan agreed, affirming that: 'There's a bunch of right of nasty cunts out there, Brodie, sorry to say.' They were protecting me – despite the fact that I had seen plenty of 'nastiness' in my line of work for years. I was too tired to be offended.

Joe had been forced to carry Duncan to the cab – he was more incapacitated through drink than illness. As we drove on, Duncan lay down on the back seat and we took a pull down each. Joe's knees were round his chin but no one could complain of discomfort in Duncan's presence. The taxi wound its way inexorably along Junction Street, with its hordes of Sikh shops, each turbaned head speaking in a broad Leith accent, passing the Vicky baths where we all used to swim. We had passed the point where Bowling Green Street used to be. I went to Brownies there in the Ebenezer church, it smelled of beeswax polish and freshly cut flowers. I loved it, principally for the fact that when you kneeled at church there, your knees were placed on a blue velvet cushion, trimmed with tassels of gold. At St Mary's Sweet Star of the Sea, where I went to nine o'clock mass every Sunday, the pews were hard and wooden, likewise the kneelers.

The journey reinforced the renunciation of my roots, and my family origins; ascending up Leith Walk we reached St Mary's Cathedral at the top, and I was back on more customary territory.

Driving from Leith to Fairmilehead is a stretched and sluggish climb. As we ascended yet further into the driveway to Mile End hospice, we seemed to be entering the clouds – but it was just another haar. The hospice is purpose built in the heart of a community surrounded by trees. Drawing to a stop, the taxi driver got out and helped us bundle Duncan inside – like a broken puppet he was all angles and bones.

A well-padded receptionist met us with a wheelchair and a smile. I followed behind gravely, as she whistled, and spoke to Duncan.

'She's got an arse like two bairns fighting under a

blanket,' observed Joe as he watched, fascinated as the mounds of flesh moved independently of each other under her uniform. Wheeling Duncan into his room she declared brightly: 'My, you've had a busy day, and a good one too from the look of you!'

Duncan flicked his eyes at Joe and myself – the jollity of the staff was probably a coping mechanism. Duncan looked like a lot of things, but a man who had just had a good day wasn't one of them. We waited in the corridor to allow her to leave, the scowl on her face when she saw outsiders saying more than her smile, before we entered.

I brought Joe up to speed with what Duncan had told me – and saw his mouth gawp open in the process. 'Is this right?' he asked Duncan.

'Aye, it's right,' he said in the middle of a coughing fit. 'Every time we told a teacher, they just hit us. Then the Head would give a speech about how we were just one big happy family.'

'One big happy family, eh?'

'He said we were all in the same boat, and we had to put our shoulders to the wheel and work together – he'd been on lots of motivational courses. The staff and the kids – he said it was always very "undermining" when the kids took it upon themselves to make stories up.' Duncan paused for a moment and when he spoke, his voice could hardly be heard. 'As if we could even imagine things like that.'

Lingering over Duncan, the odour of decaying flesh filled my nostrils, sweet, cloying, and musty. Beneath me lay a man who had the life leeched out of him, pathetically thin, a carcass hovering on the threshold of death.

'I remember the first time I saw her,' he whispered, his eyes tightly closed. 'I caught sight of a woman going into the dormitories. She didn't work there and I didn't think it was right, not at night. It wasn't my dorm she went into that night, but I still knew she shouldn't be there. It wasn't just that I didn't recognise her, it was that there was an air coming from her. She oozed something. I didn't know what it was, but I knew I didn't want to be anywhere near her. I kept my eyes open that night. I didn't want to risk falling asleep. I told the Head the next day.'

'What did the headmaster say?' I asked.

'He said she was a friend, and that it wouldn't be wise, it wouldn't be wise at all, to mention it to anyone else.'

'Did you mention it to anyone else?'

'I told another boy from my dorm the next day – he wouldn't even speak about it for a few days, then when he realised I wasn't going to shut up, he told me that his two older brothers had been in the school before him. They had mentioned the lady to him as well.' As he spoke, the fingers on Duncan's emaciated hand grasped the bedclothes. When he paused, it was only for one hand to fold over the other and lightly trace the black marks of his carcinomas.

'Turns out I wasn't the first child to complain. It had been going on for years.' His eyes were downcast.

'The lady – that's what they called her – would come and pick the kids up. I started to watch out for her.

She came regularly; I've seen her take the youngest ones half asleep from their dormitories. But most times they would be sent to the school gate.'

He looked at me to say something. There was nothing I could say. Holding Duncan's claw-like hand to my face was all I could do and he seemed to draw strength from the gesture.

'The children would stand there in all weathers. Sometimes she was late. I watched from the windows.'

'Where were they taken?'

'On their outings,' he sneered. 'That's what they called them. They said they were taken to the devil's house.'

'The lady, the devil and the missing girl? It's like a fucking tarot card, Duncan – I can't make sense of it.'

Joe tried to reason with me. 'He's not to blame, lass.'

'Do you know what you're up against, Brodie?'

I felt his breath hot and sour on my face. Tears flowed freely, dripping from his chin. 'Of course I don't. Care to enlighten me?'

'I might be dying, but I'm not stupid. Ever since that time when I was in that place, I've looked out for this sort of thing. It's become a full-time fucking job. It's everywhere. But this time, the bastards are so fucking untouchable that no one has any chance of getting them – and they know it. You tell me, Brodie, you explain things to me.'

I couldn't answer him – he was doing well at playing me at my own game.

'Have you any idea the time scale these people work to? A hundred, two hundred years – that's nothing to them.'

'Stop talking in fucking riddles!' I shouted in exasperation. 'Who? Who works to that sort of time scale?'

'The knights,' he shouted back at me just as loudly.

'The knights? Do you mean the Knights Templar? Christ, Duncan – I didn't know you were some dopey bloody conspiracy theorist too.'

'No, Brodie, that's not who I mean. There are others – the Knights of the Enlightenment. That's what they've chosen, that's what they call themselves – they're very keen on origins and heritage. If you're talking about an organisation that is controlling Scotland, that has controlled Scotland for years, you have to go back a bit. This wasn't started by some dozy hippies in the '60s.'

Concrete filled my heart, drying slowly, stopping movement, and then it spread to my lungs making it hard to gasp more than a mouthful of oxygen. I started to worry, in the blurred way that I had learned as a child, the game had swung quietly but swiftly into vulnerability and helplessness. It had been too much for Duncan. I'd underestimated him – I'd seen the druggie, in his last days, one of Maggie's brood. I hadn't seen the intelligent man who had been keeping a quiet but watchful eye on all of this for years, who had made sense of it in the only way he knew how. But how much of it *did* make sense?

I had been reared since childhood in the knowledge that *The Devil, watches waits and picks his time.* Now, I was facing the Devil and his Lady. When had the world gone so mad?

THIRTY-THREE

If I'd realised it was going to be so busy I would have suffered the inconvenience of arriving at court half an hour early. After all I'd been awake all night.

With ten minutes to go I could see everything clearly from the Hall. The doorways to court nine were on a long irregular stone-floored corridor directly leading from the Great Hall. The ground was shiny, buffed by the feet of litigants and their agents over the centuries. The two sets of wooden doors were old and had been painted to look like varnished wood.

Above the door, on the cream plaster, each entrance was marked for Counsel or Public use. Both entries had an outer and an inner door. Counsels' door had a glass partition that was used to observe what was going on in court, without disturbing it unnecessarily. I couldn't say if the public entrance had the same glass, for I never entered the court via that door.

I used to think there was something delightfully exclusive about having a special doorway, while wondering why exactly it was necessary to separate us from the public. It couldn't be on grounds of safety because the doors were adjacent, separated only by a thin wooden partition. But now I was beginning to see there was altogether too much exclusion going on in Parliament House, a lot of it for no reason whatsoever – with regards to my own situation, the only way I was going to gain admittance to the club was to do their bidding in this trial.

I pushed my way through the public throng as the almost indistinguishable cry of the Macer reverberated around the hallowed hall

'Her Majesty's Advocate against Kailash Coutts, calling in court 9.'

The black cotton felt heavy and warm as I pulled its voluminous weight around my shoulders. If I were Queen's Counsel, I would have silk, not cotton – one of the many privileges of rank. Nonetheless, I have some additional status shown by gown; an extra flap of black cotton hangs from my shoulder like a badly repaired tear. It may not look like much but it indicates to the court, and to my learned friends, that I have addressed the House of Lords in an Appeal case.

'Her Majesty's Advocate against Kailash Coutts.' The Macer spoke again over the microphone – in this garbled manner he called us to business. I hurried to court 9, almost tripping over my gown as Glasgow Joe trailed behind me, uncomfortable in a grey pinstriped suit and conservative blue tie. The stripes on his suit were too far apart to make him appear legal: with his stature and demeanour he looked more like a member of the Celtic mafia.

'Do you need so many different bits of paper? And what's with all the poncey bits of pink ribbon? You trying to give me a red face?' he said, dramatically blowing a piece of pink cotton tape away from his nose.

'You insisted on clerking to me. I didn't advertise a bloody vacancy.' I spoke to him over my shoulder whilst I was still pushing forwards.

'I'm here to keep you safe, you narky bint – not be your bloody donkey.'

It was impossible to get near the Counsels' doorway because the queue to get in the public entrance had snaked out to the Great Hall and was blocking my access.

'Joe, go in front – and see if you can make any headway here.' I pushed him in front of me and snuck in behind his shoulder blades hoping to make progress.

'Coming through, coming through,' he shouted as he shrugged his great shoulders from side to side. Like the Red Sea, the crowd parted and I scampered along in his wake.

I had already been to the toilet three times that morning, and the griping pains in my stomach told me that I had to go again. I was not unduly concerned that I would disgrace myself in front of Lord MacDonald because this is a symptom I always got before appearing in court. I tried to think of it as Shitting Herself Lawyer Syndrome rather than IBS. A rampant dose of 'the skitters' always told me that I was ready to perform. Electricity flowed through my veins and I never felt more alive than when I was on my feet before a particularly vicious bench.

Lord MacDonald was new to me; I had rarely appeared before him, so I couldn't form my own opinion. Consensus was that he was hard and appearing before him was like being repeatedly hit on the head with a claymore.

The files, papers and books that Joe was carrying reached from his groin to his chin. We had breached the outer door but we were unable to gain entry to the court because of the gaggle of young counsel peering in, hoping to get a glimpse of the infamous Kailash Coutts. Their wigs were pure white and unblemished like their skin. A white wig shows inexperience, and we all long for the dirty tarnished wigs of the weary old war-horses: which was why I had bought mine second-hand. After the purchase, I then stained it with tea bags, dried it in the oven, and dragged it round the floor for a couple of days. It looked great and no one had ever called me on it. There wasn't much difference really between that and not wanting to be called names at school because you had pressed new jeans or gleaming white trainers on.

These youngsters were not veterans; they looked like schoolboys from Eton with hairpieces. One look from Joe and they pushed through the door, and then flattened themselves against the wood panelled walls to let us pass.

Court nine is the largest; presumably it was picked for the trial by the administrators to accommodate the pack that turned to face us as we walked in to take our seats. The public gallery is all on one level, and it consists of hard wooden benches. Its front rows were filled with advocates wearing very expensive suits, their faces brown from the Tuscan sun. They wore immaculately ironed shirts, and cufflinks with the school crest, Patek Phillipe watches or Rolexes peeked out from beneath shirtsleeves.

I was reminded of the crowds that in the past attended public hangings. But who was being executed here? I harboured no illusions; many of my colleagues sitting there would just as happily have watched me brought to heel as Kailash brought to justice.

Some of my learned friends affected the dress of a bygone era. Mutton chop sideburns covered half their faces. These men wore their blacks with pride in the office, a black jacket and striped trousers. Their authentic antique fobs were hidden in the watch pocket of their waistcoat with only the heavy gold chain showing. It was a game, and they all had their costumes.

Here and there an advocate stood up to nod and acknowledge my presence. The Dean of the Faculty was one, and he was close enough for me to observe that the charm on his watch chain was a Rosy Cross. The showing of my brethren indicated that they expected me to do my duty. I searched hopefully for the libertarians, but sadly, they were absent. It seemed that individual human rights had no place here today.

Behind learned counsel sat the press pack; Jack Deans amongst them. A cold look, icy like the north-east wind, covered his face – I knew that it was actually concern for me. I didn't have time for my bowels or my libido to ponder the scene in front of me.

'Where do I sit?' Joe hissed at me, anxiously looking

for the correct place, keen not to show the assembled crowd his ignorance.

'You know I've never been on this side of the law before.' He peered around anxiously as if the two court cops present were about to collar him.

'Calm down . . . let me go in front. After all – you were the one who insisted.'

Joe had been adamant on accompanying me as my clerk – into the den of thieves, as he had renamed Parliament House after he had to pay counsel's fee for an opinion on licensing law.

I sat down on the front bench, and pointed to him that he should sit behind me. I gave him a pen and paper.

'Now if you want to be my paralegal then you're going to have to pay attention . . .'

His eyes were already straying from mine, anxious to take in what was going on behind his back. Nipping his hand brought his concentration to me.

'Write down what the judge says – write down what witnesses say . . .' I had been over this forty times before, so we said in unison:

'Especially when I am questioning – note down what the witness says.'

His eyes showed his fear of writing, of putting things down on paper. Lots of people suffer from it but it was something he was going to have to get over because I might have to rely on his notes when cross-examining. Joe had never really seen school as an educational process, more of an optional distraction. I generally switched off when people said they had been to the school of hard knocks and had a degree from real life, but, with Joe, it was actually true. He learned more in the playground for the world he would end up in than he ever did in geography or maths. Now, however, although he probably felt he was back to taking notes on *Janet and John*, he was going to be a vital part of this over-educated environment. I doubted I was the only one needing to go to the toilet at that moment.

Hector McVie and his junior counsel, a bland young woman who I knew only by sight, idled in and sat on the front bench at the other side from us. His instructing solicitor sat behind with pen poised at the ready, surrounded by papers and books.

'Are you sure you're prepared for this, Brodie?' McVie placed his arm proprietorially along the bench encompassing his junior, and acknowledging his instructing solicitor. Casting his eye over Joe he threw me a withering look. A crooked smile greased his lips. Actually, I admired his gamesmanship and recognised it for exactly that. He was basically a good guy, but he knew as much as I did that there were rules to follow and roles to play. Hector was pointing out that I was a junior; out of my league in a case like this. Silks, attended to by junior counsel, defend most murder cases. Both his instructing solicitor and junior were older than me. Smiling a cheesy grin that belied both my worries and my churning stomach, I turned to speak to Joe – ensuring that the flap of material on my gown flounced as I turned, for Hector had never been instructed to appear at the House of Lords.

'What's all that about – the smiling and the tossing

of the hair?' asked Joe. Before I could answer, Bunny MacGregor walked in, unaccompanied, and took her seat just behind Hector McVie's solicitor. There was a rumble in the court as all the advocates present stood up to bow before her. I alone remained seated. It felt churlish, and, I must admit, wrong; eyes flicked between Bunny MacGregor and myself.

'Get up,' hissed Joe. 'Everybody else is standing out of respect for the poor woman's grief – it's not her fault her man's deid – and you're in this trial, so show your manners.' Grabbing my elbow he pushed me up. As I rose all other counsel sat down; standing out, I nodded my head in the direction of Bunny MacGregor recognising her loss.

Severely dressed in black, her formidable white hair was piled high on her head making her seem taller than her five feet eight inches. Looking at me her face got redder, and redder, and her eyes watered – somehow it made her look grief stricken rather than the annoyed harridan of a widow I had hoped.

'Ms McLennan,' she squeezed out through pursed lips. Before her I wilted, and sat down, anxious not to be in her firing range any longer.

'That poor woman's had it – she'll no' last the trial.' Joe voiced his pity, and fell for the act that Bunny was plying to everyone else in the room.

A concealed door in the wooden panelling on the wall opened, and a stout female prison warden marched out. Her arrival heralded the announcement of the guest of honour.

Kailash sauntered in, her head held high, glossy black

hair rippling in the muted light of the courtroom. Collectively those on the public benches took a sharp intake of breath. A soft red velvet dress sheathed her body, enhancing, not hiding the curves. Sheer silk stockings led down to elegant Jimmy Choos. There had been no point in me advising her what to wear – she wouldn't have listened, and, anyway, she knew this type of thing much better than I did. To me she looked like trouble. Every man there would think that she was trouble worth looking for.

Bunny MacGregor's anger consumed her as Kailash walked in. Momentarily I wondered if there would be a cat fight, if Bunny would make a scene, reach over and pull Kailash's hair – and part of me wished she would, thus giving my client the victim status she so desperately needed – but the moment passed and Bunny looked as though she had won the fight to keep her emotions in check.

'At least that widow's shamed Kailash into some sense of decency.'

'Joe? Have you suddenly joined the Wee Frees? You sound like an outraged Kirk member instead of someone who makes his living pimping off bloody lap dancers.'

Joe chose to ignore me – even though I was clearly right – and continued his *Sunday Post* analysis of the situation.

'Cannae even look the poor woman in the eye.'

He'd have been as well crossing his arms and tutting – but his stage whisper probably expressed the sentiments of the court.

Kailash had scanned the court taking in every detail, but she had studiously avoided Bunny MacGregor.

'All rise.'

Before I could respond to Joe, the Macer walked in, silently announcing Lord MacDonald's arrival on the bench. An awed hush fell over the courtroom as we all stood to greet the judge. He was a young man by judicial standards, probably in his fifties; it was hard to tell, because underneath his wig, his hair had been expertly tinted to match the raven shade of his youth. When he was seated comfortably, the assembled court was permitted to sit.

In the dock Kailash was free to lock her stare onto his, for in the High Court I was not allowed to act as a buffer between the bench and my client. As with Sheriff Strathclyde I felt it was Lord MacDonald who required the protection. Shifting uneasily under her gaze, he stared straight ahead. Bunny MacGregor was the only person whose eyes Kailash refused to meet, although Lord Arbuthnot's widow was doing her utmost to ensure her dead husband's alleged killer felt her presence.

It was Friday morning and the clock showed that it was 11.39. We should have just enough time to empanel the jury and then adjourn for the weekend.

'Did you get the list?' whispered Hector McVie's junior to me.

'This trial is being rushed – and that's not my fault. I only got the jury list late last night.' It's hard to show displeasure when talking in hushed tones.

A courier from Crown Office had delivered to my house a list of all the jury members who were available

314

for this sitting. I had been dismayed to note the high proportion of women – you don't want that on a jury, they are hard, much harder than men.

'How many are you going to object to?' asked Joe quietly.

'You've been watching too many American shows – I've only got three objections, after that I've got to show just cause.'

The jury members had been sitting on the public benches so they had witnessed Bunny MacGregor's show of grief, and my obsequiousness. Christ, I'd forgotten they were in, I shuddered at my fawning before the widow. First blood to Hector McVie. And whilst Kailash's entrance was spectacular for a red carpet at the Golden Globes, I wished she'd come in like a widow about to commit suttee. Another point to Hector.

As the jury members filed forward to take their seats, a retired headmaster eagerly surveyed the scene.

'Don't bother,' I said and the judge waved him off.

The seats in the jury box were filling up; I was pleased that they were, on average, young for a jury, youth being more forgiving than silver surfers.

'Don't bother,' I said to the anorexic who was about to take her seat. I like a healthy jury; if you get too many going down sick then the jury is hung.

The clock was behind my back, so that it was in plain sight of the judicial eye. So was I as I stood up to make my third, and last, objection to a jury member. The Crown were keen to have jury member number twenty-three so that alone was enough to make me oppose it. Elaine Jones was an unmarried forty-year-old teacher.

Teachers are generally bad news anyway on a jury – they think they know everything and over-process things – but Ms Jones was looking resentfully across at Kailash, who although older than her, looked at least fifteen years younger. I wasn't having Kailash go down because of another woman's petty jealousy.

As I stood to make my objection Lord MacDonald intervened.

'Don't bother,' he said helpfully, reading my mind.

'And now we are twelve,' I said to Joe as the last jury member took his seat. 'The judge is just going to swear them in – then we'll adjourn, and have a coffee.'

'Court rise,' the Macer shouted, and we stood while the judge left the bench.

'He's got as much power as the Pope,' said Joe in awe.

'He's got a damn sight more authority,' I replied.

Tidying my papers, we waited for the crowd to disperse.

'You've not lodged any special defences – is that wise?' asked Hector. He had removed his wig and was openly scratching his head as though he had nits. It didn't stop him being condescending though.

'You wouldn't know a special defence if it came up and bit you on the arse, Hector, so no wonder you're surprised. Let's be honest – the whole criminal arena is a bit of a mystery to you isn't it?'

Joe followed me out. 'Do you have to be so rude?'

'First of all, that's bloody rich coming from you, and secondly, it's just gamesmanship – we're only playing.'

Parliament Hall was busy with advocates and their agents. The public had gone downstairs for coffee. We usually drank in the Lower Aisle, a cellar of St Giles's Cathedral that had been turned into a café, but necessity demanded we hang around to ensure we did not miss the case being called. An industrious hum echoed round the hall, and the names on everyone's lips were Kailash Coutts and Brodie McLennan. Small clumps of people were dotted around.

'They're all gossiping,' I pronounced disdainfully.

'How can you tell?' Joe sounded doubtful – he was impressed by the superficially serious expressions and I was amazed to see him so out of his depth.

'They're not working because if they were they'd be pacing up and down. They're all talking about me anyway so no one cares if they're overheard as there's only one subject.' The bobbing heads were jiggling up and down with rapt attention, and repeatedly looks were thrown over their shoulders in my direction. Hector McVie came into their midst like a redeemer. For a fat bloke he held himself well, his shock of faded gold hair was thick and sleek, kept in place by some expensive gentleman's grooming cream.

'Your opponent looks well – for his age.'

I had no doubt that Hector would consider himself damned with faint praise from Joe.

'He's having a mid-life crisis,' I replied, nodding in Hector's direction.

'Well, unless he's going to live until he's 120, I'd say he's a bit old for that.'

'There's some talk that on a recent trip to LA he had hair extensions.' We both stared at his head, as he stood alone by the empty fireplace, pulling his fob watch out of his pocket, and looking at the time, over and over again, all the while scratching his head.

'Brodie – I've been trying to find you.' Jack Deans had hold of my shoulder and was pulling me to face him.

'No surprise in the judge then,' he continued. Jack was out of breath, and peering anxiously from side to side. 'Lord MacDonald's recently been appointed a Senator of the College of Justice.' Jack's breath was steadier now. 'Do you know what the first thing he did was?'

Again a question I was not allowed to answer. I shook my head.

'He gave a speech to the Enlightenment and then resigned – before he even told his own family, he had to inform the Enlightenment.'

'Jack, it's no longer a surprise to me which judge is a member of the Enlightenment. You'd have a better chance of shocking me if you told me one that wasn't.'

'Lord MacDonald isn't just "any" judge. He's the one with the most to prove – the most biddable because he has to perform his first favour. Watch your back in there, Brodie – because Kailash isn't being prosecuted by Hector McVie; Lord MacDonald is the lead counsel.'

With that warning he disappeared off for his caffeine shot.

'The trial's getting to him already,' I said.

'Who? Jack Deans?'

'No, Hector McVie.' I was focusing on the opponent I could do something about. 'Maybe he's waiting on someone. Could be his new twenty-five-year-old girl-friend. I think that's who he's changing his looks for – no matter how much money he spends, he's no oil painting.'

'I don't think you should count on that – look...'
Joe pointed to Bunny MacGregor; the clipping sound of
her heels cut through every conversation in the hall, stopping them dead. A nippy breeze seemed to flow wherever she walked. Hector McVie greeted her effusively. It
was wholly inappropriate for the Advocate Depute to be
lunching with the victim's widow. Unlike England, our
criminal justice system is not adversarial and the prosecution has a duty to be seen to be fair to the accused.

'What could they possibly have to say to one
another?' I turned to Joe.

'If I was him – I'd be promising to nail the bastard
who killed her man.'

'I don't think he'd say it quite in those terms – but
you're probably right.'

'It's a wonder she's not come over to you – are you
no' supposed to be nailing the exact same bastard?'

'Hardly likely.'

Sufficient time had now passed for me to know that
court was adjourned until after lunch. It was standard
practice in court for the judge to inform you when court
would reconvene, but something must have happened
to prevent this. I contemplated following Hector and
Bunny to their eatery, but one look at Joe was enough
to know that surveillance would never be his forte.

'I'm going to the cells to check on Kailash – you can
come if you want or meet me at the crossroads, where
all the main corridors meet.'

Joe shivered. 'When hell freezes over – that's when
I'll go voluntarily into a prison cell.'

THIRTY-FOUR

Kailash's cell was set into the wall and the bars ran from floor to ceiling. I crept up on her unannounced. It was a tableau; her plate of stodgy prison fare lay uneaten in the corner. She sat on the narrow bench, sideways so that she could use it as a table. Intrigued I tried to sneak up on her to see what engrossed her so.

Her senses were too quick for me, and she turned to face me. Standing up she made no effort to hide her actions. The turnkey moved towards me and opened the cell. Kailash held a pack of cards in her hand as she came to shake my hand.

'You look good today. Thank you for making the effort,' she said, moving her eyes from my polished heels to my perfectly fitting suit, and politely never remarking on the fact that she had provided them.

I actually blushed at her kind words.

'I suppose it's too early to say how we're doing?' she continued.

I nodded.

'I don't like the look of the judge. He seems – uncompromising.'

'Well, we've got the weekend to think about it – we're not going to get started this afternoon. The judge will swear in the jury, and then adjourn.'

'So there's nothing to worry about then?'

Her voice was insistent.

'Well, not this afternoon – it's just a formality.'

She placed her arm around my shoulder; again her scent was delicate and sweet. Lightly she manoeuvred me over to the bench.

'If there's nothing to worry about – why do I keep pulling this card?'

Her fingers reached into the pack at random. It was done at lightning speed, as if she hoped that speed alone would save her. It did not.

In her left hand she held aloft the 'Hanged Man'. I took the card from her; it was from a very old hand-painted pack. The workmanship was exquisite.

'They're from my mother – eighteenth century, hand-painted Italian. The only thing of use she gave me – the other thing she bestowed upon me was the name Bernadette. I know which has helped me more.'

I looked at the card again. The problem was, I couldn't just dismiss Kailash's fears because I look for signs and omens too. I was glad when the case was called again. Kailash and I looked at each other, at the card that I still had in my hand, and then reassembled back in court nine.

The jury sat in their box. Kailash was wedged between her guards and I sat in my appointed place.

Even Joe was where he should be as we all waited on Lord MacDonald.

'Is he taking instructions from somewhere?' Joe's voice was loud. As if we were in church, people turned to see who was making the noise.

'Shut up or speak in a lower tone,' I hissed.

'But yer man – he's no' here.'

'Court!' shouted the Macer and we all stood as Lord MacDonald entered. Sitting down, he offered no explanation or apology for his lateness. It was approaching 3.30p.m. when he started to swear in the jury and I could see Kailash visibly relax as she realised her first day in court was almost over. At 4.20p.m. I started to tidy away my papers.

The voice came booming from in front of me:

'Mr McVie, are you ready to call your first witness?'

In stark amazement, I looked at Hector, but a silent moment of understanding was passing between him and Lord MacDonald. In Scotland there are no opening speeches. The Crown call their witnesses and get on with the case, but they don't sit late at night. Right now the alarm bells were ringing – the first witness being called at this time of day?

'I am, M'Lord. The Crown calls Roderick Buchanan.'

The Macer went out into the passageways of the court and shouted, 'Roderick Buchanan, Roderick Buchanan,' like a town crier, over and over again.

Like a rabbit in the headlights of a car, Kailash turned to me, her eyes demanding an explanation. Shrugging my shoulders, I could offer none. That sly old bastard had pulled a fast one on me, and there was no way I could say anything now. To object would be to let them know that I had no intention of being an Amicus Curae.

'Do you swear to tell the truth, the whole truth and nothing but the truth?'

Roddie's hand was on a copy of the Bible as he answered yes. He looked as shocked and nervous as I felt.

'Is your name Roderick Dougal Buchanan?'

'It is.'

'And do you reside at 653 India Street, Edinburgh?'

'I do.'

My heart rate refused to slow down. I caught Jack Deans' eye and he knew I had been ambushed. The list of witnesses and productions that had been delivered to me last night was incomplete. The new list of witnesses contained one additional name – Roddie. I had no idea what he was going to say, but whatever it was would be bad for me.

Fear caused my mouth to dry and every sound was heightened. I could hear Joe fiendishly writing away, noting everything Roddie said. I poured myself some water; it was lukewarm and fetid. I looked at Roddie through the glass. What the fuck was he playing at? From my first phone call to his wife we had fought to keep the firm free from the old scandal and now here he was where it was all bound to be dragged up again. Unless he'd been forced to come clean...

'And are you aged fifty-five?' Hector's voice was calm and commanding

'I am,' replied Roddie. I wanted to shout that he was old enough to know better. I had no idea what game he was playing or what the stakes were.

'Now, Mr Buchanan – do you know the accused?'

Roddie nodded, his voice failing him? Whoever was making him do this had tightened the thumbscrews. I almost felt sorry for him.

'Would you mind pointing out the accused?'

Shakily, Roddie raised his finger and pointed.

'Let the record show that Mr Buchanan has pointed to the accused, Kailash Coutts.'

I have always thought it was a ridiculous practice; of course the accused is the person sitting in the dock between the prison officers – who else is going to be there?

'So, Mr Buchanan, would you mind telling the members of the jury exactly how you met the accused.'

Roddie looked at me beseechingly, his eyes flicking under his lids. The sweat was running down his cheeks forming glistening pools in his beard. I couldn't bear it any longer.

'Objection to the relevance of this line of questioning, M'Lord.'

A sigh escaped from Roddie's lips that could be heard around the hushed courtroom. Hector McVie was on his feet. Pulling his gown straight, he looked directly at me as he spoke. I pulled myself up to my full height. I could not let this line of questioning be heard in front of the jury. My client would be lost as her reputation would be immediately impugned, thus making her a less credible witness. If the press got a whiff of what I was beginning to suspect Roddie was about to say then the firm was finished.

'M'Lord,' began Hector, 'I'm asking for a little leeway here. Relevancy can be established.'

The first duty that a court lawyer has is to the court; it is important not to mislead a judge, and Hector McVie had an established reputation at the bar. If he was telling the judge that he could establish relevancy, then he was entitled to be heard. I could sense the decision going Hector's way.

I jumped to my feet; it was like the last rash act of a dying man.

'M'lord could hear the evidence without the presence of the jury and the press – under reservation.'

Lord MacDonald smiled, and I knew that I had played into their hands. Roddie relaxed measurably as the jury filed out of the courtroom as did the public gallery, including the press. The judge had told them they were not allowed to speak to anyone about the case. The sternest warnings were given to the press, they were not authorised to comment on any of the evidence or witnesses who had spoken today. Failure to abide by this judicial direction would result in their paper being fined tens of thousands of pounds for contempt of court. For the moment, Roddie and the firm were safe. All that mattered to me was that if the firm was protected then so was I.

Joe stood up to leave but I pulled him down. Lord MacDonald cast a suspicious eye over him. As the last body left the court, the Macer locked the door. The room felt horribly intimate. Lord MacDonald was the first to break the silence. I noted that we had already sat beyond the usual time, and I wondered how long we would be asked to stay on a Friday night. Or what the end of the evening would bring – someone would find their reputation in tatters.

I didn't fancy the odds on whether it would be Roddie, Kailash or myself. But I knew I had enough of a survival instinct to at least try to make mine a little better.

THIRTY-FIVE

'Mr McVie – if you are ready?' Lord MacDonald raised his pen and nodded that he was anxious to proceed.

'Thank you, M'Lord,' replied Hector politely – court speech is always polite, even when you are knifing someone in the back.

Hector cleared his throat, and continued.

'Mr Buchanan – if you'd like to tell the court about your relationship with Ms Coutts?'

It was obvious from Roddie's demeanour that he wanted to do no such thing – and who could blame him?

'Ms Coutts and I had an intimate . . . business relationship.'

'So,' said Hector, twisting the knife a little deeper, 'you paid for certain services from Ms Coutts?'

'That is correct.'

There were several embarrassed coughs going on around the court.

'To the best of your ability, can you please give the court a job description for Ms Coutts?'

'Ms Coutts is a professional Madam. A dominatrix.'

'And does Ms Coutts have a place of business where she operates from?'

'Well,' stumbled Roddie, 'sometimes she would be mobile – come to a hotel room perhaps – and at other times we would meet at her club.'

'And what is the name of her club, Mr Buchanan?'

'The Hellfire Club.'

The clock's tick sounded particularly loudly now. I stared at a bee buzzing madly, hitting itself repeatedly off the windowpane. There was no escape for the bee, very little for Roddie, but how much could I bank on? The courtroom was warm and airless; suddenly I felt very tired.

'The Hellfire Club. It sounds unique,' oozed Hector, miraculously acting as the moral barometer despite the fact that he had probably been there himself. 'Are the services offered there by Ms Coutts and her staff . . . special?'

I glared at him – wet yourself and get it over with Hector, I thought.

'Other establishments offer BDSM.'

'For those of us who are not familiar with this rather particular area of life, would you please explain what . . .' Hector looked theatrically at his notes as if he could not remember the acronym from seconds before, 'BDSM means?'

'BDSM stands for bondage, discipline and sado-masochism, I believe,' came the response of Lord MacDonald, helpfully clearing up the matter. Hector and I stole a glimpse at one another and I suppressed a smile. The judge flushed appropriately.

'Thank you, M'Lord,' Hector said seamlessly. 'So, Mr Buchanan, are there other professional dominatrix in Edinburgh?'

'Oh yes – there most certainly are!' Roddie nodded animatedly.

'Objection, M'Lord – my learned friend promised the court that he would establish relevancy. Unless he intends to publish a directory to the unwholesome aspects of Edinburgh night life, I fail to see what relevance this all has,' I interrupted.

'M'Lord – I crave the court's indulgence for a few more minutes.' Hector sounded like a virtuous supplicant.

'Granted, Mr McVie – but do hurry up. Ms McLennan – your objections have been noted.' Lord MacDonald was glancing anxiously at the clock, no doubt mindful of his evening appointments.

'So, Mr Buchanan – if there are other professional ladies who offer these BDSM services, why did you choose Ms Coutts?' Hector spat out the words as if they left a sour taste in his mouth.

Roddie shifted uneasily from foot to foot, and muttered inaudibly.

'Tell the witness to speak up – I can't make out one word he's saying,' Lord MacDonald hissed angrily, oblivious to the fact that Roddie found the next sentences mortifyingly embarrassing to repeat.

'Kailash offered other services – special services that the other Tops don't.'

'Tops – what on earth are Tops?' Lord MacDonald was obviously tired and hungry for he was getting testier by the minute. As well as that, his knowledge of S&M seemed to have run dry.

'Sorry, M'Lord – a Top is a person who is dominant in sex and a Bottom is someone who is subservient,' Roddie added helpfully.

'And I take it from this that you are – a Bottom?' Lord MacDonald looked pleased with himself at mastering this new idiom.

Retrieving his examination from the judge, Hector asked the next question.

'And what services did the accused offer that others in this city would not?'

'Objection, M'Lord – all the witness has said is that the other ladies did not offer the service, not that they refused,' I added.

'Well, did they refuse?' the judge asked, curiosity showing in his eyes.

'Yes, they did,' Roddie answered.

I had just shot myself in the foot. Basic golden rule – if you don't know the answer to a question, don't ask it.

'And why did these other ladies refuse?' Hector threw me a smile, in recognition of my unwitting help.

'They said no because it was too dangerous. The practice is not recommended – unless the provider has medical knowledge and specialist equipment.'

'And does Ms Coutts have these?' Hector was looking round the court, very pleased with himself.

'Yes. Kailash has what they call a . . . a white room . . . a room where . . .' Roddie took a coughing fit and grasped for a glass of water. Without putting the glass down, he spoke hurriedly.

'Where pseudo-medical procedures are carried out.'

'And what pseudo-medical procedure did Ms Coutts carry out for you?' Hector winced with all the drama of a third-rate soap star in pantomime.

'She – erm – she injected a saline solution into my testicles causing them to swell.'

Even Lord MacDonald was shifting uneasily on the bench. I could hear Joe, and a lot of other men in the room, cross, and uncross legs.

'Does this mean that Ms Coutts has knowledge of anatomy, and physiology?'

'Oh yes, she has an extensive education on the arteries and blood supply in the body – it would be dangerous if she nicked either of those during her . . . procedure,' assured Roddie. We were all satisfied that Kailash knew exactly how to inject bollocks with saline, but I knew precisely what was coming next.

'So when Ms Coutts set out to kill Alistair MacGregor, the deceased, she knew – or ought to have known – that severing the carotid artery would lead to death. Furthermore . . .'

'Objection, M'Lord – the witness is not a professional and cannot speak as to Ms Coutts' knowledge at the time of the incident.' I was on my feet, shouting.

'Furthermore, her knowledge of the body is such that she should have been able to save him had such an accident occurred.' Hector continued to speak over me. I was still on my feet trying to drown him out, but the damage had been done.

'Your objection is upheld, Ms McLennan,' Lord

MacDonald nodded in my direction, indicating that I should now sit down.

'Very well, M'Lord, my last question is withdrawn.' Hector looked unrepentant. The information was out there. I looked around the courtroom – everyone was an insider and this was a secret kangaroo court.

'Before we move on – does this procedure have a name?' asked Hector.

'It's called "ball torture".' Roddie shook his head in embarrassment.

'So would it be safe to assume that a woman who would carry out such – ball torture . . . ' Hector stopped and pointed directly at Kailash. 'Would it be safe to assume that such a woman hated men in general or just one man in particular?'

'Objection, M'Lord. My friend is leading the witness. Furthermore Mr Buchanan is not a professional witness, and is unable to speak to the state of mind of the accused.'

'Objection upheld – Mr McVie, I must ask you to contain yourself to the evidence that the witness can speak to.' Lord MacDonald was smiling at Hector McVie all the while he was giving him this reprimand.

My mind was spinning.

Why had Roddie agreed to give evidence in the first place? Because the court knew they could rely on me to keep it a secret? They knew that I would try to stop Hector impugning Kailash's reputation. And if I did that then I was not an Amicus Curae.

I was the one who had moved to throw the jury and the press out. I was the one who had created this clandestine court. Inadvertently, I had fulfilled Eilidh Buchanan's command to keep it hush-hush.

'M'Lord, no doubt my friend will point out that the accused lacks motive to kill in this case, and so I would bring the court's attention to Crown Production number thirty-four.'

I looked up my new production list, and in particular the last item.

Number thirty-four . . . a Nokia mobile phone.

My heart stopped. The Macer handed Roddie a blue and silver mobile phone. I thought I recognised it, but hoped I didn't.

'Do you recognise the number of this phone?' asked Hector, holding it up and pushing a piece of card with the number printed on it towards my beleaguered colleague.

'Yes,' answered Roddie, looking mystified.

'Well, would you like to tell the court whose phone it is?'

Again Hector's expansive arm movements addressed the public benches – he seemed to have forgotten that no one was there.

'It's the number I used to contact Kailash on – to arrange our . . . trysts.'

'Trysts?' repeated Hector. 'How wonderfully romantic.' Sensing my objection coming and Roddie's discomfiture, he quickly went on.

'Now, you can see that there is a text message on the screen. Would you like to read the message to the court, and the date it was received by the accused?'

Roddie took his half moon gold-rimmed spectacles

out of their case and placed them on the end of his nose. They made him look like everyone's favourite Grandpa – if they just hadn't heard of his bollock debacle. Clearing his throat he began to speak.

'"Meet u as arranged. Alistair" received on 15 August.'

'The text message was received the night Alistair MacGregor was killed by the accused.' Hector's voice was pounding and suitably dramatic.

Kailash turned and looked at me accusingly. The last time that she had seen that phone, it was in my possession at Cornton Vale. The only conclusion she could draw from it was that I had handed it over to the Crown. It was an incorrect assumption – the last time I had seen it was when I placed it in a locked drawer in my office.

Roddie refused to meet my eye. He must have stolen it. What else had he taken? I could not object to this evidence because the moment it came into my possession I should have handed it over to the Crown. Failure to do so was perverting the course of justice, a criminal offence for which I had known police officers get four years. Glasgow Joe was poking me on the back urging me to get up and say something. I was being massacred. My own actions were coming back to haunt me.

One of my mother's favourite sayings suddenly came clear into my mind: 'What you dae in the night – the devil sees in the light.' I thought she used it as a warning about teenage pregnancy, now I understood her true meaning.

'Objection. M'Lord, my learned friend has no way

of knowing that the man who sent the text was Lord Arbuthnot.'

I was deliberately using his judicial title not his actual name. It was a small point, but sometimes your clients demand that you give them a good spraff, especially when their case is hopeless.

'Your objection is noted, Ms McLennan.' Lord MacDonald peered down at me, and stroked the front of his robes smoothing the red Templar cross on the white satin. In 1812 there wasn't a member of the judiciary that had not been a member of the Enlightenment. That was when the robes had been redesigned to honour their Templar past and in true Masonic tradition the meaning of their symbols was hidden in plain view.

'Now, Mr Buchanan, my friend objected when I asked you if the accused hated all men.'

Roddie nodded to show that he recalled that objection.

'But are you able to say if Ms Coutts hated any men in particular . . .' he rushed his last words out.

I was on my feet,

'Objection! Hearsay.'

It appeared that Roddie had been well coached for he shouted out too: 'Kailash Coutts stated that she hated Alistair MacGregor, and that one day she would kill him.'

'Objection!' I screamed.

'You are a bare-faced liar, Roddie Buchanan.' Kailash was on her feet, the prison guards were struggling to contain her as she tried to jump out of the dock and get to Roddie.

'Order! Order!'

Lord MacDonald was crimson in the face. The prison guards had pushed Kailash so hard that she had fallen onto the floor of the dock, where one woman pulled her up. Kailash was as red as Lord MacDonald and it was the first time that I had ever seen her dishevelled.

Calmness came over the court, like the morning after a squall, as everyone resumed their seats.

'M'Lord, that concludes the Crown's examination of this witness.' Hector flicked his gown up and sat down.

'Ms McLennan – in view of the lateness of the hour, court will adjourn and resume on Monday when you may cross-examine the witness.' Lord MacDonald then turned to Roddie. 'Thank you for giving your evidence in such a straightforward manner – you are of course still under oath, and you are not allowed to talk about this case to anyone.'

This admonition could not have been more trite. As Roddie stepped down from the witness box and was led outside, the notion of him speaking to anyone else about his private behaviour was unthinkable.

'Court rise!' the Macer shouted. Those present shuffled to their feet, and as Lord MacDonald processed out of court, the clerk began to tidy up the well.

I looked across at the window to see how my friend was doing. The bee lay with his legs up against the closed window.

Like everything else – buggered.

THIRTY-SIX

Taking a piece of paper, I walked round the front bench through the well of the court. Picking up the bee on the paper, I threw him out. I was almost caught in my maudlin mood as the clerk handed me a piece of paper.

> Meet me in Parliament Hall before you leave
>   for the evening.
> Hector

Nothing to lose, I thought and made my way to the Hall. Hector stood before Chantry's statue of Lord President Blair. As I approached him, he immediately began to talk.

'Men such as these,' he tapped the marble shoe and the tap reverberated round the walls, 'they are more than mere personalities – they represent the law, Brodie. And if a man like Alistair MacGregor is seen to be flawed then the rule of law in Scotland is also faulty. We can't allow that to happen now – can we?'

The Hall was empty, but I did not feel we were alone.

The eyes of judges past stared out of their blackened canvasses and seemed to follow me. Hector did not bother to speak in hushed tones.

He took my arm, and we began a slow procession up and down the tiled floor. The walk wasn't out of fear of being overheard, no, this was merely habit. Obviously Hector thought we had work to do, and this is how we did it.

'Why did Roddie give evidence?' I asked.

'Well he wasn't keen, let me tell you.' Hector stopped conversing to laugh as he recalled just what that persuasive talk with Roddie Buchanan must have been like.

'Oh, I am sure that you are aware of our debating society, Brodie. It brings with it rights and benefits – but sometimes one is called upon to do one's duty for the greater good – today it was Roddie's turn to sacrifice himself.'

'What will happen to him?' I asked, out of interest rather than care. I knew that news of his evidence today would leak out and his reputation – which I had fought to save – was now well and truly gone. So much depends on reputation in this game – you have to guard it with your life. Through reputation alone you can intimidate and win. Roddie had let his slip, and now he was vulnerable and would be attacked on all sides.

Roddie would know this better than anyone, for he had spent years destroying his enemies by making holes in their reputations – and then he let them be hanged by public opinion.

'Roddie did what was asked of him. He'll be taken

care of. He might get a Sheriffdom somewhere, or he could be made chairman of a tribunal.'

'It's not a bad payoff – at least the pension is good.'

'Enough of Roddie – you don't want his sacrifice to be for nothing.'

How little he understood about my relationship with Roddie Buchanan. I knew his evidence would get out because I was thinking of telling the steamie myself.

I grunted. Hector took it that I was in agreement with him.

'What we want, Brodie, is for Kailash to plead,' said Hector.

'I've told you she won't.'

'You also told me that you were prepared for this trial – but you didn't have a clue what you were up against in there, did you?'

We paced in silence.

'Look, I'm not here to make your job difficult, Brodie. I would accept a plea to culpable homicide.'

Culpable homicide – it was something. At least life imprisonment would no longer be mandatory. Sentence was at the discretion of the judge.

'OK, Hector – if I could get her to plead to culp hom then I would also want it accepted by the Crown that she had diminished responsibility.'

Hector looked interested.

'How was her responsibility for her actions diminished?' he asked.

'I don't know – I'll think of something.' And I knew that I would. I was great at doing pleas in mitigation – where an accused had been found guilty, and the court is asked for mercy. But one thing I knew, was that no matter how good I was I did not want to throw myself on the compassion of this court.

'I'll ask her to plead to culpable homicide and the Crown agrees that her responsibility was diminished – but I want an understanding that she'll get no more than four years,' I stressed.

'That would mean that she'd be out in two years – is that all the killing of the top Scottish judge is worth to you?'

'Look, Hector, no more poncing about – that's the deal I'll put to her. You still have to prove motive and Kailash swears that Lord Arbuthnot had never been a client of hers.'

'So she didn't deny knowing him – just that he wasn't a client?'

'However she knew him, nothing about this is going to look good for our legal system, so I suggest you take my offer to your superiors.'

'No need. I am authorised to agree anything – within reason.'

He shook my hand.

'I might not get her to agree before Monday,' I warned.

'You'd better – otherwise Lord MacDonald is calling the press and the jury back in and your client will go down for murder, and Roddie's career will go down the toilet taking yours with it. Jointly and severally liable, remember? You'll be working until you're my age just to pay off Roddie's debts.'

I watched him walk away. Unfortunately, the bastard

was right. Roddie had one of the most impressive art collections in Scotland. The paintings, mostly modern, had been bought with the firm's money but Roddie had been sly enough to ensure that they were all in his personal name. The current overdraft of the firm was nothing compared to the fee income; but if that should stop overnight, then we would go into free fall.

Suddenly I felt very tired. I did not know if I had the strength left to save myself, let alone Kailash. I walked to the corridor where my box was stationed as I had arranged to meet Joe there. He was unwilling to let me leave Parliament House on my own on the grounds of safety – God love him if he actually thought I was safe inside these ancient walls.

Hector McVie and the Enlightenment had just filleted me better than any butcher of a serial killer could.

Joe leaned against my open box, weariness showed in his eyes. I wasn't the only one being affected by events.

'Brodie!' he shouted, as if I could miss him. Raising his huge hand in the air, I saw that he had a brown paper parcel in it.

'Somebody's left his calling card.'

My heart sank; whatever was in that package, it was not good news.

The battle on two fronts continued.

THIRTY-SEVEN

Little Miss Muffet sat on her tuffet
eating her curds and whey;
along came a spider
who sat down beside her
and frightened Miss Muffet away.

Patch, Glasgow Joe, Fishy, Jack and I sat in my kitchen. This was becoming quite a habit, and it wouldn't take a mastermind to work out that my house had become one of the only places we all felt safe. Rich coffee in mugs, chocolate chip shortbread I'd made in the early hours of the morning earlier that week, and a parlour game in front of us. It was like playing pass the parcel. The package contained many layers, the first was the hand-written note with the nursery rhyme.

Glasgow Joe held it up.

'Does anyone know what this means?'

I took the paper from him and looked round at the usual motley crew that surrounded me in my kitchen. Nursery rhymes were not what you would expect Joe, Jack, Patch and Fishy to have intimate knowledge of.

'I've heard it argued that every nursery rhyme has a political meaning – or it records some historical event.'

Jack picked up my thread of thought.

'That's right – "ring a ring of roses" is about the great plague. But I don't know what the spider thing is about.'

I examined the nursery rhyme again.

'Miss Muffet is supposed to represent Mary Queen of Scots – and the spider is John Knox. He "frightened" her to leave Scotland and she threw herself on the mercies of her cousin, Queen Elizabeth, who beheaded her.'

'The bodies in the bag had been decapitated,' Fishy added.

'Perhaps we should look at what's inside the rest of the parcel before we comment,' said Patch. Another layer of brown paper hid the contents. Like a child at Christmas, Joe pulled it off.

'A bit of care is required here, Joe – you might destroy something.' Patch was testy as he took the parcel from Joe's hands.

'There's a newspaper clipping. It looks like an old story.' Patch put on his glasses and examined it.

'Oh, it's about that baby that was found washed up at Portobello . . .'

'Let me see it.' Fishy took the paper from Patch.

'We already have this particular article in the police file,' he said. 'This is in better condition though – I suspect someone bought a copy of the original paper and took this out. I'll follow up with the *Evening News* and see if they have a record of who bought it.' Fishy wrote down the action that he had committed himself to take; it would have to wait until morning as the payment department at the newspaper was shut for the evening.

'The person who left this – thing for you . . . do you think they didn't know that we already had the album? If so, then they're not the killer.' Joe's voice was soft and plausible.

'No – I've had this feeling for a while that I'm just not asking the right questions.' I sipped my icy Mexican beer, the lime that was inserted into the bottle neck nipped a tiny cut that I had in the inside of my mouth. The tip of my tongue was covered with incisions, where my teeth had inadvertently sliced into it whilst I was thinking.

'I can't get the answers – because we are not looking in the right direction. I think this is a reminder that this baby is important in all of this. We've been looking at the girls. Maybe the baby is the real clue.' I was tired after a hard day in court, all I wanted to do was guzzle pizza and drink beers. I had an appointment with Kailash in the morning, and I wasn't looking forward to it.

'Has anyone come up with anything on this baby because I don't have much?' Fishy looked hopefully around the table.

'I found the original report but it tells me nothing – the local bobby received a call from a woman walking her dog on Porty beach. He investigated, found it was indeed a baby, attempts to find the mother drew a blank, possibly because the baby had been in the sea for some time.' Fishy read the notes in a monotone voice from his black police notebook.

I weighed out the flour for the pizza I was making – it always relaxes me after a day in court – and Patch screamed in horror.

'Careful! We've got evidence all over the place here!'

'If we don't catch him without resorting to forensics then I'm dead,' I said.

'We can use both.'

Patch had already placed the nursery rhyme note and the newspaper article in evidence bags. He wore white cotton gloves as he unwrapped the next layer. Disappointingly, there was nothing; it was simply padding for the chief clue. Carefully, with the skill he used in dissection, Patch removed the last layer. He placed it before us. We stared in silence, horrified, because we knew what it had done.

I couldn't touch it.

'Well, now we know what that bastard meant by spider.' I opened another beer, without bothering with the lime.

'His spider . . .' I pointed at it with the bottle, 'was a medieval instrument of torture. It's made of iron – the pincers are meant to represent spider's legs.'

Their eyes followed me as I walked around the kitchen, I stopped for a moment at the stainless-steel range cooker to stir the thickening crimson pasta sauce.

'The tongs would be heated in a fire – then attached

to a woman's breast and pulled and twisted until the breast was mutilated or it came off.'

The pizza dough was rising in the heat of the kitchen; I pushed my finger deep into its gooey mass, and deflated it. The bread mixture clung tackily to my finger as I tried to push the thoughts of burning young flesh from my mind.

Fishy had opened the photograph album at the set of pictures that depicted Laura Liddell's torment. The second image in the series illustrated just what exactly 'the spider' was capable of.

'We have to stop this bastard . . .' Joe didn't finish what he was about to say but I knew that he could not bear the thought that the killer may use that instrument on me. I wasn't too keen on it either.

'We have to find Moses Tierney – and make him tell us what he knows,' I said. My appetite had gone; even the difficulties I faced with Kailash were nothing compared with this.

'Moses?' asked Patch. 'What do you want with Moses?'

'He's the boy,' shouted Joe. 'Isn't he? He's the boy in the photograph – the one watching. And you…' He looked at Jack, 'you're the one who knows where he is – he's your fucking grass, isn't he? He's the one who told you about the break-in at Fettes? He's the one who told you what was really taken?

'Don't you worry, Brodie – I'll make the wee bastard talk. He'll even fucking sing for you after I've finished with him.' Joe was growling. I was glad he had refused any alcohol, drink mellows him and I needed him to be as mean as hell.

'Joe, remember what he's been through, what he's seen. Nothing that you do to him could be as bad as the "Devil" has already done.'

I picked up my helmet, and switched off the cooker – our appetites had disappeared.

'Patch – you see if you can find any autopsy reports on the baby. Fishy – you look through the records for any assaults where the perp used instruments of torture.'

I walked up to Jack Deans, and stared at him.

'And you . . . it's about time you took us to Moses.'

'How'd you know I can find him?' he asked.

'Because we give you more credit than we should,' I replied. 'We'll follow you.' I was angry with him for still holding his sources close to his chest, even if it hadn't taken Joe that long to work out that he was Jack's informer. As soon as we saw the photograph of the young boy with the haunted eyes, we realised that information had been sitting in Jack's lap all the time. A look of recognition passed between us. We knew exactly who it was. The roar from the street almost rattled the windows. Joe was impatient; he had already started up Awesome. Fishy and Patch had already moved from the table, anxious to get started. Only Jack was slow. I glowered at him from the kitchen doorway.

'Shift your arse . . . now,' I shouted, too anxious to be polite. I was determined to find out what I needed to know, and I was no longer naive enough to think it would be either painless or trouble free.

'This may not be the best way to go about it, Brodie.'

'What do you want me to do, Jack – sit and wait

until he comes for me? That delinquent has inside information- he knew that I was the next victim, why else would he have gone to court that day?'

I pulled my bike jacket roughly over my shoulders, forcing my arms in. Taking my temper out on myself was not one of my better ideas.

'Think about it, Jack – there's only one way he knew that I was next. It's because he is still in touch with the killer. Moses can lead me to the killer.'

'I think you're wrong, Brodie.'

'Ok, Jack, if I'm wrong I'll buy you both a pint, will that do you?' The sarcasm in my voice was unnecessary but it kept the tears away, and at least Jack was heading for the door, with his car keys in his hand.

THIRTY-EIGHT

In my opinion Hillside Crescent has always been an underrated piece of Edinburgh real estate. Each time I drive past, I find time to admire its elegant sandstone tenements. The windows are long, and narrow wrought iron balconies serve as an attractive safety feature. As we approached Moses' address, I noted the Doric columns standing like graceful sentries on either side of the heavy black stair door.

Joe's voice interrupted my interior design gazing. 'Crime does pay – this is a helluva lot nicer than that poor bastard Frank Pearson's flat.' His voice echoed in the stairwell as we climbed up and up and up. A top floor flat reminds you that Edinburgh tenements were the first skyscrapers – and they don't have lifts.

The front door was neatly painted, there was no name on it. A brass laurel leaf door-knocker was just waiting to be rapped. Joe slammed it repeatedly. Even to my ears he sounded like the drug squad. I could hear feet scampering inside; they were talking in hushed voices and an eye peered out at us through the spy hole.

A decision was finally made to let us in, but it took them at least five minutes to unbolt the various locks on the door; Houdini would have had trouble getting out. One single chain was left on. Joe could have kicked through it in an instant. The door opened five inches; a cherubic face peeked through.

'What the fuck do you want?' it squeaked.

'Manners for a start or I'll skelp your arse – now open the door, we want to see Moses.' Joe was at his menacing best.

'What if he's no' here?' the foul-mouthed angel replied, undaunted.

'Well then, you'd better get him here or I'll kick this door in – and when I'm finished with him I'll come looking for you.'

A command was issued from within, and the final chain was undone.

'I'm sorry about him – but we're not too keen on strangers here.'

Moses himself had come to the door to greet us. He looked resplendent in black evening trousers and a white pin tucked shirt with winged collar. His sleeves were without cuff-links; they were rolled halfway up his forearms and I was surprised to note the thickness and strength of his wrists.

Like a child playing house, he eagerly led us through the hall into his stylish drawing room. When I say that the house was stylish, I don't mean that it was decorated tastefully – it just had its own look. If the decorating style of the Dark Angels lair had a name, it would surely be Vampire Chic. The hallway was painted blood red, ornate gilt Napoleonic mirrors hung on the walls lit by candle sconces. In fact, the whole house appeared to be illuminated by candles.

Two large zebra skin rugs lay on the thick wooden floorboards, the white stripes marked with dirt from careless shoes. The doorway to the drawing room was of generous proportions, floor to ceiling windows could have lit the room had the candles not had such a presence. There were some bizarre design features – velvet cushioned sixteen-foot benches lined the walls. They reminded me of the catacombs in Rome where the benches are stacked like bunk-beds.

'We sit in here for meetings and they double up as beds,' Moses explained as I stared at them. 'If the right kind of kid comes to the door I always find them someplace to put their head.' Moses was answering my questions without me having to ask them.

'Like a latter day Fagin?' I replied.

'Yeah – something like that.'

He was laughing at me. Black eyed androgynous kids sat on their perches. One sat high in the corner eyeing me as if I were carrion. Jack, Joe and I stood in the centre of the room, an unholy trinity.

'We've come here to speak to you, Moses. With you,' I corrected myself.

'About fucking time – what took you so long?' Moses was derisive, it could have been bravado but somehow I did think he had been expecting the call.

'Sorry to have disappointed you – where do you want to start?' Joe flexed his muscles behind me; we were obviously going to do a good cop/bad cop routine, and unusually I was getting to play the good cop.

Moses clapped his hand and shouted.

'Right, you set of radges – fuck off, I want some peace.'

He obviously went to the same charm management school as Roddie Buchanan. Moses turned his attention to Jack.

'Took your time bringing them, didn't you? Took your time bringing her,' he emphasised.

Jack ignored him, no doubt now that he had brought us here their business connection was broken; consequently he no longer had to jump to Moses' command.

'We'll kick off then.' Joe rubbed his knuckles theatrically, letting the double meaning of his words sink in. Moses ignored him, and lay on a purple velvet French daybed.

'Sit.' He gestured expansively with his arm.

'We'll stand,' Joe replied for us all.

I pulled up a small footstool, and sat at Moses' head. As I had tried to explain to Joe, there was nothing that we could do to Moses that would be as bad as what he had already survived. That in a nutshell was the secret of his success. What had he to fear? Death? I wondered how many nights he had lain awake praying for death, pleading for the comfort of an eternal dreamless sleep.

'Moses – you know what we are here for. I found the photographs in Frank Pearson's flat.' My voice was soft and soothing. I let my hand hover just above his skin, so as not to alarm him. I was letting him know that I was there, and then I placed my palm gently on his forehead.

We all have our personal space. People who live in towns have a narrower personal space than those who live in rural areas. The importance of this area, our breathing space, is that if someone comes into it, and we're not aware of his or her presence, then we can feel as if we have been assaulted. Criminologists believe that this is one of the reasons for so much inner city violence, and stress.

'Could you move over a bit, Moses?' I asked him, my voice timed to match the rate of his beating heart.

'Put your feet closer together, drop your hands by your side, and take a deep breath in. Now close your eyes – you'll feel more comfortable.'

Moses was clearly humouring me, but he carried out those simple tasks unaware of how the human mind works. Everyone should be warned about this – if you follow someone else's instructions, and carry out five or more simple commands of theirs, then your conscious mind switches off, and you obey them automatically.

Psychologists call this the 'click whirr' response. It isn't that humans are stupid, it is simply that our brain has so much information to process that it is always looking for a shortcut. I find it invaluable in my dealings with people. I was taught it in Los Angeles, during a completely different period of my life, and one which I never dreamed would come in useful in a situation like this. The Master Hypnotist who taught me made me pledge always to use it in others' best interest. What can I say? I'm flawed.

Following my signing, Jack Deans closed the shutters, and in this darkened room I began to lead Moses back to hell. I knew this was necessary. The only way that Moses had been allowed to live was if his memories had been repressed. It would have been a natural safety device for the brain to ensure survival. Consciously, Moses knew as much as I did, but your subconscious mind never sleeps – every face you have ever seen is recorded there. The conscious mind is the gatekeeper to the subconscious. If it thinks you need to be protected, then hypnosis cannot occur, so the clever hypnotist lulls your mind. I spoke softly into his ear, boring his conscious mind, urging it to switch off. Then, to deepen the trance, I lifted his arm, and threw it fiercely back down on his body. The shock of the force, and my decree, sent him down into unconsciousness ten thousand times deeper than he had been.

'Moses – we're going to go back now.' I spoke softly but with authority. I was the master. Holding his hand, I lead him back to a time when his arms and legs were shorter, when he was younger than he is now. Tapping him on his third eye I directed:

'Now you are six – tell me where you are.'

I was taking this boy back to the worst period of his life – time to go back to hell.

THIRTY-NINE

Moses didn't answer me. Joe and Jack hovered over the unconscious boy, fascinated by the primeval scene. Shamans have been putting initiates into trances since pre-history – they wouldn't be bothered by the couple of useless gawpers watching me. I tapped Moses harshly on his forehead. His eyes flickered under the lids as if he were in a dream state.

'Moses – are you inside a room or outside?'

To get people used to talking in this state you have to start with the most basic questions.

'I'm outside,' he replies.

'Where are you, Moses? What are you doing?'

'The snot's dripping down from my nose. I'm trying to lick it all away but it's really salty and slithery and there's only so much I can get rid of. My tongue's spreading it all over my top lip, it's giving me a moustache of bogies. That would be ok on any other day, it might be funny, but today I want to look my best because the lady is coming to get me.'

'Where is the lady taking you, Moses?'

'I think she's going to take me to meet my new family. I hope she comes in a Volvo. Volvos are my favourite cars, because mummies drive them. Mummies who love their children and take them to the zoo. I love to watch Volvos especially the ones with dogs in them, and children's stories in the cassettes. And I love zoos, because the animals can look all fierce and wild but they can't get you, they're all locked up and it doesn't matter if they're roaring or howling or scratching – you're safe.'

Moses was rambling – but he was only six. It was important that I let him talk in a way and at a speed that he was comfortable with – especially given the horrors that I knew I was taking him to.

'Snot's still dripping down my nose. I'm lifting my arm, and wiping it on my anorak sleeve. It leaves a slimy trail like a slug. I try to rub it away on my shorts – I usually only wear them to school, but I've got to look my best for the lady. It's lonely standing here, I wish she would come.'

'Does she come, Moses? Does the lady come?'

'Yes! She does, here she is! Maybe this lady will be my new mummy. She's a bit old, not like granny, but still pretty old. The car she's driving isn't a Volvo. "Don't put your muddy feet on the seats," she says so as I don't dirty them. She says we're going for a long drive, but she won't tell me where. Maybe she wants to surprise me – maybe there will be a whole new family waiting there; maybe I'm just what she's been looking for to make them complete.'

'What's her car like, Moses?'

'It's all stuffy and dry inside but at least my nose

356

has stopped dripping. The lady is playing some music on the radio – she says it is someone important but I don't understand what she is talking about and the look on her face makes me think I maybe shouldn't tell her I prefer *The Singing Kettle*. I don't want to upset the lady. Are we there yet? I ask, and the lady tells me to be quiet she'll tell me when I'm there. My new family must live in the country because we are leaving Edinburgh. I'm lying on my back, and watching the clouds move across the sky. I feel like an angel and I wish that I could fly. If I could fly I would be there already with my new mummy. My old mummy's gone. Granny says she's with the angels, and she'll be happy now because there's no smack in heaven. But I don't remember her smacking me, I remember her being lovely and don't think of the times when she was cross or looking for money or going out in the middle of the night or lying on the sofa all woozy from the medicine she said she had to take. When Mummy had to go to the angels, Granny wanted to keep me but she's got something that makes her bones sore.'

This child had so much to say. I looked over to Jack and Joe – the former was listening intently, but Joe could hardly bear to. His head was down and he was staring at something incredibly interesting on the floor.

'Maybe my new family will have a daddy; I'd really love a daddy, I've never had one of those. We've turned off the motorway now, and there are cows. Real cows in the fields. I can see the bridges – maybe we will have a boat. We've turned again, into a driveway. I'm nearly there! The tyres are crunching on the sparkly granite and I can see a castle. My new family live in a castle! It's a little castle but that doesn't matter. It looks over the river and the bridges.'

I keep asking questions – I have to.

'What does the lady do when you get there, Moses?'

'She's pulling me roughly out the car but she must have made a mistake because she's hurting my arm. She's never hurt me before, so it must be an accident. I want to stamp my feet and see the red lights come on in the heels of my new trainers, but she's dragging me along the ground. She must be in an awful hurry but I bet she would like the lights in my trainers if she had time to look at them. The front door is huge and scarred, as if it would protect the people inside from any invader. There are holes in the door and I wonder if they were made with arrows. Will I get to play cowboys and Indians here, do you think?'

'I don't know, Moses. What do you think? Is there someone else there who might play games with you? Good games?'

'Well, a girl answers the door; she's wearing her school uniform. Is she daft? It's Saturday – she doesn't need to dress like that. She's quite old, maybe fourteen, but she has her hair in bunches. She looks a daftie, I think I was right first time. Just above her white ankle socks I can see a tattoo. It's a butterfly, and it's lovely. If she's my new big sister, it's fine – I don't mind her being daft, she looks friendly but a bit sad. The lady has gone now and it's just me with the girl, and the girl tells me her name and smiles at me and asks if it's my first time here. I nod my head, and she starts to cry, softly, a tear just running down her cheek. Now she's hugging me – she smells nice and clean. We're going along a stone corridor; it must be terrible cold on your feet in the wintertime.'

'What else do you see, Moses?' I ask.

'Big tin men with axes line the hall, and there are paintings from the olden days of cross-looking people. They're staring at me so I keep my head down, and follow the girl upstairs. We've stopped outside a huge pair of doors and she's sat me down on a chair to wait. She's giving me some peppermint chewing gum into my hand, she's making me promise not to look through the keyhole. Just wait, and someone else will come for you, she says.'

Moses' jaw moved up and down like a cow chewing the cud. To him it was as if he had time travelled. Moses was back outside that room waiting to go in. I cannot pretend that I didn't know what I was doing, the possible consequences of where I was taking him, but in that instant I felt the outcome justified it. The result being that I would live. I have already admitted that I am imperfect. I'm selfish too.

'Now, Moses, I want you to go and look through the keyhole and tell me what you see.'

He shook his head from side to side.

'Moses.' My voice was deep and harsh. 'Nothing can hurt you – look through the keyhole. I'm with you holding your hand.'

'I promised Laura I wouldn't look.' My eyes locked with Joe's. The tension was high, we breathed in unison. Forgetting to blink, we stared at Moses.

'To the keyhole,' I urged, and squeezed his hand.

'Lots of old people are seated round the walls. The lady who has brought me here is laughing and handing out drinks. It's hard to see, because it's such a small hole, but I can see the girl – it looks like a party – she's handing out drinks – it's like one of my granny's dos 'cos they're all old. I'm getting sore kneeling down – one of the old men is getting my friend to take off her clothes. She's being really rude – they're making her be really naughty – she's touching her bottom in front of them.'

Moses looked distressed. His head was waving from side to side, as if he was possessed. Joe and Jack were scared for him. Moses' breathing was laboured, he was literally panicking. The mind cannot tell the difference between the truth and a lie. To him it was very real but I could not allow myself to feel his pain; he had to be pushed through it.

'My new friend with the tattoo is there, and another girl. They're sitting on men's knees and they've got no knickers on. I swear, their knickers are on the floor. The men are touching them and everyone is looking. This doesn't look like my new family – there are too many grown-ups and they are doing bad things. My friend starts to touch the man's bottom and she is still crying, but everyone ignores her. The door's opening now and the lady's coming for me. I hate her.'

'Tell me what the room is like, Moses,' I urged, trying to calm him down. His heart was racing at an alarming rate, and in an older person it would have led to an attack. Sweat had broken out on his top lip. I could see that his shirt was sticking to his skin. I could have taken him slower, calmed him down, but I needed to know. My impatience was my undoing again.

'I don't like the room. It's got a big picture of the devil in it and he's looking at me. His eyes are following me. The lady is takin' ma hand and we're going out of the room now – maybe she's takin' me back to ma granny.' A sense of comfort came into his body as he recalled his grandmother.

'What are you doing, Moses?' I had to ask because he was pulling his hand away from me.

'I'm trying to get away from the lady.'

'Can you get away from her?'

'No – she's too strong. She's pulling me downstairs to . . . to a . . . a dungeon. It's where the devil lives and he's in there and he's got a big fire going and it's horrible – but it's not cold outside so why has he got the fire going and what is he doing? I don't like it. I don't like it.'

Moses' breathing was still laboured but it had slowed down as the child tried to make sense of the scene around him. I could see his eyes moving around slowly under his lids, as he carefully took in every corner of the room.

'Tell me about the room, Moses,' I urged again.

'It's not a room,' he said petulantly, 'I told you it's a dungeon – a real one too 'cos it's dark and they torture in here.'

'What have they got there to hurt people, Moses? How do you know they torture people?'

'Not people, not big people – just kids. Only big

girls get hurt here, that's what my friend's telling me. She's shouting "don't cry, Moses, the devil only hurts big girls, you're safe honey, just pray to the angels."'

'What is the devil doing to her, Moses?' I asked. When people are in a trance you have to get into their mind-set; I couldn't argue with him that it was just a man hurting his friend.

'He's got her tied to a cross – not like the one Jesus died on though. This one's like the one on a Scottish flag.'

'What's your friend's name, Moses?' I asked, keeping my eyes on Joe and Jack.

'Laura. She's called Laura.'

I closed my eyes, for I too had seen Laura Liddell tied to a St Andrew's cross.

'What's happening now, Moses?'

He clenched his eyes twice, as if he could not quite believe what he was seeing.

'Tell me, now!' I tapped my finger on his forehead, bringing the same effect as hitting a dog on the nose with a newspaper – although it doesn't hurt, obedience follows.

'He's got a stick in the fire – and he's shooglin' it about. The lady's in the background with a camera – he's taking the stick out of the flames and it's got prongs on it, they're hot, they're burning hot, they're glowing.'

Moses sighed deeply. He needed a rest; his nervous system was exhausted. I could have no pity – I needed to know more than he needed to tell.

'Go on, Moses.'

I squeezed his hand harder. Glasgow Joe could see

362

the pain the boy was in and he hit me across the back as if to say, 'give it a rest'. In spite of the tears freely flowing down Joe's face, I continued. I tapped Moses yet again.

'Laura's crying, she's begging him to leave her alone. She tells me to look away but the lady holds my head – so I have to see. She makes me see. I hate her. I hate her so much.' This was all whispered. Silence followed, Moses was alone in his shock. Hot fat tears escaped from under his lips.

'They're hurting Laura so much – her skin is burned away and it smells like ma granny's Sunday roast. I don't want to see any more, Laura can't speak to me, they're pulling me beside her, they're chopping her up like some deid cow, and the lady's taking pictures,' he continued, shaking his head.

'I know it must hurt, Moses, but you must go on.'

'It's the wrong girl. What I can't understand is – I think they hurt the wrong girl.' He kept shaking his head. 'They hurt the wrong girl. Laura could have lived. They got the wrong one.'

'Moses?' I steadied his head.

'Moses?' I said in a firmer tone.

'Why do you think the devil hurt the wrong girl?'

He considered my question for a moment and then replied:

'Because he kept calling her Kailash – and her name's not Kailash, it's Laura.'

FORTY

I did not turn to see Joe or Jack's reaction. I didn't even
have time to check my own. I continued to work with
Moses. Rocking his head back and forth, I told him
that he would wake on the count of five. I threw in a
gamble by telling him that he would recall everything
that had happened. In addition I gave Moses a post-
hypnotic suggestion that any time I snapped my fingers
and told him to sleep, he would immediately go into
a trance deeper than the one he was in today. If he was
agreeable to that he had to raise his forefinger on his
right hand. Silent body acknowledgements are the most
effective.

Tired and drained, Moses wearily opened his eyes.

'What the fuck have you done to me?'

'Where do you sleep, Moses?'

Staggering up, he led me to a large room with a
double bed in it. Pushing him down, he fell softly like
a baby. I snapped my fingers, and told him to sleep. As
I left the room he was mercifully unconscious.

On the way home Jack and Joe bombarded me with

questions. Too tired to answer, I ignored them for the entire journey – that doesn't mean that I didn't hear Jack's incredulous praise or Joe's warnings.

'Are you sure that laddie's gonna be OK? Should you not have told him just to forget everything again? To bury it down deep and never, ever think of it again?'

I didn't need their questions, I didn't need their noise. I just needed to get home, rest and then try to make some sense of it when I woke.

When I finally got there, I fell into my bed and needed no hypnosis to make me sleep soundly. I intended to sleep like the dead. I must have done for a while, but then, as usual, the phone rang. Automatically, again as usual, my hand reached for the receiver.

'Is that Brodie McLennan?'

I screwed my eyes tightly, trying to force some fluid into them, for my lids were stuck to my eyeballs. My life was like a psychotic Groundhog Day. Fumbling I found a pen, and muttered that it was Brodie McLennan speaking.

'PC Fulton here. Ms McLennan, we've got a young man on the Forth Road Bridge threatening to jump unless you come out to see him.'

I needed no name from PC Fulton.

'Tell Moses I'm coming.'

FORTY-ONE

Orange and pink streaks cracked the sky over the Firth of Forth. It looked like a celestial tie-dye gone wrong. I didn't need a shepherd's warning to tell me this was going to be a difficult day.

It was dawn and the Forth Road Bridge was practically deserted. The motorists who did pass Moses were either too tired or too focused to notice him standing on the edge of the structure holding on to a thick steel suspension wire.

The Forth Road Bridge was built in 1964, and opened by the Queen. A smaller version of the Golden Gate Bridge, it spans the river Forth, providing a gateway to the north. It sits parallel to the beautiful maroon cantilever bridge, the Forth Rail Bridge, built by the Victorians in the heyday of railways. It's the scourge of commuters but a favoured haunt of suicides.

In the distance, to the north, I could see the hills. It was such a clear morning I felt as if I could see forever. But as soon as I fixed my eyes on Moses, all thoughts of views and scenery quickly disappeared. He was dressed as I had left him, standing in a slight breeze swaying with exhaustion and nerves. His knuckles were bloodless with tension; in spite of appearances he had a tight grip on that rope. He wanted to live.

PC Fulton was an older bobby, a couple of years shy of retirement; he knew how to handle the situation, although I doubted if he had ever been on any negotiation courses. Having made the decision to manage the state of affairs, he made a judgement call to keep it low key; this principally meant that there was no ambulance standing by. There were only the three of us, and thankfully the elements were being relatively kind. Far, far down below I could see the blue grey river swell and lap against the enormous posts that held up the bridge. To my mind it looked hungry for Moses, and if I couldn't talk him down there was no one else to save him.

The roar from Awesome's pipes made him turn to see me. I raised my hand in salute to him before I dismounted. I had come alone. I gave myself the excuse that I did not want to wake Joe – in truth I couldn't bear the thought of him saying 'I told you so'.

PC Fulton moved towards me, a stout comforting figure. Over his arm was a rough grey prison blanket.

'Sorry to wake you – but I got the call. I know the lad and headquarters thought I could handle it. It's not even my beat – I'm Muirhouse, this is South Queensferry.'

I put my hand out to shake his.

'It's OK – I know him. I don't mind.' Like rapid gunfire, my words came out – broken. I didn't want to say that I felt responsible or to offer any explanations. Moses had coped with this for years – even if it had been buried. I had screwed that up, messed whatever delicate balance he had, and now a boy who had dealt with his demons for years was trying to end it all.

'Moses – get your arse down from there now,' I barked at him, the wind carrying my words. I wasn't sure what to expect but I could see that PC Fulton had been trying the softly, softly approach for the last five hours.

'Fuck off, Brodie – I'm going nowhere till you promise.' His voice was bitterly strong.

'What do you want me to promise, Moses?' I asked, anxious to agree to anything so that I could get him down quickly and without PC Fulton asking me any awkward questions.

'I want you to swear you'll make me forget again – and I want your word that you'll get those bastards.'

PC Fulton looked at me quizzically but I was in no mood to offer chit-chat.

'I'll do everything I can.' I shouted but under my breath I whispered, 'But not today for I have to see Kailash.'

'What was that?' PC Fulton asked.

'If you want to keep him safe – do us both a favour and lock him up. I'll come down to St Leonard's as soon as I can – but it might not be until tomorrow morning.' The breeze muffled my words, and PC Fulton blinked, convinced that he had misheard me.

'You want me to lock that laddie up?' He looked at me doubtfully.

I nodded. 'I want you to lock him up to keep him safe – if you take him to the Royal Ed he can walk straight out again and finish what he started.'

'The boy needs help not prison. He'll get more of that from a psychiatrist at the Andrew Duncan Clinic than down the nick. As I said, I knew his family. I want to do what's right for him.' PC Fulton was adamant.

'If you want to keep him safe then the only place for him is St Leonard's – then I'll come and take him off your hands and get him the attention he needs.'

It may have been beginner's luck, and the fact that he was ready to come down, but Moses allowed PC Fulton to get near him. His thin limbs were frozen stiff from holding one position for so long. We approached him cautiously, I was more wary than the constable because I suffer from vertigo. Like the pull from a magnet I felt myself being drawn to the edge. A cold trickle of sweat ran down the inside of my arm, dizziness threatened to overcome me, but I made myself keep moving. PC Fulton had climbed the barrier as elegantly as his chunky thighs would permit; I was in no position to criticise style. I was several feet behind the constable praying that, by the time I reached them, there would be no need for me to go over the side. My eyes kept being dragged to the water as it greedily lapped the posts.

With the expert cast of a fisherman the constable threw the blanket around Moses, swaddling him like an infant he effortlessly bundled him over to the safe side of the bridge.

Half carrying, half pushing him, Fulton got Moses

to the car. As Moses sipped the hot coffee that the constable's wife had made for his break, PC Fulton charged him with breach of the peace, and read him his rights.

I told Moses exactly how I would protect him. What I would do to help him adjust in the future, and why those bastards that hurt him and the girls were going down. The trouble was, he was ten miles down the road by the time I thought of words adequate enough to express my opinions.

As I watched the Panda car driving off, guilt ripped my heart to shreds. It was too early to go to Cornton Vale, and I couldn't face Joe round the breakfast table. When I have bad feelings, I try my damnedest to ignore them. This was one of those times. Fast driving, hard liquor and sweet food are the best panacea. Even if it hadn't been dawn I had work to do so I headed off to do it – and get a couple of Mars bars along the way.

FORTY-TWO

Tempus fugit. Well, it might for some people at some times, but it didn't for me that morning.

I sat on the hard kerbstone beside Awesome waiting for ten o'clock so that I could be allowed into Cornton Vale. A probationary prison officer eyed me suspiciously as I thumped down my scraped bike helmet on the counter.

'Agent visit,' I answered the unspoken query in her eyes.

'What firm?' Disbelief rang soundly in her voice.

I looked around for someone I knew, an old hand was coming on duty.

'How's the bike running, Mike?'

'Sound as a pound, Brodie.'

He nodded to the new officer and the agent signing-in book was passed through the grille.

'Kailash Coutts. She's on remand – she should be in D Hall. Mike, can you bring Kailash out for an agent visit?'

The echo of heavy doors being unlocked resounded

through the prison walls. I sat in the agent's room, and waited.

Her scent preceded her. Prisons generally stink. Male prisoners are worse than female, and the strange thing is, it's not because they are dirty. An odour of hopelessness emanates from their skin. It's horrible, but Kailash was different.

In spite of the debacle that was the first day of her murder trial she floated in, her emotions hidden behind a mask of exquisite grooming.

'You came.'

It was a statement, not a question, almost as if she expected me to abandon her, and resign from acting before the court on Monday morning. Perhaps I would have done if my own options were not so limited.

'You don't expect much of me,' I replied.

'I knew what I was getting before I asked for you that first time.'

That could have been taken as a compliment, but I decided not to press her on it. As I pulled the cheap wooden chair away from the table, its legs scraped along the floor, making a screeching noise that set my nerve endings tingling. I took her file out of my bag, and placing a pen in my mouth, tried to think of a way to start to broach all that I had to say.

'Take that pen out of your mouth – you look like an imbecile. I hope that's not a habit you've got,' she chided me.

I placed the pen, dripping with saliva onto the table. It was a bad habit of mine but no one except Mary McLennan ever told me off for it. Miffed, I decided to spit it all out, starting with the court case. Kailash might have known what she was getting when she asked for me but I had no idea. I still wasn't sure what I was dealing with.

'The evidence against you yesterday was pretty damning,' I began.

'He's a lying bastard,' she replied.

'So what? No one's going to believe that Roddie was double-dealing. You set him up. Everyone thinks he pays for ball torture. Why for God's sake did you do it?'

I had never fully bought into the idea that Kailash used the photographs as a marketing tool. If the rumours were true she was richer than Croesus and didn't need to resort to cheap stunts.

'Roddie might not be into the "white room" scene – but he's into pretty much everything else. Stuff that I don't approve of.'

I almost choked. 'What could be so bad that you don't approve of it?'

'My motives don't matter at the moment. I deemed it necessary that Roddie be brought down a peg or two – they needed to be shown that I could get to any one of them if I chose.'

Sullenly, I stared at her as she continued.

'Roddie was drinking red wine. He didn't know who I was. I slipped Rohypnol into his drink – it was simple; the red wine camouflaged the blue dye that's supposed to act as a safety device. In a few seconds he was unconscious.'

'And then you could do what you wanted?' I shook my head, remembering I had heard similar words and how they had come from me talking about my own situation.

'I don't apologise for my lifestyle.'

'I could almost understand it if you needed the money – but you don't.'

'Ever read Freud?' Kailash asked derisively.

'No jury is ever going to believe you. The affidavit you signed – you said Roddie only wanted one testicle injected. Why didn't you tell the truth then?'

I shoved the photograph of her and Roddie across the table at her. Unconcerned she picked it up and examined it, a sly smile crossed her face as if even now she did not regret what she had done to him.

'Not even you believed me when I told the truth. I knew what I could get away with and it worked.'

'Well – you're not going to get away with it this time. Hector McVie wants you to plead to culpable homicide – I've got him to agree to that.' I coughed to cover my unease. 'On the basis that you had diminished respon-sibility.' I finished hurriedly, but started up again so that she did not have a chance to speak. 'Hector also said that he could guarantee that Lord MacDonald would sentence you to four years – you'd be out in two; it's the deal of the century.'

Kailash stood up. The chair fell loudly on the floor.

'The deal of the century?'

She spat it right back at me.

Turning her back to me, I thought she was going to leave. Instead she pulled her white silk trousers down, just enough to show me a well-toned brown buttock. On the pert muscle was a keloid scar.

'When you can tell me what that is,' she screamed, jabbing her finger into it, 'then we'll talk. You've got a lot to learn, Brodie.'

Looking at the scar made me feel faint. It was still so vivid, so raw. Time hadn't made the wound heal in any way that could make what I was looking at acceptable. Kailash had been branded, and my sympathy for her was only reinforced by the fact that she was being so emotional for the first time in front of me. But, like my client, I had a professional duty – and being horrified or empathetic didn't come into it.

'I've seen one before. Not as distinct but I haven't been able to get much information on it.'

Something in my voice made her relent. Softly her zip screeched as she refastened her trousers, and sat down. In my mind's eye all I could see was the scar.

'It's a brand. Like a cattle brand. The symbol was constructed out of very fine metal and then it was heated to 1400 degrees Fahrenheit. Branding is very rare – in New York it seems that everyone has a tattoo and yet there won't be many people who have a brand. For those that do it's an art form – mine was not.'

Standing up to talk, it seemed to me that the symbol was still burning Kailash. Her voice was distant, unaffected by emotion.

'The mark is caused by a third degree burn – hence very few people willingly brand themselves.'

'When was yours done?' I probed.

'I was seven – and it didn't heal well, that's why the brand is raised on me.'

'What does the symbol mean? I take it that's important?' I asked.

'I'm surprised you didn't work it out,' Kailash replied.

'The one I saw was not as . . .' I fought for the correct word, 'distinct as yours.'

'Because it was a lot older,' she answered, taking a deep breath like a swimmer going under water.

I kept quiet, forcing her to continue speaking, but she didn't – she got up and dropped her trousers again; too fascinated to be embarrassed I examined the keloid scar.

'It's a pentacle. A Masonic, and Templar mark. Sir Robert Moray – the first known Mason – used it when he signed the minutes of the Edinburgh lodge in 1641. He called it his Mason's mark.' If I was expecting her to be impressed by my knowledge, then I was sadly mistaken.

Kailash shook her head.

'Look again,' she hissed. Turning round, she caught my eye. 'You're always jumping to conclusions – you're too impatient, Brodie.' I'd heard that criticism before, but I still couldn't believe that patience is a virtue.

Placing my thumb and forefinger on her warm soft skin, I stretched the scar, irrationally afraid that I was hurting her. Closer examination revealed the error of my previous discourse.

'It's reversed! The pentacle is upside down!' I was excited by this discovery.

'And . . . ?' Kailash moved her hands in circles in the air, signing for me to continue.

'And a reversed pentacle is the sign of Baphomet – the goat-headed god.'

'More,' she said simply.

'The Templars were accused by the Inquisition of worshipping Baphomet and . . .' I pre-empted her next prompting, trying to buy some time; there was something else that was niggling me, and her too, I thought.

'Baphomet is an old French word the origin of which simply means Mohammed.'

'Interesting, Brodie, but not relevant – think of where you saw the sign last. And what manner of man it was on.'

'Well, obviously it was Lord Arbuthnot – and he was a legal man.' I shrugged my shoulders.

'No!!' Kailash's scream ripped through the air. It was as if a lightning bolt had struck my subconscious, jolting it into action.

'Eliphas Levi and Aleister Crowley claimed it had an esoteric significance. If one point was upwards it represented good and if one point was downwards then it was evil.

'Then if Alistair MacGregor chose that symbol – and opted to have it burned into his flesh at 1400 degrees – what type of man do you think he was?' Kailash was frustrated with me, but I was reluctant to give her the answer she wanted.

'For God's sake, Brodie, look beyond the uniform the man wore. Think of what you have discovered about him since his death.'

'His drug damaged heart; your accusations of him cottaging in the East End . . .'

'You're not asking the right questions, Brodie. Think, think. Just ask the questions that your intuition tells you to ask.'

That was the heart of the problem for me, for any lawyer. You don't go to university to learn the law; you go to have your mind trained. All my education had instilled in me never to ask questions that I did not know the answer to; such preparation disconnects your heart, that's why lawyers have spawned a million jokes in every language. *What's the difference between a lawyer and a vampire? A vampire only sucks blood at night.*

Sitting there in that prison room, listening to Kailash's erratic breathing, I knew my life was hanging in the balance. It seemed a ridiculous directive. What did I need to know to save myself, never mind Kailash?

It was after all very simple.

As soon as I opened my mind, it was staring me in the face – it had probably been there all along.

'God, Kailash – I've been trying to find out what's going on but you know all the answers. You always know them, always have known them but have held back.

'Kailash – you're the missing girl, aren't you?'

FORTY-THREE

My words were, in truth, a statement of fact which I had finally recognised, but yet again Kailash evaded me.

'Thank you for the compliment, Brodie – but surely I'm too old to be classified as a girl?' With that, she smiled her set smile, her public smile, and continued to hide from me.

'Look, you can play all the games you want to – maybe you get some weird kick out of all of this – but don't take me down with you. Don't do it, Kailash.'

I got up to walk, to stride across that tiny room. I needed to pace. Kailash remained silent. I tried to wait her out; it was just too damned hard and she was too good at it.

'You're the key to all of this – Moses, the girls. How does the abandoned baby fit into it all?'

Gripping the table, her knuckles went white. Was the show over, or had it just begun?

'That's where you're wrong, Brodie McLennan. I'm not the key – that baby is.'

'Please tell me. I'm getting lost in all this.' I was ready to beg. Kailash's eyes flicked over me. Sensing my distress, she laid a hand on my curls and smoothed them. Was it back to the professional Ms Coutts, always there to do whatever the punters needed? Was she working me now?

'Brodie, Brodie, Brodie – do I need to spell it out to you? There were always girls – there were always pregnant girls. And when you get pregnant girls, you get babies. Not as often as you should – but sometimes, someone slips through the net.'

'Stop talking in riddles, Kailash. Did you? Did you slip through the net?'

'In a way, yes. There was a baby once, a baby who was mine,' she said flatly.

'Who was the father?' I asked – but inside I already knew the answer.

'You know who the father was. You know who the father was to all of those babies of all of those girls – me included.'

She was going to make me say it, and then she was as good as saying she was guilty of murder. With me roped into withholding evidence and everything that went with it.

'OK – it was Lord Arbuthnot.'

'No,' she replied.

My breathing stopped.

I was completely lost.

'No,' she said again. 'It wasn't "Lord Arbuthnot" – it was just plain old Alistair MacGregor.'

'But you said he'd never been a client,' I shouted at her. More lies, was that all she was capable of?

'For Christ's sake, I was thirteen when my baby was born – do you really think the devil pays for his privileges? I was Alistair MacGregor's slave and I was marked by his brand. The brand you have just seen, the brand you have just touched.'

So again I had asked the wrong question. I might have got to this point a lot quicker if I had asked if she had ever had sex with Alistair MacGregor. But then again, she would have denied that. The only thing she would admit to was that Alistair MacGregor had sex with her.

'Why did you throw the baby into the sea?' I asked, although I think I could understand why a thirteen-year-old who had been repeatedly raped and brutalised would throw away the spawn of such an encounter.

'I did no such thing,' she stated and the way she said it made a chill run down my spine. Both her hands were placed on the table, like a feral cat she was facing me down, furious that I could suggest she had taken such a step.

'He did it, or his people did – they threw the baby into the water to get rid of the evidence.'

'There must have been plenty of other evidence to convict him?'

She grunted at me. 'You'd think so – groups of children complaining over thirty years. No one listened – he wasn't acting alone, you know. There was a ring of high-powered men with influence. High-powered people with influence.

'I was left for dead after I had my baby. I was pumped full of heroin. It was their intention to dump me somewhere, probably in a bag like the other girls.'

'Do you think they were pregnant too?'

She nodded. 'There is absolutely no doubt in my mind. I'll bet amongst the body parts that were recovered – I bet they never found any wombs.'

I would have to ask Patch; he had not been forthcoming with information, but I wasn't going to be fobbed off now.

'You can't win against these people, Brodie. They've got the law on their side. But I will not plead – Alistair MacGregor is not being deified as a result of my actions.'

'There is one way that we can verify what you're saying, Kailash.'

I reached over and pulled a strand of hair from her head.

'DNA testing. If you were raped by him, if you did have a baby by him, and if that baby was thrown into the sea… these things can be proven. We'll test the baby's DNA and Alistair MacGregor's – it will confirm that he is the father.'

'You'll do DNA testing on a baby that has been buried for years, Brodie. Dead and buried a long time.'

'I know that and I know that this might be distressing for you – the baby will have to be exhumed for us to get a DNA sample.'

Shrugging her shoulders she sighed: 'Is that what you really think will solve all of this? You're going to waste time getting an order to get an exhumation? You'd never get it anyway. What are you going to say? That you've got a hunch? That you've got a notion to dig up the bones of a long-dead child to satisfy your curiosity?'

I had to think on my feet. 'I know that, I know we'd never get it – that's why we can't go through official lines.'

She caught my drift quicker than I would have liked.

'You'd be robbing a grave, Brodie – if you were caught. You would be stealing a baby's bones. Is that how far you're willing to go to get to the bottom of this? That baby – the key to all of it: but at what cost?'

Her voice trailed off.

Thoughts of Burke and Hare came to me; they got away with it for some time before detection. But they did it under cover of darkness, we still had long light nights, and I would be visible if I attempted this.

'If I was caught, I'd be arrested – my life as I know it would be over. But I'd still be alive.'

There was nothing else for us to say to each other. We both knew the implications of what I was suggesting and we knew that I would carry the burden of it.

I left Cornton Vale knowing that the night ahead would change my life – one way or the other.

FORTY-FOUR

I drove from Cornton Vale to Edinburgh, yawning all the way. I had become obsessed with sleep – I wanted the trial over for many reasons, the whole business over, but none so much as the fact that I just wanted to lie down and rest. Preferably somewhere without phones always ringing in the middle of the night.

When I got back to the flat, it was clear that the usual suspects were still there. Fair enough for Fishy – he lived there after all – but did the others not have homes to go to? I swear when this thing is over, I thought to myself, I'll move away and give none of those buggers my address. It was only after such a glib and normal thought had passed through my mind that I remembered exactly what I had planned for myself in the much nearer future. Christ, if I managed to successfully grave-rob, the whole shower could move into my room in celebration if they wanted to.

As soon as I walked in, Fishy was on me.

'I know where you were,' he said accusingly.

I stared at him – which part did he know? Joe's big gob came to the rescue.

'Aye – PC Fulton phoned. Was it really necessary to have Moses arrested?' Joe pushed Fishy out of the way so that he could glare at me.

'We've got too much to do to get caught up in personalities,' I snapped back at him. I was stripping out of my bike jacket as I walked into the kitchen. Patch and Jack looked at me reproachfully.

As I took my seat Jack handed me a cup of steaming espresso perfectly made with just a touch of golden froth on top. At least he hadn't started on at me – yet.

Patch had photographs from Lord Arbuthnot's post-mortem on the table, the series of pictures that detailed his back and buttocks. I pointed to the inverted pentagram.

'Can you just go over this again, please?' I asked. I needed to collect my thoughts again and assimilate all I had learned since my visit to Kailash. The hour-long trip back from Stirling was a blur of sleepiness; I hadn't done much thinking or analysing – or even plotting.

'I've explained to the boys the significance of the mark, and we've been over it before,' he said, putting another picture up on the makeshift board inside his briefcase.

'But we need to consider it in conjunction with this. Laura Liddell – note the mark on her right buttock . . . and here,' he placed another image up for us to look at.

'A section of the second body found in 1985. The same mark visible.'

'Now, note the marks on the deceased's back.'

He pointed to Lord Arbuthnot's image.

'These marks are old – they have been made by cigarette burns. Initially they concerned me because most likely they came from the deceased indulging in a sexual game known as smoking where he in effect becomes a human ashtray.'

'And anyone who would allow himself to be used as an ashtray would not be dominant,' I said, following Patch's line of thought.

'Precisely.' Patch looked around the table.

'What kind of nutcase does these things?' Joe shivered involuntarily. 'I can understand people giving – and getting – a good kicking; but this kind of pervy stuff? Christ, I've a lot to learn.' I remembered the last time I had heard that phrase – when Kailash had spat it out at me in Cornton Vale.

'More people do this than you would imagine,' I said.

'Well, the fact that anyone does it is more than I can fucking imagine,' answered Joe.

'Anyway,' said Patch, 'I've been researching this stuff and there are some people known as switches – they change from submissive to dominant depending on who they are with.'

'Arbuthnot was a paedophile. So with helpless kids he was a dominant, sadistic torturer, but when it came to himself, he was the victim?' I said.

'No, that wasn't what I meant,' Patch said huffily. 'Don't twist my words, Brodie. Dependant on who his companions were – what they encouraged him to do – that would decide which role he took.'

We were back to a killing team. One of the only explanations that had ever made sense for the attacks on me starting after Lord Arbuthnot's death.

As I looked round the bunch of misfits in my kitchen, I wondered how much more of this they could take – we were all in way too deep. Could I push them deeper still?

FORTY-FIVE

'How the hell did I let you bully me into this?' Joe gasped as he climbed the high wall surrounding Seafield Cemetery.

'Christ, this must be twenty-five feet – and you don't see many climbers that weigh as much as me.' Sweat rolled down his face as he attempted to get a foothold on the wall. It was difficult, as it was intended as a deterrent to keep grave-robbers like us out.

Jack Deans sat in his car listening to the police radio – our early warning system so that he could alert us if we were likely to be receiving police attention. The thud as Joe fell off the wall into the graveyard made me certain that someone would notice something soon to announce our presence.

'I don't want to do this, Brodie – it's sick. Have you thought it through? If you need to do a DNA test on this poor bairn's bones, what do you hope to find? That Kailash is the mother or isn't she? That Arbuthnot is the father or isn't? I don't get what you want, Brodie. I just don't get it.'

Joe was expressing my own thoughts, but as I looked around the tombstones, I knew I didn't want to join them. I'd take confusion and illegality over that option any day.

'Piss off then, and I'll do it myself,' I said, secure in the knowledge that he would stick to me like glue.

I ran in front, crouching down so low that my thighs screamed and my lungs were fit to burst. Naturally, I arrived at the grave first. The six-foot marble angel stared down at me from her plinth. As I moved her eyes followed. The ground was wet and clawing. I started to dig with my bare hands straight away, the black earth sticking to my fingers, creeping under my nails. It felt cold and damp beneath my touch, chilling my heart. I knew the words on the gravestone off by heart the dark made no difference – they were burned into my vision:

> *Remember man that thou art dust*
> *and into dust thou shalt return.*

The priest put ashes on my forehead and uttered those words on Ash Wednesdays.

'Well, I don't want to be dust yet,' I muttered at the angel.

'Will you stop tickling that ground?' Joe was beside me as I continued to try to get through the earth. 'Move so that I can get on.'

I had merely scratched the surface, but I didn't see how Joe could do much more. He might have muscles, but he hadn't brought any tools.

'Christ, Joe,' I whispered as loudly as I could. 'Some help you are – where's the shovel?'

'Fuck!' he said, a bit louder than I felt comfortable with. 'I'll have to go back and get it. That fucking wall'll do me in one way or another. If I'm not back in... God. How long would it take for me to get arrested, do you think?'

'Piss off, Joe – the sooner you get the shovel and the crowbar, the sooner we can get this over with.'

As soon as I saw the back of him, any streak of bravado I had left me.

It was dark, it was cold, and I was alone in a grave-yard intending to dig up a baby's corpse. Images poured into my head – what would it feel like to pull a tiny white coffin out of the ground, where it had lain for almost three decades? The wood would be rotten, the brass handles tarnished. Would I touch worms? Rats? Would I be sick?

As soon as I let myself think about it, I knew I couldn't do it.

There were steps too far even for me.

And this was one of them.

How could I throw a coffin lid onto the ground? How could I look at a skeleton covered in a tiny white gown and a pink teddy eaten by God knows what? I knew too much from old newspaper reports – that baby was still real to me.

I heard something move, I thought I heard some-thing from the direction of the stone angel above me. My mind was racing – everything seemed alive in this place of death.

I thought I heard the angel scream.

I thought I heard my mother cry.

That baby.

That baby.

That baby.

That was what she had called it.

That baby.

Not 'my' baby.

Not 'my' child.

She was cold, but was she that cold?

The silence I needed to keep didn't matter. The noises I thought I could hear seemed less threatening.

'Joe! Joe!' I shouted as I ran towards the gates and the wall.

I was running as fast as I could. Trying to get away from what I carried, the knowledge that I was bearing, rather than what I had left behind. Joe was clambering over the top just as I reached the entrance to the cemetery. I reached my arms up to his and, vaulting the wall, barely noticed the drop. Jack drove off whilst the passenger door was still open.

My mother's cries rang in my ears – and I was sure I heard the fractured weep of a newborn soul.

They drove me on.

The end was coming.

FORTY-SIX

Soft goose feathers encased in linen cradled my head, the pillow was worth every penny I had spent on it, for it lulled me into a sleep that, at many points, had seemed as if it would never come.

The alarm must have gone off but didn't wake me. The desire to sleep late was too strong even for the threat of imminent death to break.

'Get up you lazy toe-rag – your breakfast's out and the Prof's on his way.' With one tug Joe had pulled the covers from my bed. Curling more tightly into the foetal position I tried to ignore him, until his words permeated my coma-like slumber.

Jumping up and down on one foot I pulled my socks on. My balance had improved by the time I was forcing my second leg into my jeans. The t-shirt from last night lay rumpled on my chair, lazily; I was about to put it on, then I recalled where I had worn it last, and what exactly I had considered doing.

I went the extra step and pulled a fresh one from the drawer. My hair could wait; getting rid of that t-shirt could not. Holding it at arm's length I walked into the kitchen, not stopping until I reached the bin. I threw it in.

Joe had a blue striped butcher apron on, he was frying sausages. Jack and Fishy were already seated round the table looking as if they had been up all night. Starving, I grabbed a piece of hot buttered toast from the pile. Joe slapped my hand.

'Wait till it's ready – have you washed your face this morning?'

Holding on to half a slice of toast, I stared in the large mirror on the wall behind the kitchen table. Mud smeared my face, from temple to chin. Grave mud. Slowly, I looked at my hands fearing confirmation of my thoughts. True enough my fingernails were still black from the baby's burial place.

Standing at the table I threw the toast, aiming for the bin. I missed.

'Clean yourself up – I'll get this,' Joe shouted. I was already on my way to the shower.

Through the streams of cold water running down my head I heard the muffled sound of the doorbell. My fingertips had been scrubbed so hard they bled, and it was difficult for me to dress quickly for my legs were still wet; the jeans got stuck half way up my thighs.

In the hallway I could hear Patch's voice. Pulling my zip up, I ran out to greet him. They were all sitting round the table. Glasgow Joe was turning into Delia Smith before my eyes and Patch gratefully received a steaming mug of coffee, and a bacon sandwich. They were all waiting for me – even Jack and Joe didn't know everything as I had been so overwhelmed on the way back from the cemetery that I hadn't told them all of my thoughts. Frankly, I had been borderline hysterical and I needed to be a sight more together before they would take me seriously.

'I don't believe that Kailash is the mother of the baby found in the sea,' I began.

'Well, what does that matter anyway?' asked Patch. 'We don't need to know how many pregnancies she had, and God knows how many abortions,' I raised my eyes at his religious morality and presumptions, 'but we do need to find out how to keep you safe.'

'That's what I'm trying to tell you,' I sighed, resting my head on my forearm on the table. 'Kailash was pregnant. Lord Arbuthnot was the father – he'd been raping her for years. But Kailash could never have thrown a living child of her bones into the sea; she could never have murdered her own.'

'With all due respect, my dear,' interrupted Patch, 'she seems pretty adept at killing to me.'

'But not her own child, Patch,' I countered. 'Rape victims don't always have terminations. Some want to get good out of evil; to prove that they are different to the bastards who attack them.'

'And that's Kailash?' he asked, eyebrows raised. 'She is repeatedly sexually abused but believes that her baby will be a sign of a happy new life? I think not.'

'Kailash Coutts is a whore, Brodie,' interjected Fishy. 'She only cares about herself. She's ruined enough lives over the years – another one wouldn't make much difference to her tally.'

A heavy weight fell upon my chest and it felt hard to breathe. My chest lifted painfully in short little bursts.

Joe stroked my head as I lay it down further.

'What makes you so sure, darlin'?' he asked.

I felt stupid even as I prepared to say it.

'She kept saying "that baby", never "my baby", never "my" anything. It was as if she was trying to distance herself. And as if she couldn't get too attached to what she was saying. I'd bet my life on it – she isn't the mother of that child.' I shuddered as I said it.

I didn't want to bet my life on anything, but this time I was sure Kailash wasn't playing me. This time I felt I had seen behind the mask. Why wouldn't they believe me?

I looked around at the table of men – I had my answer really. I wasn't a mother, but I knew where the gap lay – they couldn't imagine it, couldn't contemplate something so primal as the need to protect your own.

'I saw the mark, Joe!' I shouted, clutching at anything. 'The brand links Kailash, Lord Arbuthnot, and Laura Liddell.' I was biting back the tears. I hadn't cried since my mother died and I didn't want to break that record here in front of a room of men.

'I need to see Kailash. I'm going up to Cornton Vale to tell her – I don't have time to wait until court.'

I flew out of the flat before Joe or Jack could stop me; I had already driven hundreds of miles because of Kailash; normally it was a joy, but today the heavens opened and the rain flooded the motorway to Stirling. Driving was treacherous and the wheels were aquaplaning as they crossed the puddles; more than once I feared that I had lost control.

Soaked to the skin, and in no mood to joke, I entered Cornton Vale prison.

'Have you nothing better to do than come here two days running – or are you looking for a bed here?'

I growled at the attempts at familiarity from the probationary officer. In silence she showed me to the consulting rooms. We went through the same dreary process of getting Kailash from her cell.

Standing with my back to the door, I heard her come in.

'That baby's not yours, is it?'

'What?' she asked, unused to being thrown straight into a conversation she had not controlled.

'I don't know who that baby did belong to – but I know it's not yours, maybe not even Lord Arbuthnot's for all I know.'

I wasn't prepared for the sight of Kailash's tears or for her whimpering.

'He told me . . . he told me that was my baby.'

'Who told you?' I asked

'Lord MacGregor.' She could see the confusion in my eyes.

'His father? Alistair's father?'

She kept shaking her head in disbelief.

'He saved me – he broke into the house after I'd given birth, he took me to Newcastle and got me medical attention.'

'How noble of him – with you out of the way there

was no evidence of rape or attempted murder against his son,' I sneered.

'Ah, Brodie – we're not so different, are we? Exactly what I thought. I may only have been thirteen, but I knew men's lies, men's ways. How could I trust the man who had fathered… *that*? He got me away so far, but it was me who saved myself. I broke out of the safe house, I didn't really believe such a thing existed. I … liberated some of the old man's cash before I left and got a friendly lorry driver to smuggle me on to a ferry to Amsterdam. So kind of him – who could blame him for not bothering to ask why a thirteen-year-old child with blood caked all over her was running away? Who could blame him for ignoring her tears and pain when he got his payment for his altruism? Who could blame yet another man taking what he thought was rightfully his?

'Lord MacGregor had promised me he'd search for my baby – some months later he sent me the newspaper cutting. I never knew how he found out where I was – but I was grateful that he hadn't arrived in person. By that time, I had learned a few things. Not enough – but it got me by. I got Malcolm to send one of those cuttings to you so you'd understand.'

'Malcolm? Well, Malcolm didn't put his name on it so I assumed it came from the killer.'

'Yes – well – that's Malcolm; sometimes he's a bit too much cloak and dagger for his own good.

'So you've no idea who the baby in the grave belongs to?' she asked.

'No – but I've a good idea who does,' I answered her. 'Lord MacGregor.'

'Brodie, he can confirm all of this. I'm not lying to you. He found me close to death in his son's house in Heriot Row. The midwife who tended me? She might still be alive – she knows I'd just given birth.'

'That's always supposing that Lord MacGregor will speak, Kailash. Blood is thicker than water.'

'Brodie – this falls to you. You have to make him tell the truth. Some poor mother doesn't know where her long-dead baby rests.'

Kailash's last phrase rang in my ears as I drove back to Edinburgh. It seemed out of character for her to be so concerned about anyone, much less someone who was anonymous, but I was discovering that Kailash Coutts wasn't quite the closed book I hade initially imagined her to be.

I had no idea where Lord MacGregor was even residing, but I knew a man who would.

FORTY-SEVEN

Jack insisted on driving, and Joe insisted on tagging along. I pointed out it was impossible to park in Ramsay Gardens. Naturally, it was one of the most exclusive addresses in Edinburgh, situated right next to Edinburgh Castle. It was designed in 1892 as a reaction to the New Town of Edinburgh. In stark contrast to the regimented lines and geometrical symmetry of the new area, the old was a whimsical – but often murderous – concoction of closes and ramshackle buildings. The turrets and fairytale gables of Ramsay Gardens mimic the architecture of the Old Town, originally designed as a group of tall apartments for intellectuals. I loved it.

Tourists were still swarming around Castle Hill. I refused to drive in circles to see if we could get one of the elusive parking spaces.

'Drop me here, Joe – come and get me when you've parked.'

I jumped out of the car in Ramsay Lane, a steep hill next to the Assembly Hall; it overlooks Princes Street, and on a clear day you can see right across to Fife. The flowers were out in full bloom in the courtyard; it was impossible not to be impressed. I wondered where the old man parked his Morgan roadster.

I ran up the steps, not bothering to hold onto the black iron hand rail. The faster I moved the easier it would be. I was torn between praying he would be in, and hoping he wasn't. A shiny ebony black door greeted me. The thud of the heavy and recently polished brass knocker reverberated round the hall. My heart which had jumped six inches, was hammering in my throat; wiping my clammy hands on my jeans I readied myself.

Slowly the door swung open as if it was a great weight. A nose peered round its edge, I knew that it did not belong to Lord MacGregor – it was too white and unwrinkled. One eye stared at me unblinking, black painted nails dug into the door.

Moses Tierney had moved up in the world.

Pushing my foot against the door I forced it open, although in truth, Moses was not excluding me. In fact they had been waiting on my arrival.

'What are you doing here?' I asked grumpily.

'Come in – come in – don't stand at the door.' Lord MacGregor was moving down the hall towards me. 'Moses phoned me from the police station – they were happy to release him into my custody.'

'I am very, very pissed off with you,' Moses hissed into my ear.

'That makes two of us,' I said. Poking him in the chest to move him out of the way, I felt his bones beneath my finger. Flashes of other bones came into my mind and I pushed them away. Moses was behind me as I followed Lord MacGregor into the drawing room; on edge, I sensed every move he made.

'It's magnificent,' I said, looking at the scene from his window, a living million-pound postcard. To the left stood the castle, sweeping down to the old Nor' Loch which had been drained to form Princes Street gardens.

Lord MacGregor stood in front of the window, blocking my view down to Princes Street and the Forth. I could hear the sound of the fire crackling in the grate. I presumed his age meant he suffered from the cold, for the room was stiflingly hot.

Lord MacGregor stood staring at me, drinking in every detail as if he had never seen me before. Walking towards me he reached out and touched my hair, gently, enjoying the springiness of my curls.

I stepped back out of his reach. 'What the . . . ?'

'I'm sorry,' he muttered, tears filled his rheumy old eyes. 'I'm sorry, Brodie. So sorry for so many things, but where do I begin?' It was towards Moses he looked.

'Oh, for Christ's sake, tell her the truth. Ever thought of that? There are too many lies in your bloody family.' Moses spat the words out.

Lord MacGregor slumped down in a chair.

'But where do I begin?' he asked the boy again.

Moses fumbled about in a drinks cabinet; the Edinburgh Crystal glasses sparkled like diamonds as he poured a twenty-five-year old Laphroaig into a glass, and handed it to Lord MacGregor.

'Get me one of those,' I nodded at the glass in Lord

MacGregor's trembling hand. Wordlessly, Moses did as I had asked.

I walked up and down, pacing. The heels of my bike boots clattered. I winced in case I was marking the ancient dark oak flooring, but Lord MacGregor seemed blasé, he was too wrapped up in his own thoughts.

Moses handed him a locked walnut marquetry box. Lord MacGregor pulled out the gold chain he wore beneath his shirt. It lay accusingly on his chest, weighed down by a key.

'I suppose you've come about my son?' His voice cracked with unshed tears.

'I'm surprised you're still willing to acknowledge ownership of that bastard after hearing what he's been getting away with for years,' I answered.

'I've been expecting you,' he continued, as if my words hadn't even registered.

'Have you now? Well, I'm sick as fuck of everyone expecting me to find out things – why the hell didn't you all just tell me all you knew in the first place?'

'Don't swear here – he doesn't like it.' Moses nodded in Lord MacGregor's direction, leaving me to wonder just how close their relationship was given that the boy seemed to know every nuance of the old man's personality.

'To answer your question – my dear, when you've covered up the truth for years . . . it can be, shall we say, difficult to bring it out into the cold light of day.'

'Cover up the truth? Lie. You mean lie – when you've lied for years,' I said.

'I suppose I mean both,' he said, as his arthritic

fingers fumbled with the key in the lock. Exasperated, he threw the chain, and key down; humbly Moses kneeled at his feet, and picked it up. With the skill of the artful dodger, Moses opened the box in a trice. Contemplatively his fingers were stroking his upper lip, as he stared into the box, which my prying eyes could see was filled with old papers.

'It's not going to get any easier – and she's not going away in a hurry,' Moses said as he squeezed Lord MacGregor's bony old knee encouragingly.

'He's right – I'm here for answers,' I said as he spurred into action, rifling through the documents. His tongue poked through his thin lips as he concentrated. I didn't want to say a word in case I put him off. This was what I had come for, this is what I hoped for: Kailash's travel documents or a doctor's report on her condition. He must have had something on his son in that box, something I could use to free Kailash and prove her story.

'Brodie, my dear, you need to be sitting down,' he said, pausing with two documents in his hand.

'I'll stand, thanks, and Moses . . .' I said, brandishing my empty glass at him, 'I'll take another one of these if you're offering.'

'I'm not. You'll need a clear head for this,' he replied.

The old man handed me two old affidavits. I decided to read them at random. And I decided to sit down after all.

At Edinburgh on 30 November 1976
My full name is Jane Montgomery McIntyre

403

and I reside at 23 Bellevue Road Edinburgh.
I hereby confirm that on 29 September 1976
I was present in Heriot Row after having
been instructed by Mr Alistair MacGregor to
attend a home confinement. The mother was
one Kailash Coutts, aged approximately thirteen years. At 9.04a.m. she was delivered of a
healthy baby girl weighing 5lbs and 8oz.
I do not know what happened to the mother.
I left with the baby and arranged a private
  adoption.
All of this is the truth as I shall answer to God.

I looked at the testing clause.

The affidavit was signed in the offices of Lothian
and St Clair before two witnesses. I didn't recognise
the first signature – Gregor MacGregor – but that of
the second, Roderick Buchanan, felt like it was scalding
my eyes.

FORTY-EIGHT

Lord MacGregor looked at me expectantly.

I remained calm.

'It says nothing about doping her with heroin. It doesn't take the court much further. It doesn't really help.'

The old man and Moses looked at each other.

'Get real, Brodie – of course this McIntyre woman wouldn't confess the full extent of what she had actually done. It's an affidavit not a fucking self-signed death warrant.' Moses was looking at me as if I was an imbecile.

'I see you're feeling more like yourself again,' I snapped at him.

'The value of that affidavit can only be seen when read in conjunction with the second one.' Lord MacGregor was more deferential; with eyes cast downwards he handed me the second document.

'Thank you,' I muttered, already busily reading ahead, anxious to prove that these papers were of no real import.

At Edinburgh on 2 December 1976
I, Mary McLennan, residing at 42g King
    William Court, do hereby solemnly swear
    that on 4 October I was delivered of a baby
    girl.

That's right, I thought, that's my birthday. Hardly
surprising that my own mother should remember when
her only child had been born. But why had she needed
to sign an affidavit to that effect? And why did Lord
MacGregor have it in his possession?

The baby was delivered at home.
In attendance was Nurse Jane McIntyre.

My heart ran cold.

My baby girl was 4lbs in weight. Prior to her
    delivery I was told that she had Porters
    Syndrome, which meant that her internal
    organs were missing or damaged, she was
    not expected to live.
Nurse McIntyre found out about my sadness,
    and told me that she was attending a home
    confinement. The patient was a young girl
    from a wealthy family who was not keeping
    her baby. Nurse McIntyre had been asked to
    place the baby for a private adoption to save
    the family from scandal.
I gave her my life savings of £2000 to cover her
    expenses. Nurse McIntyre advised that it

would be best if I registered the baby as my own child.

I took possession of Brodie on 7 October. Nurse McIntyre took my own sweet child to get the proper hospital treatment. I subsequently learned from Lord MacGregor that she threw my baby into the Forth.

Lord MacGregor has asked me to continue to care for his beloved grandchild, as it is the only way he can see to keep her safe.

As God is my witness I promise to love her and care for her more than any mother to make up for the great sin I have committed.

It was signed and witnessed as before.

Tears streamed down my face as Lord MacGregor held my hand.

'You're the missing girl, Brodie.' Moses had his hand on my back, patting it as if anything in this moment could bring me comfort. 'The truth's out now and that should serve as some sort of comfort to you.'

I turned on him, screaming.

'Comfort? And where exactly do you think the fucking comfort lies, Moses? That Mary McLennan wasn't my mother? That a thirteen-year-old Kailash Coutts is? Or that my father was this old bastard's perverted son? What sort of monster am I with those parents? And when does the comforting begin?' I cried, because I didn't know what else to do.

Lord MacGregor had his eyes averted from me. He

was holding a letter and an envelope. He handed me the first one, which was dated January 1986.

Dear Lord MacGregor,

I am writing to you to make amends. I have lung cancer and I don't expect to see the summer.

As you know, your son employed me as a midwife to attend at a delivery ten years ago.

He told me that the girl was to deliver a baby that he and his wife intended to adopt. I did not know how young the girl was when I took the job.

My instructions were to keep the house clean, deliver the baby and take it to a safe place to check it out; if the baby was healthy then your son wanted it, if not then I was to dispose of it. He left me a syringe of morphine to sedate the girl.

I didn't like your son and I liked his wife even less. That is why I gave the baby to Mary McLennan. Her baby was going to die anyway – I was just quickening its end.

I had to get this off my chest before I die – I hope I may be forgiven by those greater than yourself.

Yours truly
Jane McIntyre. SRN

'Does that mean Mary's baby was alive? McIntyre drowned it?' I asked. Somehow I had always imagined that the baby girl washed up on the shore was still-born. I gave my empty glass to Moses, and asked for a refill – I wouldn't take 'no' for an answer this time.

I was getting no answers from Lord MacGregor – for he had more to show me. He handed me an envelope addressed to me in my mother's hand. I tore it open.

Dear Brodie –

If you are reading this then I am dead, and I never found the nerve to tell you the truth about your birth. I would have liked to have found the courage to have introduced you to your grandfather, but in fairness to myself we were worried about how your father or his wife would react.

You were meant for a better life than the one I could give you, but your grandfather decided that it was best if I brought you up in my ways. I am very proud that you have achieved so much, my only wish is that I could have given you more.

Your grandfather, Lord MacGregor, wanted to give me an annual allowance for your care, but I said that would make me feel like your nanny not your mother, and so I refused.

I hope you can forgive me. I made a vow once to love you, I kept it.

I could not love you more if I had given birth to you myself.

Lots of love always – Mum

FORTY-NINE

Four eyes stared at me expectantly, but what was there to say?

I just sat there holding the letters; accidentally dropping the one from Nurse McIntyre, it slithered across the floor stopping at Lord MacGregor's toes. He picked it up, and placed it back in the box.

Was that it? Was everything to be put back in the box again? I wished that it could.

Wished that the box had never been opened.

That Kailash had never killed Lord Arbuthnot; or more accurately that my mother had never killed my father.

Even at a moment like this, I realised that my new life, my new identity, sounded like something from a Jerry Springer show.

'Does she know? Does Kailash know?'

I stared straight into Lord MacGregor's eyes. He couldn't answer me as he was so choked with tears. I suspect he believed I might fall into his arms and caress him, the homecoming grandchild. It was the furthest thing from my mind. He finally nodded and Moses spoke.

'Of course she knows – why do you think she asked for you? Why do you think she bought you those new clothes? Why did she send Malcolm to fix you up?'

'That's a good question, Moses – how did she know? How did she know I'd been hurt?'

'Because she's been paying me and the Dark Angels to keep an eye on you for the past few years.'

'I've seen you around, at court, in the streets near my offices, but always assumed that was just because you were pretty good clients for my world. I never thought you were there for me – it never seemed like that at all.'

'We're only spotted when we want to be.'

'When did she find out?' I couldn't help it – I wanted to know why she hadn't got in touch after my mother died. My mother. That was still Mary McLennan to me.

'Roddie Buchanan knew – he told her and he threatened to ruin you. That's why she got in first. Then Roddie phoned me to apologise – I'd sworn him to secrecy for your sake. He begged me to call her off – I'm one of the few people Kailash listens to.'

Lord MacGregor finished speaking and was now sipping on his whisky, staring at my features as if mesmerised.

'I pointed out to Kailash that the publicity could bankrupt you – she then agreed to sign an affidavit, but she didn't want to completely exonerate him because she knows that it is always important to be able to turn the thumbscrews.'

'Why did she kill Alistair MacGregor now? I mean he last abused her twenty-eight years ago? Why did she wait until now?'

'Can't you guess?' sneered Moses. I stared at him blankly.

'The fucking photograph, Brodie. She showed you the picture he sent her the week before we killed him,' Moses mocked.

It was very hard to swallow, my tongue seemed to have swelled to twice its size. Gulping I tried to breathe in.

'We? Who's "we"?' I asked.

Moses nodded, circling me, his wolf eyes flashing demented sparks in my direction.

'Finally the right questions, Brodie. We killed him to keep you safe – all of us: Kailash, me, the Dark Angels. We had to live with what he had done to us – but you, you had to be protected. Kailash's little girl had to be protected at all costs.'

'I didn't ask you to,' I said sulkily.

'No, you didn't – but do you think you could have survived? Even if he hadn't killed you – could you have lived with the memories that we have to live with?' Moses was persistent with his questioning.

I took one look at him and remembered the time I had spent in his lair, forcing him to relive his past.

'No,' I answered and it was the truth.

Lord MacGregor interrupted. 'I'm too old, Brodie – but you are my kin. Like it or not. We MacGregors don't renege on our responsibilities. You have been helped by a lot of people. However, there is still a lot to do – and it's time for you to take the lead.'

'OK, I admit it, I owe them my life.' I was slurring, the whisky and tiredness taking effect.

'Then you agree – it is your duty to save Kailash. I'll set up the necessary meeting.'

'But I've – she's got court tomorrow,' I muttered.

'Haven't you learned yet, lass? The only way to save her is blackmail – an old and honourable family tradition.'

He was sombre.

'As I said, I'll set up the meeting – the only condition is that you will have to come alone.'

'Of course I'll go alone.'

I did not want the truth of my parentage to leave those four walls. The doorbell rang. In the time Jack Deans had parked his car, my life had changed forever.

I was left with one question and the knowledge that it could never be answered:

How can you clean your own blood?

FIFTY

'Graves? You shook my bones for four hours in that bloody draughty old car of yours for this?'

The tight wind had bitten into me, shortening my temper. Driving over nauseatingly winding Highland roads had filled me full of loathing for my driver. My pleas to Lord MacGregor that he put the roof on his Morgan had been summarily dismissed. At least now I had some idea of what it would be like to travel in a Spitfire. Every other car on the road was a foe, which had to be beaten. It crossed my mind that the car was fuelled by testosterone and adrenalin. I was short on both.

'Don't be impatient, Brodie, my girl – open your eyes; drink in the scenery.'

'I've seen scenery before. Why did we have to meet them here? Wouldn't it have been more appropriate to have met at Parliament House or the Old College?'

Like nails on a blackboard the whingeing tone in my voice was even irritating me. But I had a point. The hamlet of Kilmartin is situated in the Highlands on the west coast of Scotland. It is remote and tiresome to get to. And I still didn't know why we had to have this meeting here – or who indeed I was meant to be blackmailing.

'It wasn't always like this,' said Lord MacGregor. 'Once it was an important centre, easily accessible by sea. Their lordships thought it would be more appropriate and safer for the meeting to take place here. I want you to meet them – they can help you. They wanted to meet here – this place is important to them. Now I'm going off to keep watch for them – you think about what you're going to say.'

Wearily he walked off to stand guard at the steps that led into the graveyard, leaving me to think of mysterious lordships and even more mysterious things to say to them. I felt as if I was observing him through semi-precious stones. As the sun set behind the hills, the sky was aglow with soft tones of red and orange.

This time of the evening is known as the gloaming, it is a period that fosters intimacy as the world quietens, ready for sleep. Left alone, I wandered through rank after strictly regimented rank of weather-beaten flat stones. Some were so old that they had sunk deeply into the ground, and grass was growing over them. Others were clearly defined, set amongst more modern tombs and family burial plots.

An owl hooted, it was the only sound apart from my breath, and heartbeat. Running my fingers over a seventeenth-century mottled stone, feeling the roughness of the lichen and velvety moss, I noticed that it was in better condition than some of the earlier ones.

Jamie Sinclair lay beneath the sod; his memorial proclaimed to the world that he had been a Freemason. It showed Masonic tools, a skull and crossbones.

Edgily, Lord MacGregor paced, waiting for his cohort. The older flat stones called to me, some of them worn smooth by time. Others were anonymous, apart from the engraving of the deceased's sword. This intrigued me, for I knew that in the Middle Ages, lineage and clan allegiance was even more important in death than in life, and I could not conceive why eighty fighting men would choose to be buried anonymously.

These knights were obviously wealthy because swords were very expensive in the Middle Ages. In addition to this these weapons were not the traditional ones used in Scotland at that time. The Scots favoured the claymore, which was longer, heavier, and more unwieldy than the swords shown on these stones.

Seeking clarification of this, I looked for my newly-found grandfather but he had gone, probably to the pub across the road to phone his associates as there was no mobile signal in this area. Every cell in my body seemed to ache, as I suddenly realised I was completely alone.

The hills around Kilmartin are wild and primeval; desperate to shake off this feeling of foreboding I began in earnest to examine the graves. Who were the fighting men buried here? The land surrounding Kilmartin belonged to the Campbell clan; Sir Neil Campbell had been the brother-in-law of Robert the Bruce, but the majority of the land belonged to the MacDonalds.

Maybe that explained the way I was feeling. The

MacDonalds and the Campbells have hated each other for centuries. In some parts of the Highlands, which are dominated by MacDonalds, there are signs up in public places, which state 'No Campbells Allowed' much like one would ban a dog.

The rocks and soil in Scotland give off a strange energy, as if they reflect the memories of the past. To understand this you only have to drive through Glencoe, known as the 'Weeping Glen'. The crags themselves still resound with MacDonald tears after they were massacred as they slept by the Campbells.

There was still no sign of my grandfather; I had to trust him, he must have had his reasons for arranging the meeting here, presumably one that had something to do with those ancient fighting men and one that went beyond the need for secrecy.

Sitting on a tombstone, I racked my mind going over history lessons given in stuffy classrooms at school. Staring without blinking at the shape of the sword I did not notice the cold of the grave seeping through my jeans.

The point of the knife on my jugular pricked my skin, causing a tiny red bubble of blood to flow freely to the surface. I almost sensed the blade rise and fall as my blood pumped quickly round my body. An unknown assailant yanked my head back so that I was unable to see their face. A handful of my hair lay on the ground around my feet, like a piece of sheep's wool caught on barbed wire.

Forcing my face down, the stone grazed my cheek. The rawness of the wound hurt as the tiny pieces of grit and lichen were rubbed in.

'Are you giving into fate? Or do you want to fight? In other words – are you a lamb like your mother or a lion like your father?'

From behind me, a woman spoke, her cultured tones ringing throughout the burial place. Squinting my eyes until they hurt, I tried to see round corners. My heart punctured my ribs, making it difficult for me to hear my own thoughts.

The scent of my fear was acrid, and pungent like rancid vinegar, it choked me as it mixed with the fresh night air. Feeling warmth on my thighs I panicked that in my confusion I had wet myself. Struggling to assess the situation, pulling my head round to see, I felt my hair being ripped out, follicle by tiny follicle.

Fleetingly out of the corner of my eye, I saw that the heat, which had not diminished, was coming from a flaming torch. Bizarrely, I was relieved that I had not shamed myself.

Roughly yanked to my feet I was hauled and dragged across the graveyard to a ruin that housed yet more grave-stones. A Hermès silk scarf was tied around my eyes. It smelled of stale Chanel No. 5. Rough hemp rope chafed and burned my wrists as my hands were tied behind a flat stone that had been excavated, and now stood upright against the wall. Just before the blindfold was applied, I saw the engraving on the stone, a cross of equal lengths, useless for torture – the cross of the Templars.

The ruin, which had no roof, was surprisingly warm. The wind carried the smell of the burning wood to me. Although I had not seen it, I sensed that there was a brazier, with a fire burning intensely.

Hands that were male, but soft and unused to manual work, ripped my shirt open. The palms felt clammy and feminine as the knife slit my bra. It popped open and my breasts swung free as the lingerie was cut from my body.

His face was close to mine as he worked; I could smell Rennies and expensive whisky on his breath. A big man, he towered over me, but I did not feel embarrassed standing there half naked in front of him for he had seen me that way before.

'Why are you doing this?' I asked. 'Why, Fishy?'

FIFTY-ONE

Trembling as I spoke, I prayed that I was wrong, knowing all the while how unlikely that was.

'You told me she didn't need to see me – you promised you would take care of all of this.' Droning and stamping like a two-year-old child, he loosened his grip on me as he spoke to his companion.

'Whether she's seen you or not will be of no consequence after tonight.'

The lady spoke and Fishy paid heed.

'Why the fuck are you doing this?' I screamed.

A heavy hand slapped me flat across the face making my ears ring, causing the blindfold to slip from my eyes.

'You're in the presence of a lady – don't use language like that.'

'Tell me, you fucker . . . why?' Yelling at him I was hopeful that someone might hear.

'They're not always wrong, Brodie.' Tiny pieces of his spit flecked my face as he snarled at me.

'I don't understand what you're getting at. Who's not always wrong?'

'Of course you don't understand what I'm getting at . . . but then I've never thought you were as bright as people gave you credit for. Makes sense you had someone helping you along all this time, smoothing the path. Still, notwithstanding that, even I thought you would have sussed me before now.'

'Sussed you? Sussed you? Christ, Fishy, what do you mean?'

'Think about it. Think about all that's been happening to your poor old pal, Fishy. How the nasty coppers have made his life so horrible recently.'

The penny dropped. 'The details on that child porn site? It was you. You were never set up, were you? You stupid bastard -you used your own credit card for that filth.' I barely finished my sentence before he punched me in the guts stealing my breath.

'Who sent you the photograph album, Fishy? Where did you get that from?'

'I did. I sent it.'

Lady Bunny Arbuthnot, the widow, floated into view.

'For his entertainment and edification. Unlike you, I think Richard has possibilities.' Her manicured fingers caressed his face. She dug her forefinger into his cheek, drawing blood. He made no protest and I knew then that it would be no use appealing to Fishy.

'But when you sent the photographs your husband was still alive.'

Her face hardened, emotions frozen in an icy mask.

'He had become aware that Kailash was back. He was always obsessed with that whore. He had some ridiculous thoughts of replacing me, so I needed an alternative companion.'

Bile rose in my throat as I saw her stroke Fishy's crotch; to my disgust he was stiff.

'So, are all paedophiles pretty much interchangeable to you? Do you just swap them around, one for another? Just tell me why – explain to me please – why – why I must die?' I moved my head from side to side trying to sense her; fear stopped my heart when I did. The heated tongs were hovering just above my left breast.

I knew exactly who was pulling the strings here – and I also knew that Bunny MacGregor would hate to kill me without explaining her motivation. Her pleasure in murdering me would be diminished if I were not able to share, or to be a part of her master plan.

I remained motionless as Fishy untied my hands and then retied them so that I could move. I did not dare to do so because 'the spider' glowed red hot, centimetres above my nipple.

'Did you send me that fucking thing?' I spat at her.

My head bounced off the gravestone as Fishy smacked me in the mouth.

'Shut up, Brodie! I warned you about swearing in front of the lady. I sent it to you and I took it from your room this morning.'

'Are you aware of the significance of this place?'

With one hand on my ear Bunny MacGregor pulled me out into the graveyard again.

'Look at these stones – do you have any idea what these men did?'

She twisted my ear so hard I had to answer 'No'. As she released me, the side of my face stung as if I had been lashed. My best chance to remain alive would be to keep her talking until the others arrived.

'When was the Battle of Bannockburn?' she asked, twisting my ear again like some demented history teacher. The Battle of Bannockburn is probably the largest battle ever fought upon British soil. The Scots were outnumbered three to one, and at the last minute they secured victory and their independence. Scotland remained independent for 289 years until the crowns were joined through inheritance. Every Scottish school child knows it, and even in the middle of all this, my early history lessons stayed with me.

'The Battle of Bannockburn was on the 24 June 1314,' I stuttered.

'St John's Day, a very important day for these men.'

My liver was crushed as, bent double, Bunny MacGregor dragged me to the next site. Pushing me down she banged my head off the flat stone. Dragging me by the hair to the next grave she was slightly out of breath as she spoke again.

'This man . . .' she kicked me hard in the ribs; I feared that the toe of her pointed shoe had pierced the skin between the ridges of bone, 'rode up through the Scottish ranks and onto the field at Bannockburn. The enemy were exhausted – when the English soldiers saw that a band of Knights Templar were fighting for Scottish freedom, they fled the field.'

Bunny MacGregor's eyes flashed with fervour as she spoke.

'The Knights Templar were the richest, most influential force . . .'

'Not that powerful because they were wiped out,' I hissed, interrupting her speech. There was blood pouring from the side of my mouth. The same shoe that had kicked my chest, now landed on my chin knocking me backwards.

'Whilst it may be true that on the 13 October 1307, Pope Clement V issued orders for the arrest of the knights, some had warning – and escaped.'

Bunny MacGregor circled me as I lay on the ground, inhaling the sweet smell of the burning pine logs, unable to wipe the moist grass stuck to my face, tickling and aggravating my wounds.

'Of course the Pope was in the pocket of Philip IV. The knights who had escaped the torture had nowhere to run – except Scotland.'

'Why?' I asked, desperate to buy time.

'You ignorant peasant. Before the reformation, the Papal Bull overrode the law of the land, that's why Henry VIII had to ask the Pope's permission to get married to Anne Boleyn. When Henry refused to obey Papal orders he was excommunicated.'

Pulling my eyelids open was difficult, for it was as if my eyeballs were made of slow-setting concrete. I blinked several times, to clear the blood on my eyeballs, trying to see Bunny MacGregor. Dressed like part of the hunting set, her dreary green quilted jacket was set off by the jewel-like colours in the patterns on the Hermès scarf, which now poked cheerily out of her pocket. Severely thin, Bunny still looked elegant in spite of her exertions: immaculately groomed, her white hair was too afraid to move. As was I, lying half naked in a graveyard in the middle of nowhere, while my tormentor was lecturing me on world history. I spat out a piece of my tooth on the grass.

'Of course this place is nothing now – but then it was easily accessible by sea, and the Templars were great sailors you know.'

'They discovered America,' said Fishy, and Lady MacGregor threw him a condescending nod. I tried to spit on his shoe but ended up coughing blood instead.

'Of course he's quite correct – Columbus used Sir Henry Sinclair's Templar maps – proof of this fact is Rosslyn Chapel built 100 years before Columbus discovered America. The ornate stone friezes show corn on the cob and other vegetables indigenous to that land.'

I must have passed out for a second or two, her hand was cold and skeletal as it hit my face.

'For self preservation these warrior monks had to forego their oath of celibacy – did you see on the grave-stones that they intermarried with the great clans? They kept their knowledge and wealth intact – from these roots Scotland has been led.

'When Robert the Bruce died, he asked that his heart be buried in Jerusalem – trusted nobles set off to the Holy Land to carry out his wishes. On 25 March 1330 at the battle of Tebas de Ardales, the Scots riding vanguard were surrounded. Lord Douglas, who carried the casket containing the Bruce's heart around his neck, took it off and threw it into the battle shouting:

> "Braveheart, that ever foremost led,
> Forward as thou wast wont. And I
> Shall follow thee or else shall die."

'All of them died except one – and he retrieved the heart from the battlefield and buried it in Melrose Abbey. In the nineteenth century Robert the Bruce's body was dug up and it was said that his leg bones were crossed under his skull – and that's a Templar sign.'

Fishy bent down, and whispered into my face.

'Is it any wonder that they still run this little country – they run the world! In the American Presidential Campaign, George Bush and John Kerry both belonged to the Skull and Bones society – are you starting to see the connections?'

Bunny MacGregor bent down, and placed the knife on my jugular again.

'Stand up – carefully,' she hissed.

I did as I was told.

'But I still don't know what all of this has to do with me – or the other girls.'

Staring into her eyes I did not hear him approach.

'Let her go, Bunny – take me.' Lord MacGregor stood with his hands in the air.

'Where are the others?' I screamed at him, for the knowledge was beginning to dawn on me. In spite of the force she put into her kick I barely felt it as it landed on my chin, either I was concussed or impervious to

426

pain. More likely it was what she said next that numbed me as I prepared to stare God in the face.

'You fool . . . but as they say the apple doesn't fall far from the tree.'

Bunny MacGregor turned to her father-in-law.

'You tell her what you've done.'

He could not look me in the eye and I knew then that no one else was coming. Bunny had cancelled the others and had come in their stead with Fishy in her shadow.

'Take me,' Lord MacGregor implored again.

'What difference would killing you make – your life's almost over as it is?'

'But you've hated me for years – think of the satisfaction you'll get laughing on my grave.'

'I'll laugh on your grave anyway – and I will get more pleasure knowing that you will have to live with the knowledge that your line ended at my hand.'

'Why must I die?' I asked.

Strangely, I knew that this was the correct question, the question that my grandfather expected me to ask.

'The Templars discovered scrolls under the Temple of Jerusalem. These scrolls showed that Jesus had married Mary Magdalene and had a child. After Jesus was crucified, Mary Magdalene and her daughter went to live in France where they were protected. The bloodline of Jesus runs in the Merovingian line – one of the families that contain this blood are the St Clairs or Sinclair as they are now known.'

Lord MacGregor stopped and looked at his daughter-in-law.

427

'History says that the Templars protected the Holy Grail – and that the holy grail is a cup or a chalice. We believe that the old word for womb is chalice – the Holy Grail was the womb of Mary Magdalene. The Sang Greal is the Royal blood that is carried in these families descended from Jesus and Mary Magdalene.

'My husband carried the Sang Greal – his mother was a Sinclair. I could not allow these pregnant girls to desecrate the blood – to preserve the Holy Grail their wombs had to be cut out.'

Her face was earnest, like a zealot carrying out the word of God.

'And you must die because you are an abomination – the child of a whore carrying the blood? It's unthinkable.' The knife moved up to underneath my chin cutting my skin. She was playing with me, shredding the skin on my neck as she moved the knife up and down.

The blade nicked my jawbone as she fell backwards.

The stone that Joe had dropped on her skull fell to the ground before he untied me.

I'd never been so pleased to see the renegade old bastard in my life.

FIFTY-TWO

'What took you so long?' I shouted at Joe. As I pulled my ripped shirt about me, he handed me his jacket, the sleeves of which ended six inches past my fingertips.

Lord MacGregor lifted the knife from the gravestone. A ceremonial dagger with a twelve-inch long blade, the handle was inlaid with twenty-four carat gold, carved to resemble leaves and a bursting spring bud.

'She obviously wanted to carry out a ritual murder to mark the death of a great warrior or king – it's an old tradition, one that she has warped to suit her own ends.'

'Where's Fishy?' I asked Joe.

'C'mon … I'll show you.' He picked Lady Arbuthnot up like a sack of potatoes and swung her over his shoulder. It was dark now and I held onto Lord MacGregor as we walked behind Joe to his Jeep Gladiator pick-up truck. He pulled back the retractable canvas roof, and there lay Fishy bound and gagged. Unceremoniously he threw Lady Arbuthnot in beside him. Joe handed me the dagger as he pointed with his finger to the jugular vein on her neck.

'Hold it here.'

Hard and emotionless his voice would have cracked glass.

Opening the passenger door, Joe pulled down the glove compartment and took out a camera.

'Say cheese,' he said, poking Bunny MacGregor until she turned to face him. 'We owe this to a dying pal – it might be the only justice he gets.' And as I thought of Duncan lying in the hospice, and her other victims, I was sorely tempted. The white flash scalded my optic nerve. Tears ran down my face as I spoke.

'Promise me the court won't be too lenient with her.' I stuck my face in Lord MacGregor's ear; he was now sitting in the front passenger seat beside Joe.

'A problem with this case is that society doesn't see women – particularly elderly women as serial killers, but ten to sixteen per cent of all serial killers are women. Many of them are elderly carers preying on the weak and infirm – their first weapon of choice, like Bunny's, is poison. That's why she used heroin. The girls were drugged with heroin, and then she tortured them. They died from the overdose not their injuries because Bunny dissected them post-mortem.' I paused to catch my breath and tried to shut out the images of those poor girls flooding my mind.

'God, Joe – how could I not have seen the links? She kept Fishy onside by providing him with enough material to make a paedophile think he'd died and gone to heaven. She killed those girls, and then she finally tracked me down with Roddie's help. When Kailash knew what was going on, when Moses got word to her, she came back from Amsterdam. All the while, Bunny MacGregor was watching me through Fishy – he was the one who visited her when her husband died, he was the one who ran me off the road and then kept the whole threatening theory going by saying someone had got his mobile number.'

'Brodie?' Lord MacGregor jumped in. 'There is no way that she will be tried – or go to prison. We simply couldn't allow the scandal.'

'You mean she'll just be allowed to walk free?' I asked.

'No; because as long as she is alive and at liberty then your life is in danger. She'll be placed in a private, secure hospital where she will be watched and guarded twenty-four hours a day.'

'Not much justice for the kids she killed and abused,' I shouted.

Poking his finger in his ear, Lord MacGregor answered.

'Justice must not be done – it must be seen to be done,' he quoted his son at me.

What would happen if the general population knew that Lord Arbuthnot of Broxden, Lord President of The Court of Session was a paedophile and that he did not stop at murder to protect his liberty and reputation?

The question roiled around in my head like an angry black sea.

Finally, I said, 'I guess the truth wouldn't be good for business.'

'That's an understatement, my dear. That's why the Enlightenment didn't support me earlier – to be fair I don't think they believed the allegations and they thought they could contain his worst excesses.'

'Well they were wrong,' I snapped, 'and children died because of their mistake.'

'Brodie, I don't think you can blame them – it's not the organisation that's bad. It was one individual – my son and your father – who was rotten to the core.'

'So I will suffer for the sins of my father?'

The thought chilled me, as I continued. 'They say in the Bible that the sins of the father shall be visited even unto the third and fourth generation. Will my unborn children be punished?'

'Don't be foolish, girl – the Bible was talking about syphilis. Now you get some sleep.'

The banging from the back had stopped.

'What are we going to do with Fishy?' I asked.

'Don't worry about him. As his colleagues would say, he's going away for a very long time. I intend to contact the Chief Commissioner as soon as I get a signal.'

'What are you going to charge him with?' I asked.

'He's already been charged,' he replied.

'I never liked the man . . . but in truth I would never have pegged him for a beast.' Joe shook his head in disbelief.

'Well, you always say that unless you've got that sin you can't see it in others but in his case it was true.'

I knew that Fishy would be placed before a 'friendly' judge; bail would be denied, he would be pressurised into pleading guilty, and then be sentenced for a very long time, but I still couldn't believe what he was; what

'd lived with. I was a lawyer. I was a reasonably intelligent person. I was a woman. Why did I not see it?
What was lacking in me that I could so easily live with
someone like that, be their friend for years, and yet
pick up nothing? Maybe at the moment it was better
for me to focus on my own failings rather than the fact
that I had shared my life with someone so twisted.

'Sleep now – I'll take care of the baggage – you still
have to appear before them tomorrow.' I was convinced
that I would not doze, but the car was warm and I was
exhausted. I did not even wake when Joe carried me
into the house.

I slept the sleep of the righteous dead.

FIFTY-THREE

There was nothing to rouse me from my slumber. I knew that Joe was dozing on my sofa, and his presence made me feel secure in the midst of what had turned into a living nightmare.

Any time I did stagger to the loo, or rolled over to get comfortable, he was there like a flash. I had taken the nondescript pills which Malcolm had left for me and a wave of peaceful doziness washed over every part of my body. Flashes of what had happened broke through – how could they not? – but the time for unravelling my history, my lineage, could wait.

By the time morning broke through, I had given up on pretending that I wanted to be anywhere but beside Joe. So many cups of tea and coffee, followed by plates of buttery toast and bowls of soup, had been brought to me by him that the mountain of untouched offerings indicated what my words denied. I was not all right, and I didn't know whether I would be ever again – but I was alive.

Joe stroked my forehead as I lay swathed in his

arms, and I know that I wept many times. As the light of Monday's dawn crept through the wooden blinds in my living-room, I sat up knowing that the day ahead would change everything forever. I had given little thought to what was going on in other parts of my new world as I slept – I had no idea what my grandfather or mother were doing (how those normally innocent titles of family ownership confused me), but I doubted they had spent any time resting. The only thing that I knew was that my request to gather the Nobile Officium would not be ignored.

I put on my court armour and a further barrier of make-up. Leaving Joe behind, I left my flat and headed for the Royal Mile, walking the first mile to clear my head. I hailed a taxi when I felt ready and blocked out the driver's chatter about roadworks and the state of Edinburgh as much as I could, finally arriving back where so much had already taken place.

They were waiting for me.

I ascended the stairs weighed down like Christ on the Via Dolorosa, burdened by the knowledge that I was going in to plead for my mother's life. The sound of my feet as I climbed the bevelled steps was hollow and heavy like lead coconut shells.

I shouldn't have been surprised when I saw that Joe had got there before me. He had no doubt bribed his own taxi driver to go quicker. He sat on a chair at the foot of the staircase and did no more than wink at me as I walked by. There was no need for anything else – we knew each other too well. He would always be there for me, and at that moment, I planned to always be there for him.

The room I was going to was far above him, high in the WS library. The stairwell had a soaring ceiling but it was unpretentious, a part of the building that only the initiated see. When I reached the top, I stopped to catch my breath. Like a fish on land, I gulped the air around me greedily to no avail. Swaddled in barbed wire, my side hurt marginally more than the rest of my body, which was saying something.

Shifting from foot to foot outside the door, I harvested my thoughts.

The walls were at least a foot thick, the door was old, white and heavy. Inside the room, the greatest legal minds in Scotland sat waiting for me. I hoped that they were nervous, for I had it in my power to destroy them. I wanted to, but it was like the sword of Damocles; if I took that course of action I would be acting like a suicide bomber. One thing I could guarantee was that the message would not get out.

I had instructed my grandfather to convene the Nobile Officium, the oldest court in Scots Law, one that is rarely used. Its origins are found in ancient Roman law, there is a three-fold test that must be applied to summon the Nobile Officium.

Firstly, there has been or there is the possibility of a miscarriage of justice. Secondly, the circumstances are extraordinary or unforeseen. Thirdly, intervention does not interfere with legislation.

Knocking once on the door, I entered without waiting for their permission. It was an unprepossessing room in need of a paint or at the very least a dust. An eighteenth-century walnut bookcase covered the back wall, it almost reached the ceiling and I paused to consider how the servants had fetched it up those stairs. The upper half of the bookcase was glass fronted, all the books were leather bound first editions, naturally the titles were tooled in gold.

Three old men, like tortoises without shells, watched me as I walked across the fraying Abusson carpet. The judges sat at a plain oak bench table, their backs to the long Georgian sash and case windows.

The new Lord President sat in the middle, his hooked nose and high cheekbones gave him more than a passing resemblance to his great-grandfather. I knew this because an oil painting of his ancestor was on the wall, and its eyes seemed to follow me as I moved to take my seat.

For the first time I understood that in some quarters it could be argued that my lineage was the more august since my great-grandfather's portrait was hanging on a wall that people actually looked at.

The clock showed that it was 7a.m., we were alone in the building. The Law Lords wore no judicial robes. Their bespoke suits were sombre. They continued to eye me suspiciously, but no emotions were betrayed on their faces.

A sorry sight.

I caught a glimpse of my reflection in the glass. My face was bruised and swollen. Malcolm, who had arrived to tend to me, at Joe's request this time, did not have time to apply the leeches to reduce the swelling, which was considerable. Malcolm had, however, gently washed my hair, and he was unable to conceal his horror as the sink filled with my red locks. My hairstyle today was not up to his customary standard; it was somewhat unusual as he had attempted to cover bald patches the size of ten-pence pieces.

'Ms MacGregor?'

The new Lord President had called me by my father's name. I knew that it was not a mistake, he was acknowledging the unspoken facts. By that simple gesture the Lord President let me know that it was within judicial knowledge that I was the daughter of their colleague, and a thirteen-year-old girl.

My grandfather came up behind me and stood at my right hand side.

'Ms MacGregor?' the Lord President said again. 'We have been briefed on this matter before us.' He nodded at my grandfather. 'And as the matter is sub judice we have decided to refer it back to the court of first instance. This case will be dealt with in court nine in the usual manner.'

He cleared his throat, this decision had been made off the bench and they had no intention of allowing me to speak.

Murmuring inaudibly, they left the room in single file. Adrenalin heightened my sense of smell, and in their wake the room was filled with the scent of Havana cigars and spicy gentleman's cologne.

I couldn't help myself, I shouted after him.

'M'Lord – the facts in this case could destroy the judiciary.'

The Lord President turned and looked at me withringly. The College of Justice had stood for centuries, 1 that time it had witnessed plots and wars, yet it had scaped unharmed.

'Ms MacGregor – we have made our decision.'

With that, the last of the old men disappeared and he door swung shut in my face.

I grasped my grandfather's elbow and the silky wool of his suit mopped the cold sweat from my palm as I moved to lead him down the stairs. He had aged visibly before my eyes, strain had bleached the colour from his withered face. I could think of nothing that would comfort him as we walked down to Parliament Hall. f his son's sexual perversions were given a public airing, well, that was something that perhaps neither of us could recover from. Now that would give the steamie something to talk about.

As he saw us approach, Joe opened his mouth to speak but the look on our faces silenced him.

'If I have to argue this case, Kailash will go down for murder. So what if his reputation is ruined? Mine will be too. I'll be damned by association with them. No good can come of it.'

I could not bear to say my father's name, at least when he was unknown to me he only haunted my sleeping hours.

I paced up and down the hall talking to Joe. My grandfather had disappeared because it was not seemly that we be spotted together prior to the trial.

I hadn't gone to see Kailash yet. I wasn't ready for a mother and child reunion in a prison cell. Perhaps,

I wondered, it would soften the blow when she went down for life. It would certainly provide a basis for conversation, other than that I had failed her. Nor was I ready to consider the magnitude of what had unfolded in front of me. It wasn't just a matter of not knowing how to approach Kailash, it was also the fact that I had to grieve for Mary all over again. How should I now think of them? My real mother and my adoptive mother? But there had been no adoption, and Kailash had never mothered me. My birth mother had never chosen to get pregnant, never wished a baby on herself, and I wondered whether I would ever be able to think about my true parentage without feeling disgust and guilt. What would Kailash's life been without me? What had I done to her? And what would she now do to me? I was pulled back to reality by the official matters in front of me.

'Her Majesty's Advocate against Kailash Coutts starting in court nine.' The Macer called us to action. I pulled my gown around me, and Joe clutched his papers.

'Break a leg,' he said.

'Chance would be a fine thing – at least I could bugger off to hospital. God, Joe, I'm going to need all the help I can get with this one.'

Hector McVie and his entourage were already assembled on the front benches. Hector looked solemn. No one in the Faculty was looking forward to the evidence in this trial. A side door opened and Kailash walked in.

Serenity had smoothed any slight line that may have marred her countenance before, and I knew then that he had had her justice. Nothing else would have soothed her soul but that Alistair MacGregor die at her hand. It was worth any price she would have to pay. Kailash did not expect Lord MacDonald to mete out any retribution on behalf of the forgotten children, of which she was only one.

'She's got your eyes, right enough,' Joe whispered in my ear, maudlin even without drink.

'Will you shut up – and I think it would be more appropriate to say that I had her eyes.' I stared at her afresh; she smiled at me, recognising that I knew the truth. Her hair was as black as coal, as had my father's been in his youth. Red hair often skips a generation.

'Court rise,' the Macer shouted and I was ready to fight for the ignored and neglected.

Lord MacDonald processed slowly and gravely onto the bench, his red silk gown rustling in the stillness. Hundreds of eyes watched him; holding their breath waiting for him to sit. The jury leaned forwards into the body of the room, the edge of their seats cutting into their behinds. The informed public were desperate to hear the evidence that had been put before the court on Friday.

I stared at Roddie. A grudging respect lit his eye, as he met my gaze. Holding his own hand for comfort, like a child about to perform, he was sickeningly afraid. Beads of sweat peppered his brow.

Lord MacDonald picked up his pen and focused his eyes on the prosecution team.

'Mr McVie.' His voice was low and polished, each

vowel neatly rounded to eliminate any trace of Scottish accent, he nodded at my colleague to begin.

Hesitantly, Hector got to his feet. I felt my stomach tighten, as if some long-nailed woman had me in the palm of her hand and was wringing my guts.

Hector cleared his throat again. The court was hushed.

'M'Lord . . . taking into account new evidence that has come to light the Crown has decided to accept the accused's plea of not guilty.'

My eyes darted about in my head. Lord MacDonald did not look surprised. The public benches were emptying as reporters rushed to break the news.

Banging his gavel, the judge demanded order.

His voice was lost in the mêlée, he shouted again and a few stragglers returned to their seats.

'Ladies and gentlemen of the jury – I thank you for your assistance in this matter – you are released from your duty as jurors.'

'Court rise,' the Macer bellowed.

Those who remained stood up on cue when Lord MacDonald left the bench. As he did so he smiled conservatively in my direction. His teeth were crooked and yellow, it was an intimacy I did not relish.

As soon as he was gone I jumped into the well of the court, heading for the dock.

I felt her arms around me, as I buried my face in her hair. The scent of rose oil enveloped me: as I recalled its healing powers I blessed her under my breath.

The warmth of her tears wet my cheek. Kailash pushed me back, still holding my face in her hands.

Locked in love we recognised each other. Again.

'At last,' was all she whispered, as she looked into my eyes. She did not let me go, even when Joe wanted to get in on the act and threw his arms around us both. Like a bear he crushed us with his enthusiasm, refusing to let go.

She kept up her litany.

'At last, at last,' she murmured, as she rocked me in her arms.

FIFTY-FOUR

We accompanied Kailash to get her belongings from the police cells. A strange ménage á trois, processing through the corridors. People gawked from secret crannies, looking at the lawyer, the giant paralegal and the dominatrix. The onlookers believed that I had scored a great victory in the courtroom on Friday afternoon.

'Look – there's gonna be a shiteload of press out there,' Joe warned me, literary as always.

'Get some more make-up on – and make sure this scarf is covering your neck. We don't want anyone speculating in the press.' Kailash was all business again and walked out first into the barrage of flashing bulbs. Television crews waited to give me my fifteen minutes of fame.

I stepped forward and was pushed aside. Lord MacGregor stepped in front of me.

His sonorous voice informed the world:

On behalf of the family, my granddaughter and I . . .

He pulled me to his bosom, the strength in his arm belied his age. 'Smile,' he whispered into my ear. In spite of the soft tones, I was left in no doubt that it was a direct order.

My granddaughter and I . . .

He repeated the phrase, rolling his rs over his tongue, as if he enjoyed the sound of the words.

We would like to say how pleased we are that justice has once again been served. My son and Brodie's father, died a hero – rushing to save Miss Coutts' life – forsaking his own safety . . .

He coughed, as he brushed his rheumy eye with a fine lawn handkerchief. As a sign to the press that his tears would not be far away, he clutched the hanky firmly between his fingers. Shakily, he continued to speak.

Not only was he one of the finest Lord Presidents that there has been in this country's long legal history – but also as a son – and a father- he was a man to be proud of.

'What's going to happen to the youths who attacked Miss Coutts?' Jack Deans shouted from the press pack, grinning from ear to ear. Moses, who stood at Jack Deans' shoulder, raised his cane in salute. Lord MacGregor ignored them both. The initiated knew Moses would continue to walk free, he had the evidence in a safe place.

We bear no grudge to Miss Coutts as witnessed by my granddaughter's decision to represent her.

A torrent of flashes, battered my optic nerves.

No further questions please – we would like to be left alone to grieve as a family.

My heart had stopped shortly after he called me his granddaughter.

By publicly claiming me for his bloodline, he had drawn me in. My new personal history was that I was

445

the product of an affair between Mary McLennan and Alistair MacGregor.

Of course the family had always been involved in my upbringing – that was why I chose law, and why my grandfather had been a governor of my school. I did not know where the heritage of my blood would take me – standing on the precipice I was almost afraid to find out. Kailash squeezed my arm, and led me off down the Royal Mile. Alone and free we walked down the cobbled street. I stopped her outside the City Chambers, with Lavender shaking her head behind us.

'Just one thing . . . why did you make me dig up the grave?' I found it hard to keep the anger from my voice.

Brushing the hair from my face, she spoke:

'*Mo Cridhe* . . . would you honestly have believed me if I had told you everything that night in the police station, or any other time?'

In my heart I knew she spoke the truth, the foundations upon which I had built my life had to be shattered before I could even attempt to accept my heritage.

'Don't reject your birthright, Brodie. These men are not all bad – but they all are one thing: pathways to power.

'This is your birthright. This is your inheritance.

'Now is where your life starts – see where your bloodline takes you – but, always know, that I'll be there beside you.'

My heart filled with emotion, but my head said only one thing:

Christ help me if this is just the beginning . . .

446

Read on for an exclusive extract from *Blood Lines*, the new Brodie MacLennan novel, coming in summer 2008.

PROLOGUE

Ruthven Barracks, August 2005

The Jacobite ruin stands high in the evening mist. Ruthven Barracks, set on a mound in the Scottish Highlands, echoes with ghosts and lovers' tales. The settlement which had existed there for over a thousand years is long gone, but the rumours of betrayal and obsession are as fresh as if whispered yesterday. Alisdair Mor mac an Righ once made his home here, but few round these parts referred to him by that name then or now. One of the blackest bastards ever to walk through Scotland's history, the son of King Robert II lived in barbarous times – times which he, the Wolf of Badenoch, made darker and more murderous every day he lived.

Now the earth which the Wolf walked is hard from the constant tramp of tourist feet. The day buses and walking tours have long gone as the low evening clouds scurry past the moon. It is almost midnight, but it is as bright as day in this land where the light does as it pleases. The lovers walk up the steep gravel path from the roadside and, hand-in-hand, enter the stony ruins. They sit down amongst the ancient stones, their heavy voices echoing with lust and revenge.

A hip flask is taken from the backpack of its owner. It is handed to the other, who fingers it anxiously, thinking of past indiscretions.

'Take the whisky and seal the deal,' come the words as the dark fluid is thrown down a throat parched from the wanting. The breath of the lovers is sweet in the night air. They search for words, for an appropriate toast to what they feel for each other. Both seem content to drink in the surroundings and the presence of the other alongside the liquid from the pure waters of the nearby Drumguish distillery.

This is a betrothal. A consummation. The reverberations of words exchanged and vows underscored will last beyond this night.

The Earl of Badenoch had ruled these lands in a cruel way – always taking more than he was entitled to, yet never satisfying himself. He knew the meaning of betrayal, he knew the cost of love. When he deserted his wife for his mistress, the Church ruled against him – and entire towns paid the cost. The Wolf sought revenge in an orgy of ransacking, burning and murder, eventually offering superficial repentance in order to win his way back into society.

But he, more than most, knew that what lies on the surface matters nothing compared to what lurks beneath. His final visit to Ruthven was for his infamous chess battle to the death – with the Devil. As the Devil called 'checkmate', a terrible storm of thunder, hail and lightning surrounded the place. In the silence of the morning, all of the Wolf's men were found blackened and dead outside the castle walls, with their master discovered lifeless in the banqueting hall, unmarked but with the nails from his boots ripped out. The Devil had won yet again – as the Wolf had always known he would.

'Don't you want me?' comes the voice from the seated woman who raises the hipflask to her lips once more as soon as she has whimpered the words.

'Don't you want me?' she asks again, her craving for love more overwhelming than the feeling of fear which batters these walls. The betrothal is not going as planned. Where are the dual commitments? Where are the exchanged vows of lifelong adoration? As the woman reaches out to touch the face of her beloved, she also raises the pewter flask above her head as a sign of dedication. Her voice echoes around the ancient stones, joining the many pledges made there over the centuries.

'Join me,' she says, but her words do not invite, they beg.

'May the hinges of our friendship never rust, nor the wings of our love lose a feather,' she continues, trying to ignore the silence of her beloved. '*Slainte.*'

The whisky warms her heart as she takes another sip. Warms her heart more than the presence of her beloved. As it trickles down her throat, the taste awakes demons. It dribbles down her chin as she tries to wipe it away with the back of her hand. Her co-ordination is all wrong – has her old friend affected her so quickly?

She drinks more, but the dribbles increase, and the woman looks to her love for help.

The words which reach her do not comfort.

'You greedy bitch. I should have known. That stagger-water was the one thing I needed to rely on – and the one thing I couldn't control. You didn't disappoint me, did you?'

The woman beseeches her lover with her eyes. Why is there such cruelty in the words? Why is there such hatred in the face of the one she worships?

'My legs aren't working properly. Help me.'

Even to her own ears, the words sound slurred as she falls heavily to the ground. The woman's tights rip on the rough stony hillside of the barrack floor, but her darling moves towards her and brings hope. Her arms are pulled together above her head and held there as she is dragged still further. There is no help, there is no hope. The soldiers' latrines await her as she is hauled round a corner.

'This is for you,' whispers her darling into her ear. The woman fleetingly thinks of love, of surprises prepared by the keeper of her spirit. As she is thrown into the hard-packed six-foot trench, her hopes are dashed and her heart knows that it has been betrayed. Silently she screams, incapable of making a sound.

'If I'd known you were so fond of the taste of sodium penthanol, I'd have tried it years ago,' come the words, but the woman is too busy watching what is happening to pay attention to the one-sided conversation. Her lover has picked up the spade resting on the rough stone wall and starts to dig afresh.

'Normally it's injected – but I find needles really... unpleasant . . .'

The pile of earth is considerable now. It has also managed to change the channel into something else. With the presence of the woman within, it is no longer a trench.

It is a grave.

Such alchemy.

The legs and the arms of the woman are useless. They are drugged into stillness, numbed into inefficiency, but it is the loss of love which immobilises her totally. The voice she once adored now drones on as the owner of it continues to dig.

'Truth serum. That's what most people know it as. Isn't that funny? Isn't that ironic? I couldn't be less interested in your truths, my darling. I've had to put up with them for long enough. I think it's much more worthy of reflection that this stuff is also used in executions.'

The face of the woman manages to contort with fear – no mean feat given the amount of paralysing drug she has willingly swallowed.

'You betrayed me. You put your truths before everything. Before me. Before our love. Do you know what that does to someone? To me?'

She cannot answer, she cannot plead for her life or use her words to escape the fate she knows is awaiting her. Flecks of spittle foam around the mouth of the one she loved to kiss. She longs to wipe them away, to show a caring touch even with the knowledge that her lover has become her executioner. Pins and needles start in her fingers as the feeling spreads throughout her entire body. The winding sheet starts at her feet as her beloved ineptly wraps her in a shroud. This will be her bridal dress, this will be the culmination of their love.

'My love, my love – why did you make me do this?' asks the undertaker of her heart.

A tear escapes the woman's eye as her beloved tenderly wraps her in their arms and, struggling with the dead weight, lays her roughly in the grave. Still the woman cannot speak. The tear runs down her face unchecked – her hands are close enough to scratch her nose but they are bound and crossed on her chest where there is no strength to break free.

The shovel of earth hits her heavily, knocking the wind and the life out of her body. Painstakingly, the grave is filled, each load crushing her body and stealing her soul.

There is hope.

Her head and neck are uncovered. She tells herself that this is no more worrying than a game children will play at the beach when they bury each other in the sand.

At any moment, her love will release her, they will embrace and their betrothal will continue.

As the knife pierces her cheek, the sensation returns to her body as pain slices through – as does the awareness that this is no childish game, this is no lovers' diversion. The metallic smell of blood joins the stench of terror. The woman's face is warm and wet as her beloved rubs dirt into the open wounds over and over again. Finally, strength returns to her fingers – as the first dirt lands on her face.

She tries to claw her way out.

She breaks her finger nails to the quick.

She feels the blood run down.

She cannot see for the suffocating darkness.

She cannot breathe for the earth in her nostrils.

She cannot scream for the muck in her mouth.

What starts in pleasure always ends in pain.

As the final words of the treasured one scrape against the ancient stones, the Wolf of Badenoch enjoys what he sees, savours what he hears.

'Who will love you now?' asks the beloved one as the knife cuts, the blood pours, and the Wolf howls with delight.

Enjoyed *Dark Angels*? Prepare to be terrified all over again…

Close Enough to Kill

Beverly Barton

Welcome to Adams County, Alabama – Population 10,374 – and falling . . .

Adams County, Alabama is the kind of town where everyone knows each other's business, the kind of place where doors stay unlocked. Until a **psychopath** comes calling.

Dubbed '**The Secret Admirer**', he **woos his victims** with phone calls, love letters and gifts, before **stalking, kidnapping** and then **brutally murdering** them.

A **terrifying game** is underway. Sheriff Bernie Granger – in her first big case and following in her father's footsteps – is desperate to stop this **depraved serial killer** before he **slaughters** another young woman. But is she getting closer to catching him – or being drawn even deeper into his **deadly web**?

ISBN: 978-1-84756-000-1